WICKED LOVELY
DESERT TALES
SANCTUARY

Story by
MELISSA MARR

Art by
XIAN NU STUDIO

HAMBURG // LONDON // LOS ANGELES // TOKYO

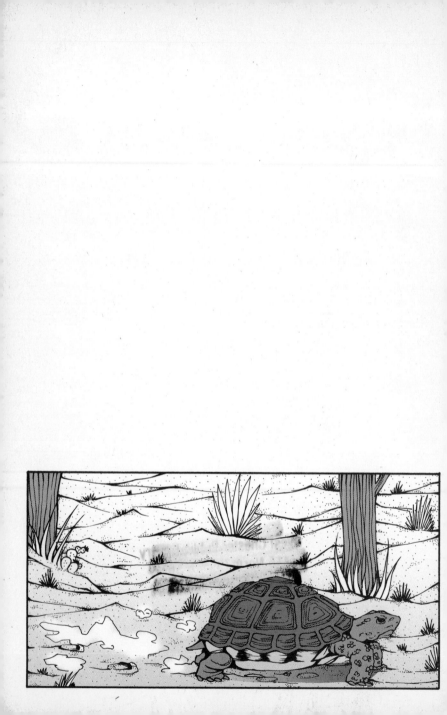

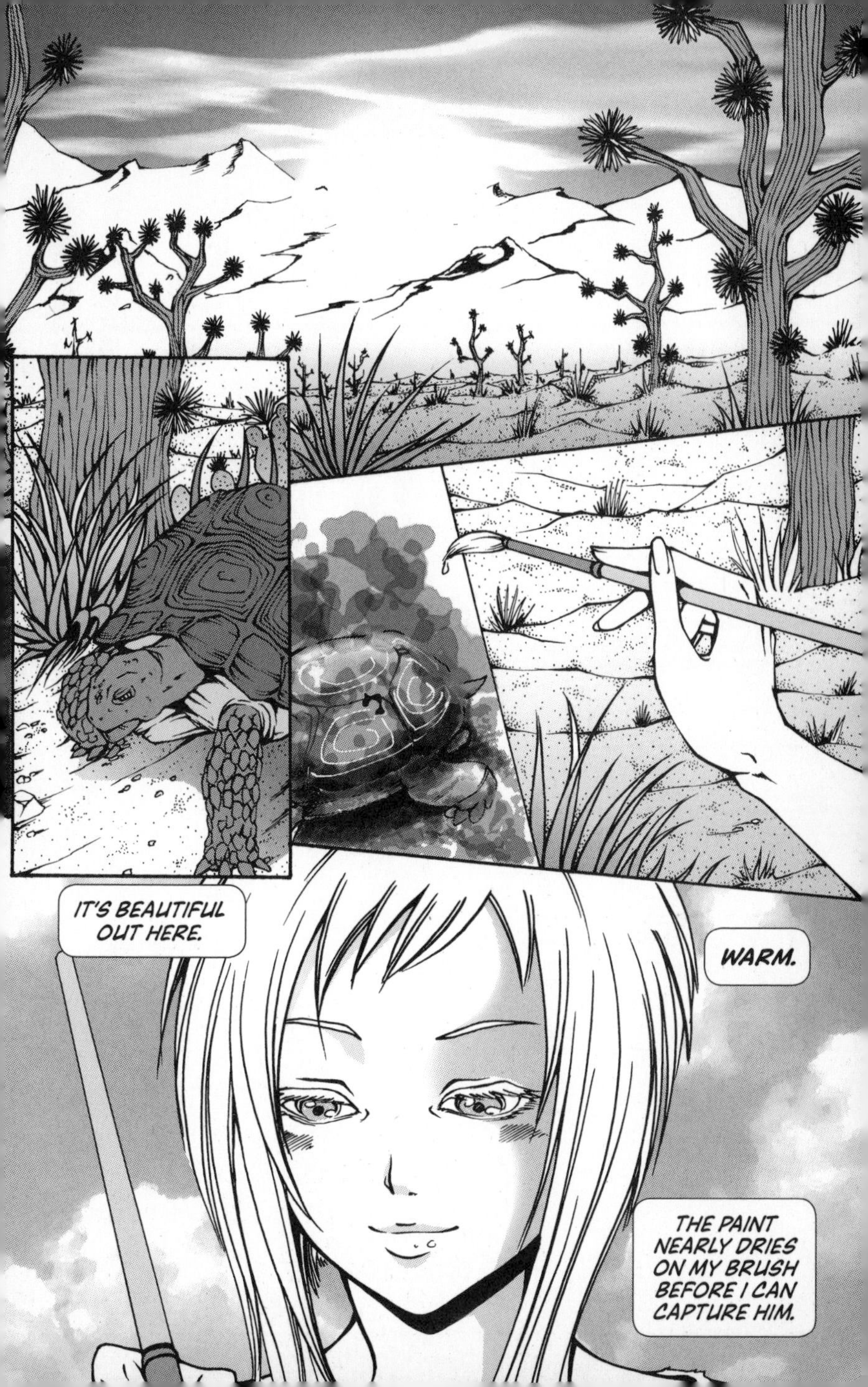
IT'S BEAUTIFUL OUT HERE.
WARM.
THE PAINT NEARLY DRIES ON MY BRUSH BEFORE I CAN CAPTURE HIM.

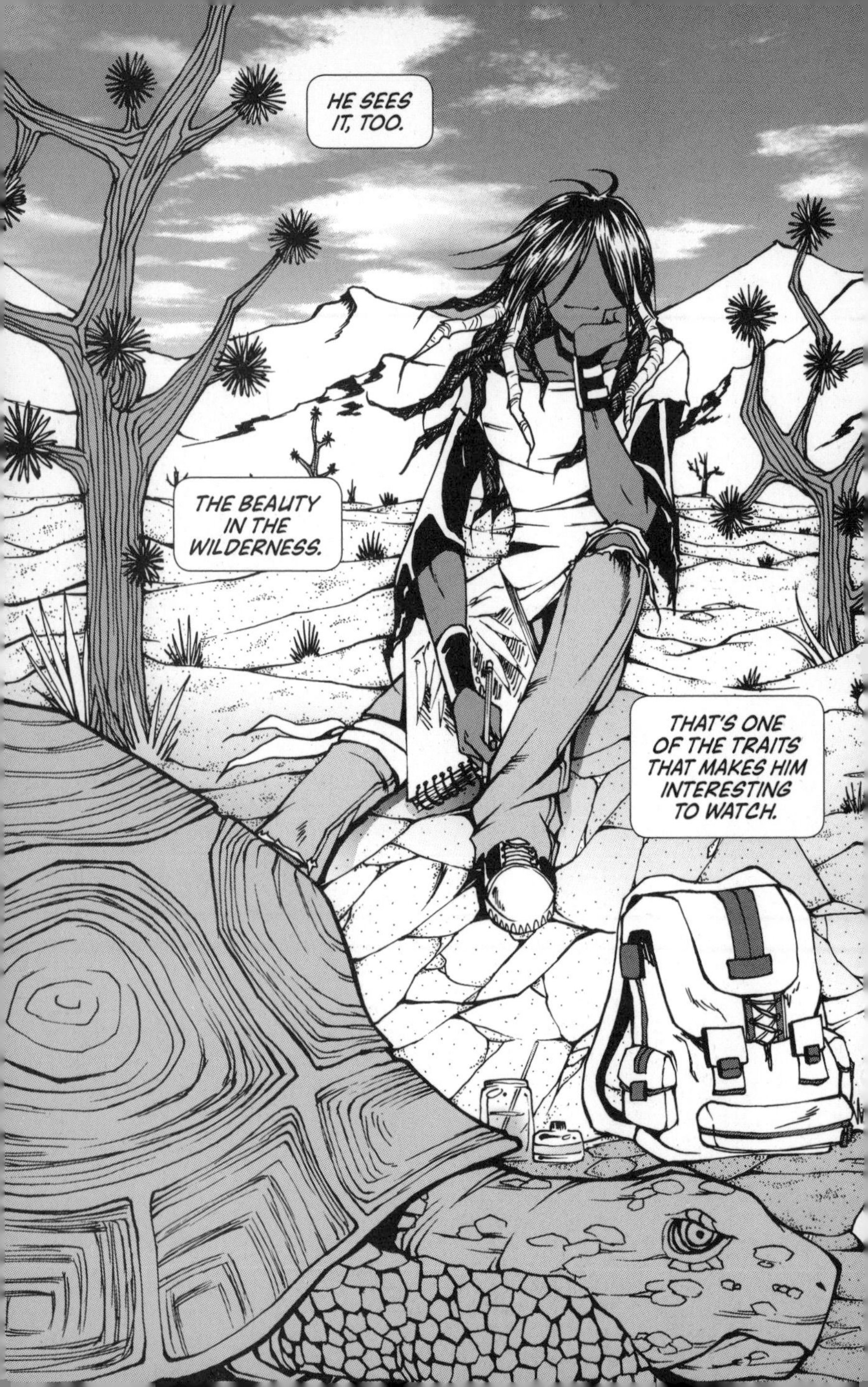
HE SEES IT, TOO.
THE BEAUTY IN THE WILDERNESS.
THAT'S ONE OF THE TRAITS THAT MAKES HIM INTERESTING TO WATCH.

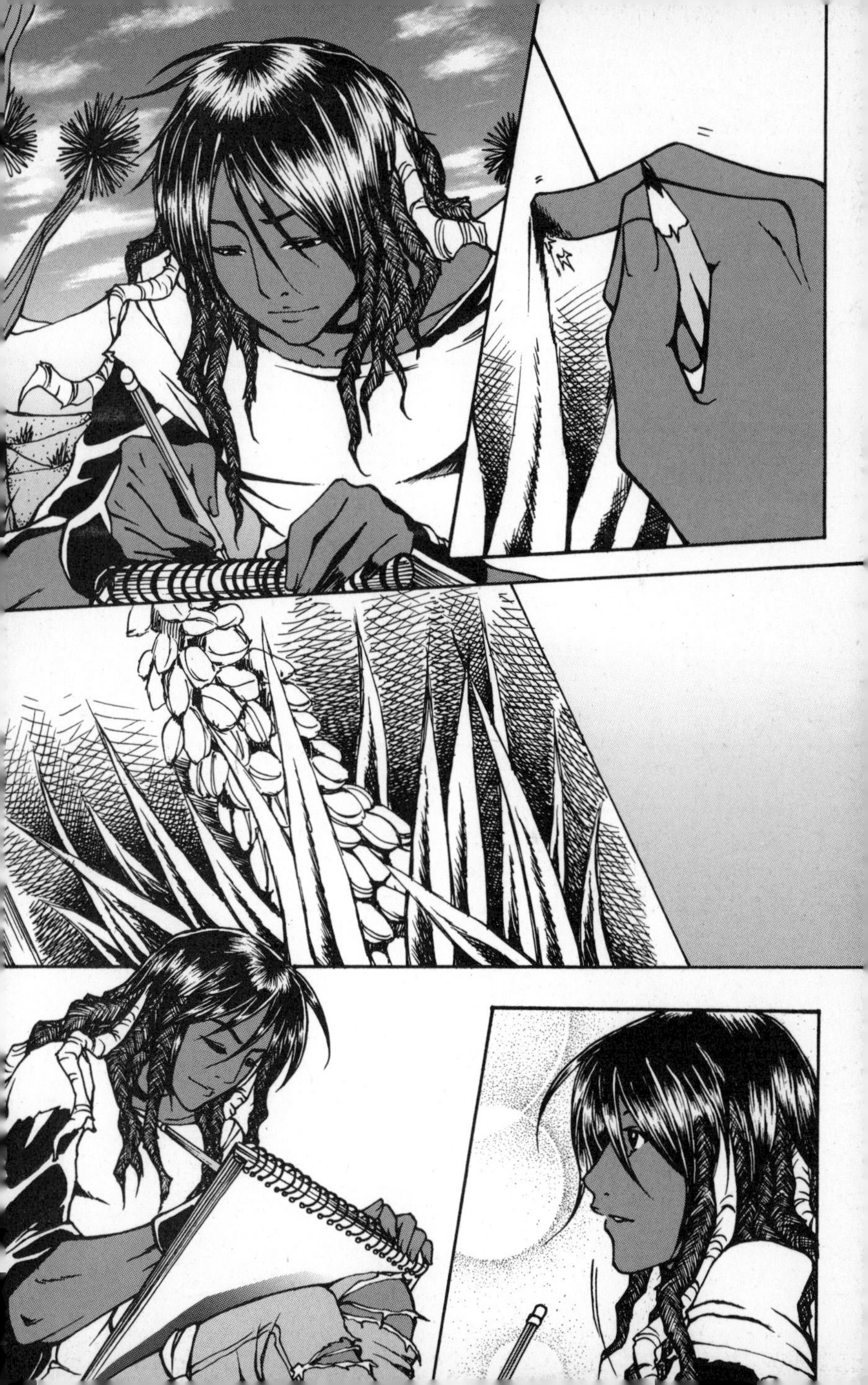

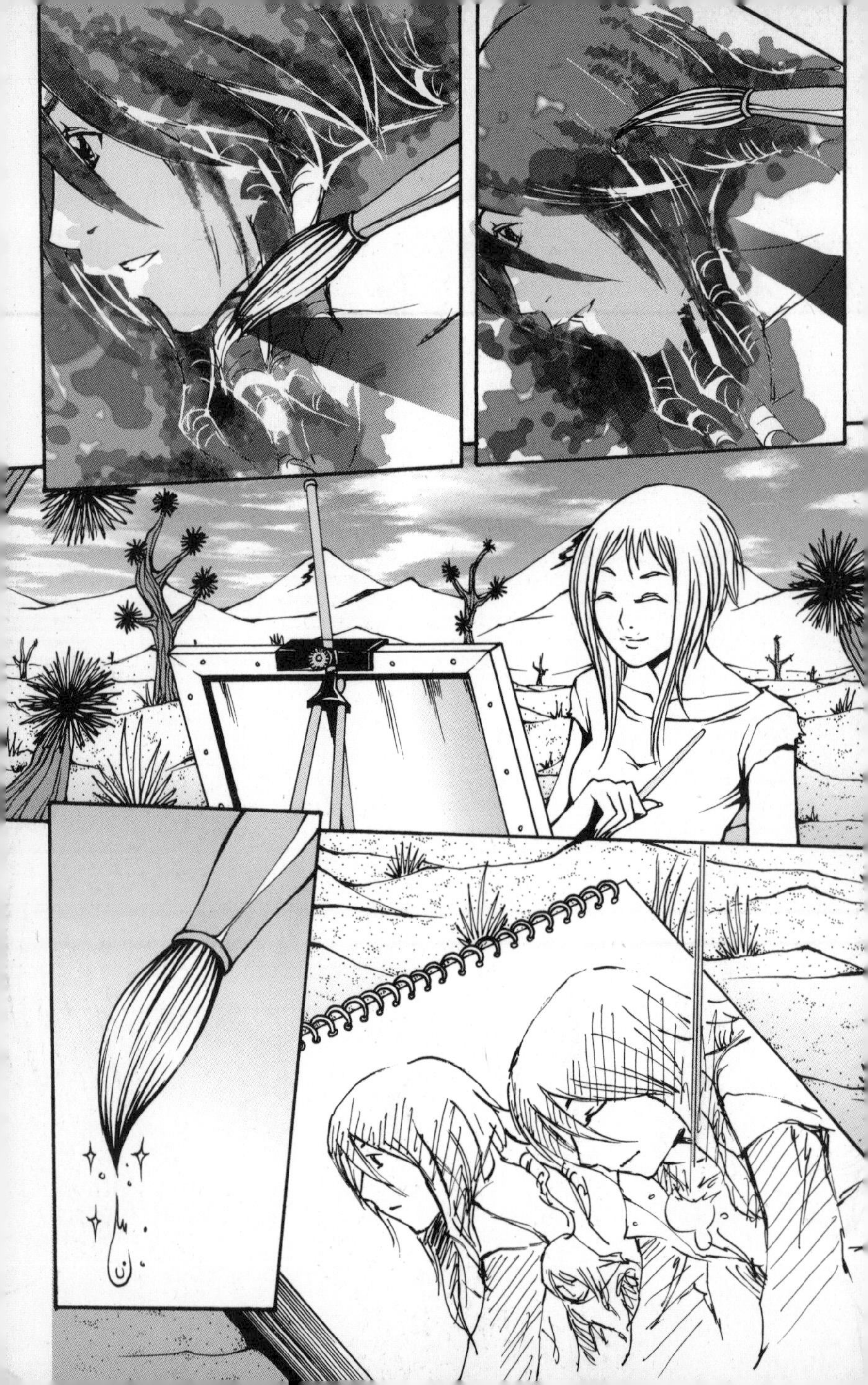

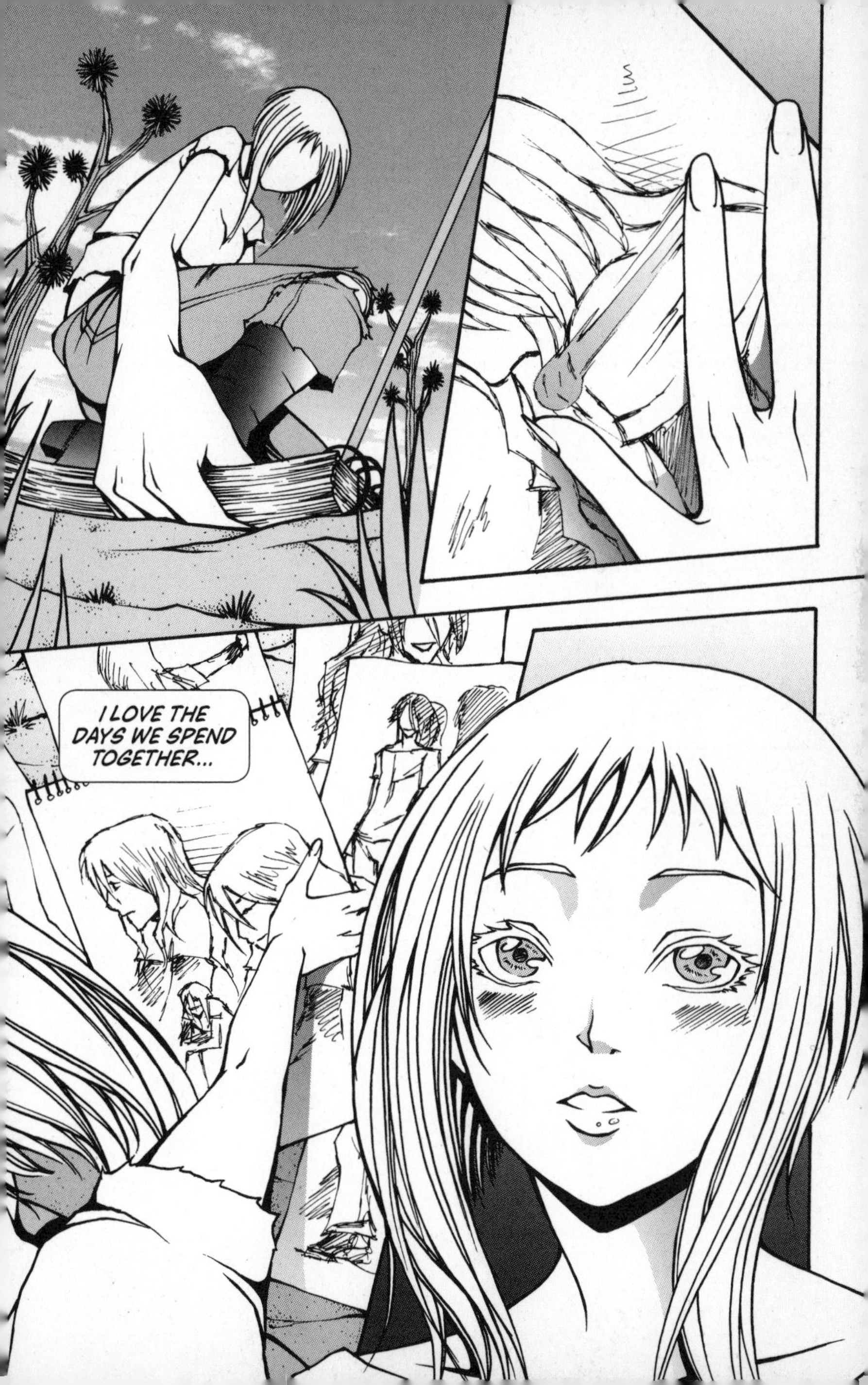
I LOVE THE DAYS WE SPEND TOGETHER...

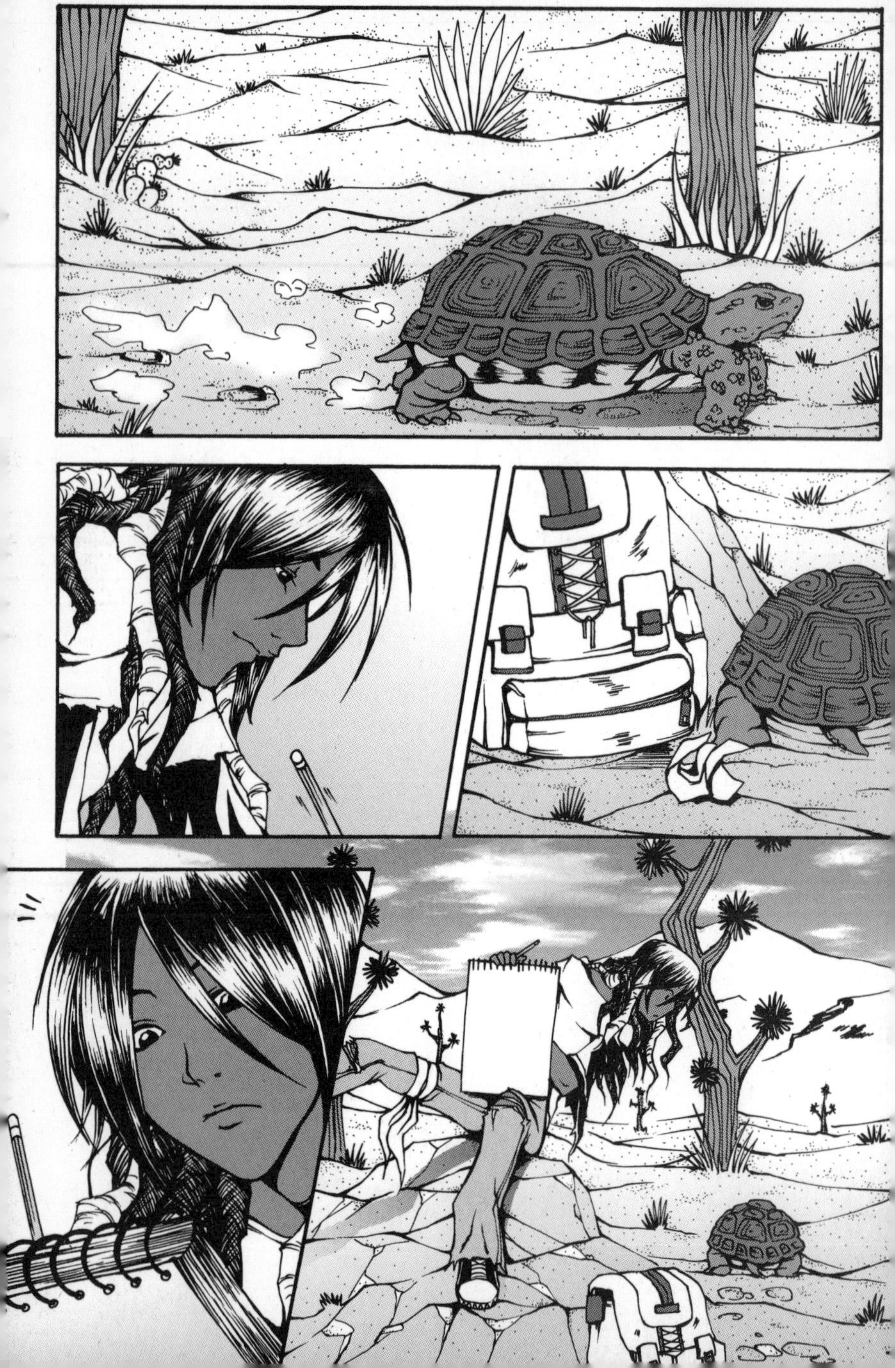

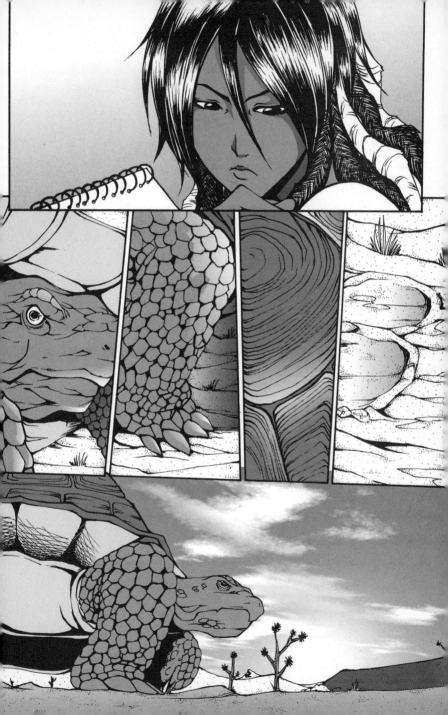

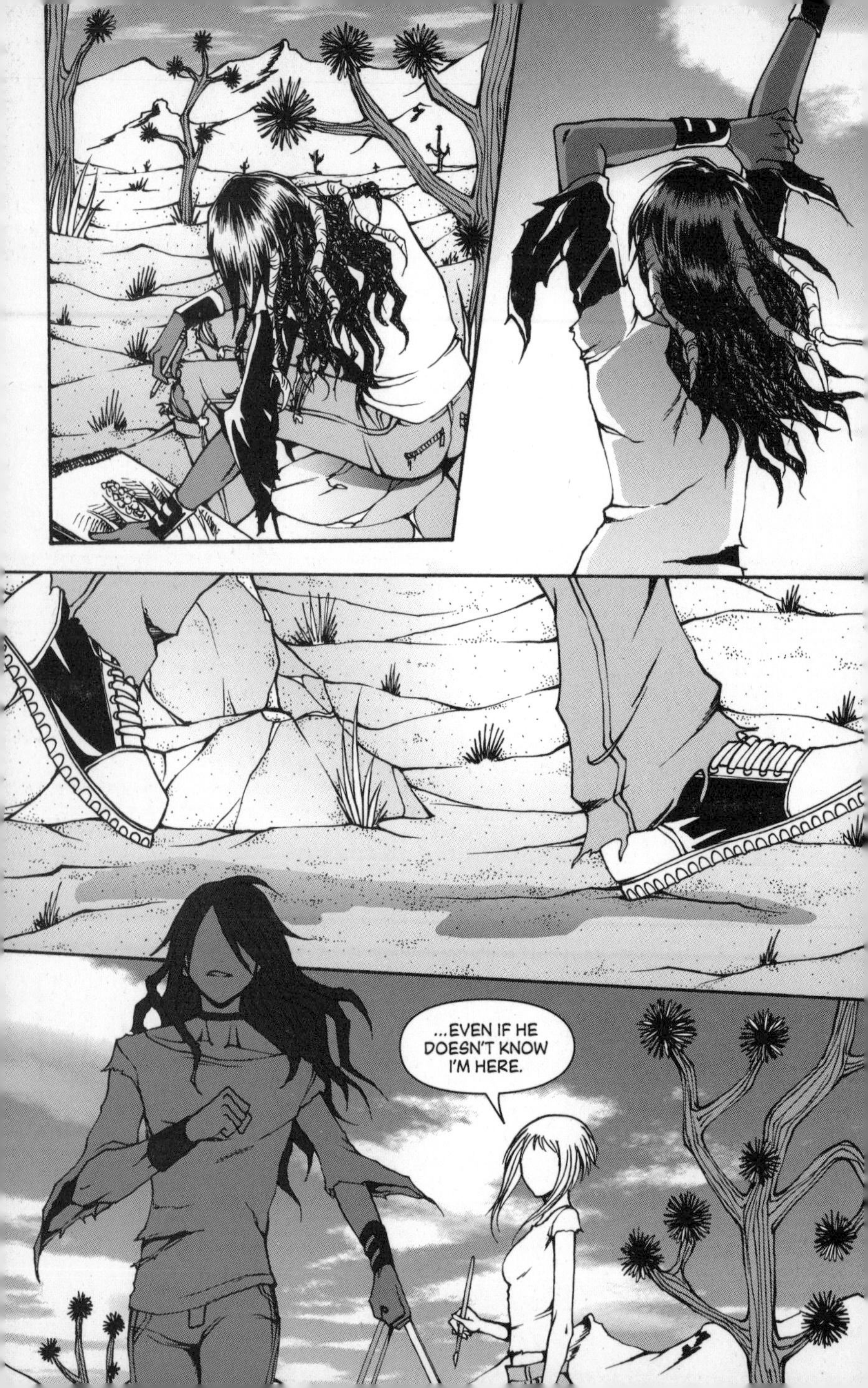
...EVEN IF HE DOESN'T KNOW I'M HERE.

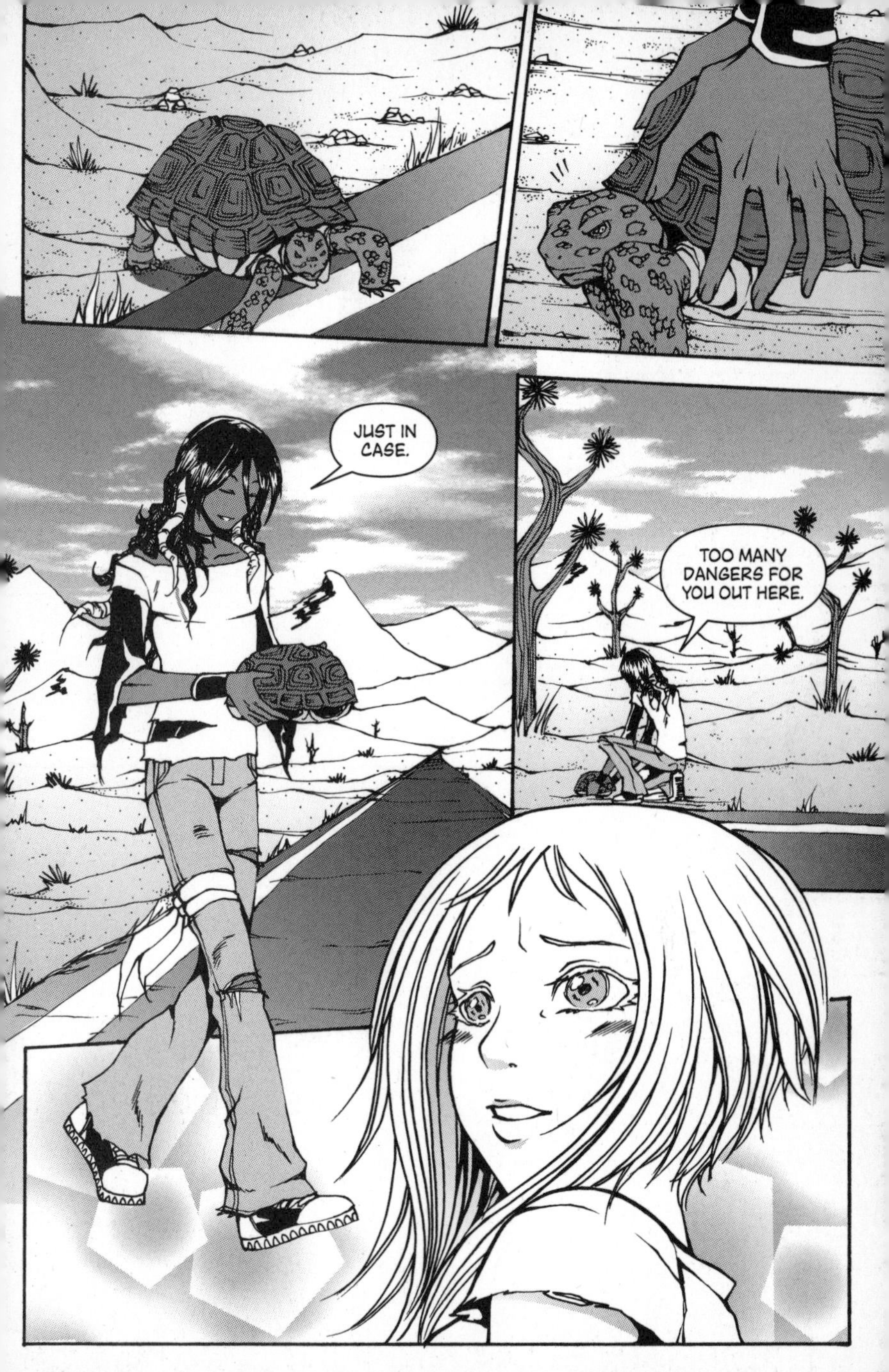
JUST IN CASE.
TOO MANY DANGERS FOR YOU OUT HERE.

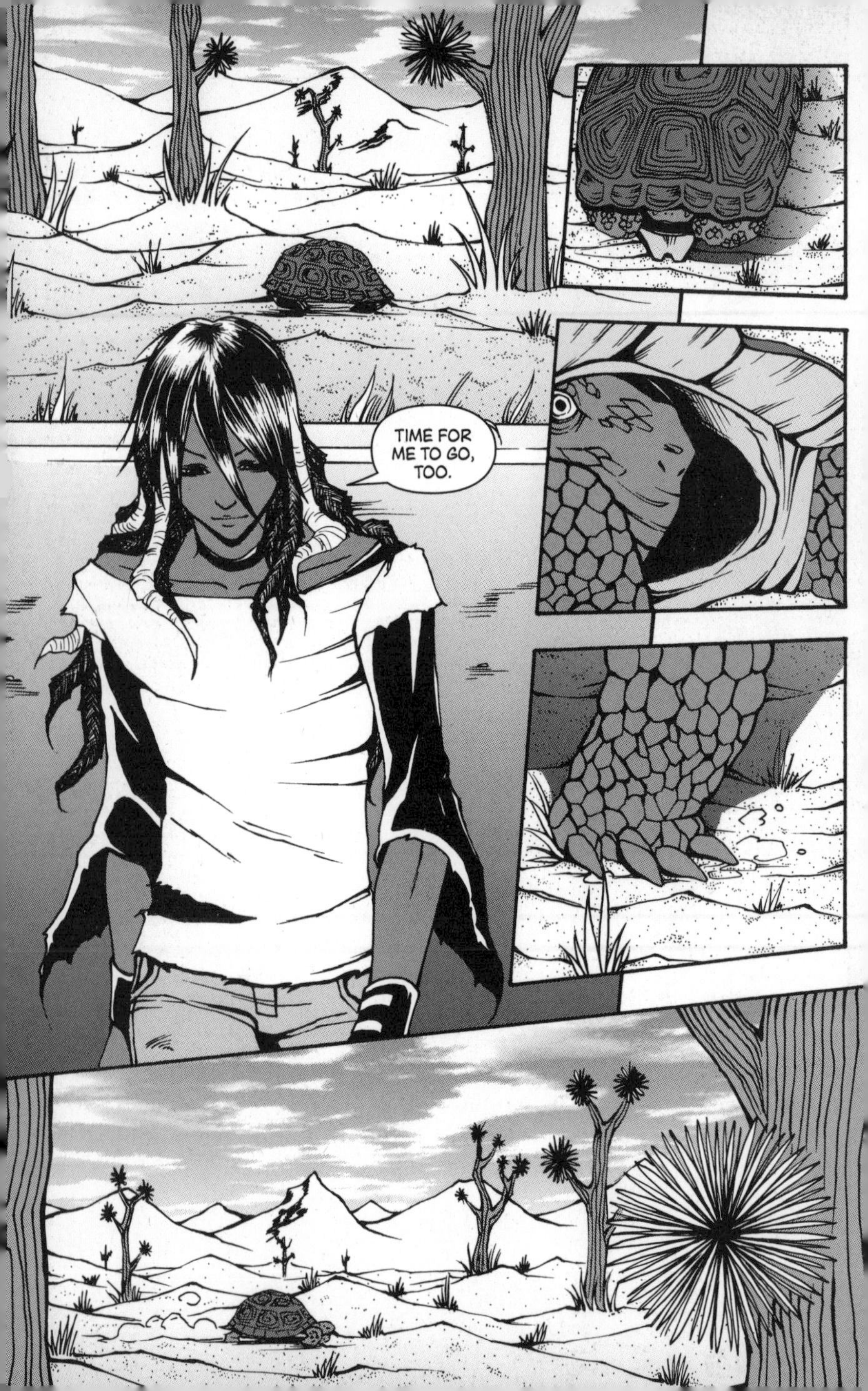
TIME FOR ME TO GO, TOO.

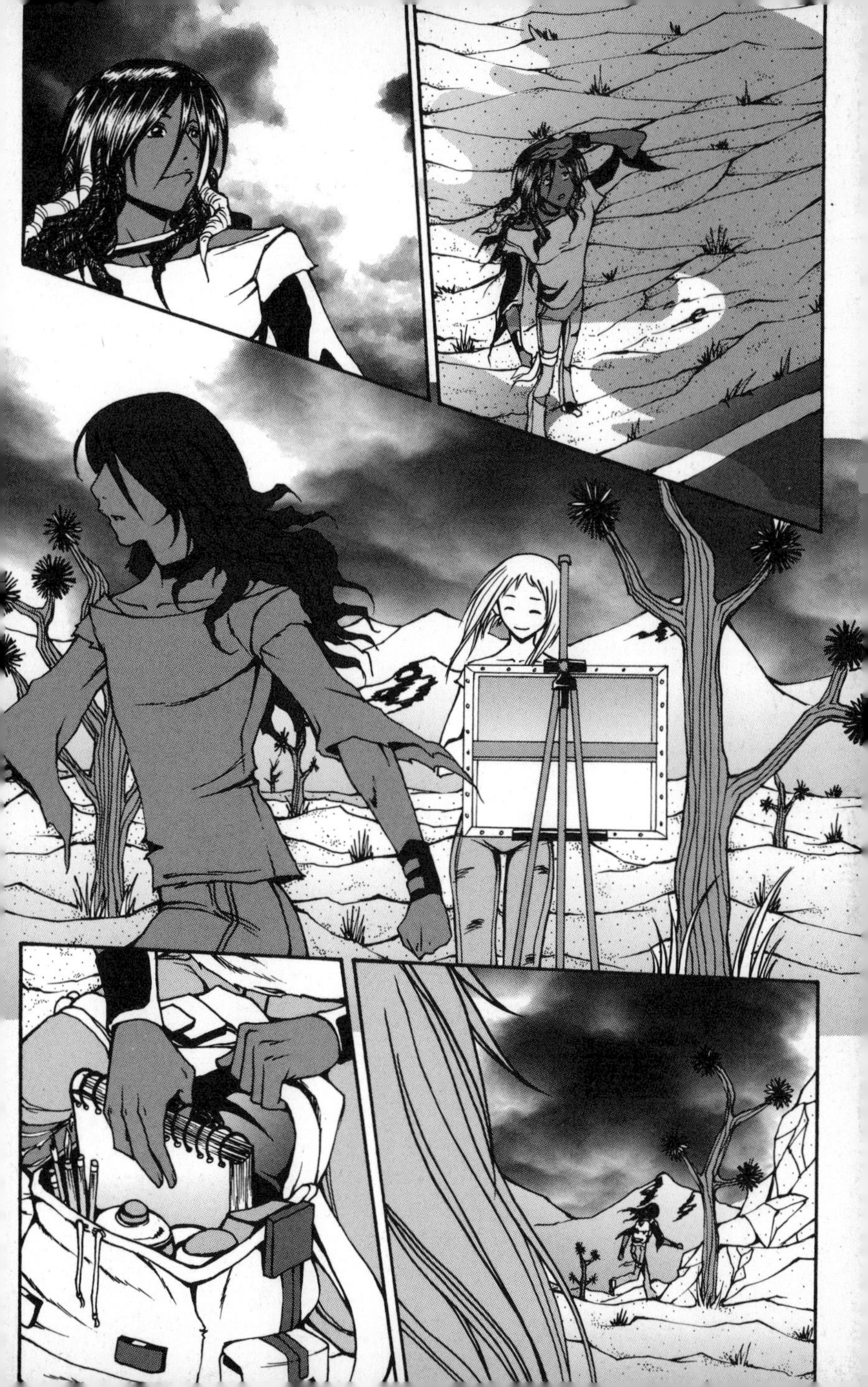

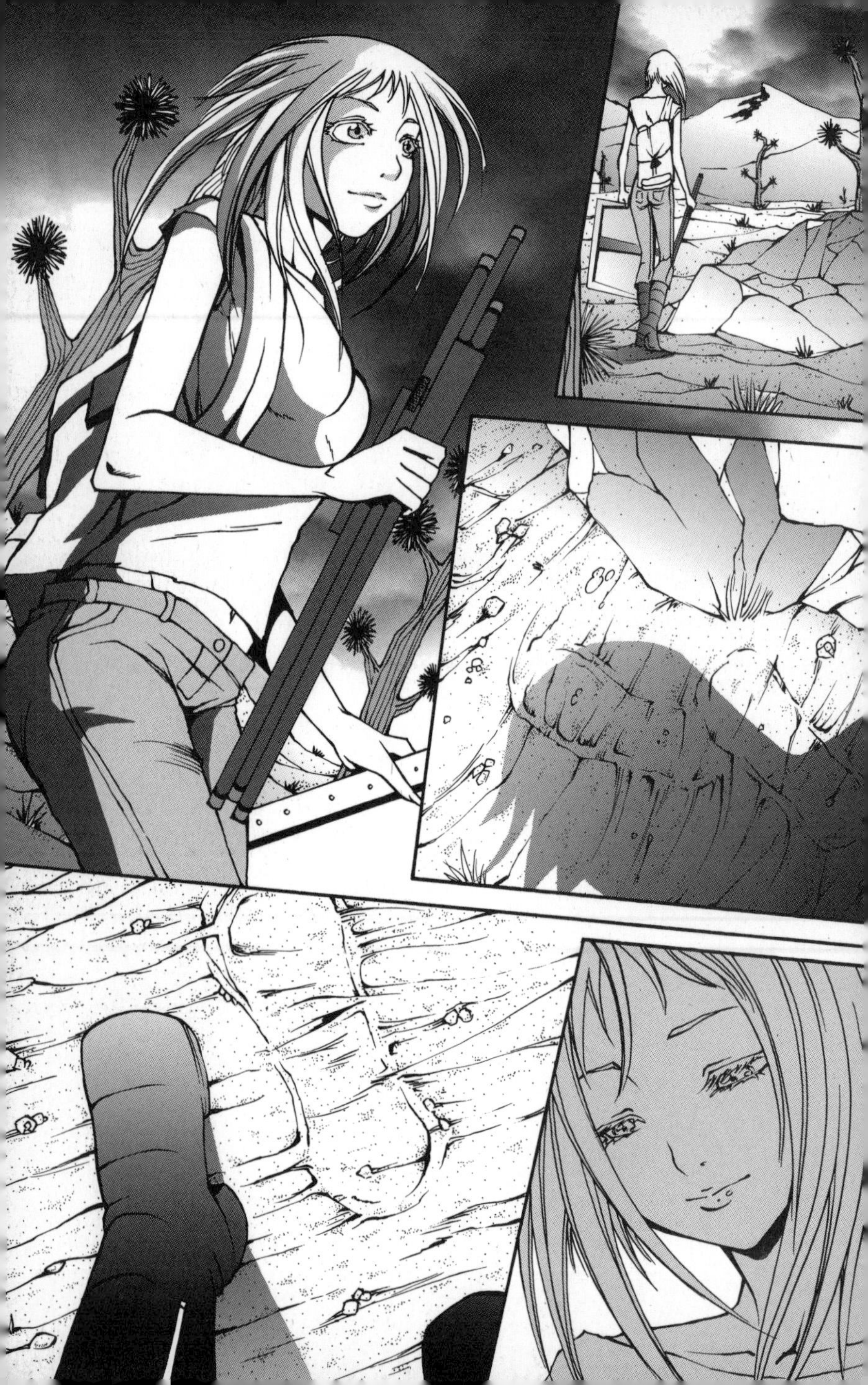

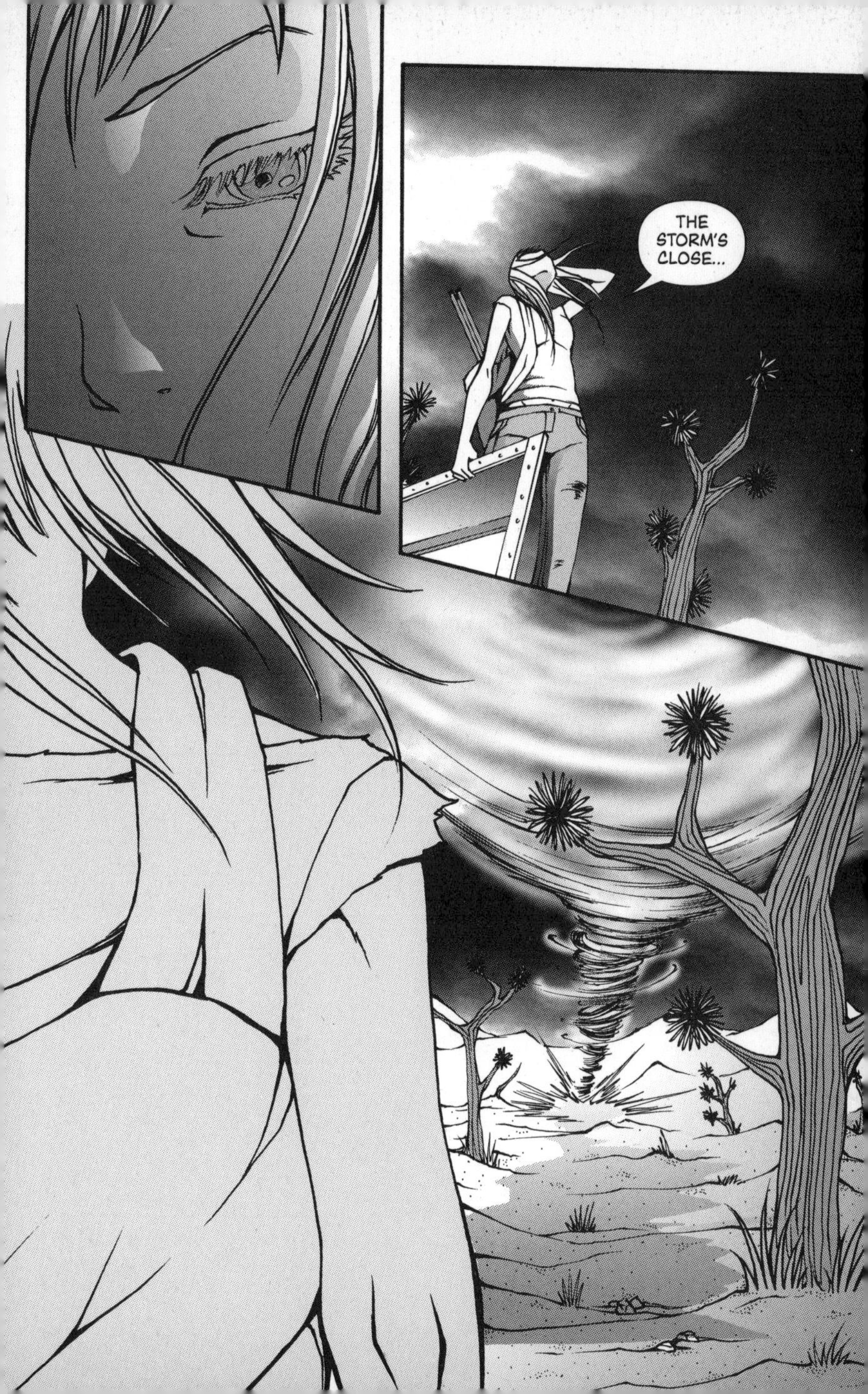
THE STORM'S CLOSE...

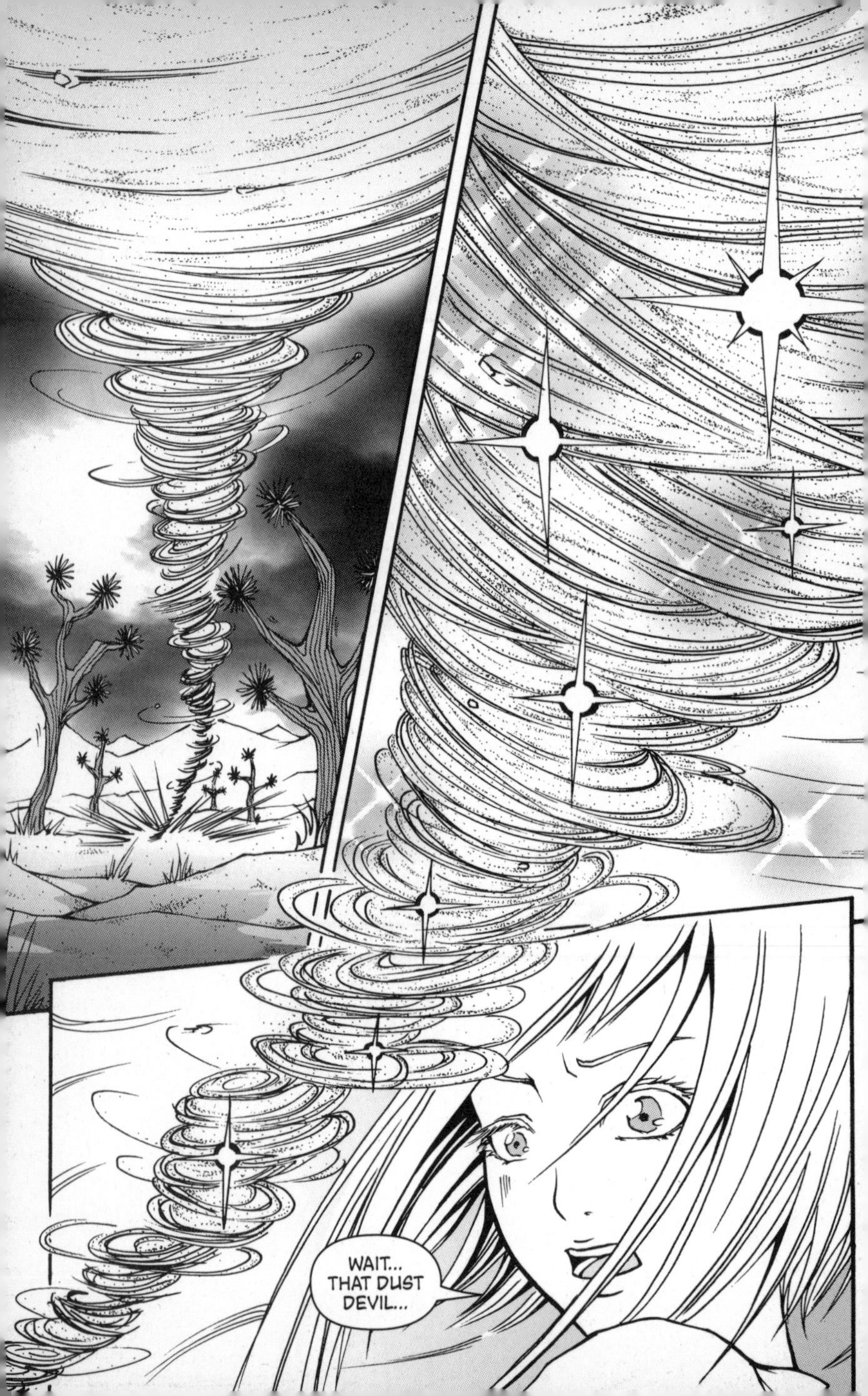
WAIT...
THAT DUST
DEVIL...

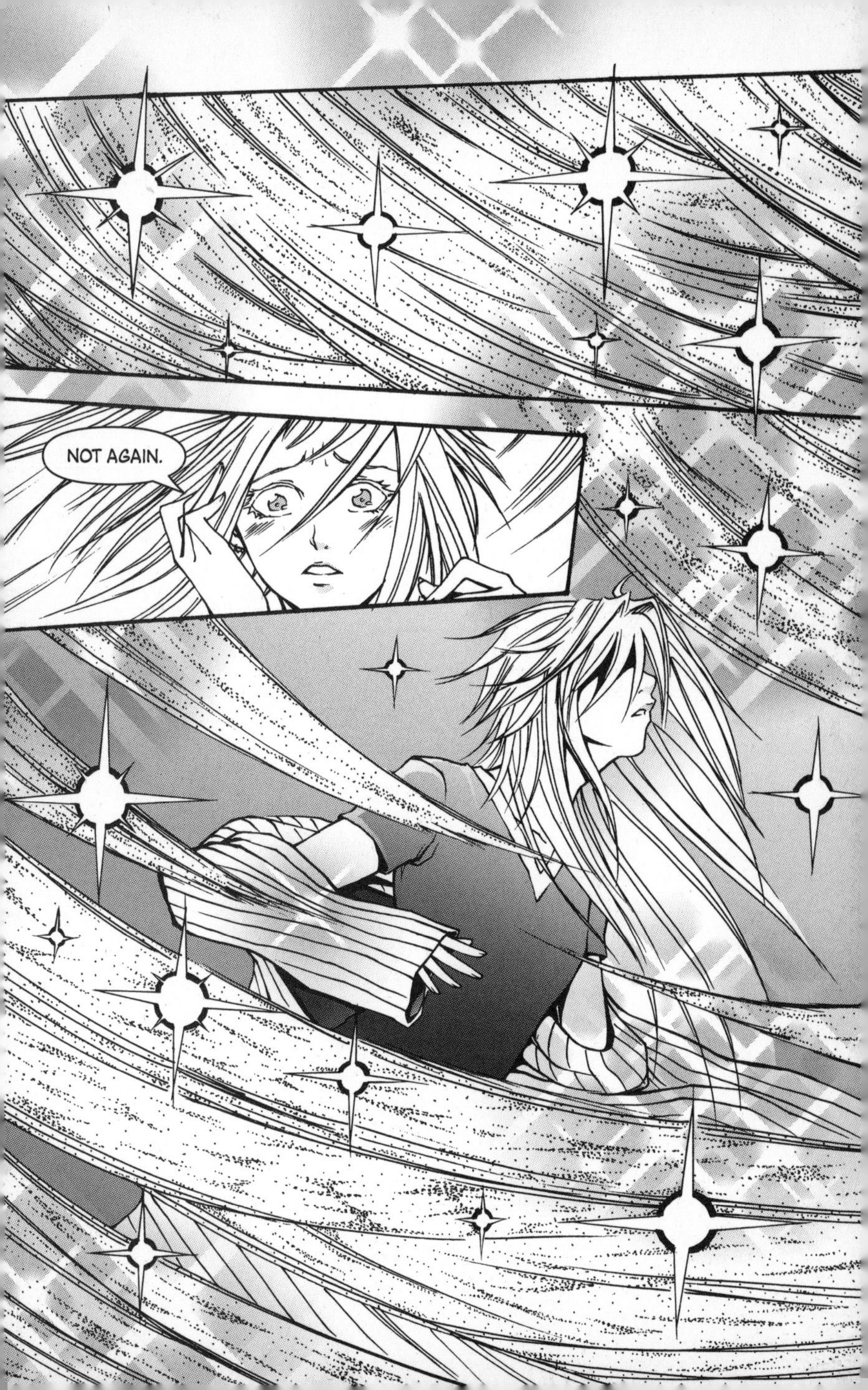
NOT AGAIN.

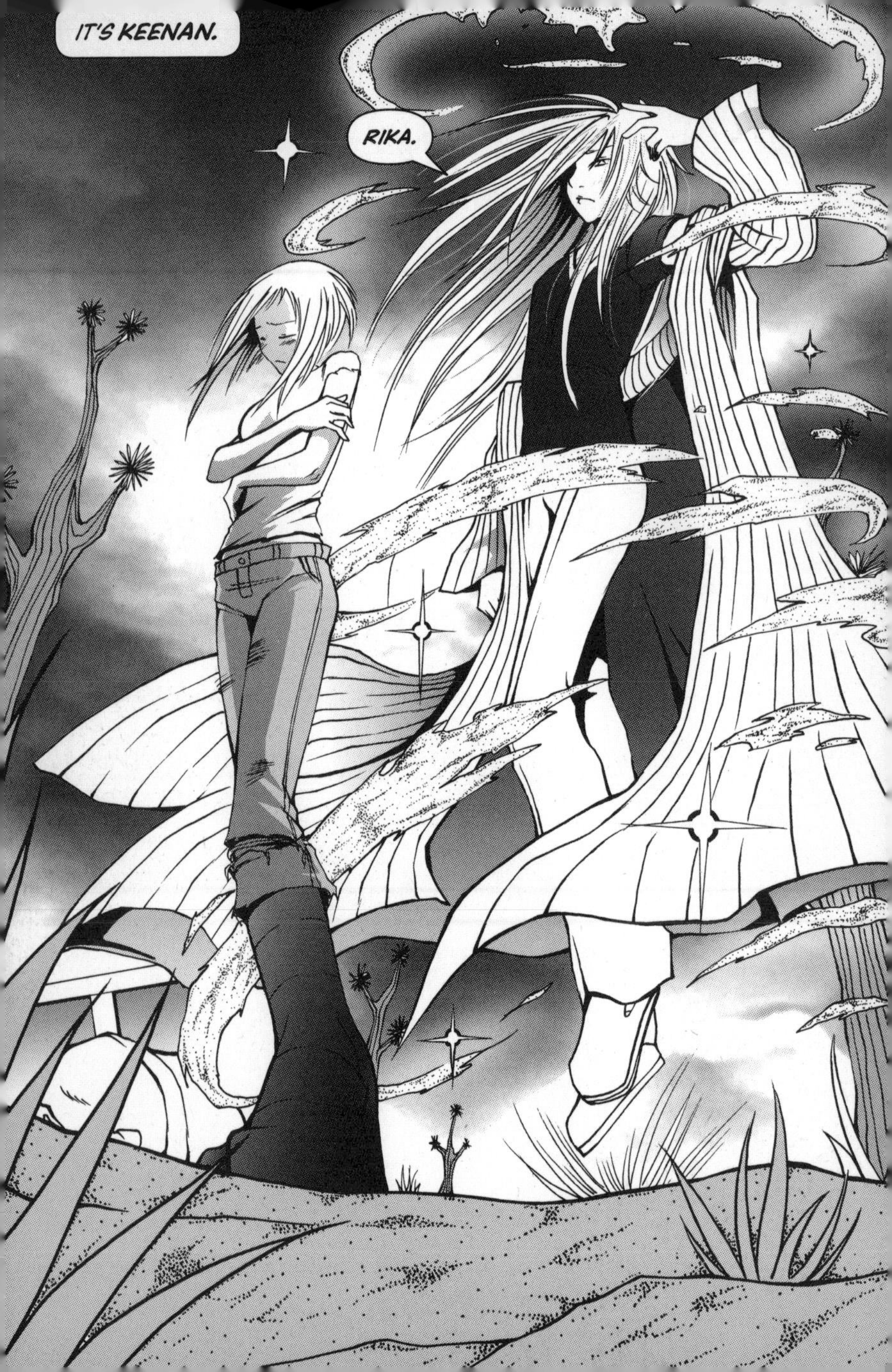
IT'S KEENAN.
RIKA.

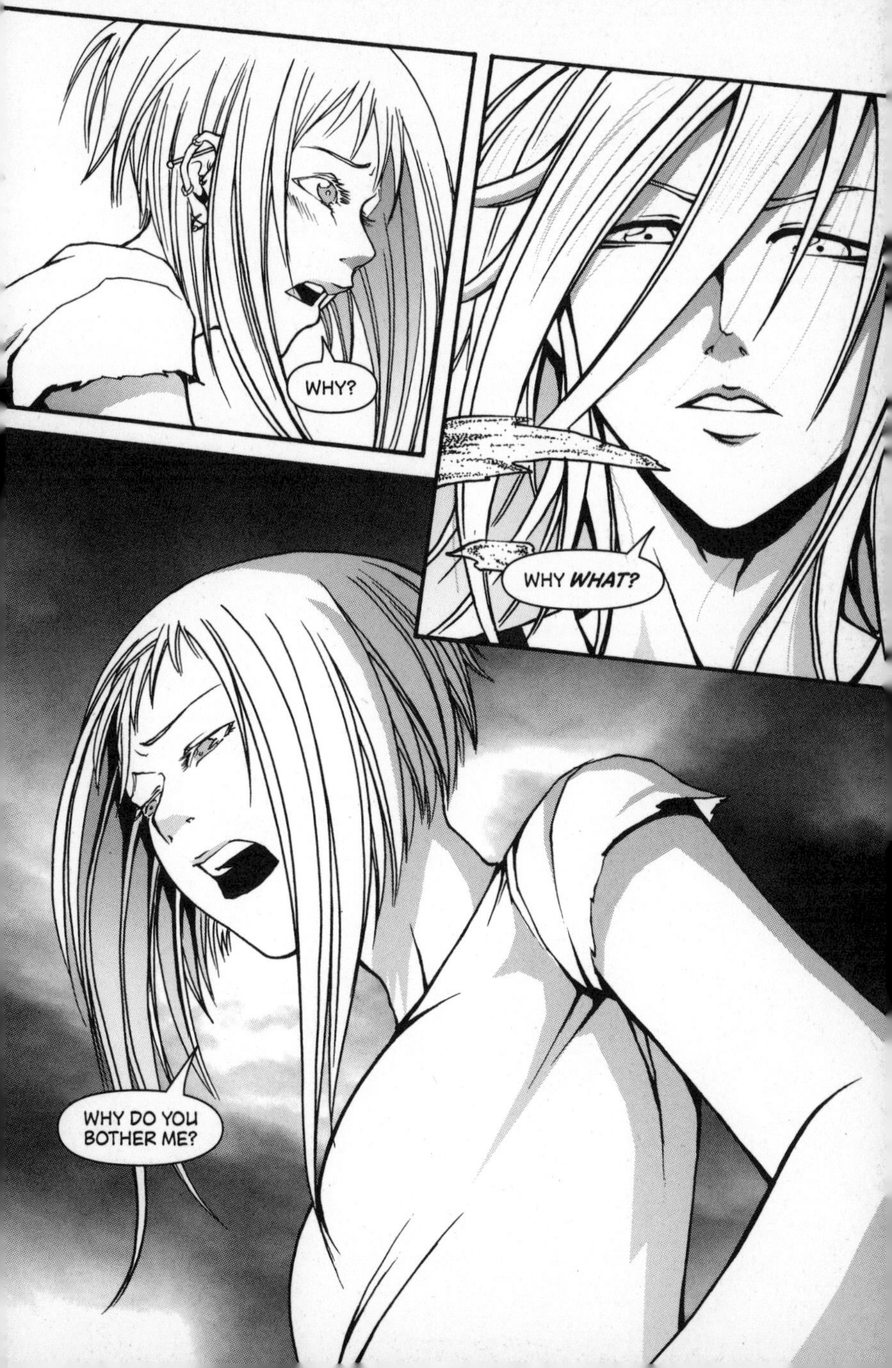
WHY?
WHY *WHAT?*
WHY DO YOU BOTHER ME?

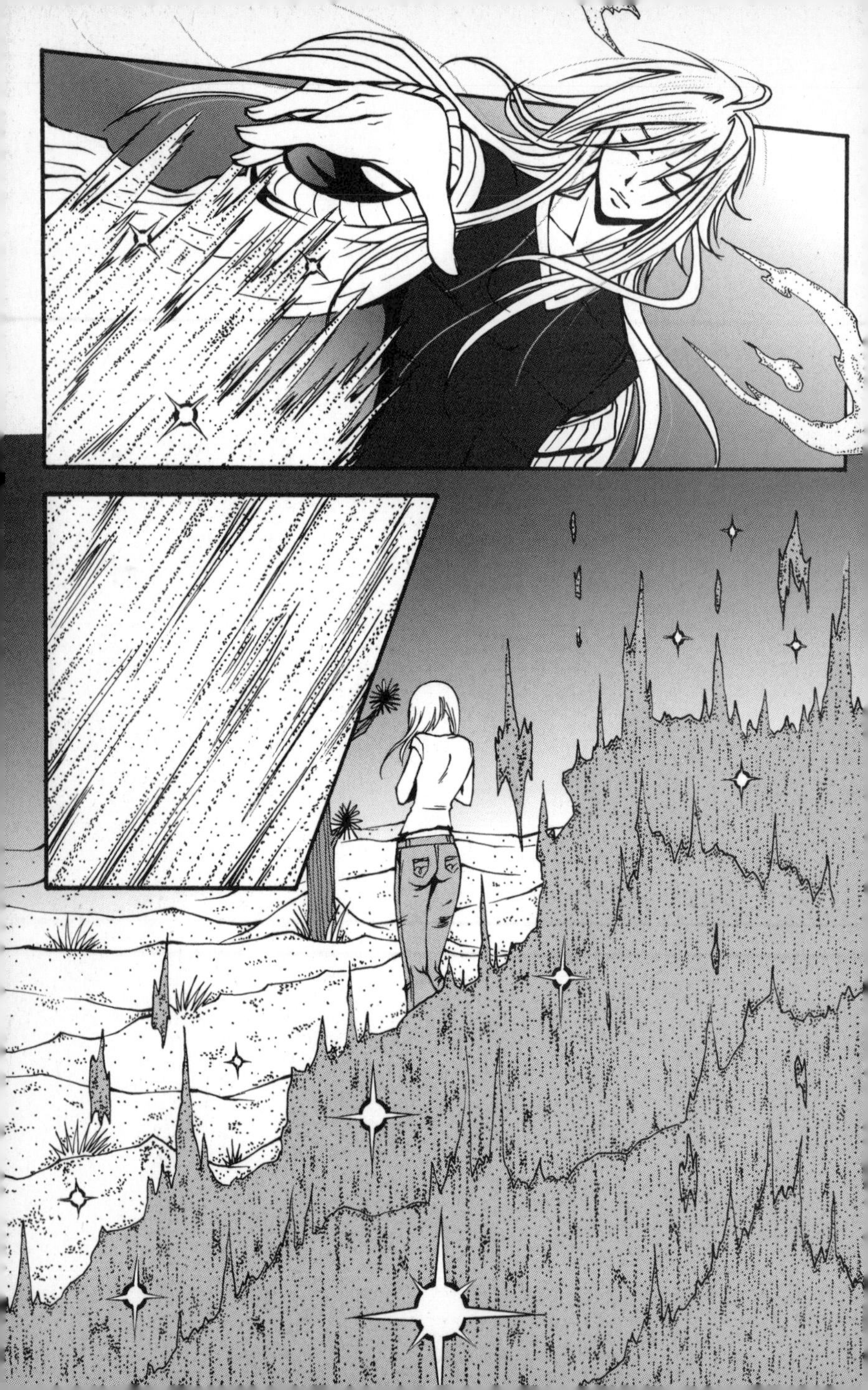

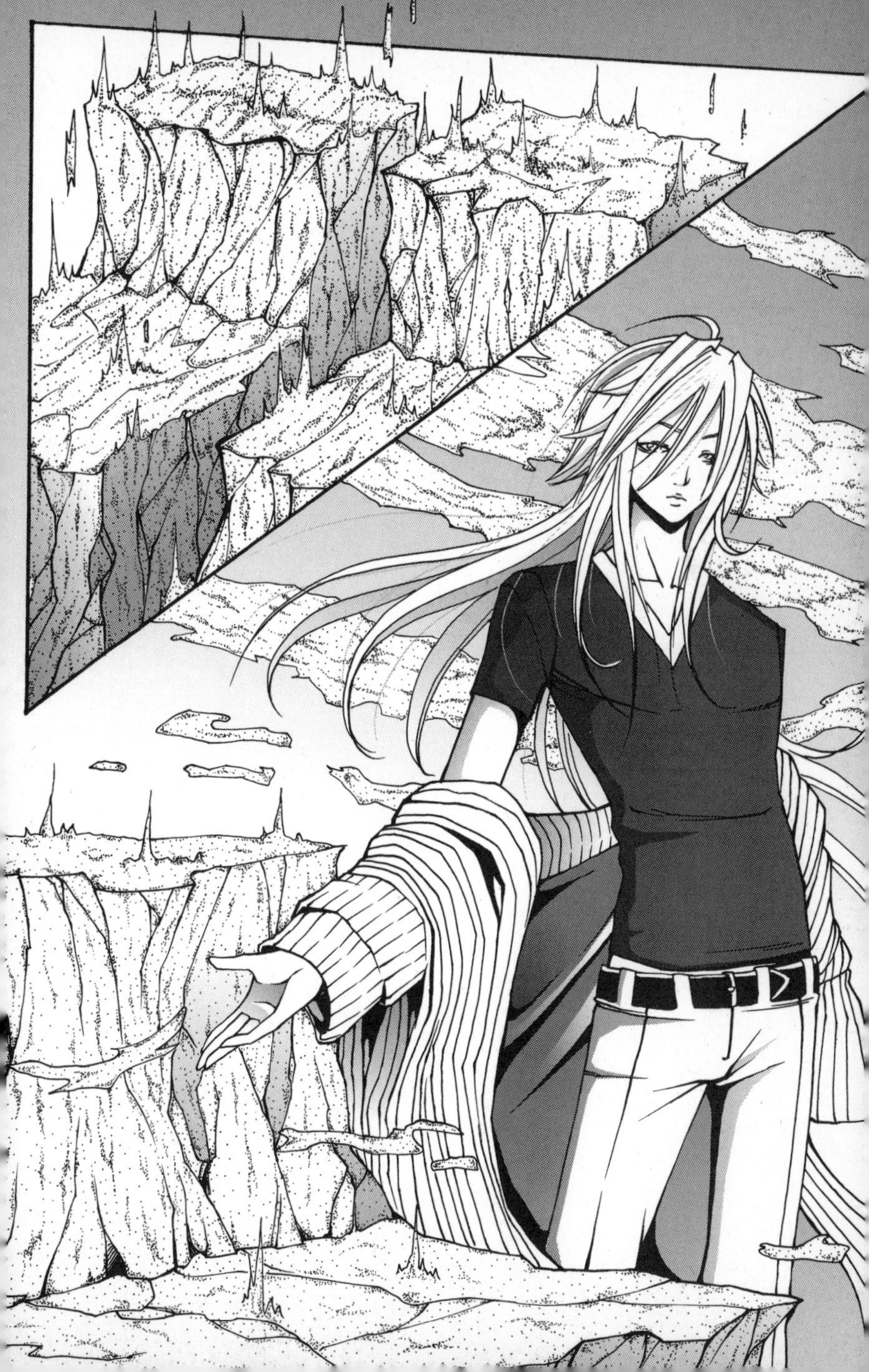

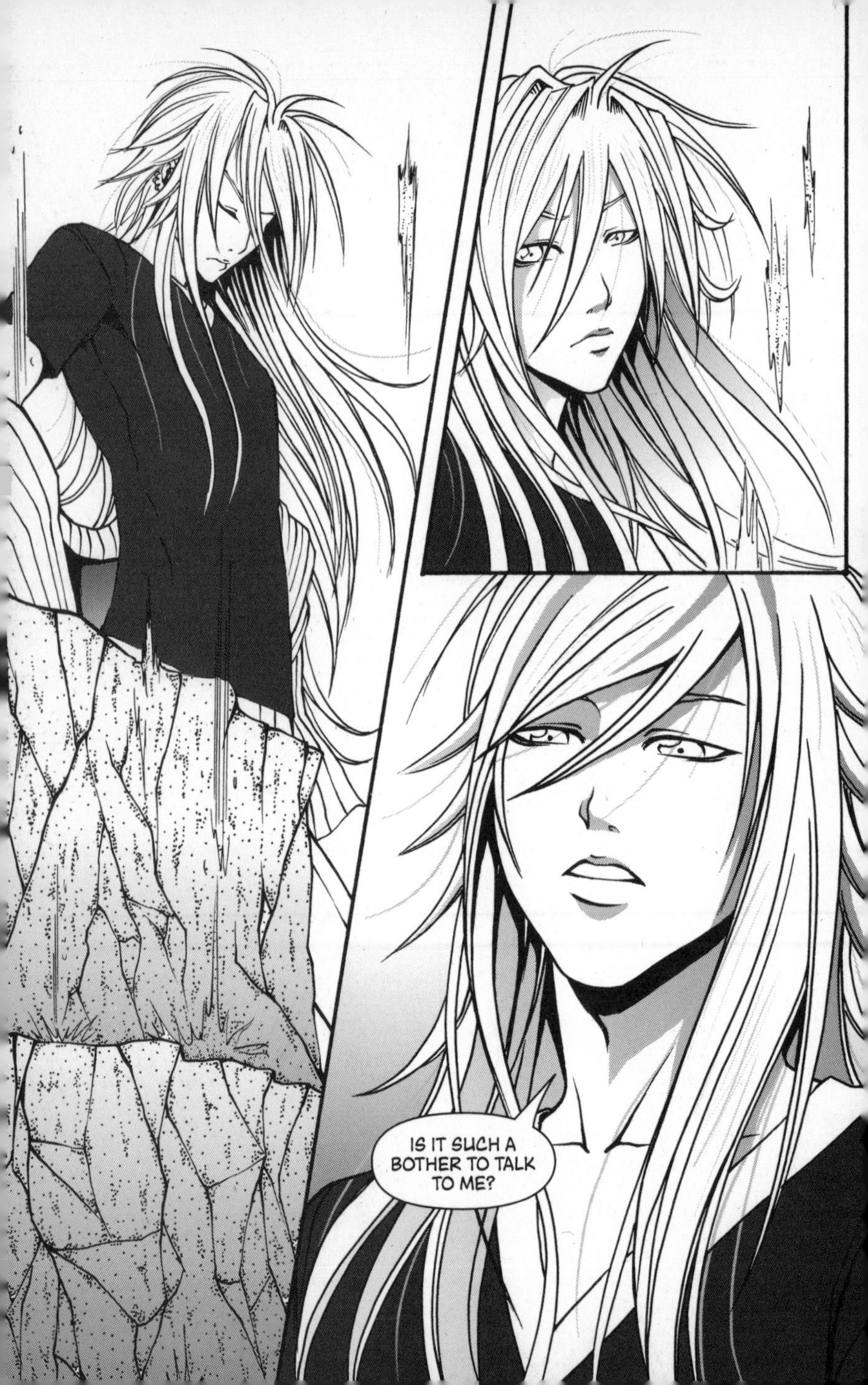
IS IT SUCH A BOTHER TO TALK TO ME?

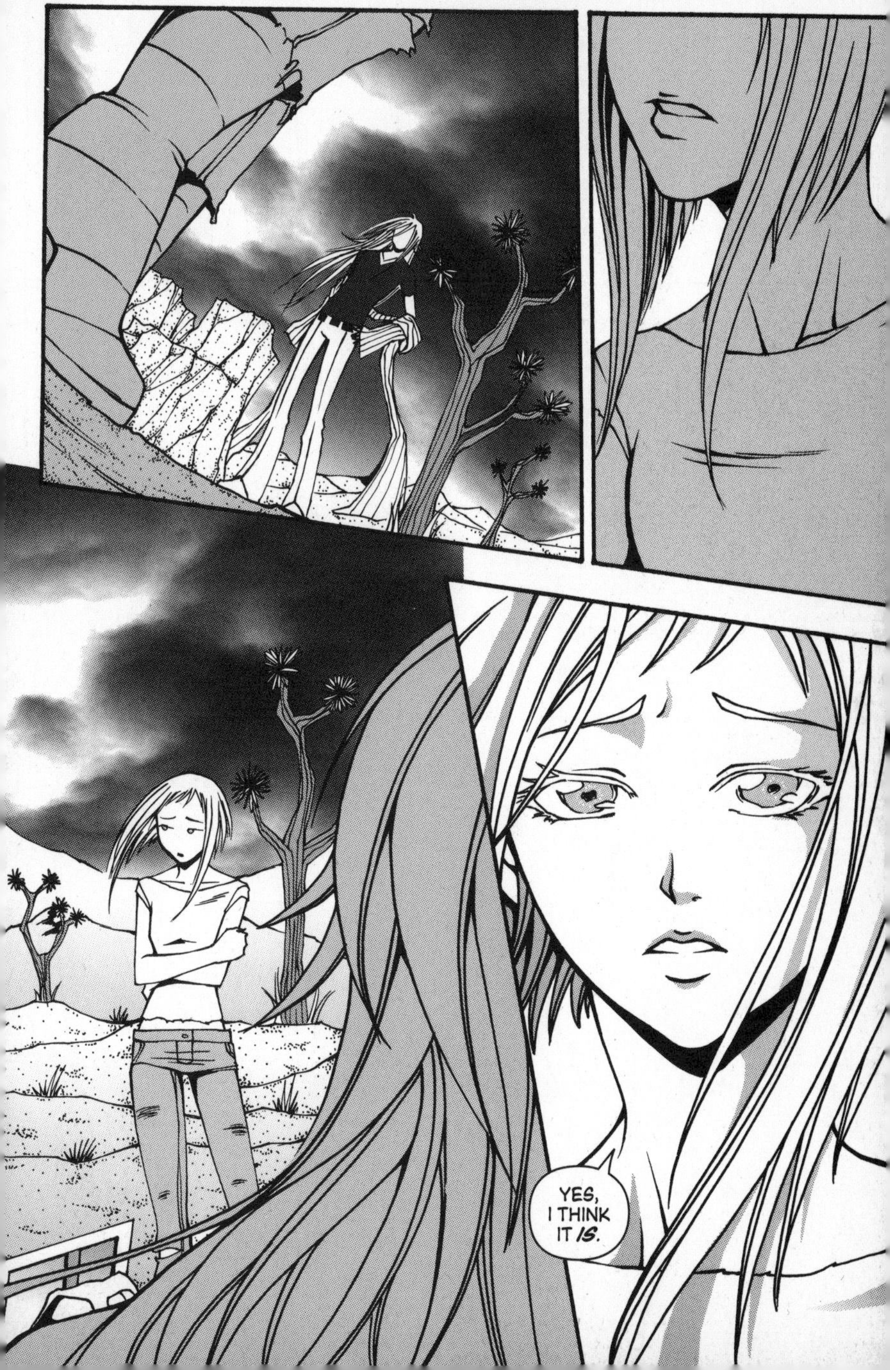
YES, I THINK IT *IS*.

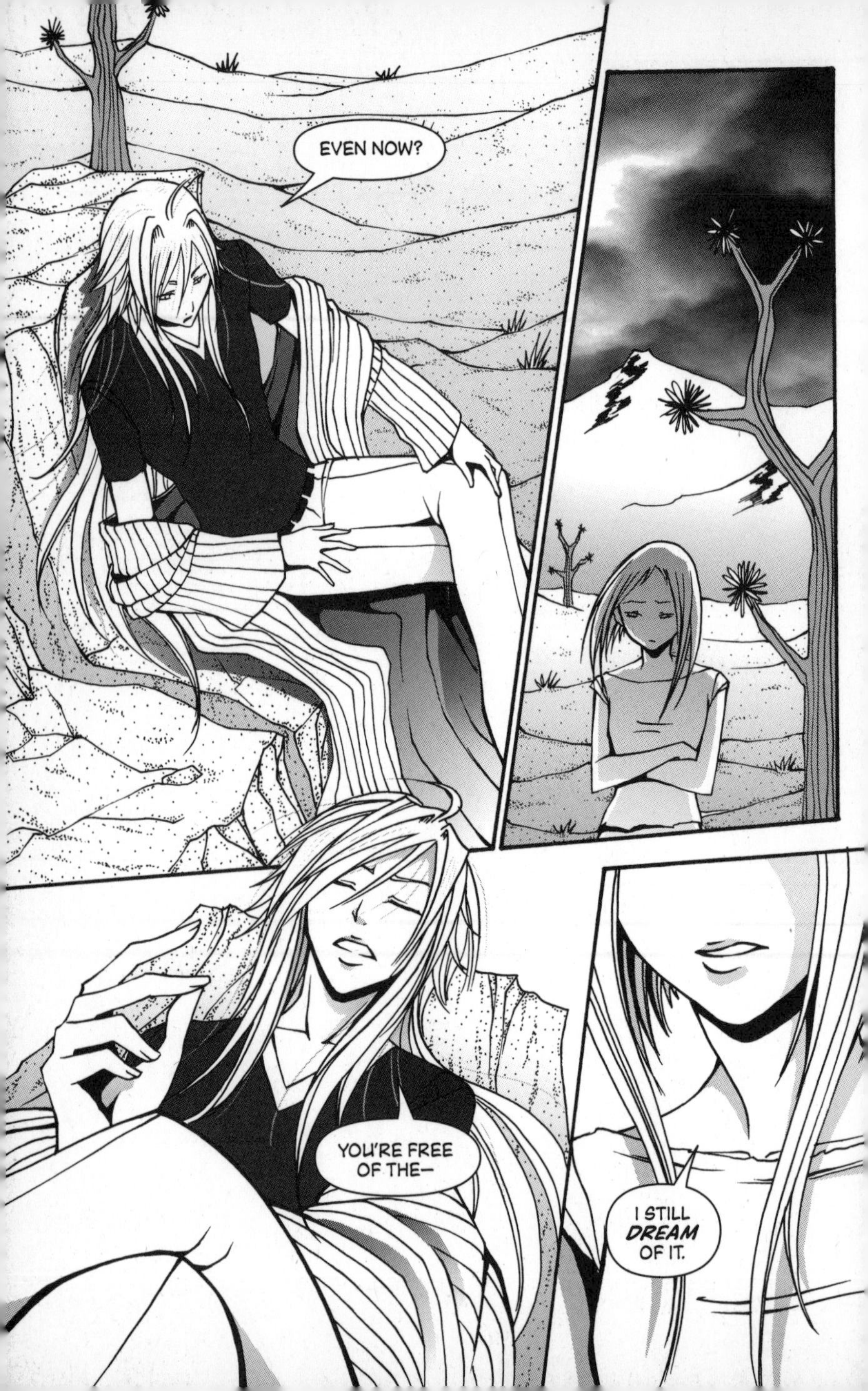
EVEN NOW?
YOU'RE FREE OF THE—
I STILL *DREAM* OF IT.

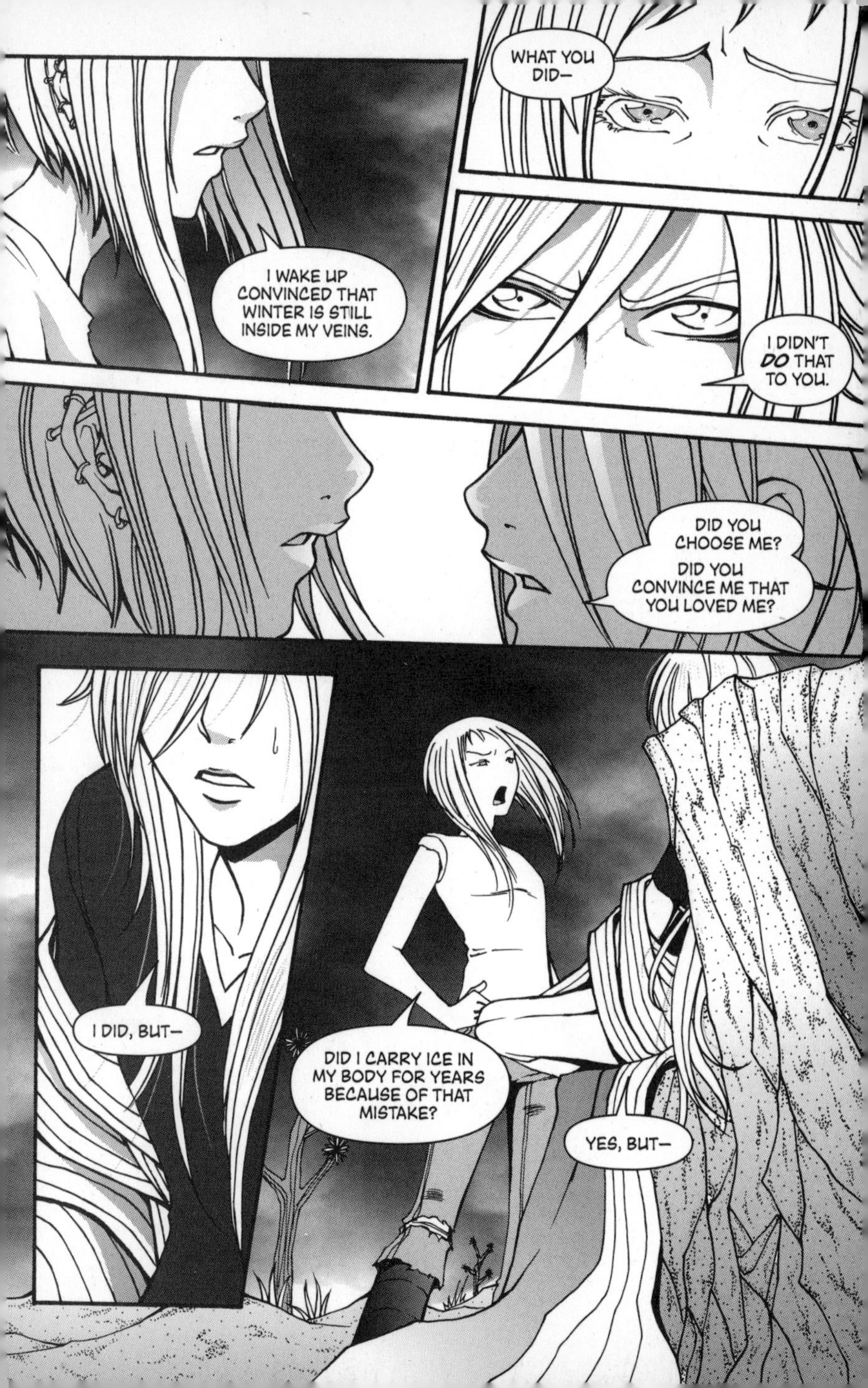
I WAKE UP CONVINCED THAT WINTER IS STILL INSIDE MY VEINS.
WHAT YOU DID—
I DIDN'T *DO* THAT TO YOU.
DID YOU CHOOSE ME?
DID YOU CONVINCE ME THAT YOU LOVED ME?
I DID, BUT—
DID I CARRY ICE IN MY BODY FOR YEARS BECAUSE OF THAT MISTAKE?
YES, BUT—

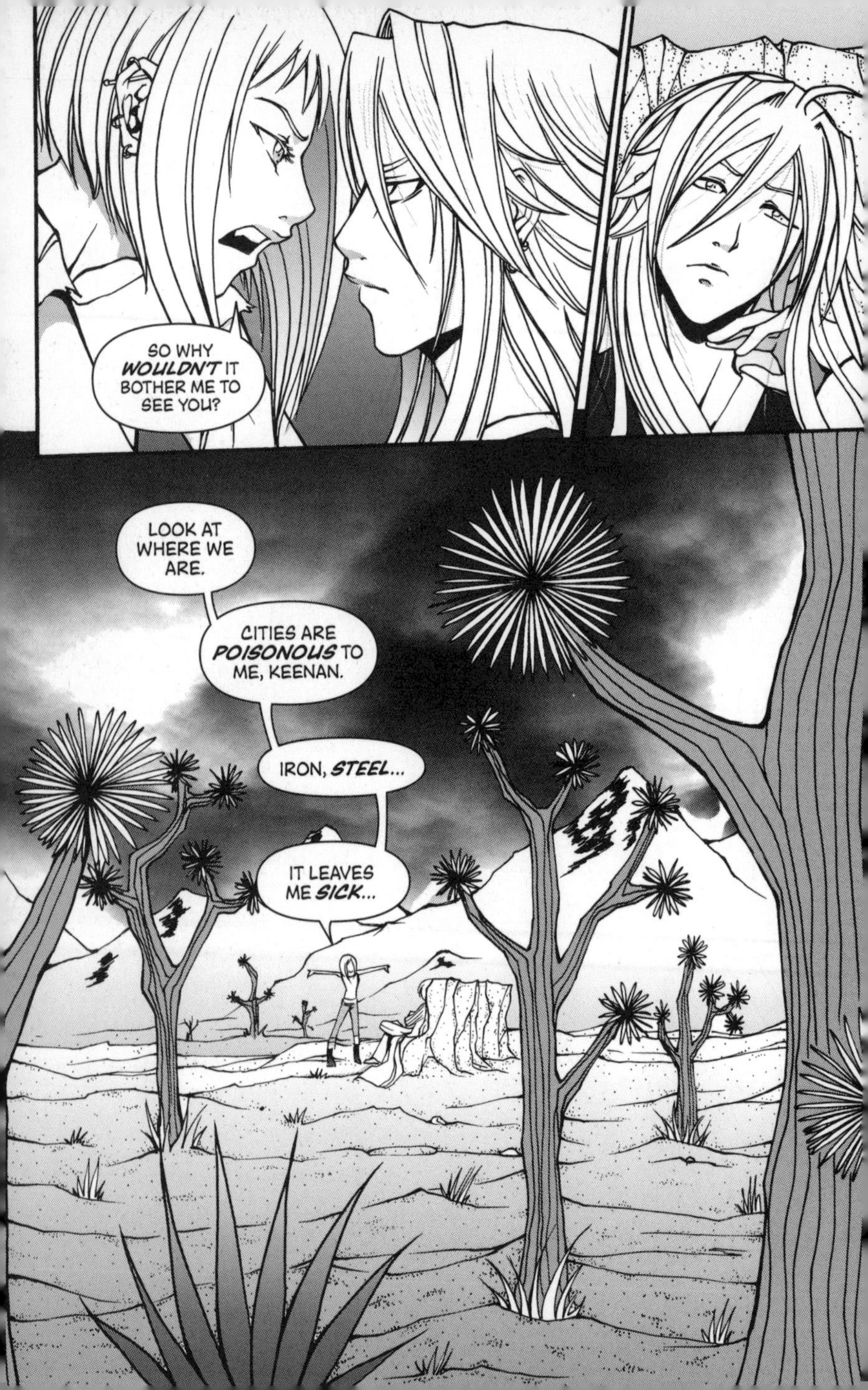
SO WHY **WOULDN'T** IT BOTHER ME TO SEE YOU?
LOOK AT WHERE WE ARE.
CITIES ARE **POISONOUS** TO ME, KEENAN.
IRON, **STEEL**...
IT LEAVES ME **SICK**...

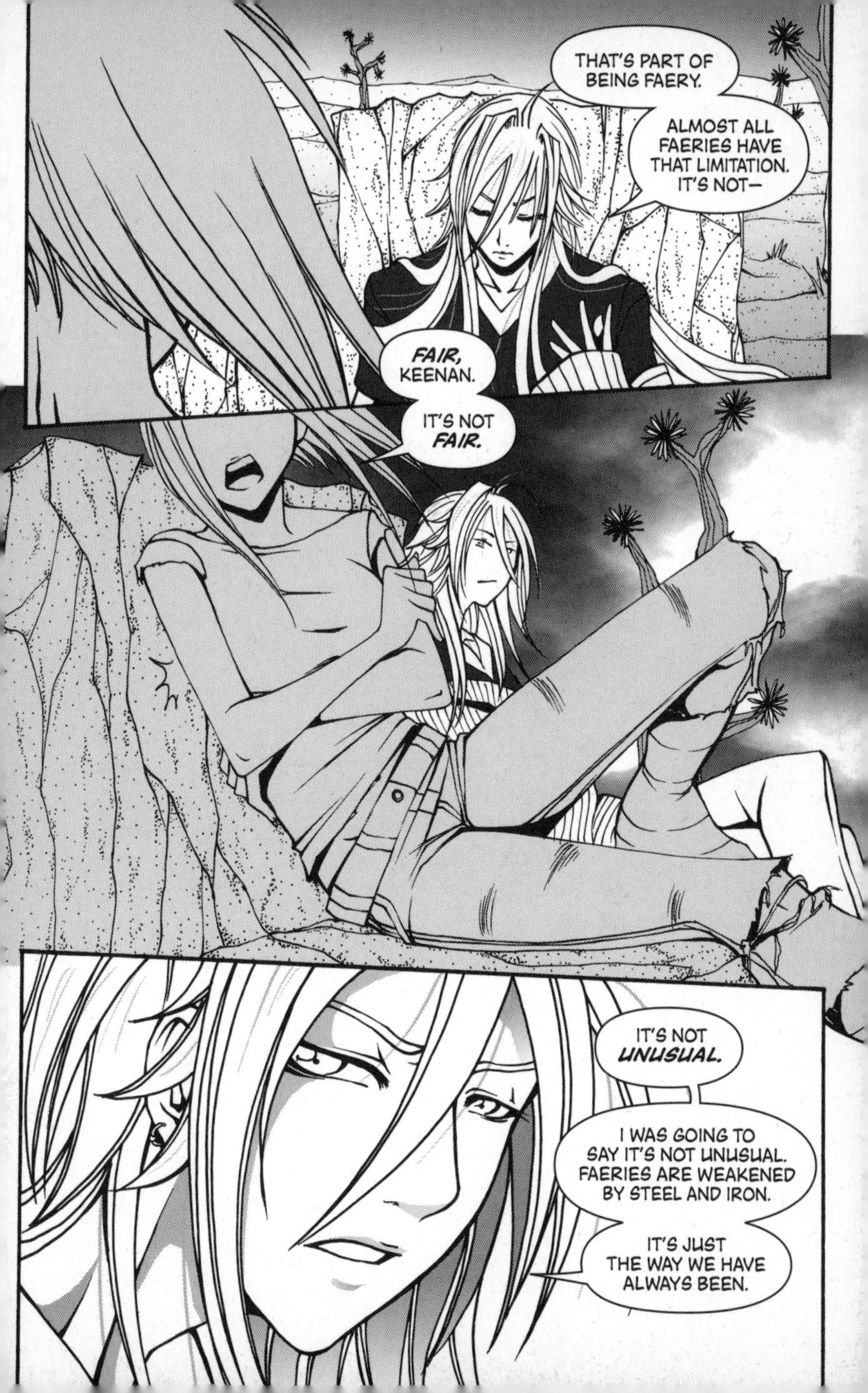
THAT'S PART OF BEING FAERY.
ALMOST ALL FAERIES HAVE THAT LIMITATION. IT'S NOT—
FAIR, KEENAN.
IT'S NOT *FAIR.*
IT'S NOT *UNUSUAL.*
I WAS GOING TO SAY IT'S NOT UNUSUAL. FAERIES ARE WEAKENED BY STEEL AND IRON.
IT'S JUST THE WAY WE HAVE ALWAYS BEEN.

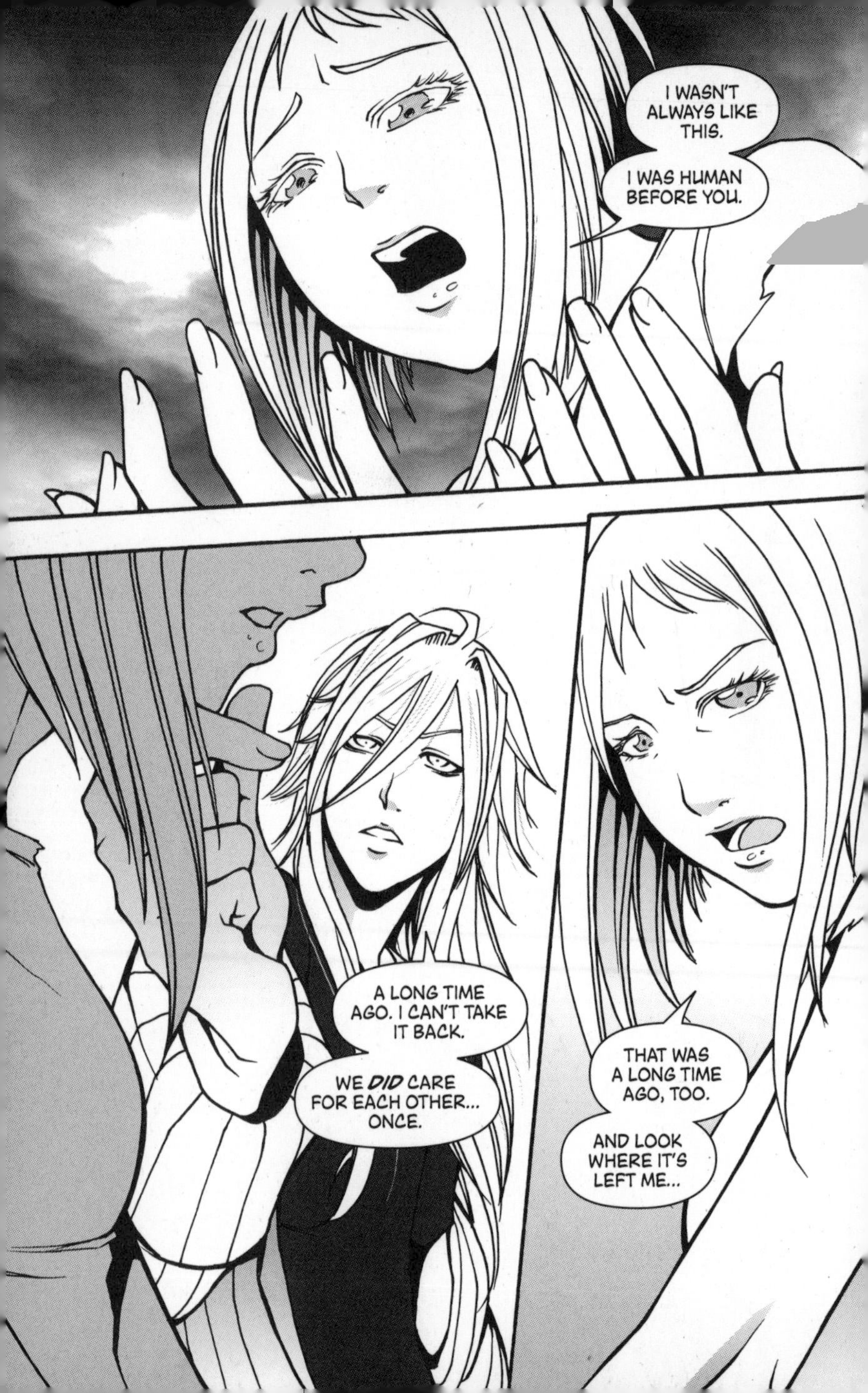
I WASN'T ALWAYS LIKE THIS.
I WAS HUMAN BEFORE YOU.
A LONG TIME AGO. I CAN'T TAKE IT BACK.
WE *DID* CARE FOR EACH OTHER... ONCE.
THAT WAS A LONG TIME AGO, TOO.
AND LOOK WHERE IT'S LEFT ME...

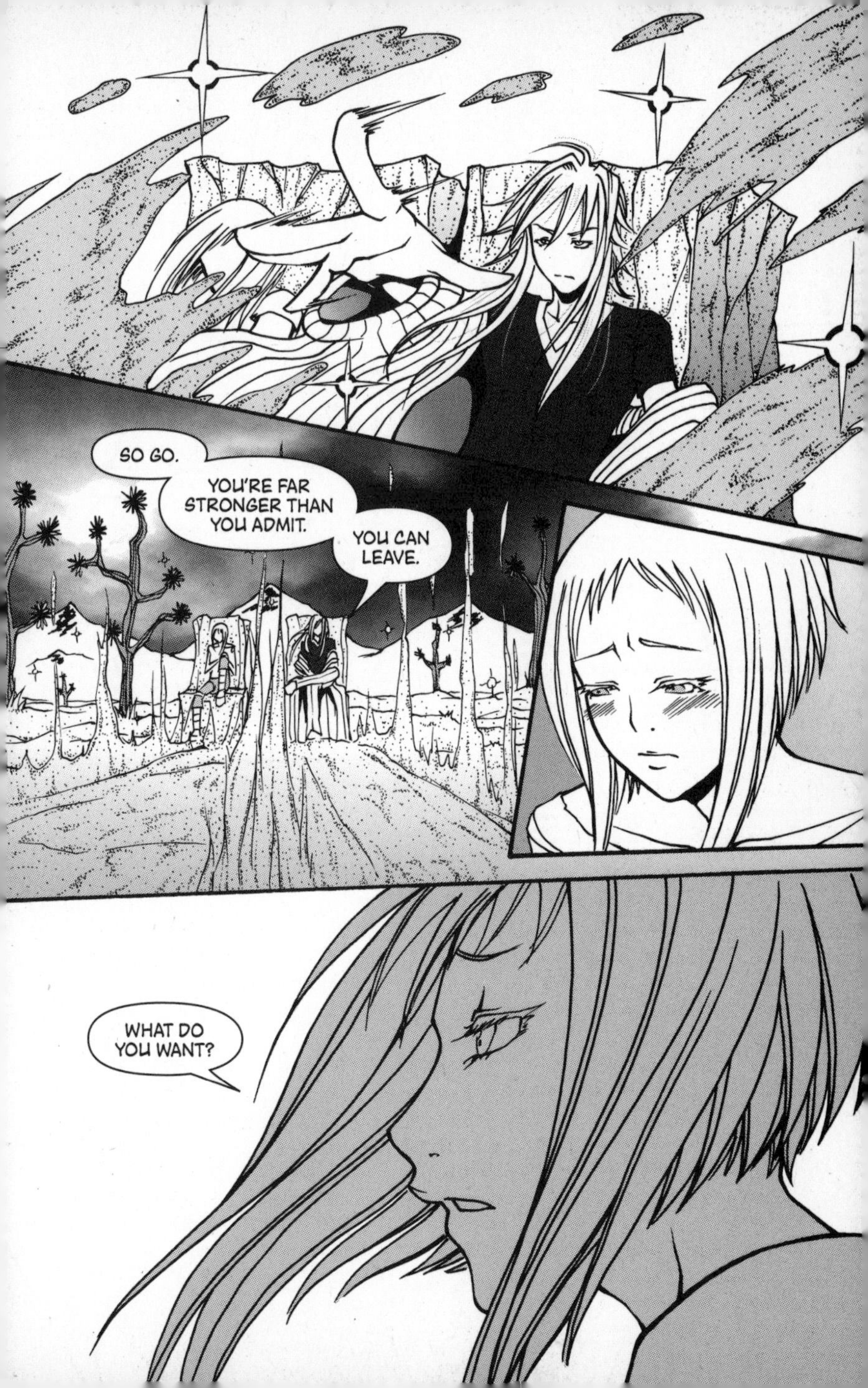
SO GO.
YOU'RE FAR STRONGER THAN YOU ADMIT.
YOU CAN LEAVE.
WHAT DO YOU WANT?

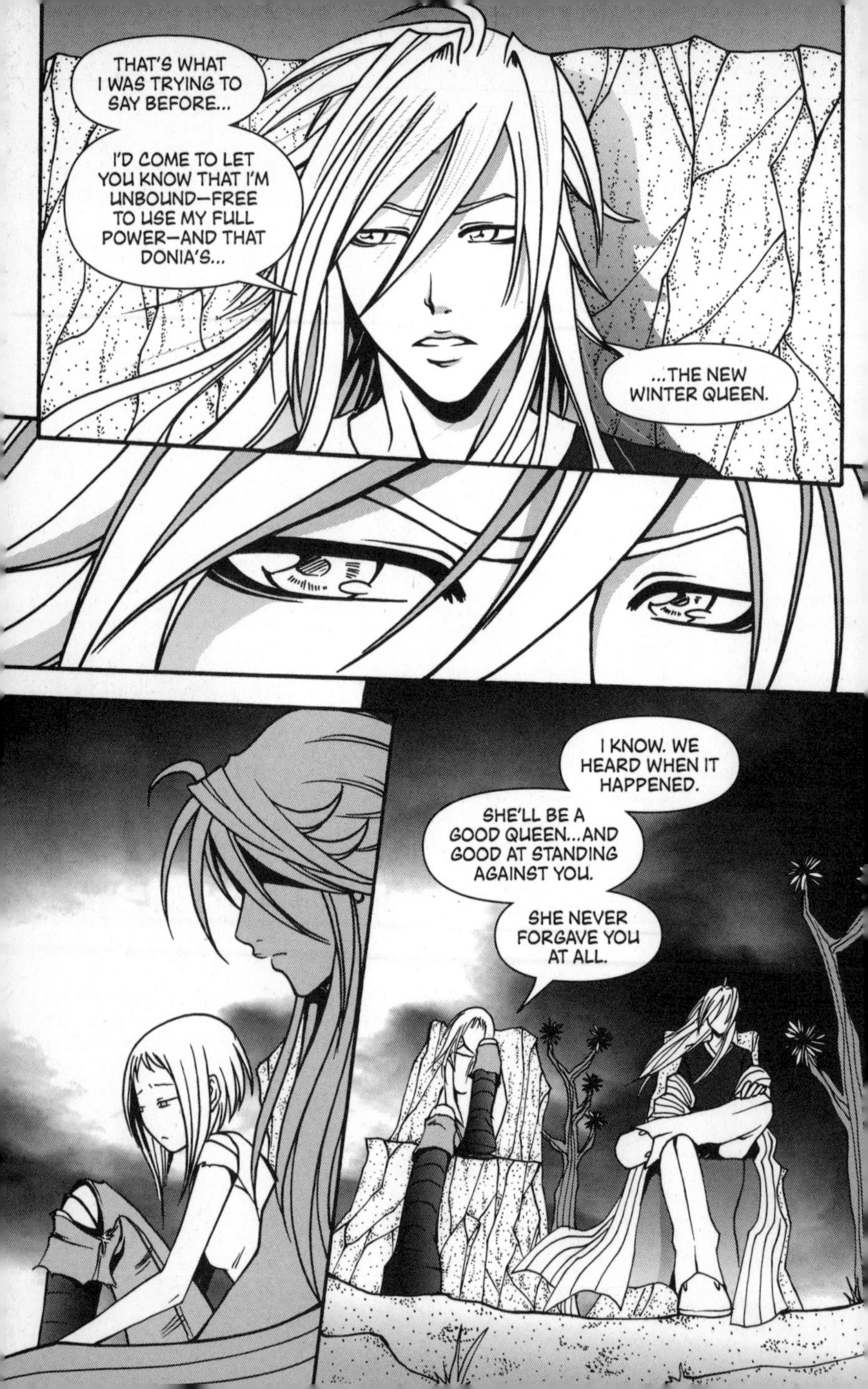
THAT'S WHAT I WAS TRYING TO SAY BEFORE...
I'D COME TO LET YOU KNOW THAT I'M UNBOUND—FREE TO USE MY FULL POWER—AND THAT DONIA'S...
...THE NEW WINTER QUEEN.
I KNOW. WE HEARD WHEN IT HAPPENED.
SHE'LL BE A GOOD QUEEN...AND GOOD AT STANDING AGAINST YOU.
SHE NEVER FORGAVE YOU AT ALL.

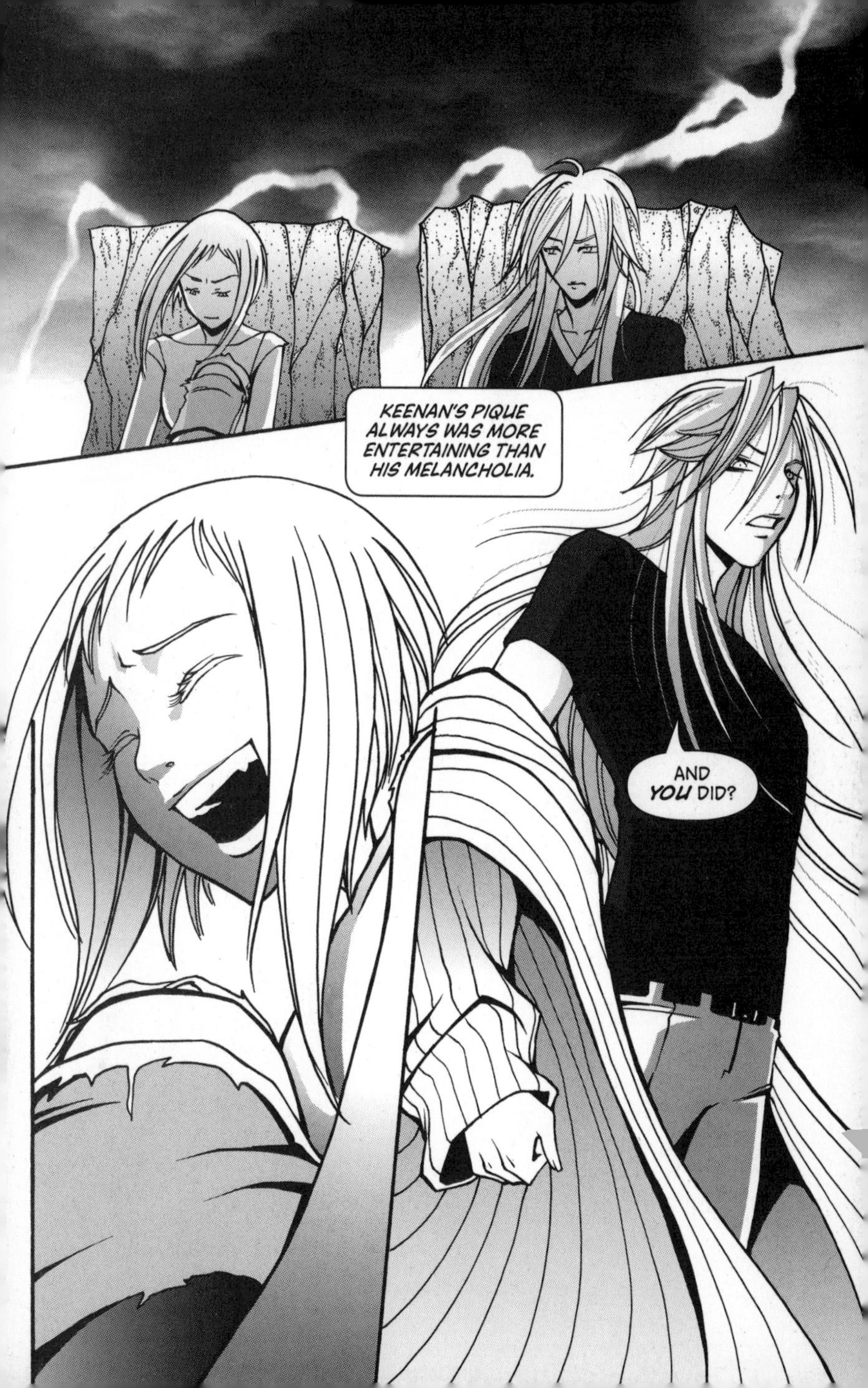
KEENAN'S PIQUE ALWAYS WAS MORE ENTERTAINING THAN HIS MELANCHOLIA.
AND YOU DID?

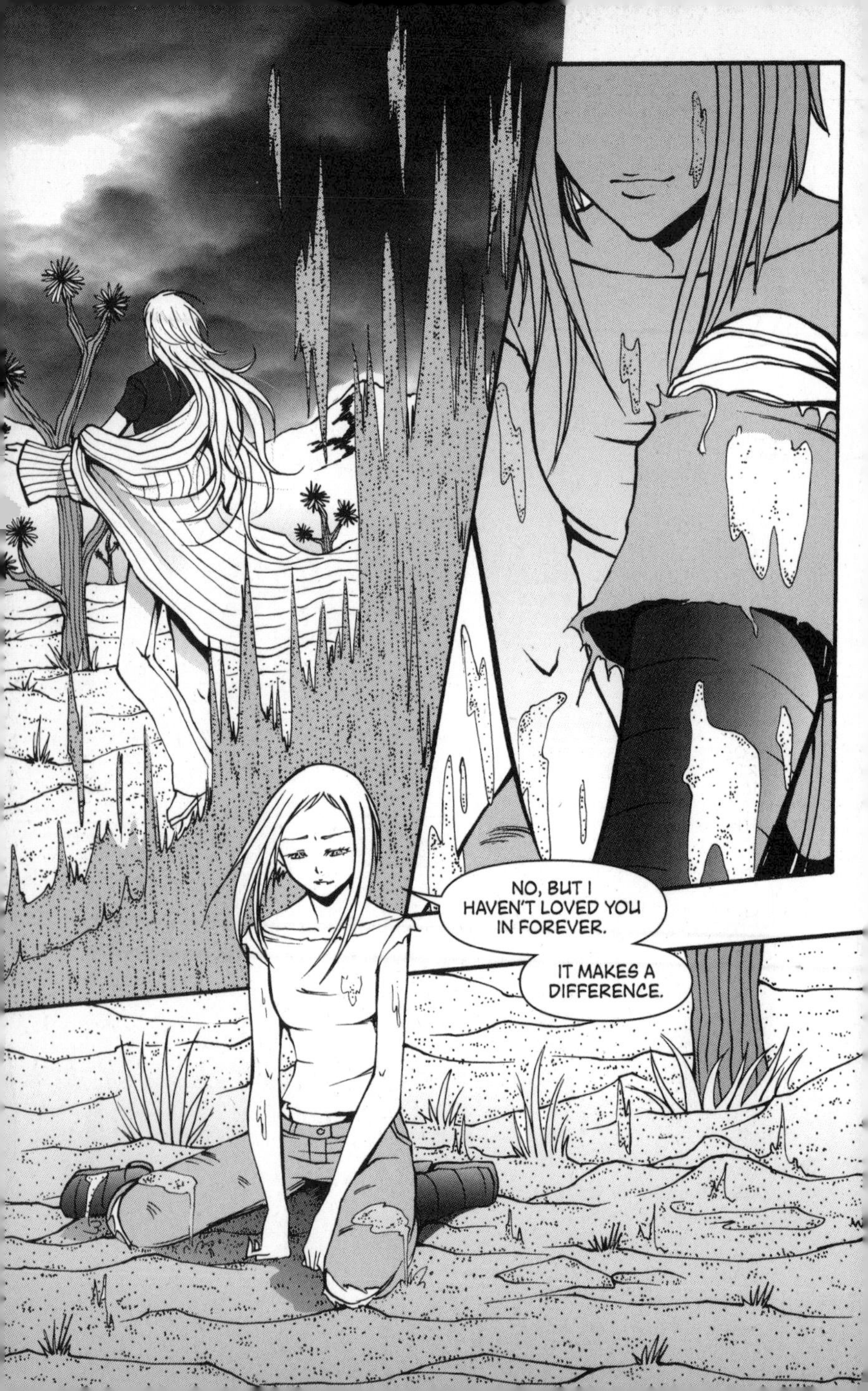
NO, BUT I HAVEN'T LOVED YOU IN FOREVER.
IT MAKES A DIFFERENCE.

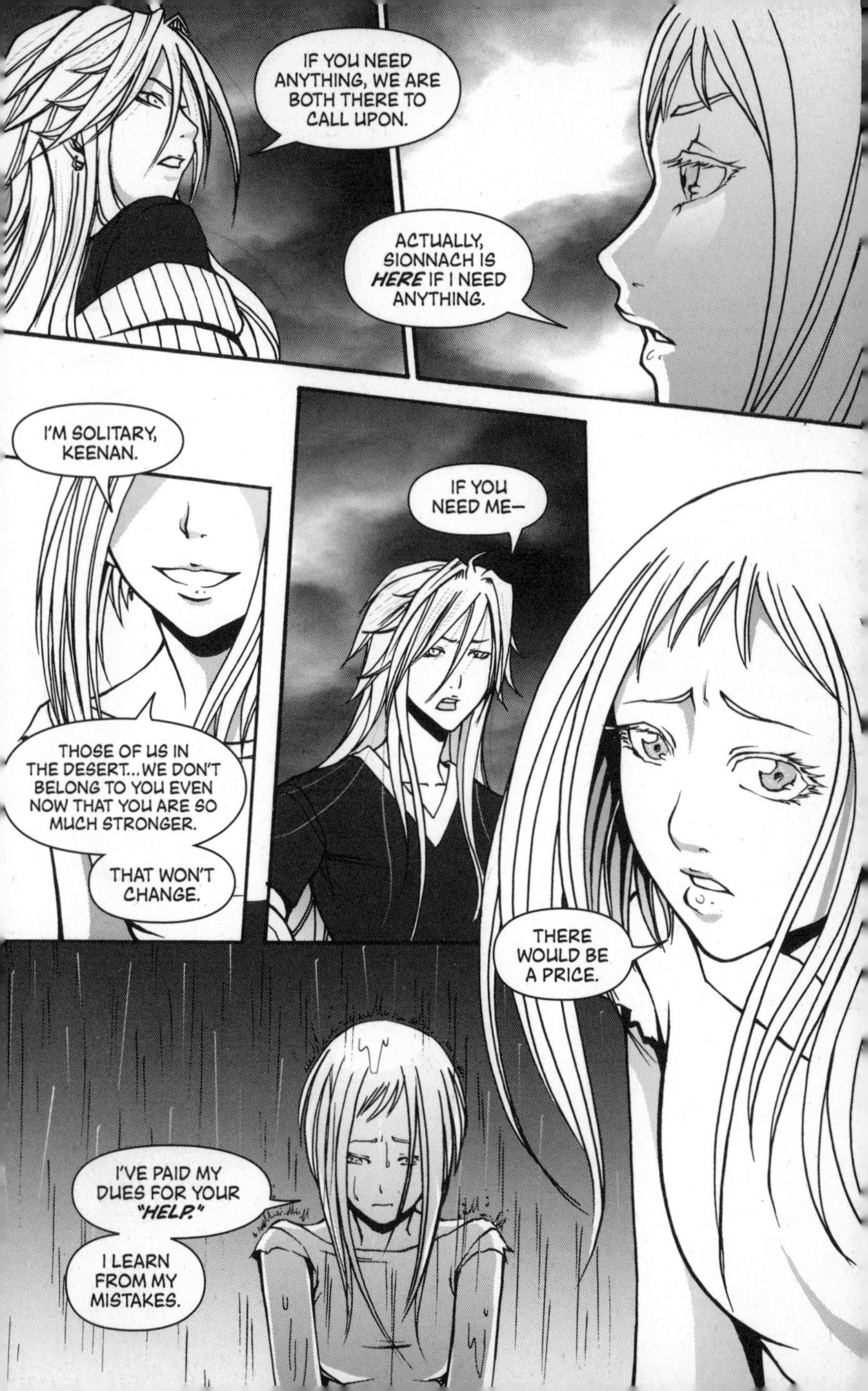

IF YOU NEED ANYTHING, WE ARE BOTH THERE TO CALL UPON.
ACTUALLY, SIONNACH IS ***HERE*** IF I NEED ANYTHING.
I'M SOLITARY, KEENAN.
THOSE OF US IN THE DESERT... WE DON'T BELONG TO YOU EVEN NOW THAT YOU ARE SO MUCH STRONGER.
THAT WON'T CHANGE.
IF YOU NEED ME—
I'VE PAID MY DUES FOR YOUR ***"HELP."***
I LEARN FROM MY MISTAKES.
THERE WOULD BE A PRICE.

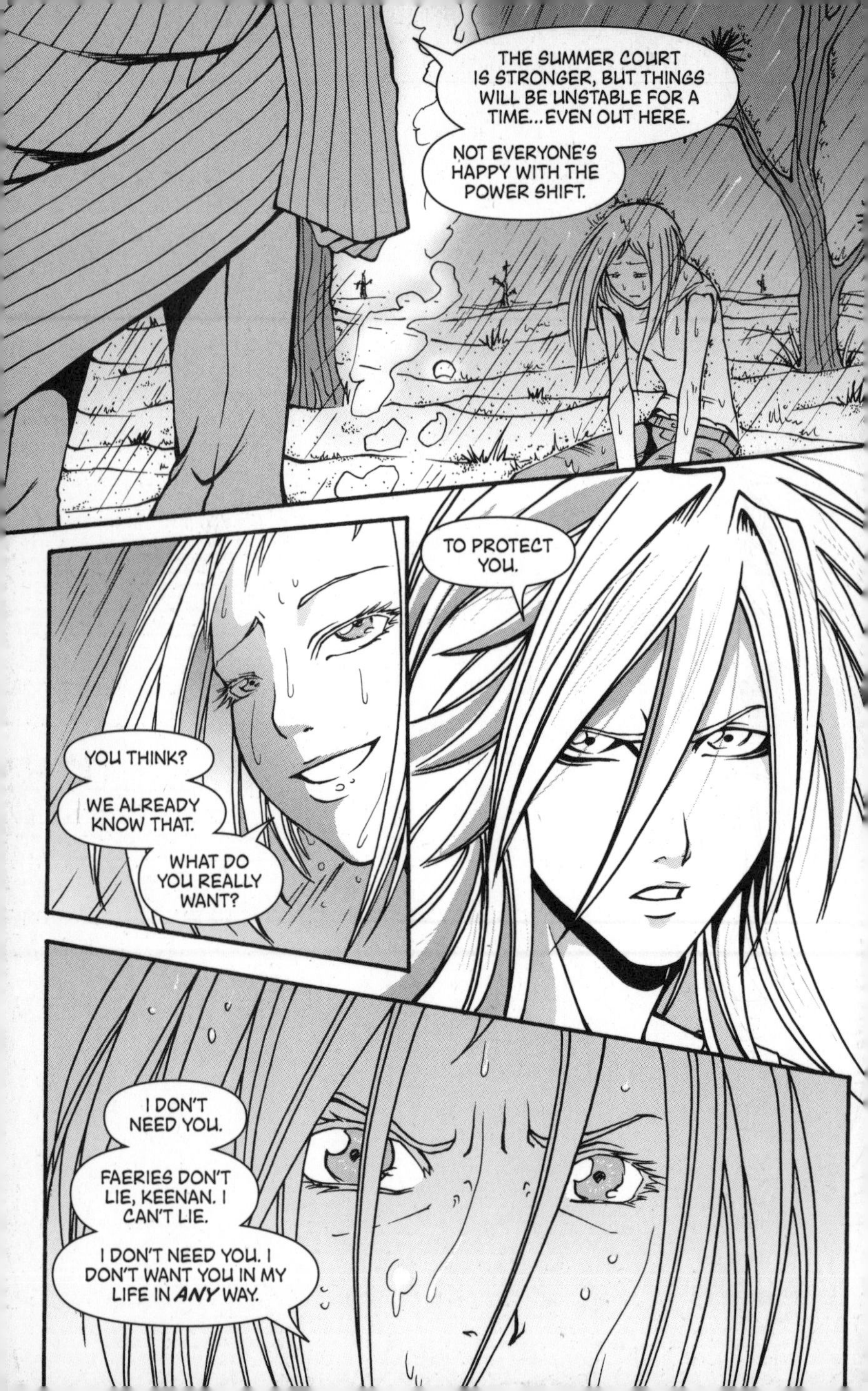
THE SUMMER COURT IS STRONGER, BUT THINGS WILL BE UNSTABLE FOR A TIME...EVEN OUT HERE.
NOT EVERYONE'S HAPPY WITH THE POWER SHIFT.
YOU THINK?
WE ALREADY KNOW THAT.
WHAT DO YOU REALLY WANT?
TO PROTECT YOU.
I DON'T NEED YOU.
FAERIES DON'T LIE, KEENAN. I CAN'T LIE.
I DON'T NEED YOU. I DON'T WANT YOU IN MY LIFE IN *ANY* WAY.

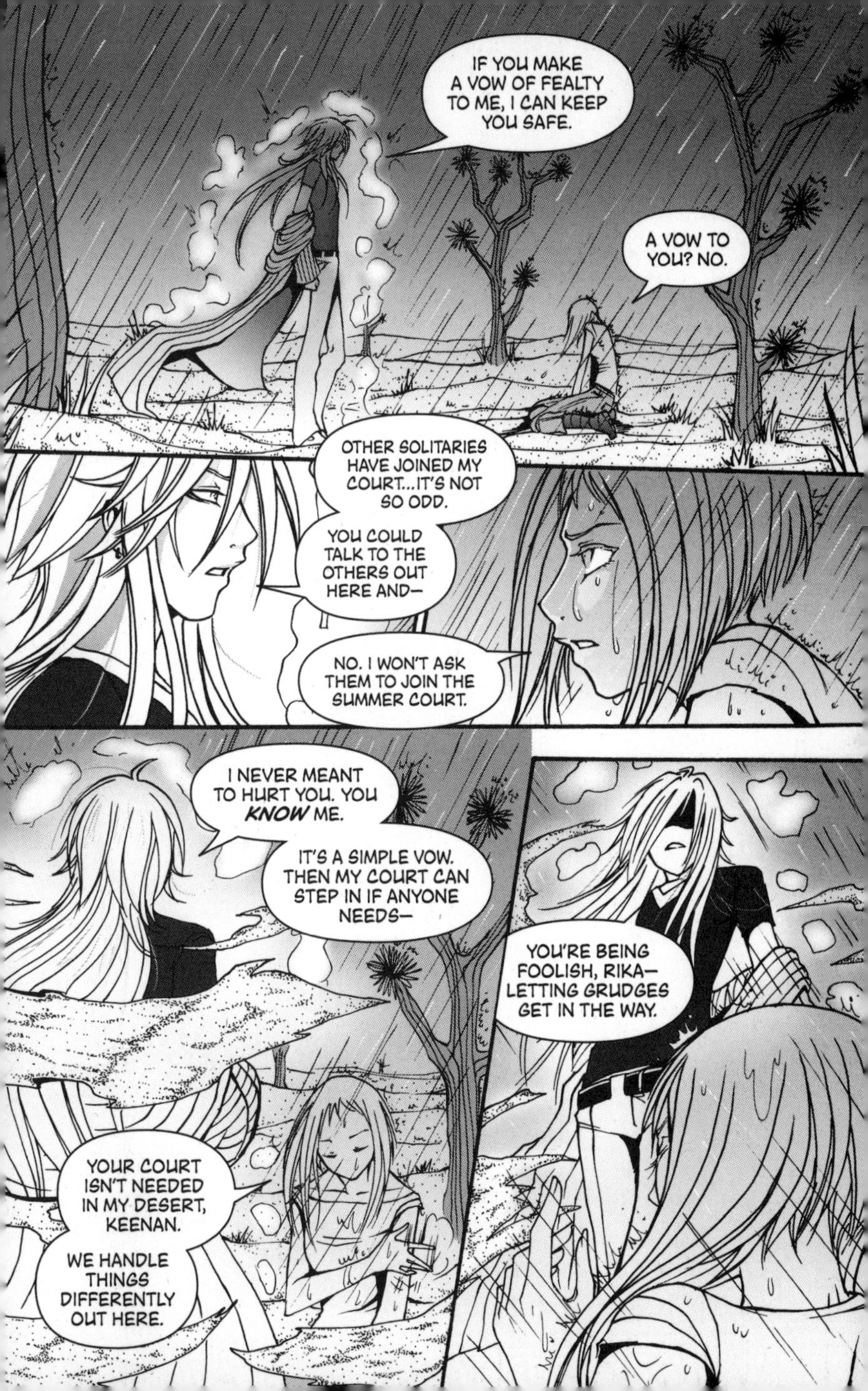
IF YOU MAKE A VOW OF FEALTY TO ME, I CAN KEEP YOU SAFE.
A VOW TO YOU? NO.
OTHER SOLITARIES HAVE JOINED MY COURT...IT'S NOT SO ODD.
YOU COULD TALK TO THE OTHERS OUT HERE AND—
NO. I WON'T ASK THEM TO JOIN THE SUMMER COURT.
I NEVER MEANT TO HURT YOU. YOU *KNOW* ME.
IT'S A SIMPLE VOW. THEN MY COURT CAN STEP IN IF ANYONE NEEDS—
YOUR COURT ISN'T NEEDED IN MY DESERT, KEENAN.
WE HANDLE THINGS DIFFERENTLY OUT HERE.
YOU'RE BEING FOOLISH, RIKA—LETTING GRUDGES GET IN THE WAY.

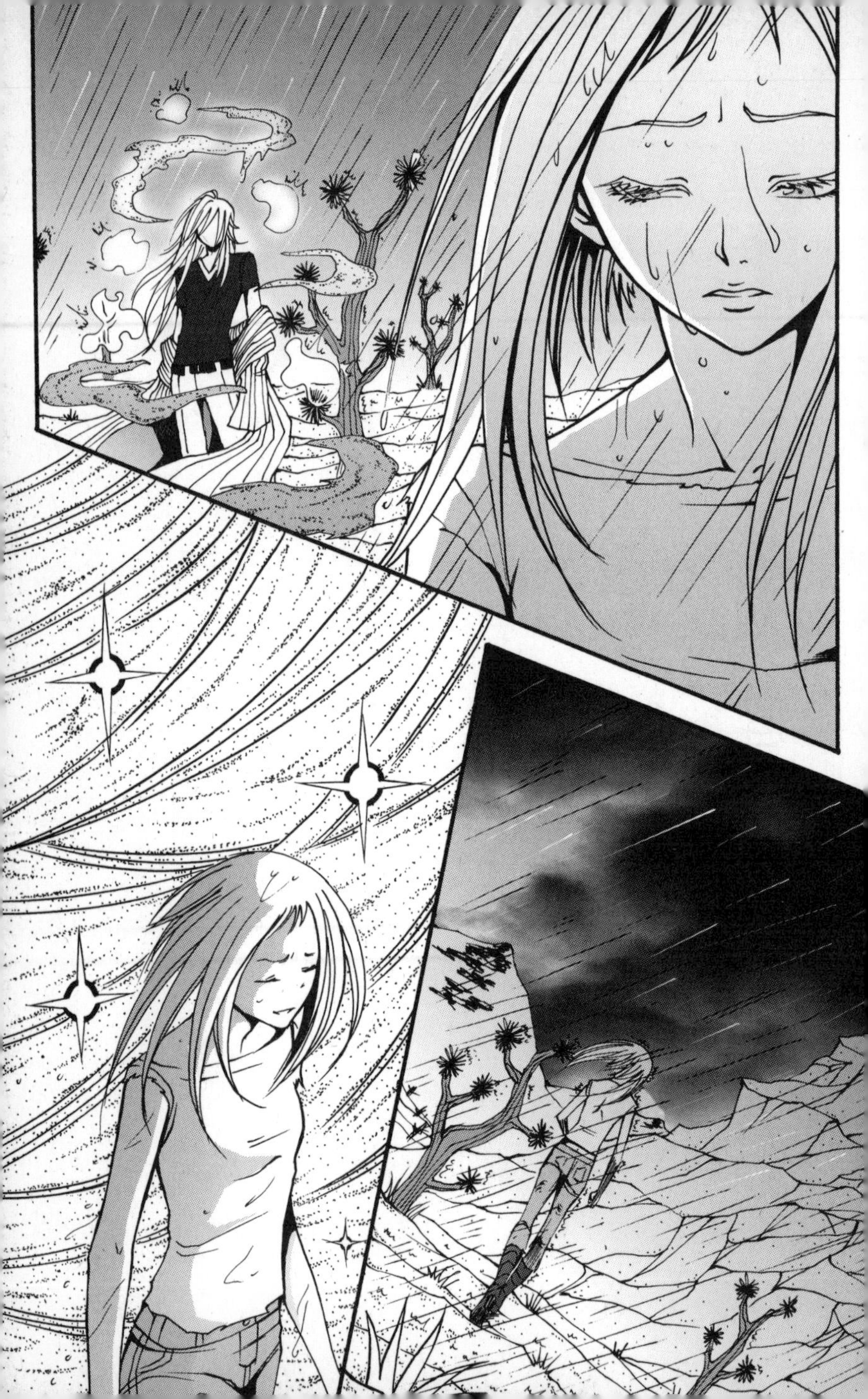

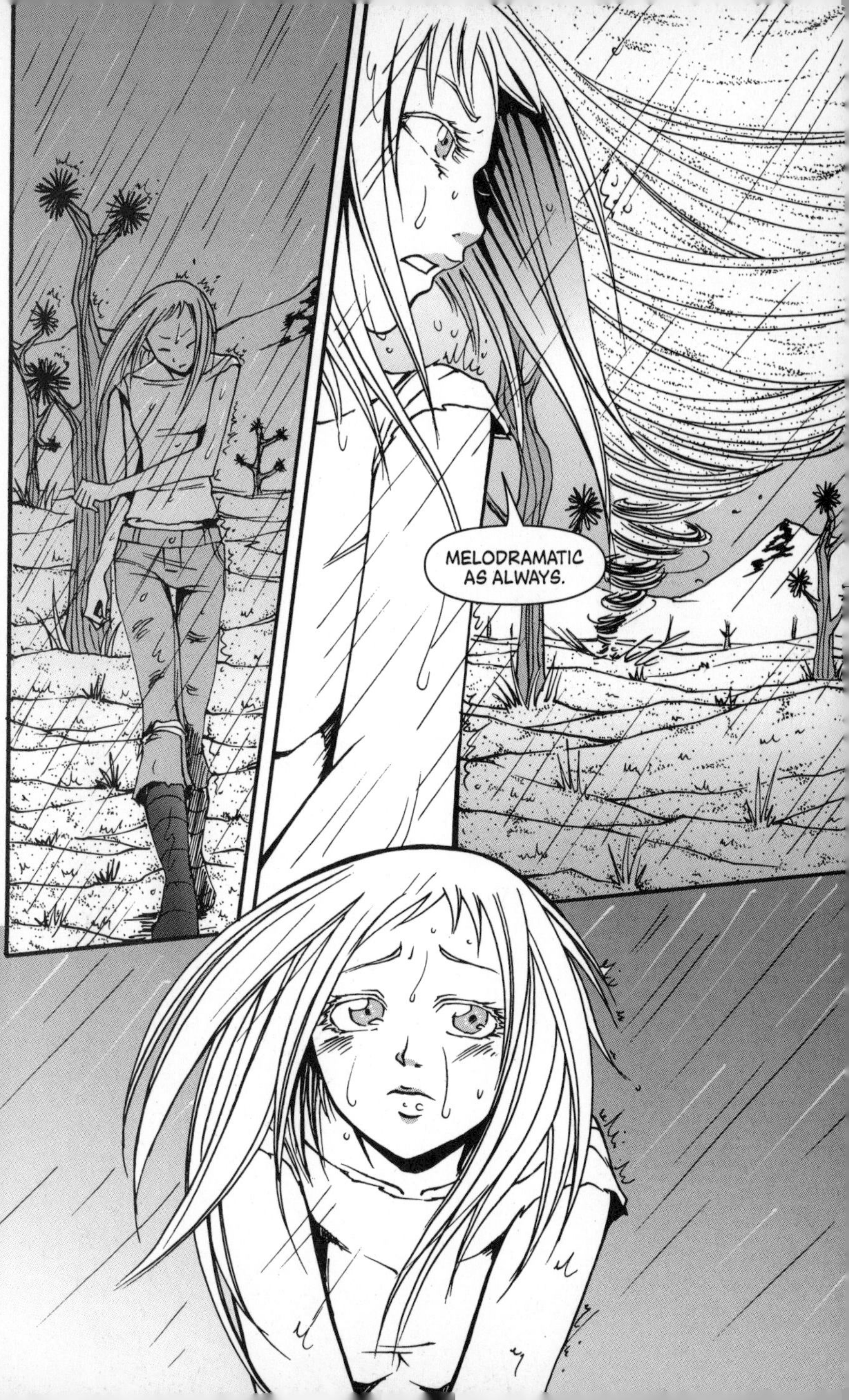
MELODRAMATIC AS ALWAYS.

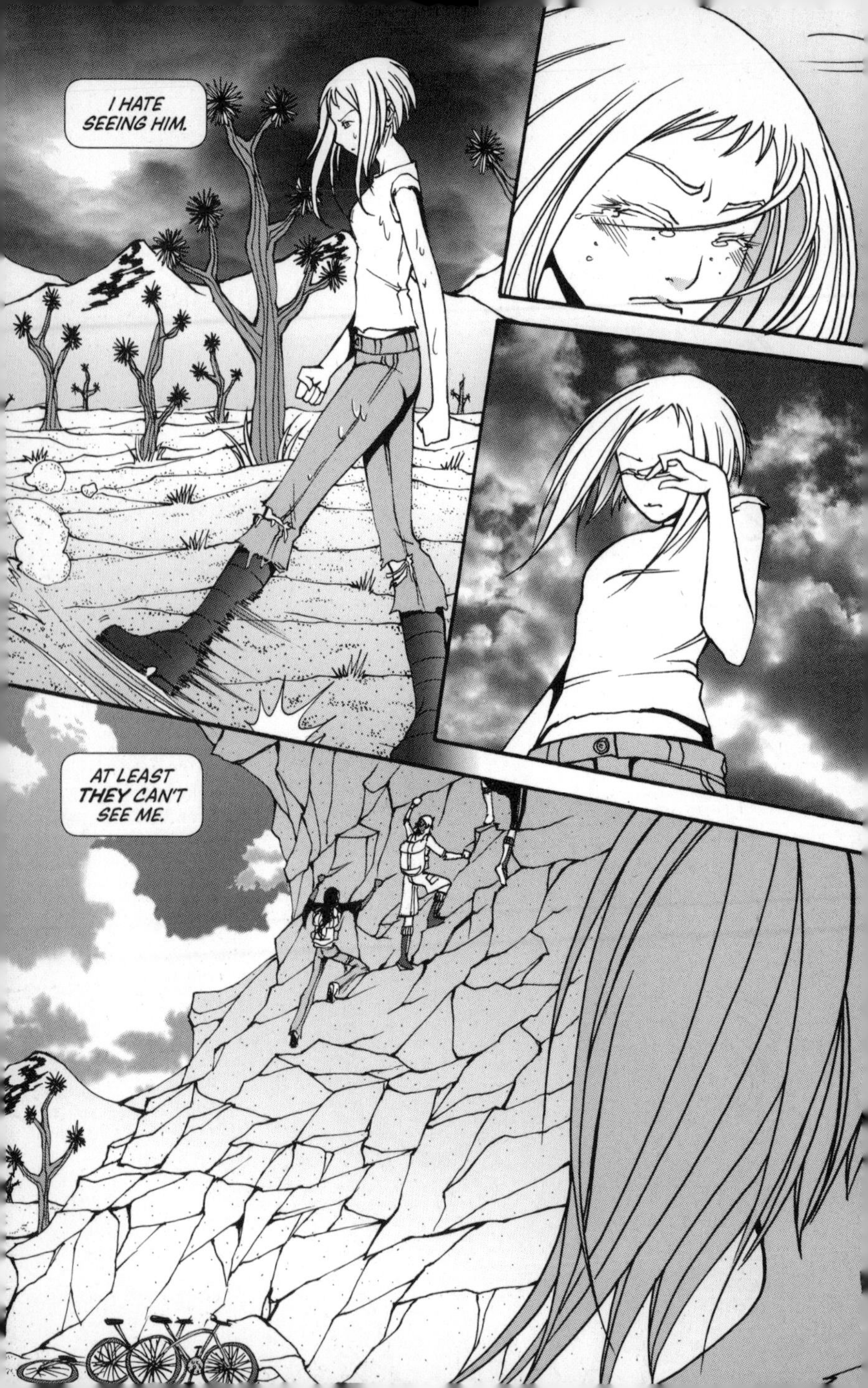
I HATE SEEING HIM.
AT LEAST THEY CAN'T SEE ME.

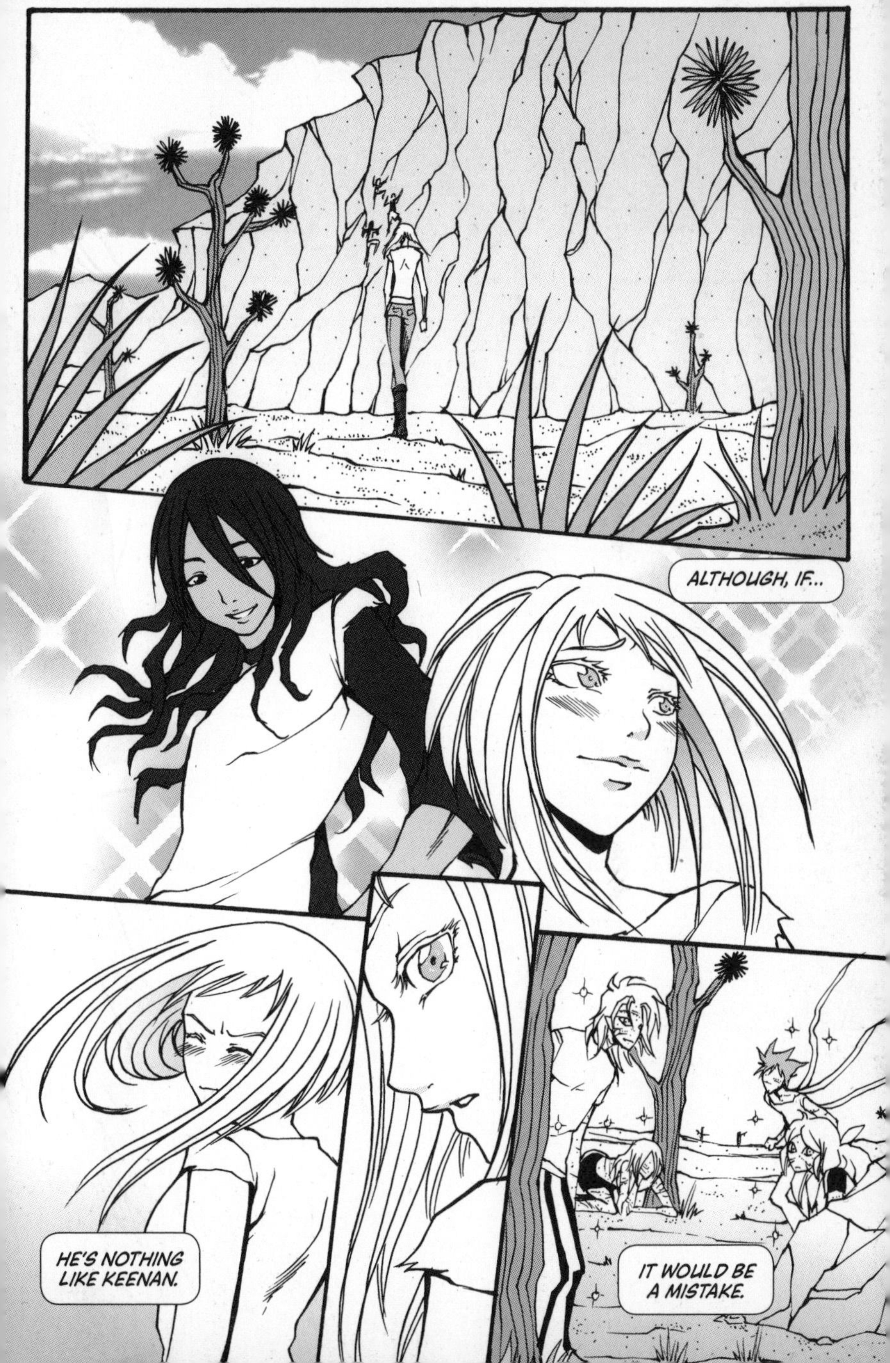
ALTHOUGH, IF...
HE'S NOTHING LIKE KEENAN.
IT WOULD BE A MISTAKE.

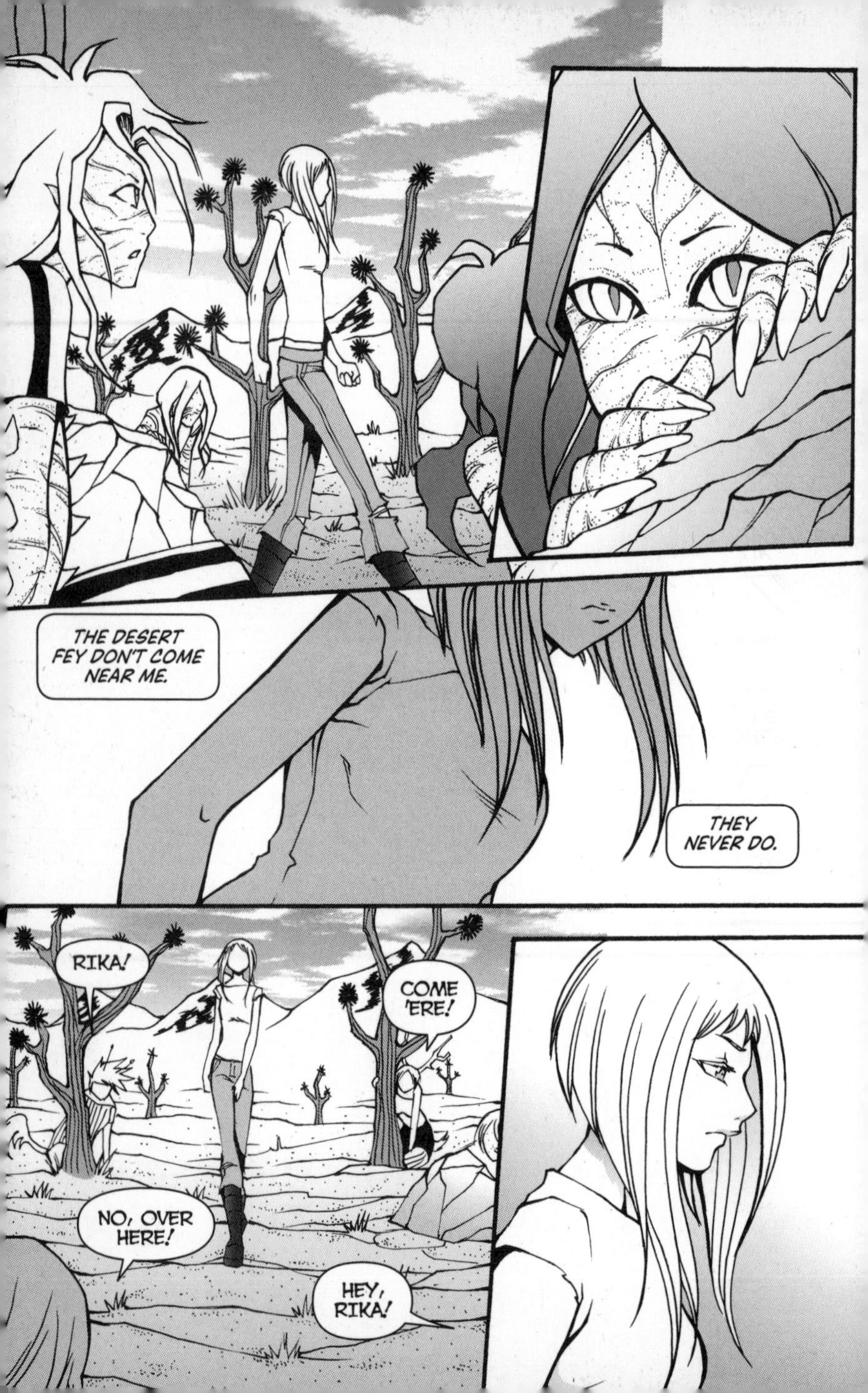
THE DESERT FEY DON'T COME NEAR ME.
THEY NEVER DO.
RIKA!
COME 'ERE!
NO, OVER HERE!
HEY, RIKA!

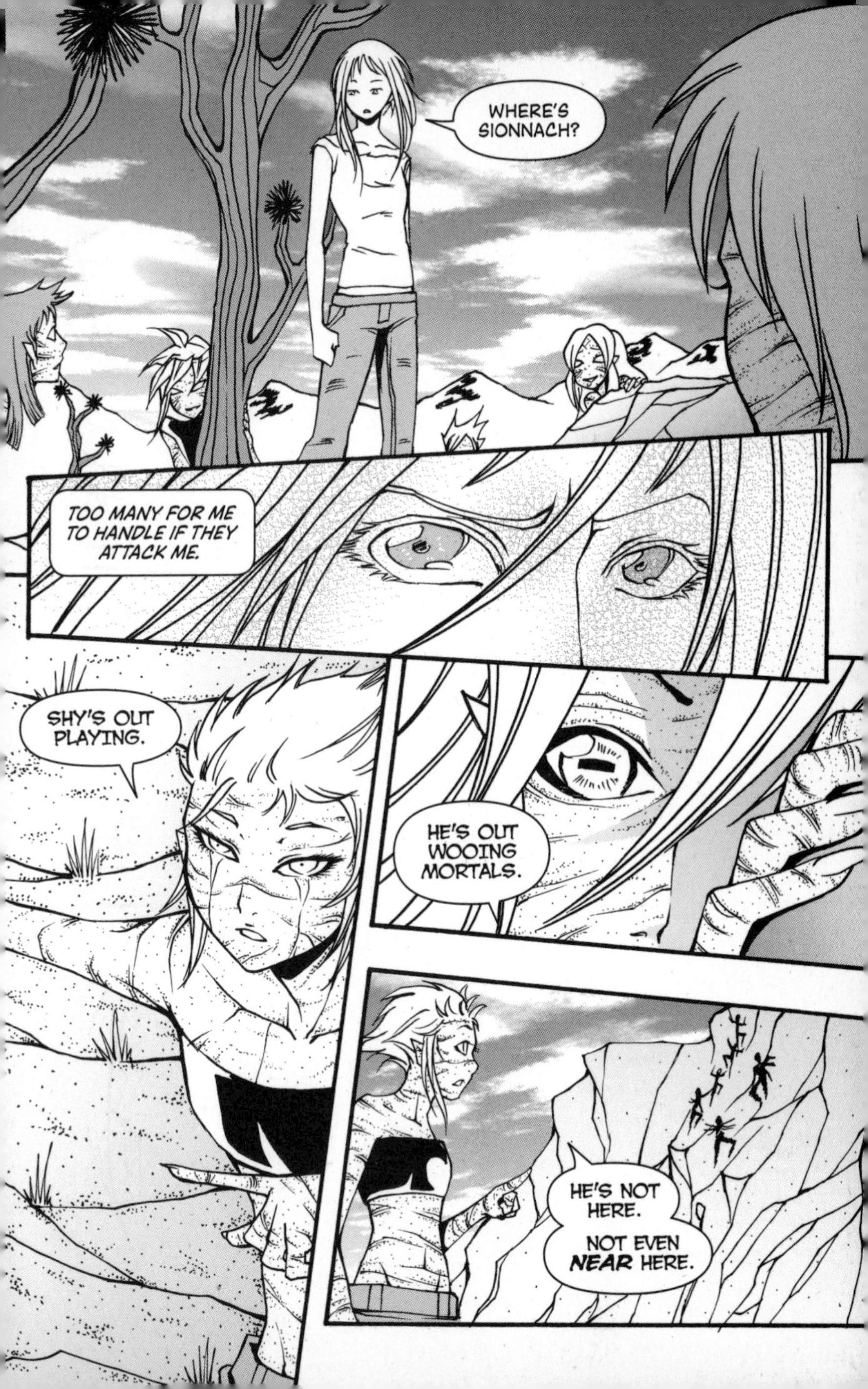
WHERE'S SIONNACH?
TOO MANY FOR ME TO HANDLE IF THEY ATTACK ME.
SHY'S OUT PLAYING.
HE'S OUT WOOING MORTALS.
HE'S NOT HERE.
NOT EVEN **NEAR** HERE.

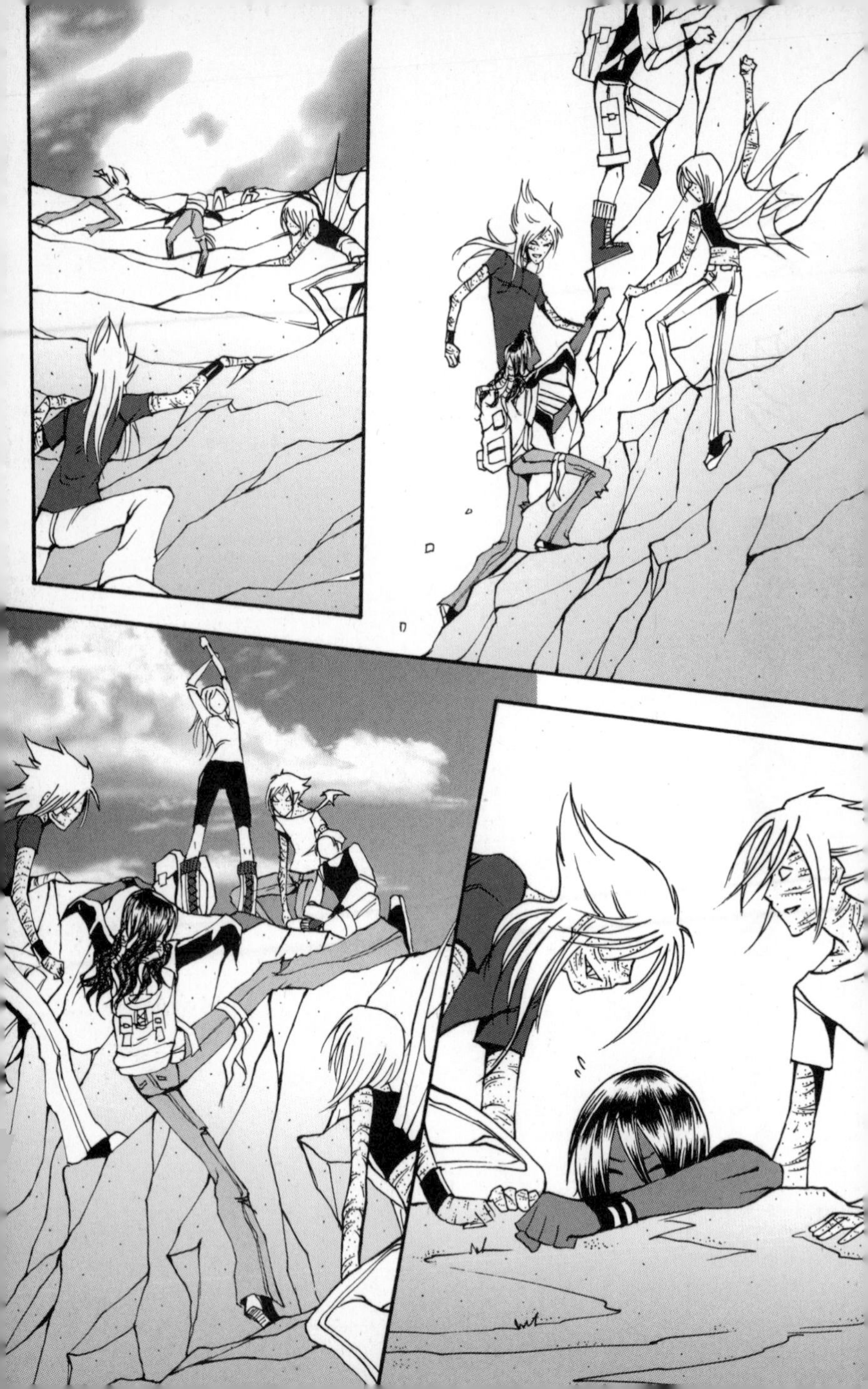

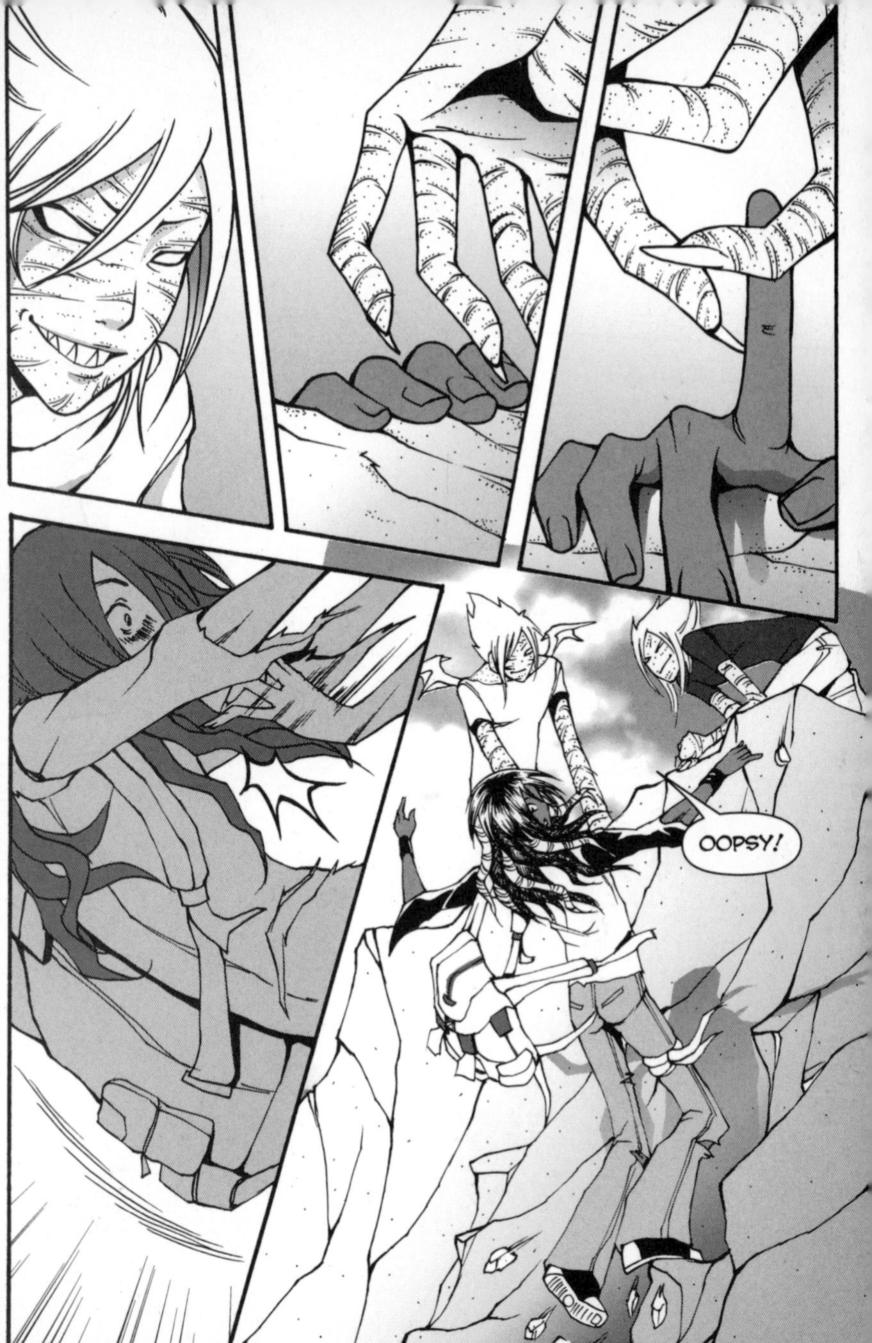
OOPSY!

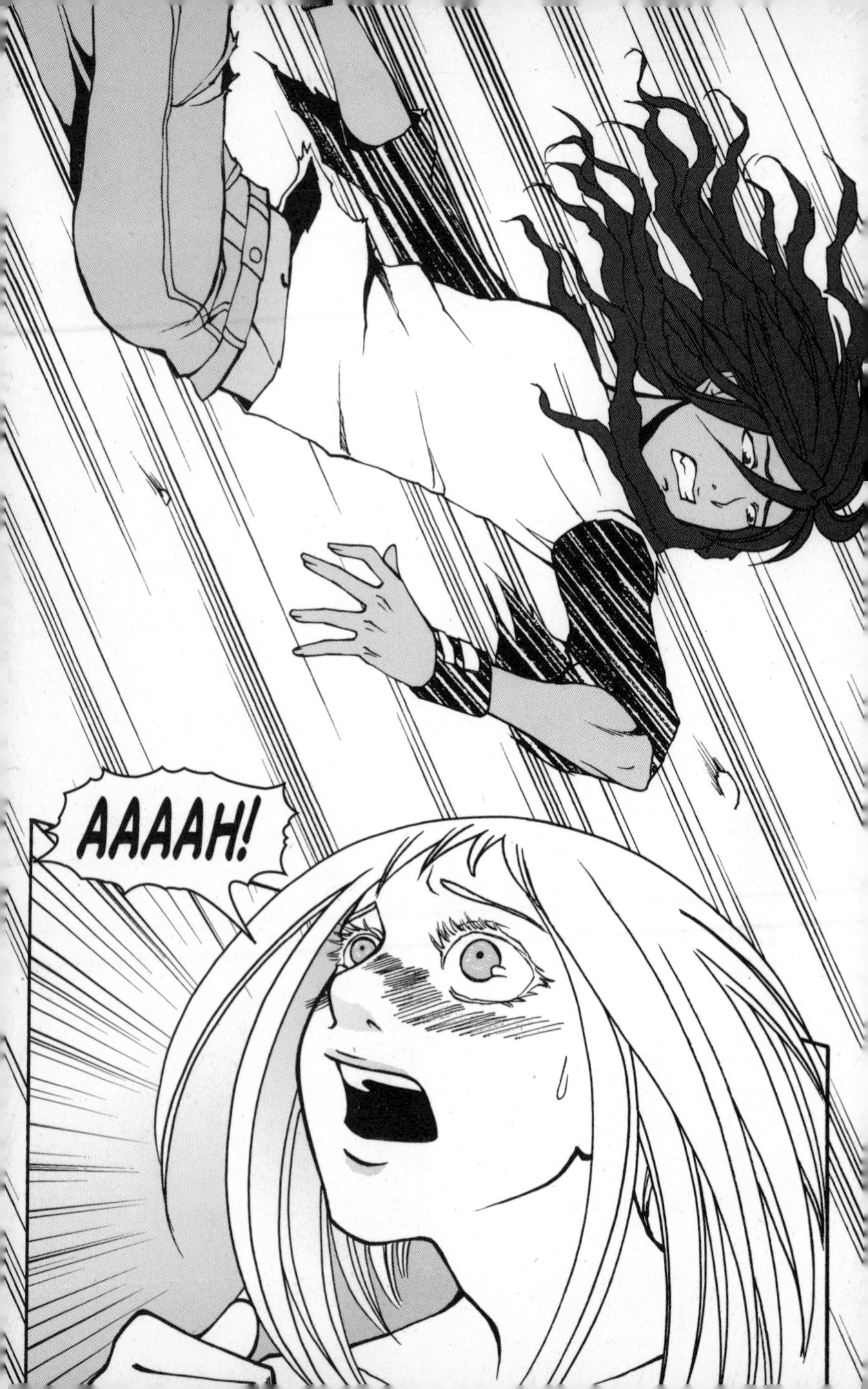
AAAAH!

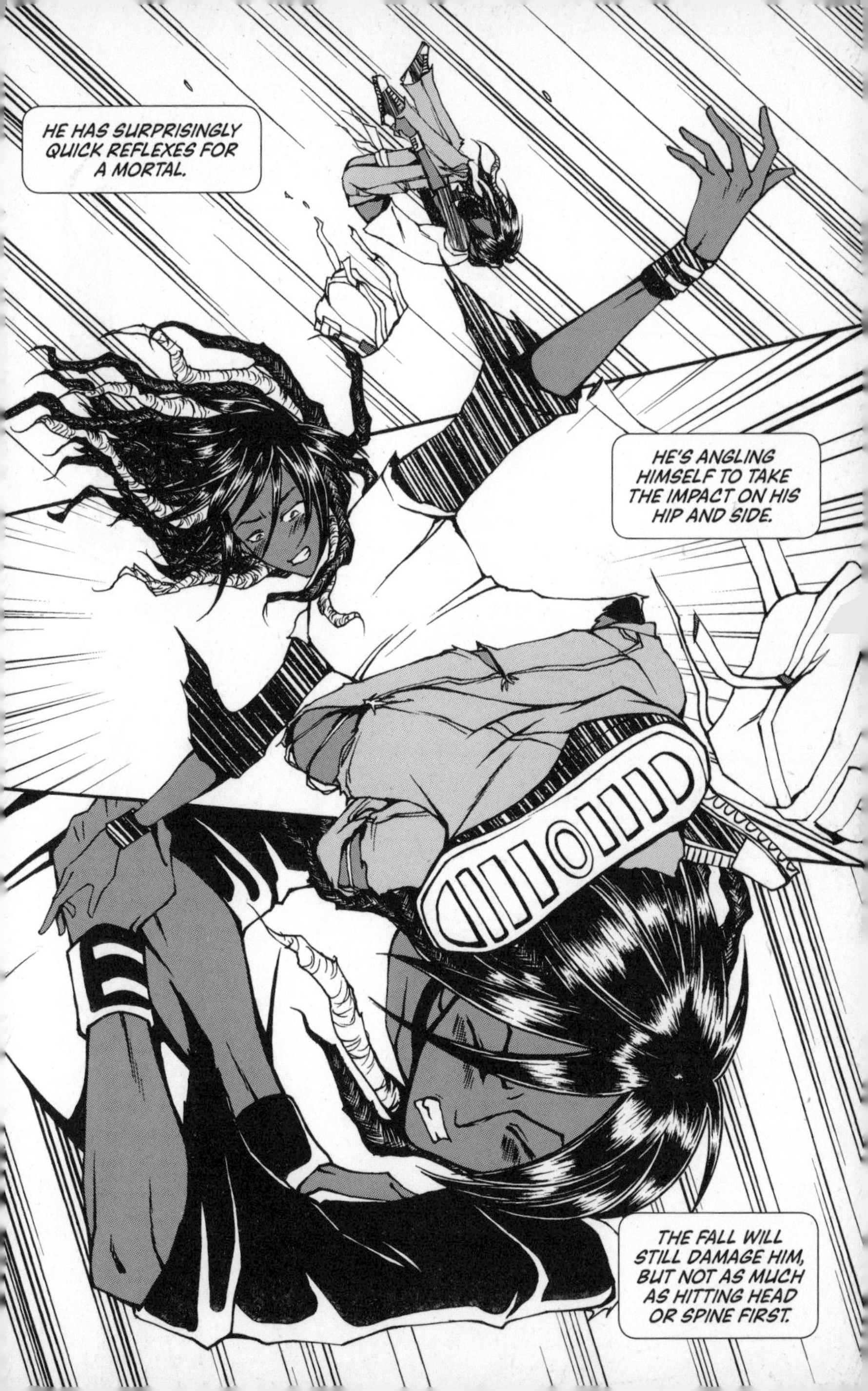
HE HAS SURPRISINGLY QUICK REFLEXES FOR A MORTAL.
HE'S ANGLING HIMSELF TO TAKE THE IMPACT ON HIS HIP AND SIDE.
THE FALL WILL STILL DAMAGE HIM, BUT NOT AS MUCH AS HITTING HEAD OR SPINE FIRST.

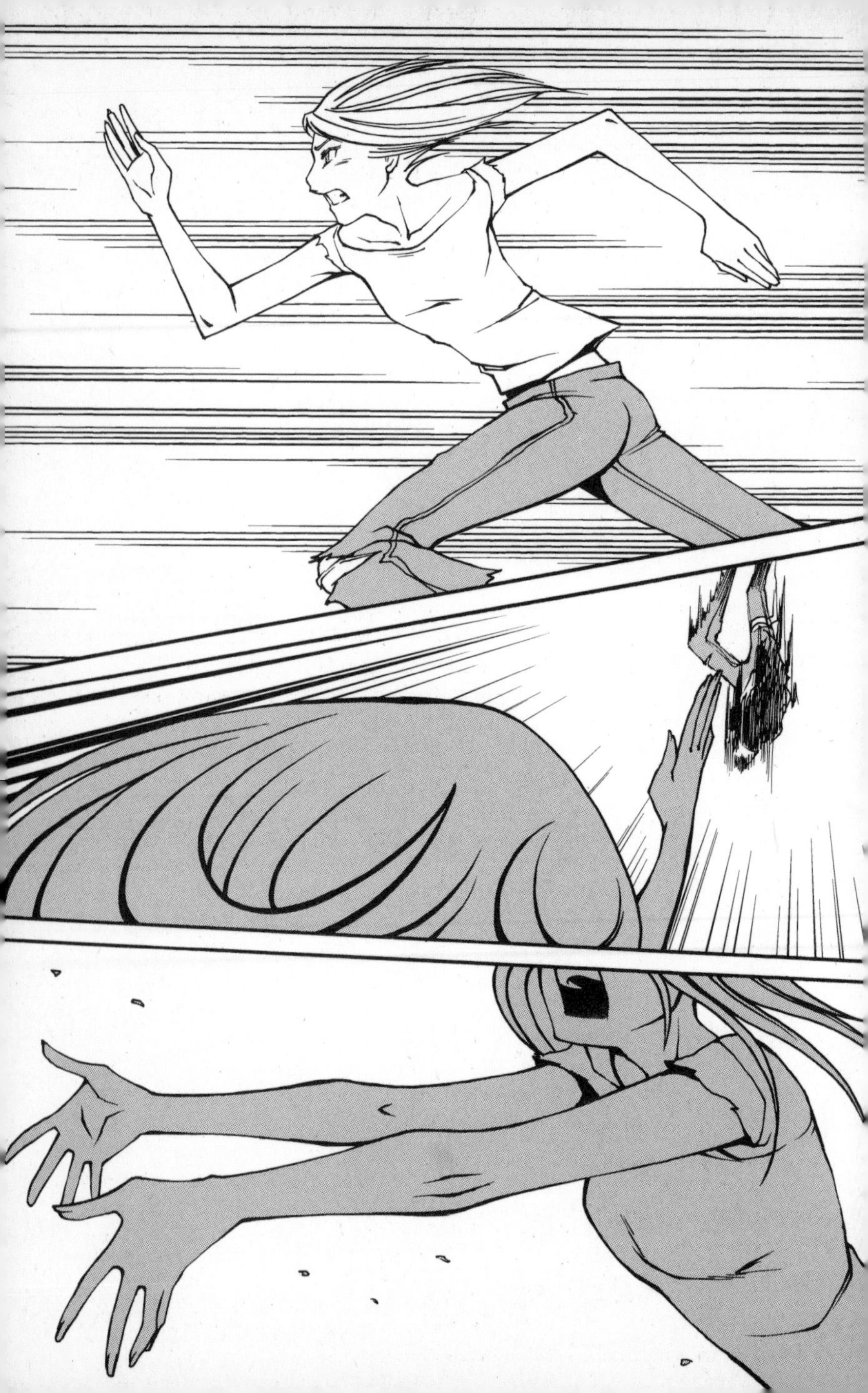

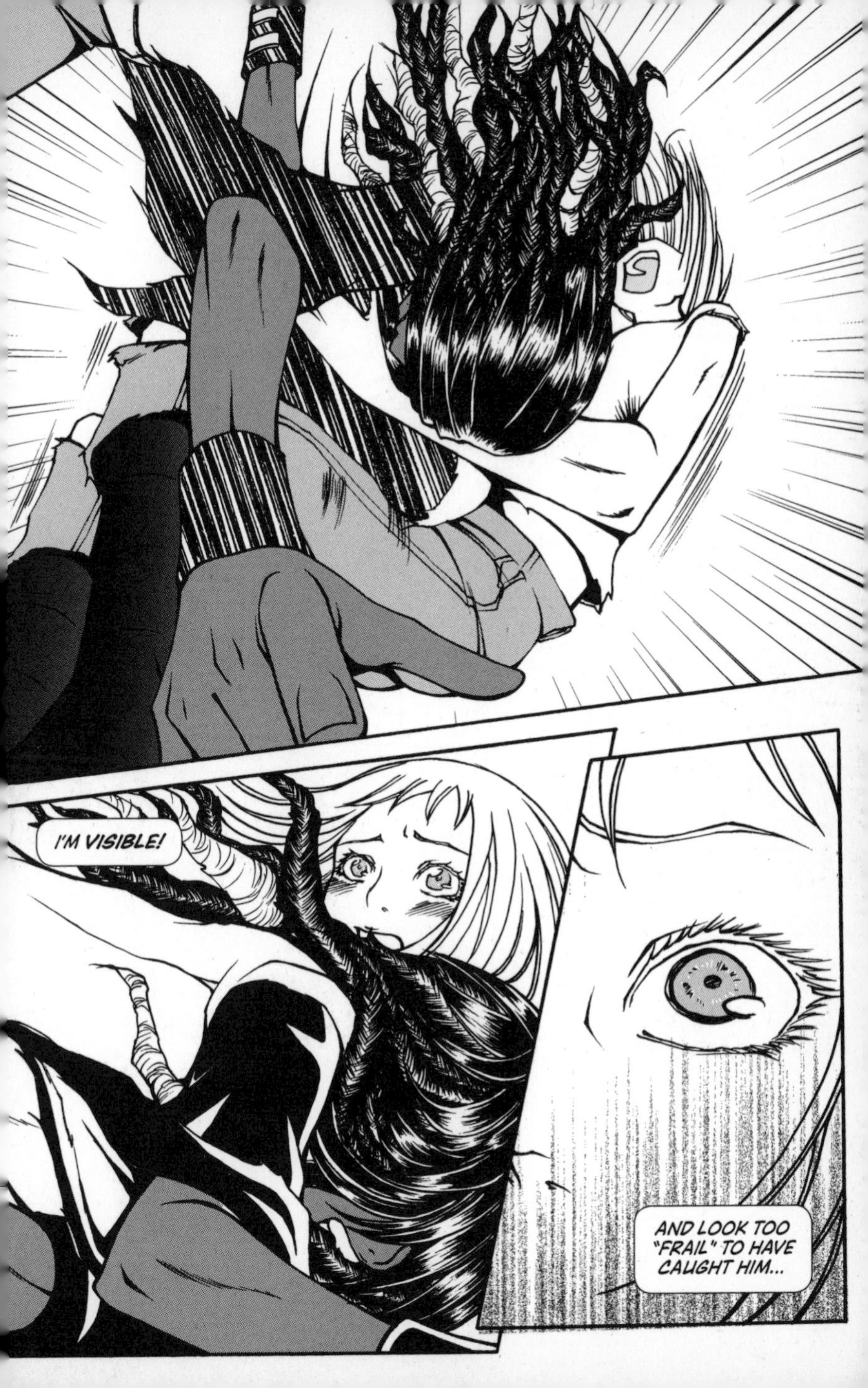
I'M VISIBLE!
AND LOOK TOO "FRAIL" TO HAVE CAUGHT HIM...

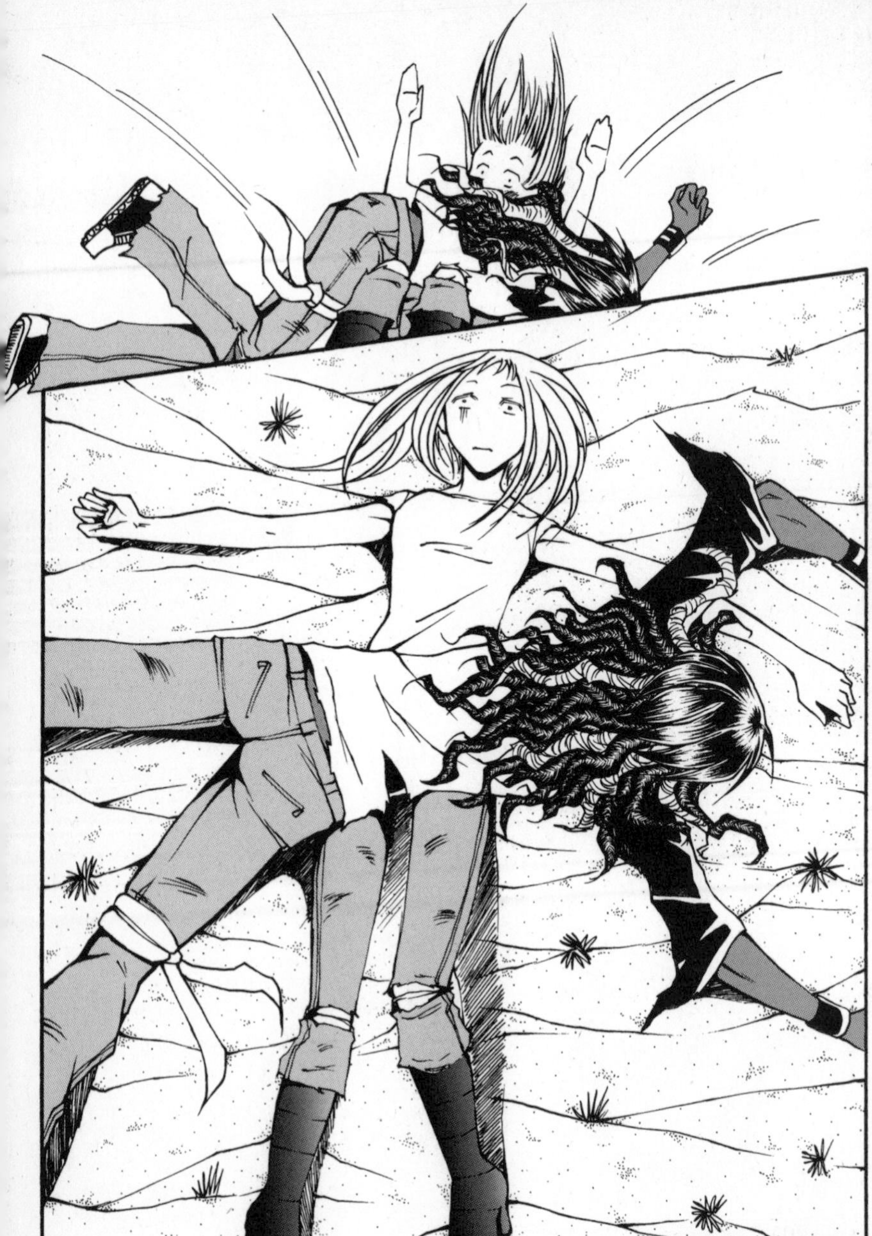

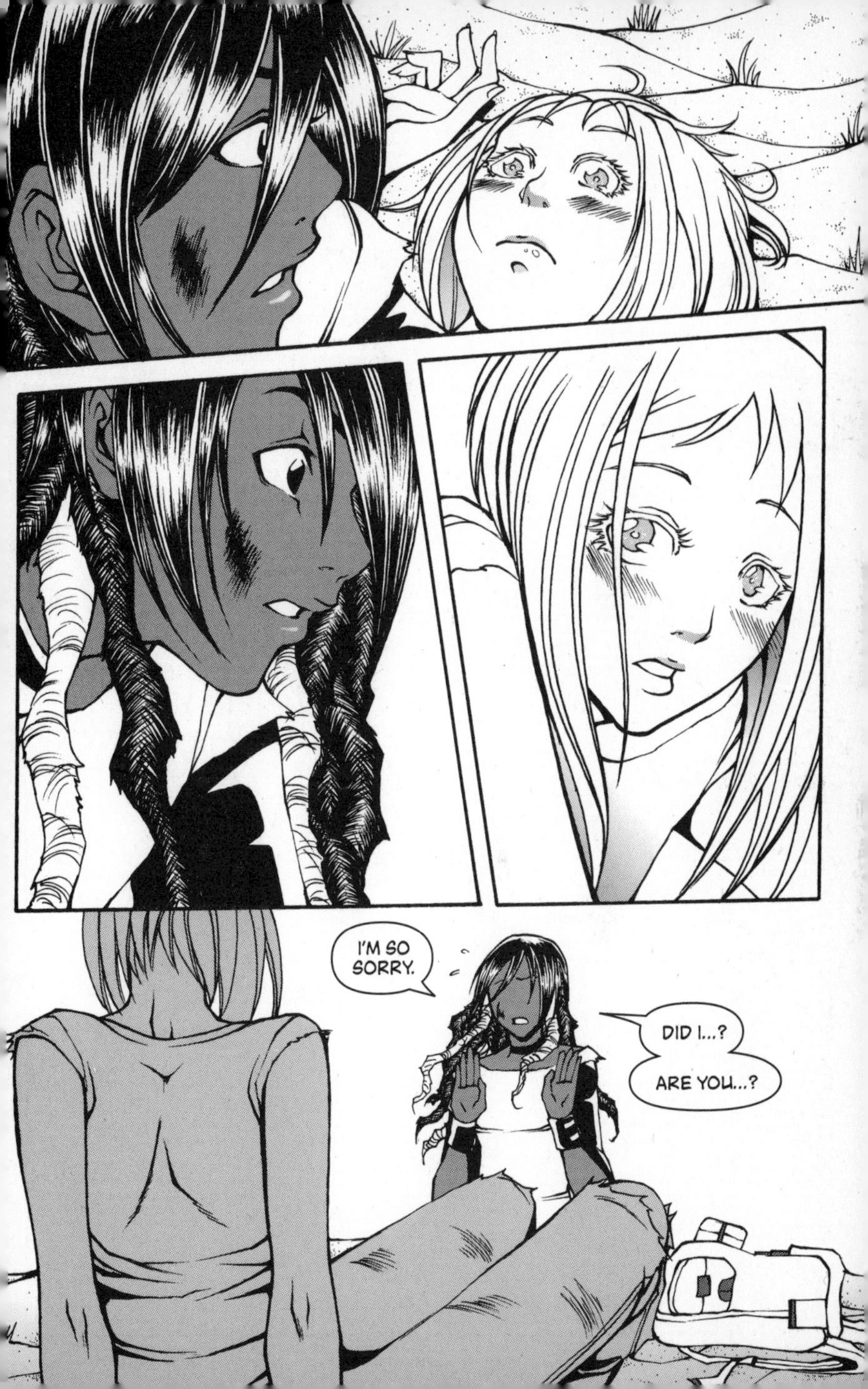
I'M SO SORRY.
DID I...?
ARE YOU...?

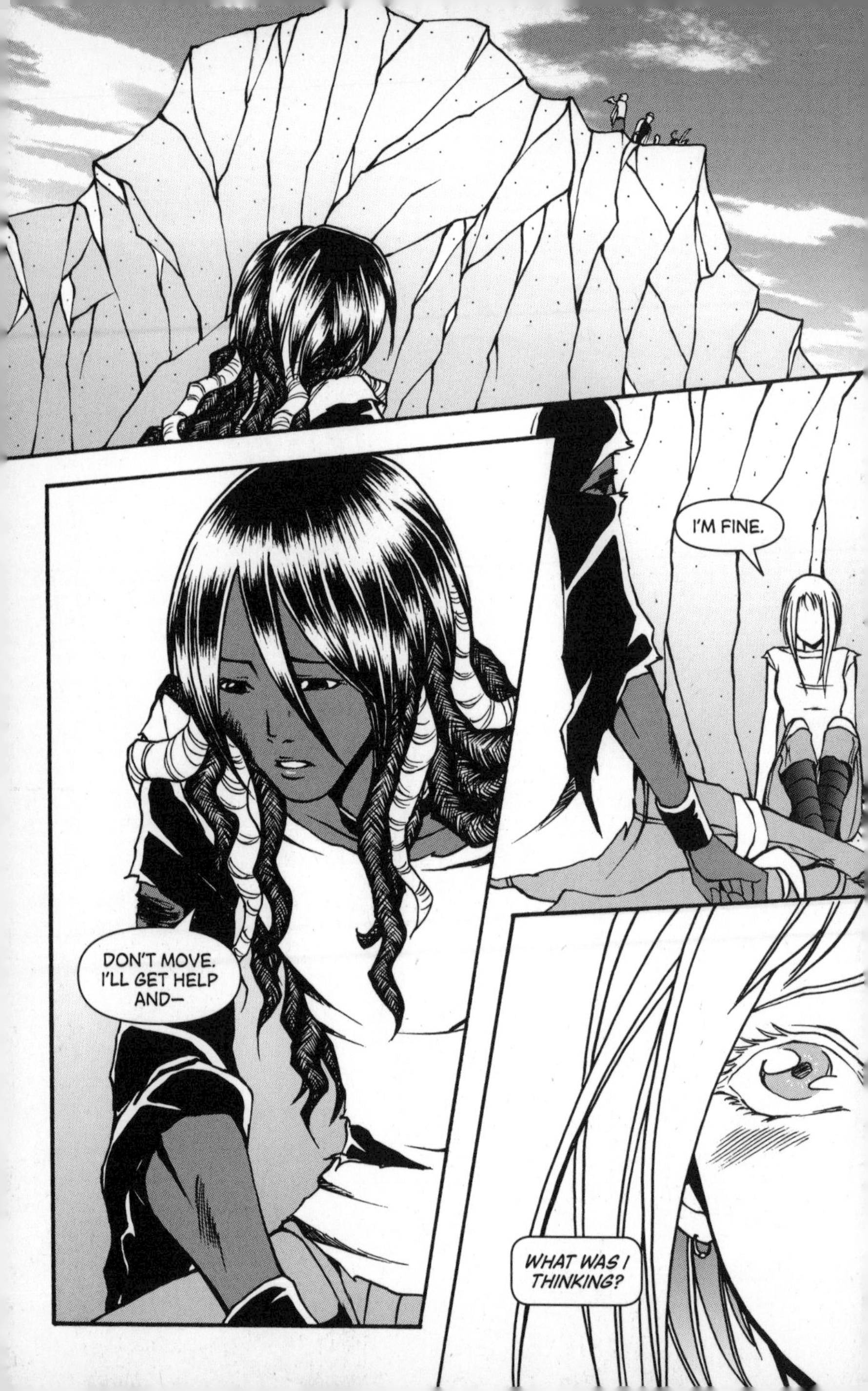
DON'T MOVE. I'LL GET HELP AND—
I'M FINE.
WHAT WAS I THINKING?

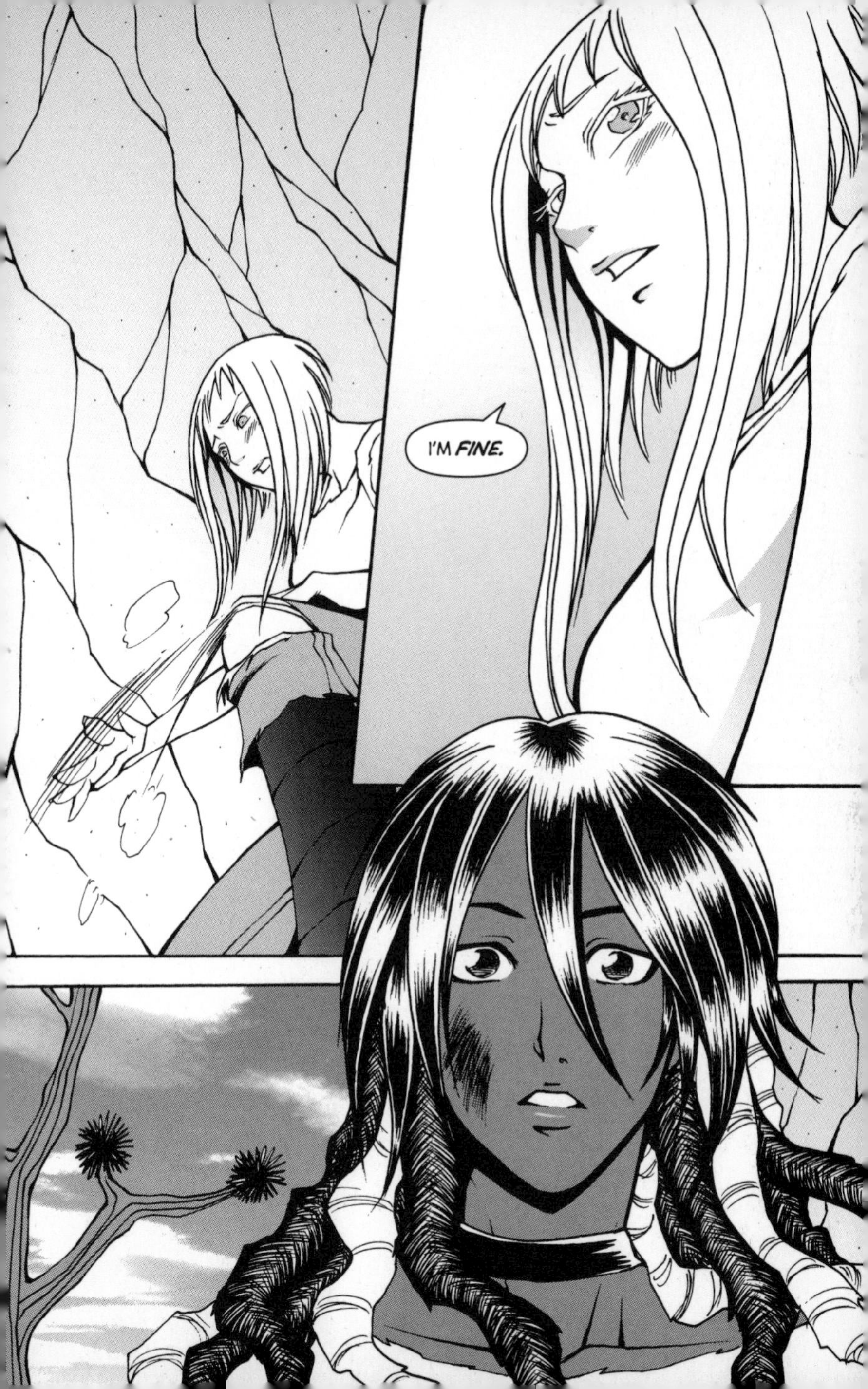
I'M FINE.

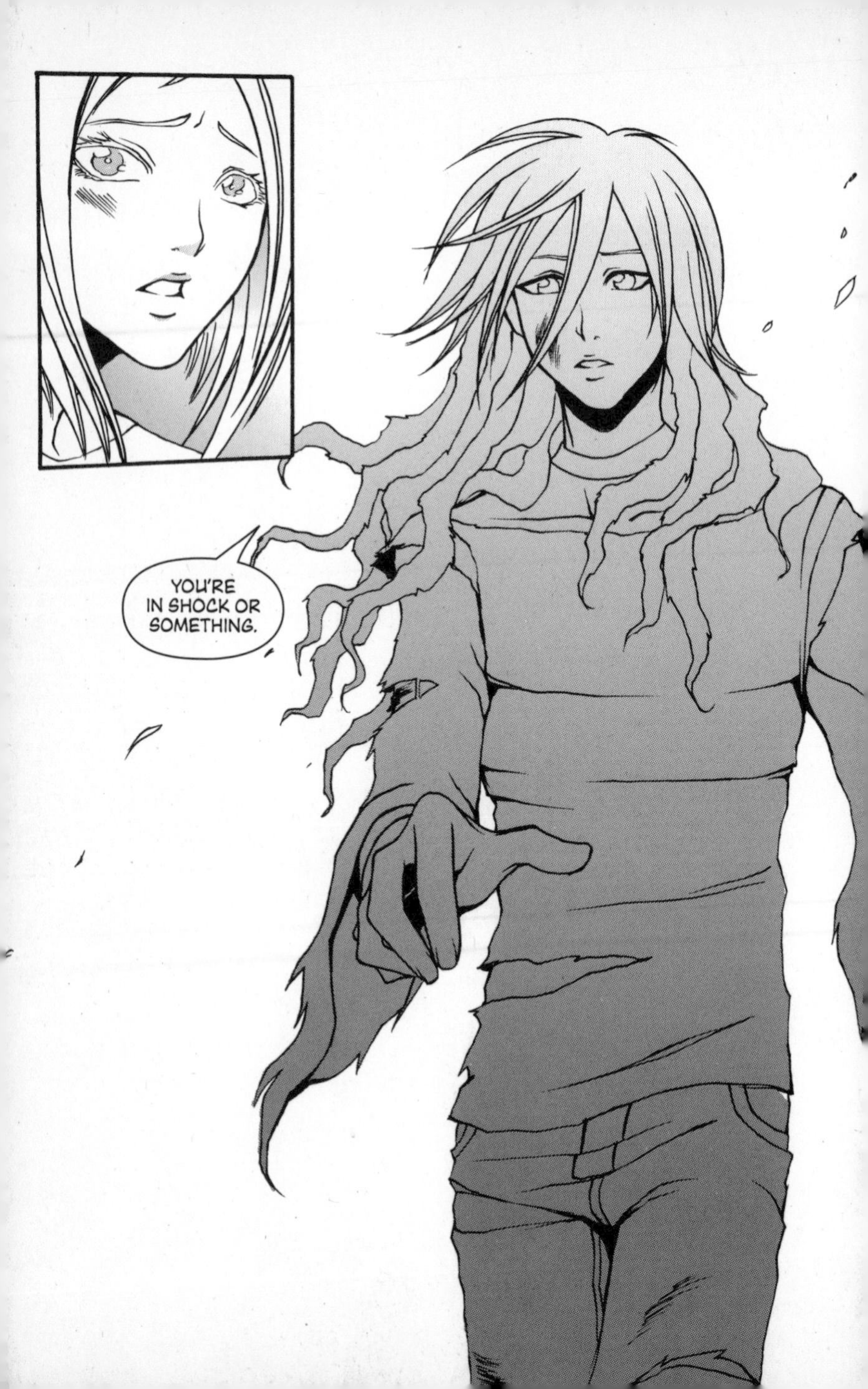
YOU'RE IN SHOCK OR SOMETHING.

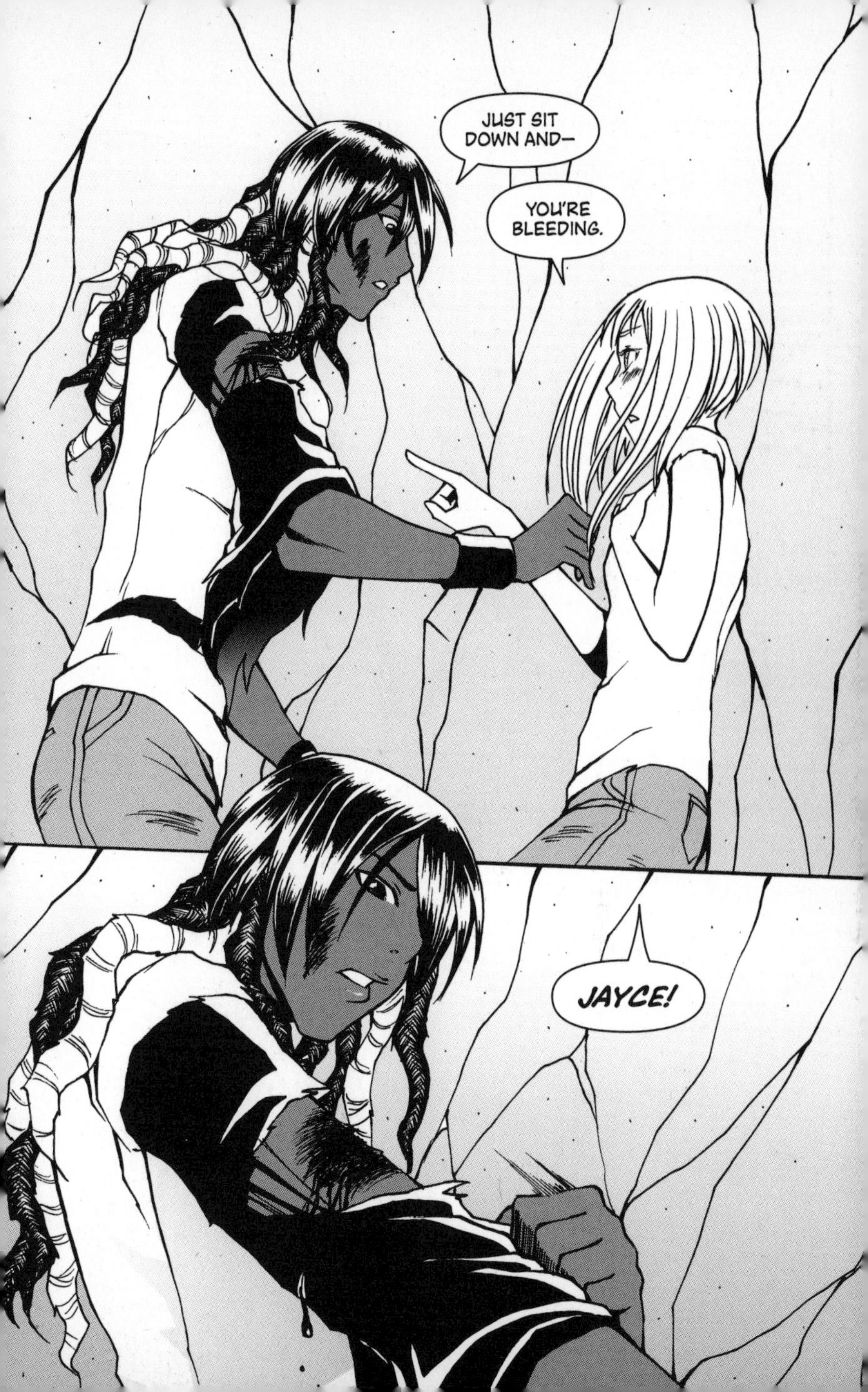
JUST SIT DOWN AND—
YOU'RE BLEEDING.
JAYCE!

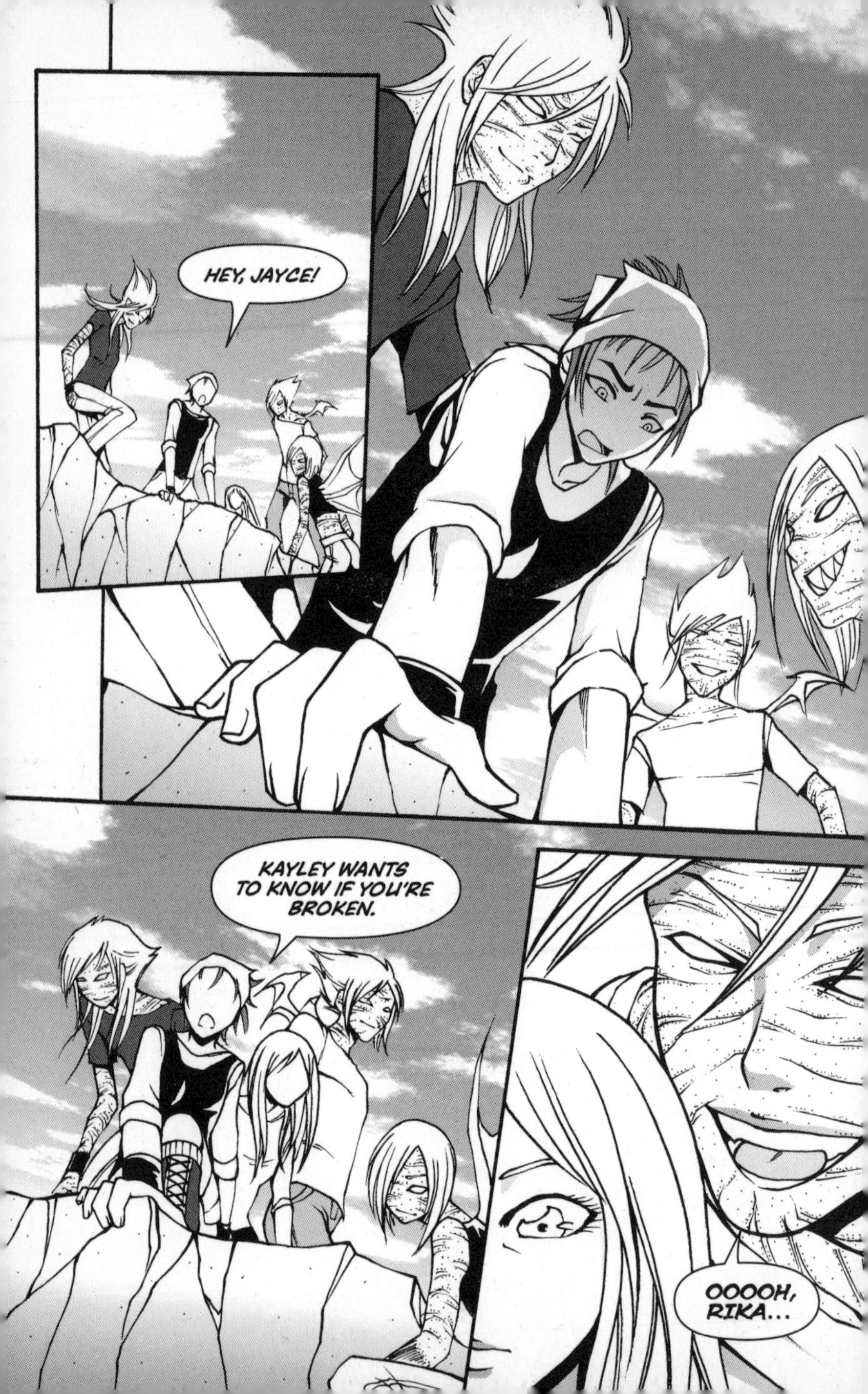
HEY, JAYCE!
KAYLEY WANTS TO KNOW IF YOU'RE BROKEN.
OOOOH, RIKA...

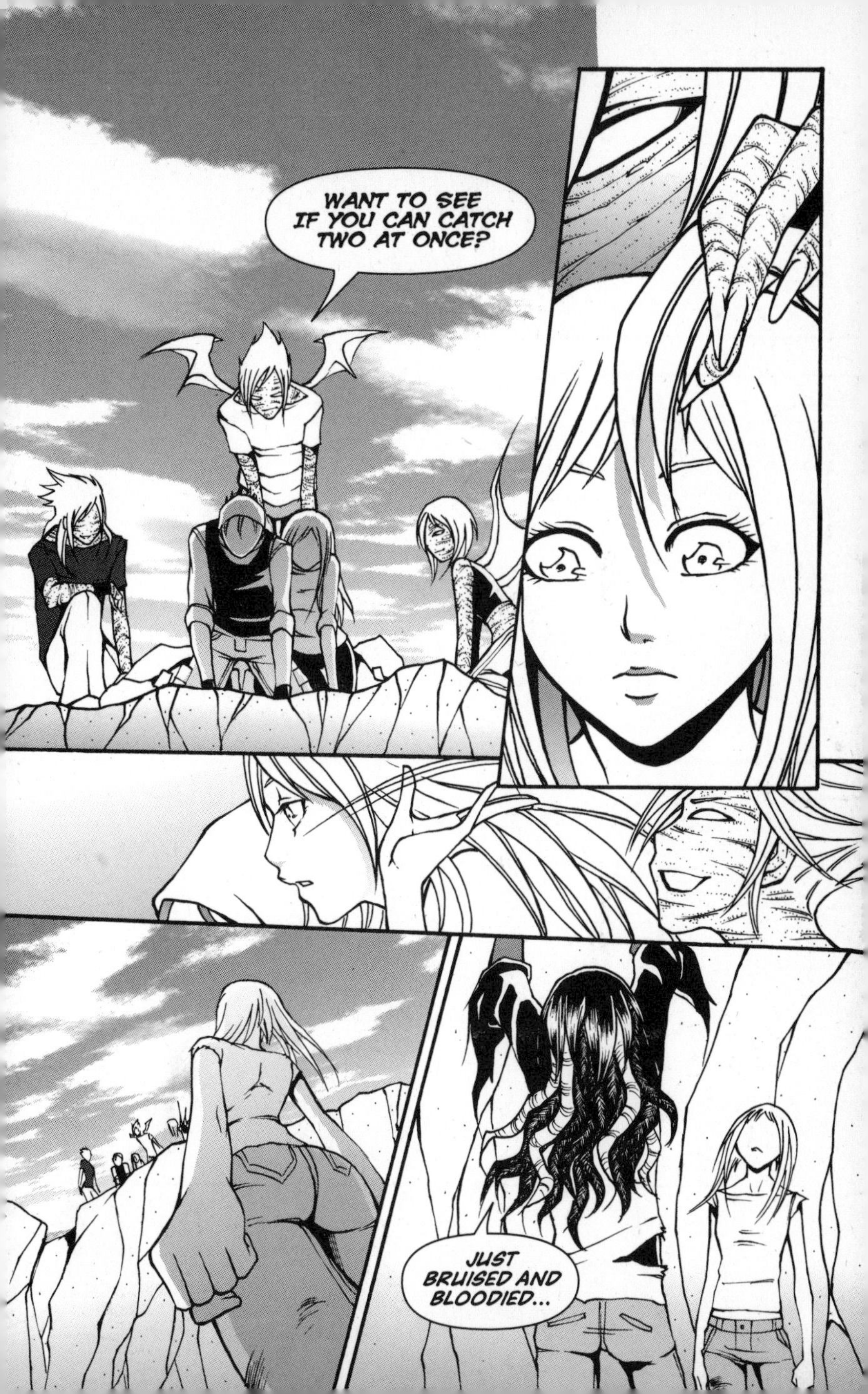
WANT TO SEE IF YOU CAN CATCH TWO AT ONCE?
JUST BRUISED AND BLOODIED...

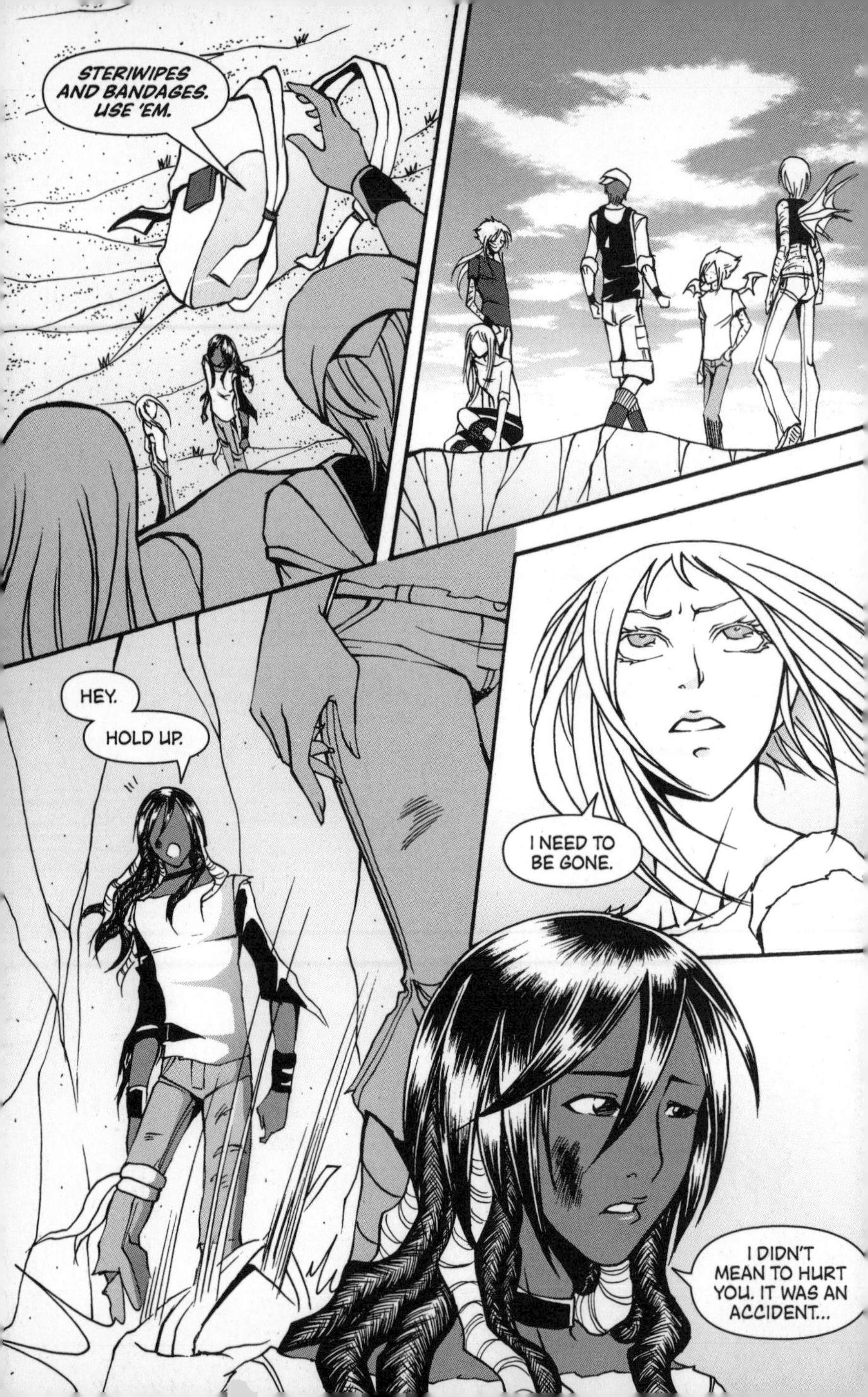
STERIWIPES AND BANDAGES. USE 'EM.
HEY.
HOLD UP.
I NEED TO BE GONE.
I DIDN'T MEAN TO HURT YOU. IT WAS AN ACCIDENT...

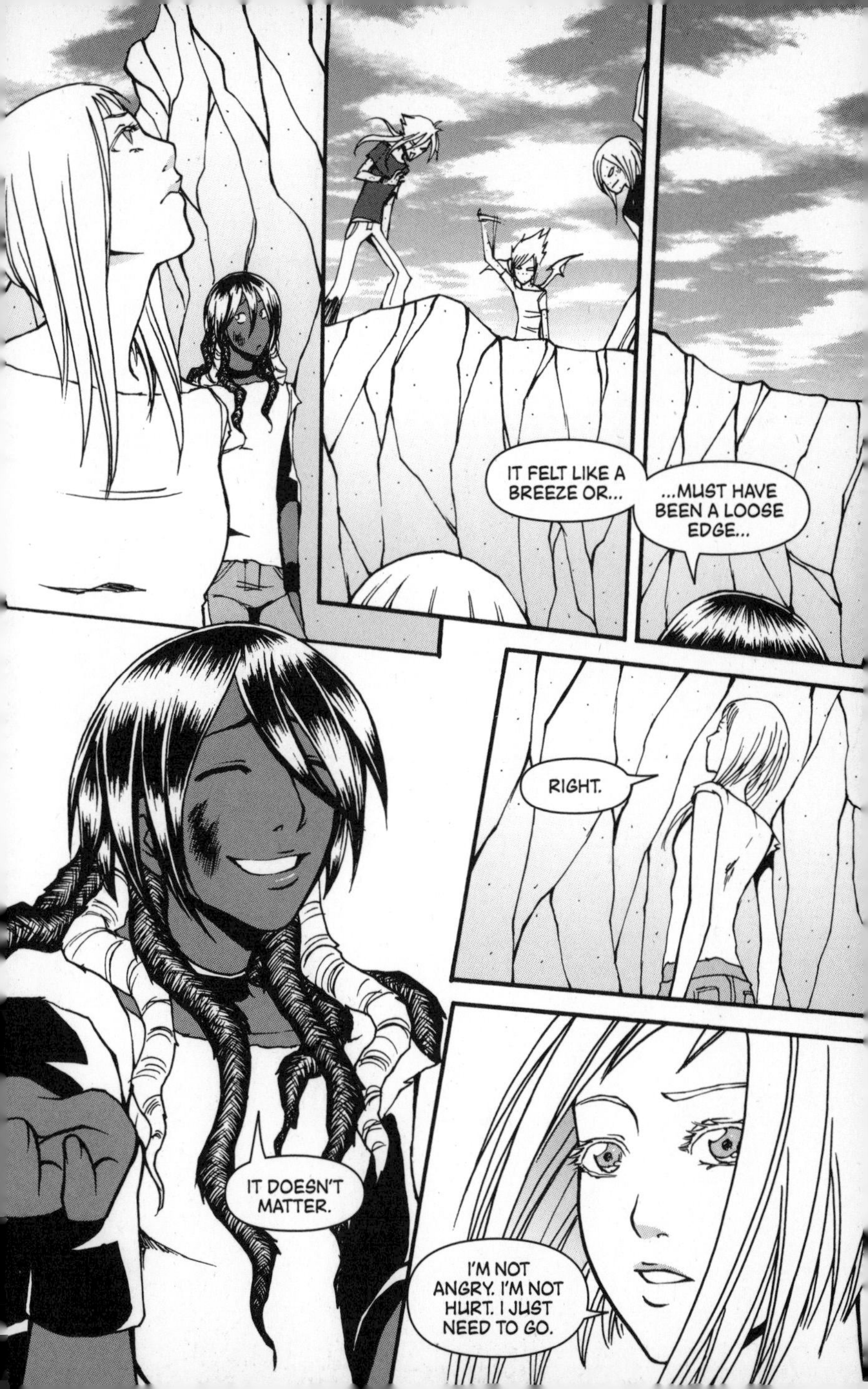
IT FELT LIKE A BREEZE OR...
...MUST HAVE BEEN A LOOSE EDGE...
IT DOESN'T MATTER.
RIGHT.
I'M NOT ANGRY. I'M NOT HURT. I JUST NEED TO GO.

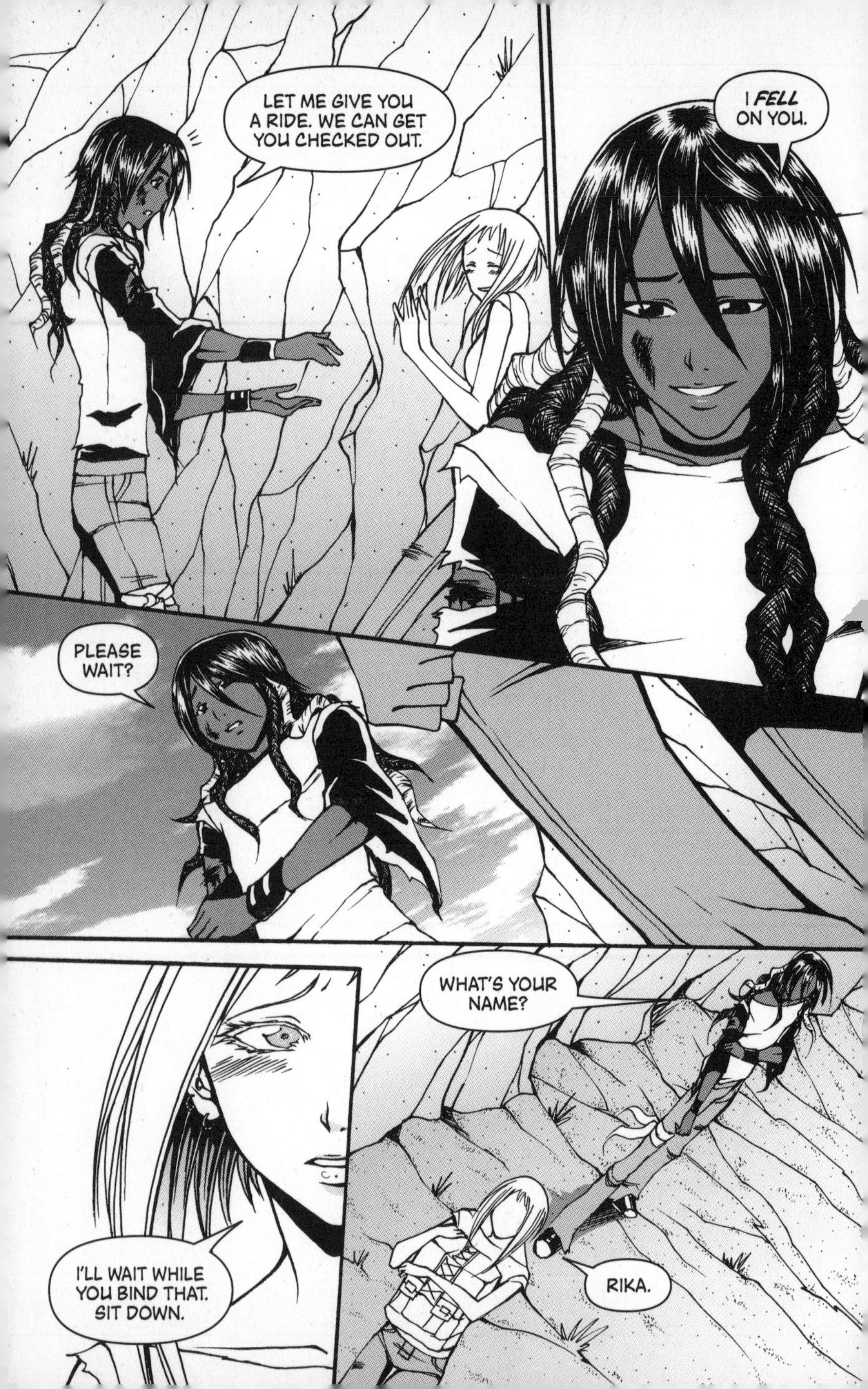
LET ME GIVE YOU A RIDE. WE CAN GET YOU CHECKED OUT.
I *FELL* ON YOU.
PLEASE WAIT?
I'LL WAIT WHILE YOU BIND THAT. SIT DOWN.
WHAT'S YOUR NAME?
RIKA.

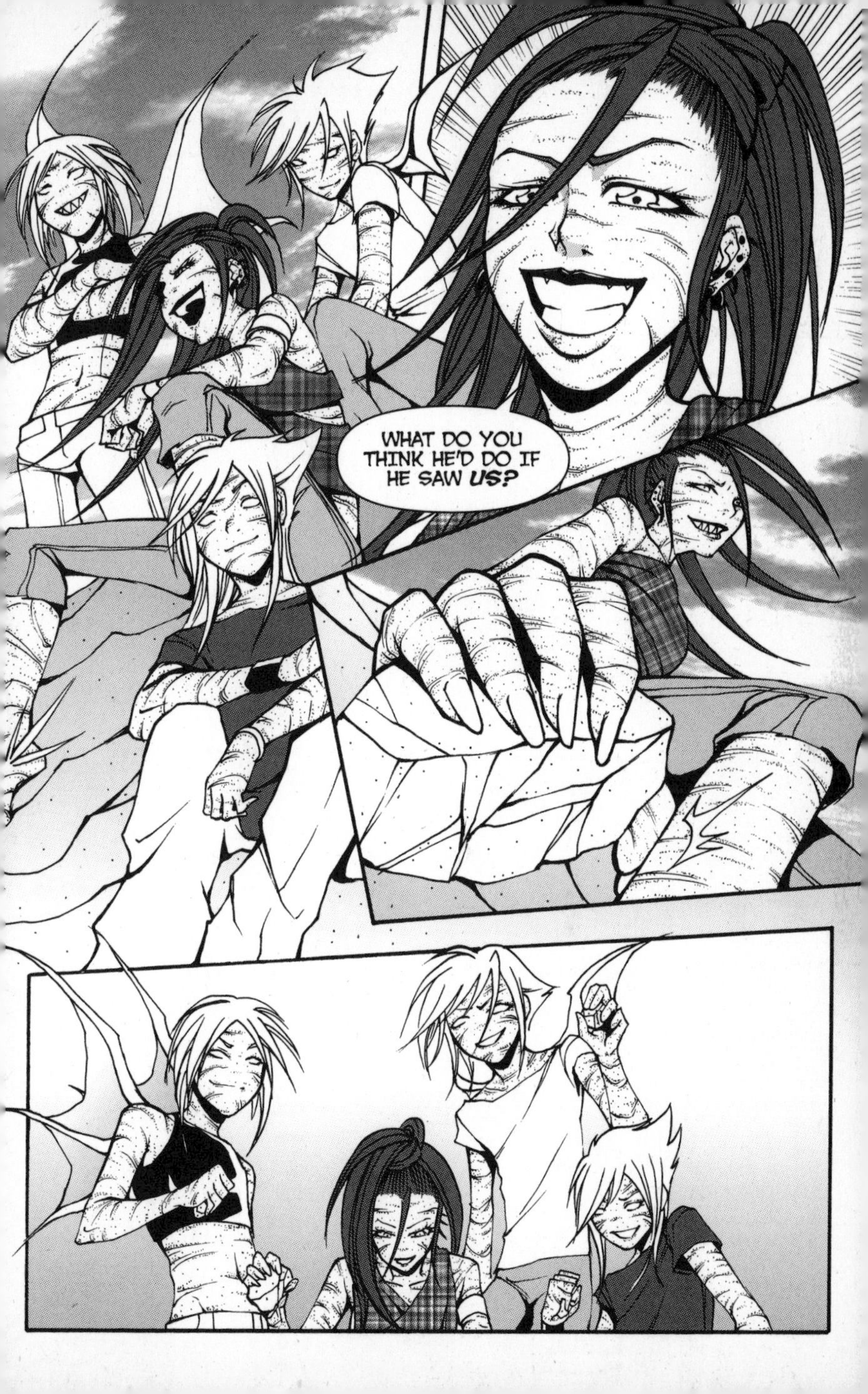
WHAT DO YOU THINK HE'D DO IF HE SAW *US*?

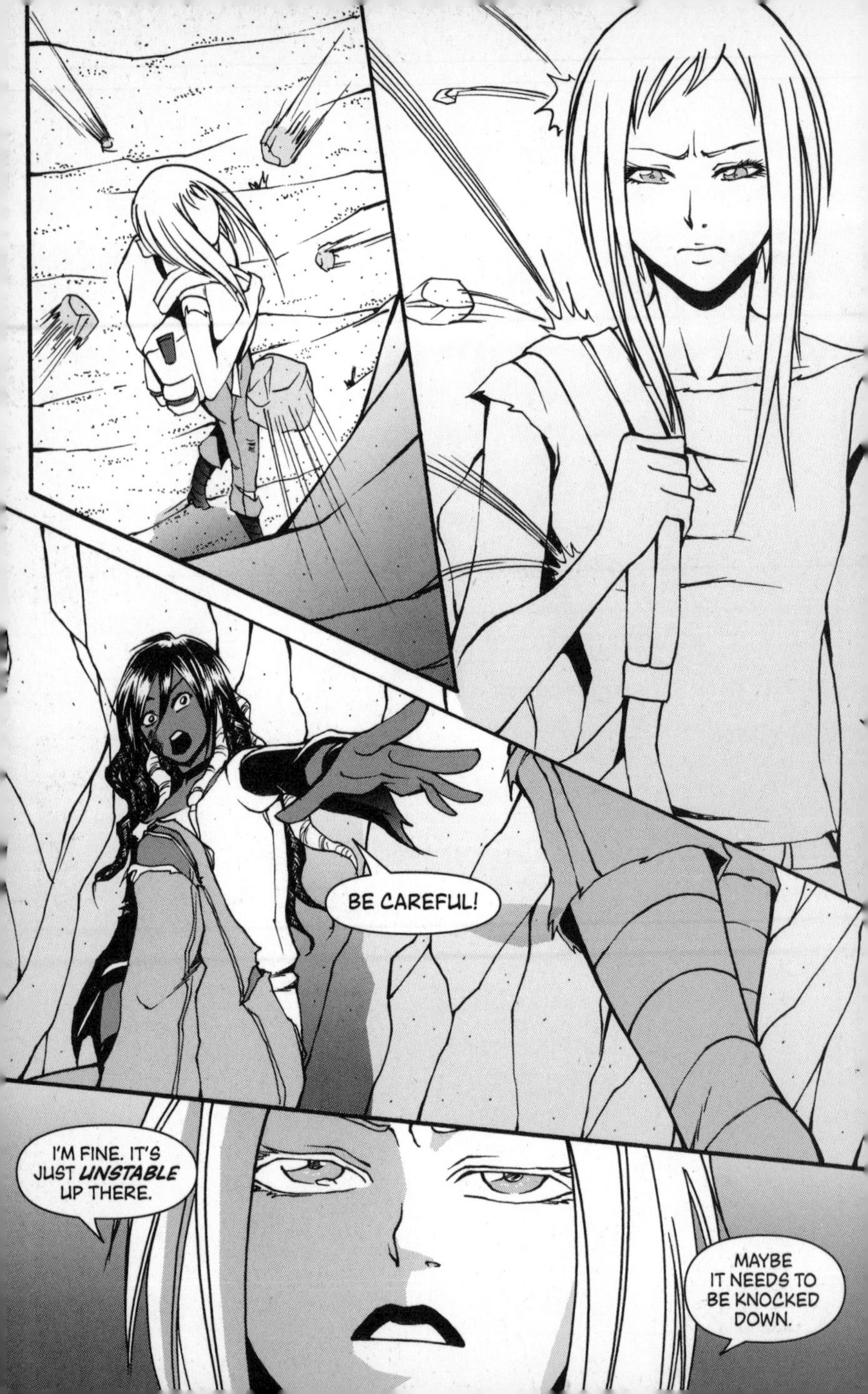
BE CAREFUL!
I'M FINE. IT'S JUST UNSTABLE UP THERE.
MAYBE IT NEEDS TO BE KNOCKED DOWN.

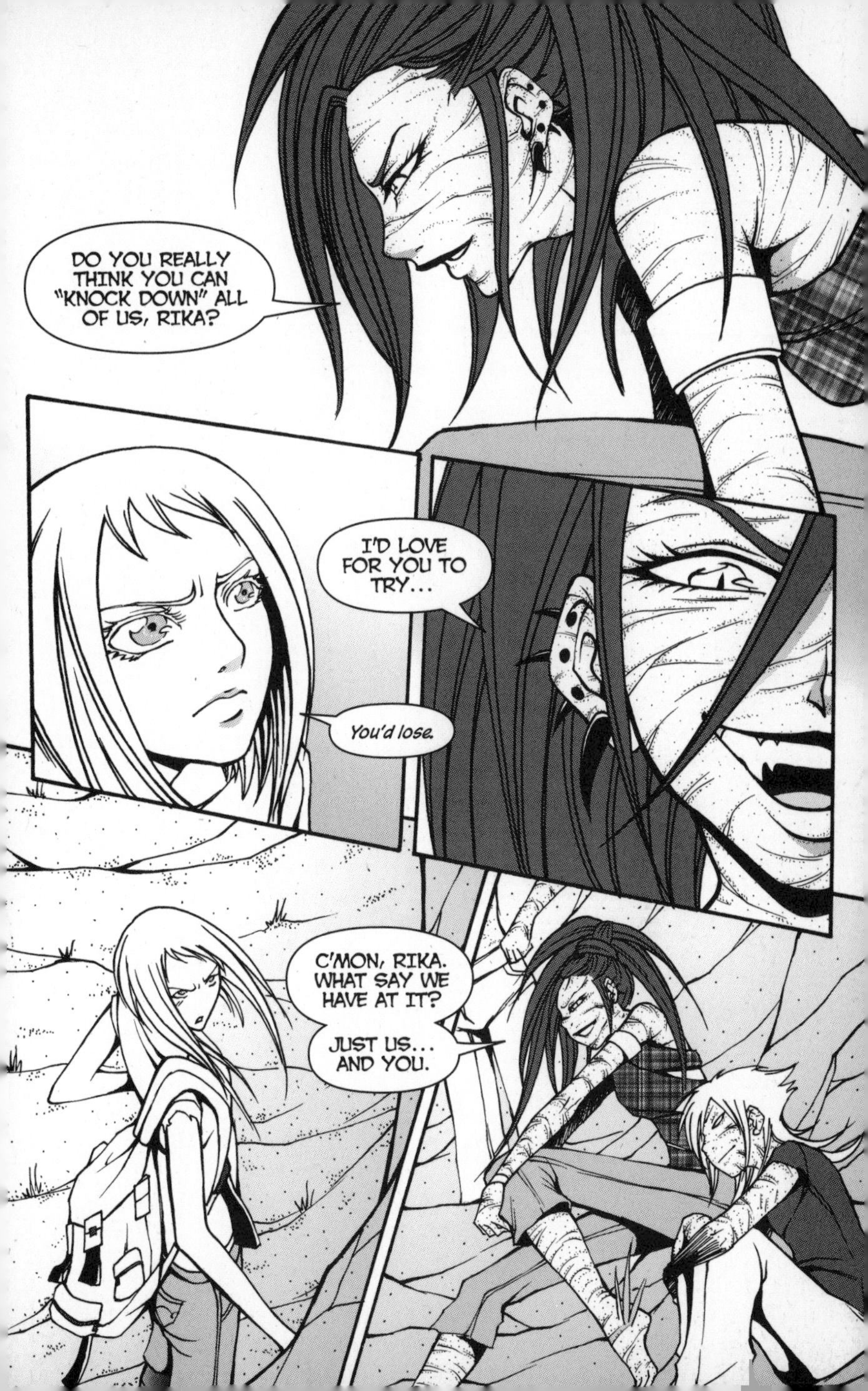
DO YOU REALLY THINK YOU CAN "KNOCK DOWN" ALL OF US, RIKA?
I'D LOVE FOR YOU TO TRY...
You'd lose.
C'MON, RIKA. WHAT SAY WE HAVE AT IT?
JUST US... AND YOU.

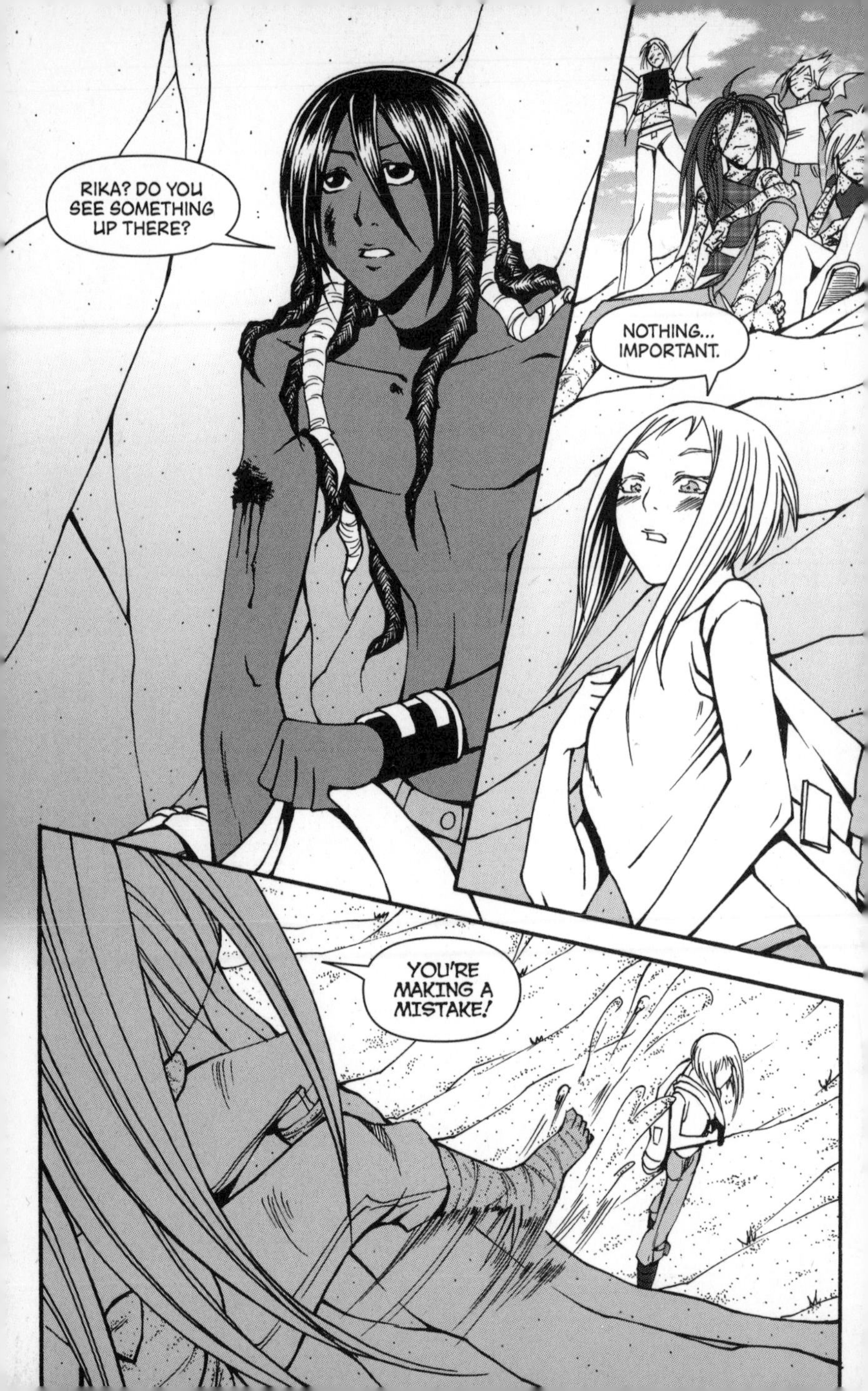
RIKA? DO YOU SEE SOMETHING UP THERE?
NOTHING... IMPORTANT.
YOU'RE MAKING A MISTAKE!

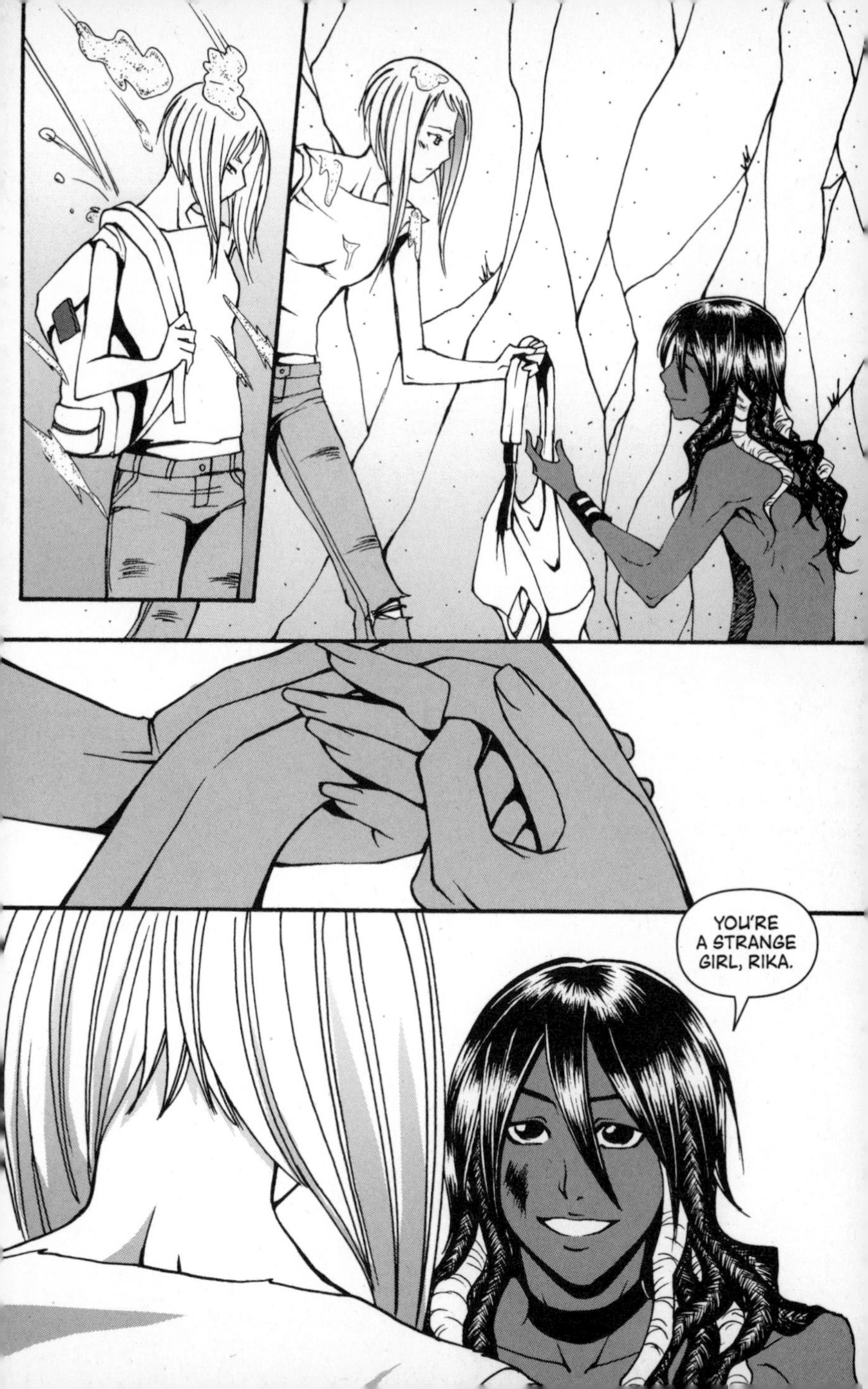
YOU'RE A STRANGE GIRL, RIKA.

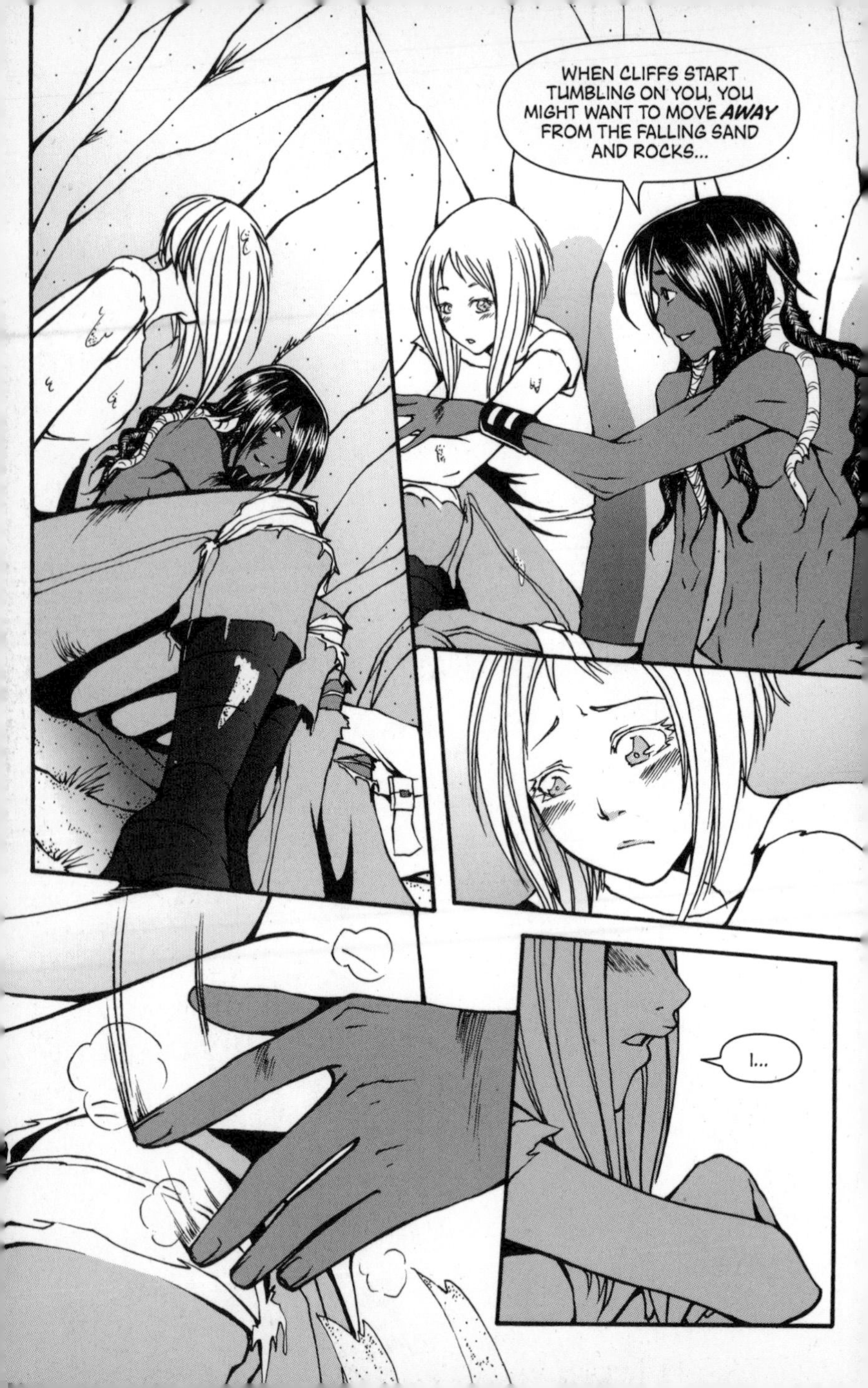
WHEN CLIFFS START TUMBLING ON YOU, YOU MIGHT WANT TO MOVE *AWAY* FROM THE FALLING SAND AND ROCKS...
I...

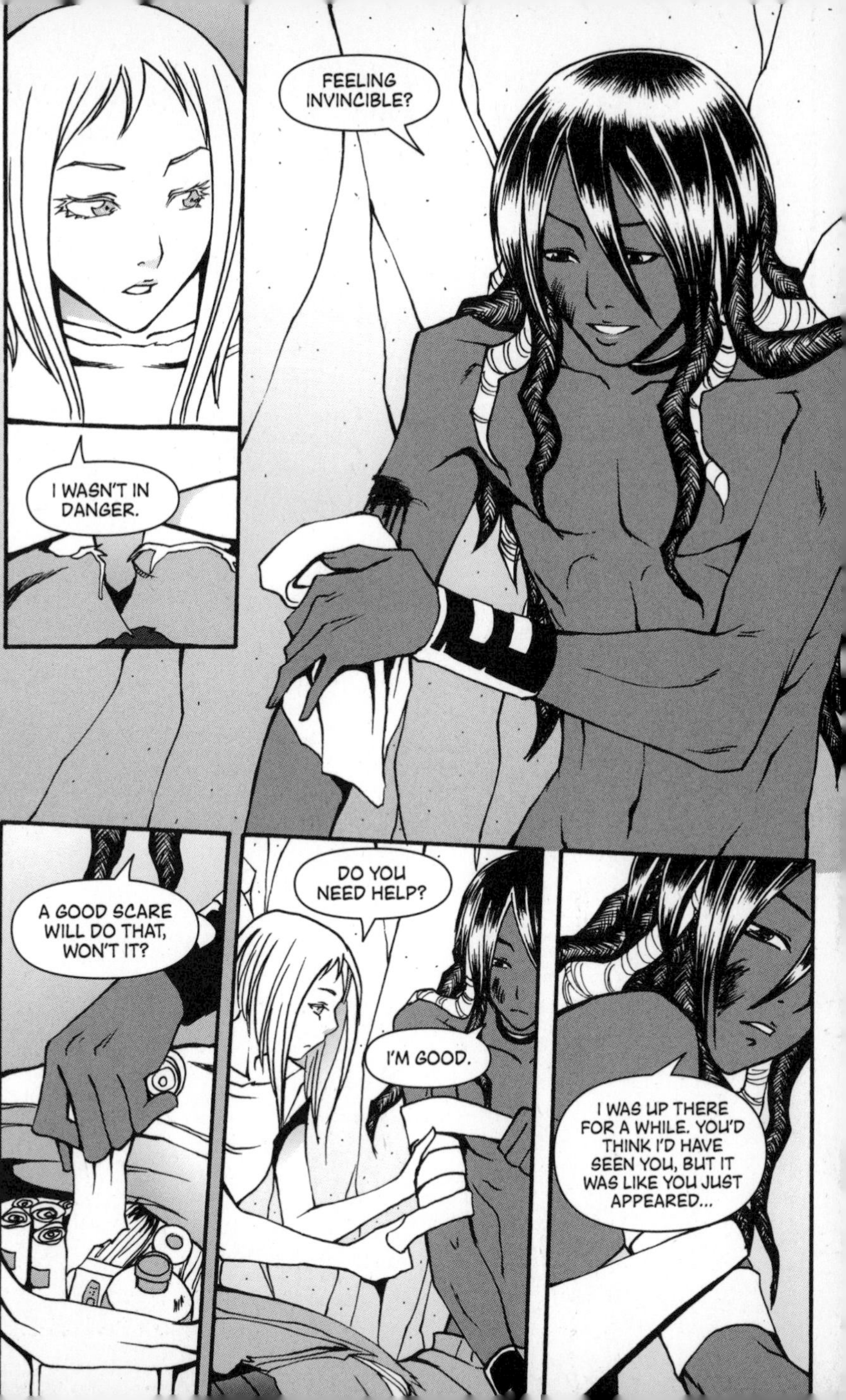
I WASN'T IN DANGER.
FEELING INVINCIBLE?
A GOOD SCARE WILL DO THAT, WON'T IT?
DO YOU NEED HELP?
I'M GOOD.
I WAS UP THERE FOR A WHILE. YOU'D THINK I'D HAVE SEEN YOU, BUT IT WAS LIKE YOU JUST APPEARED...

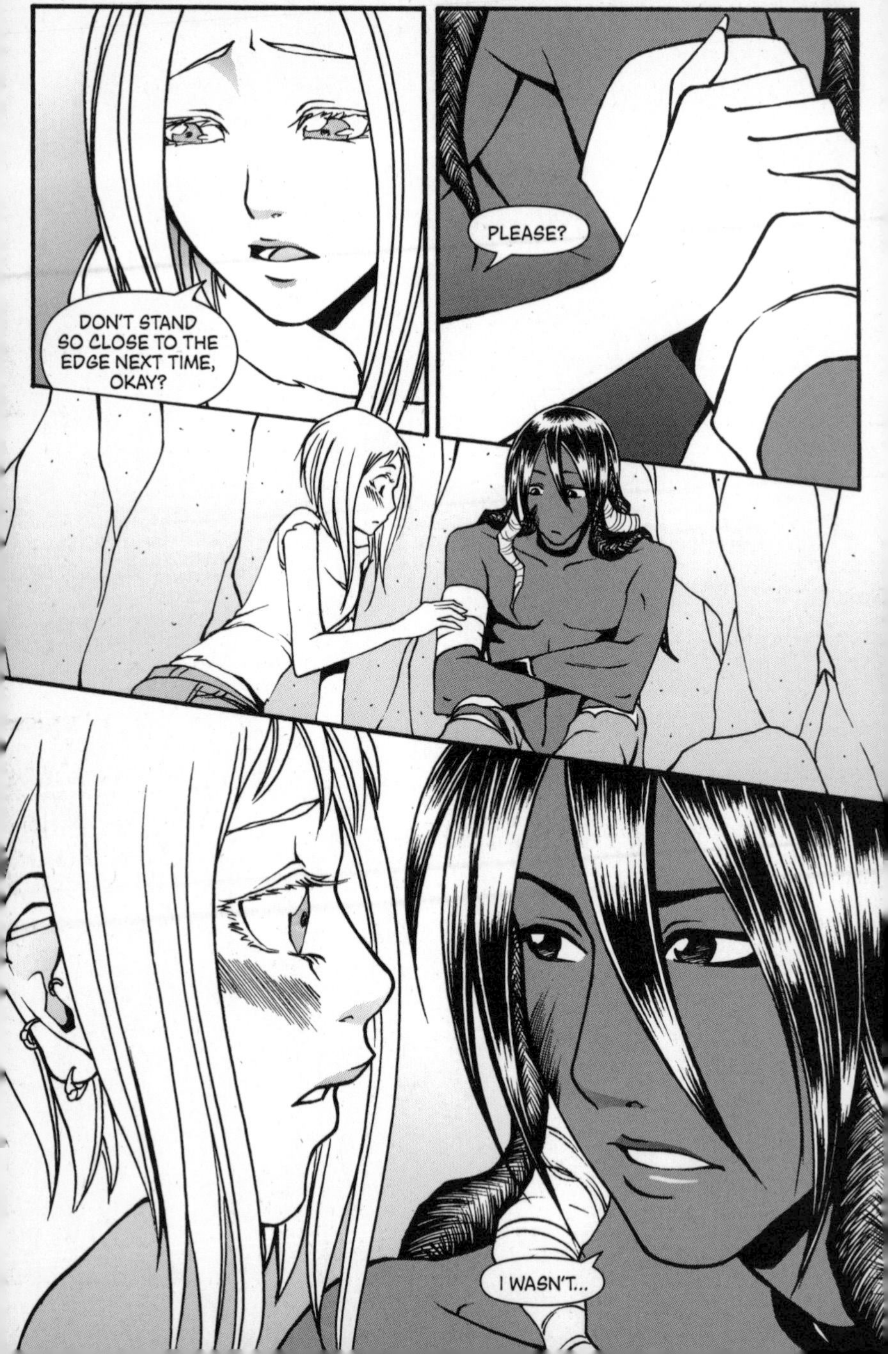
DON'T STAND SO CLOSE TO THE EDGE NEXT TIME, OKAY?
PLEASE?
I WASN'T...

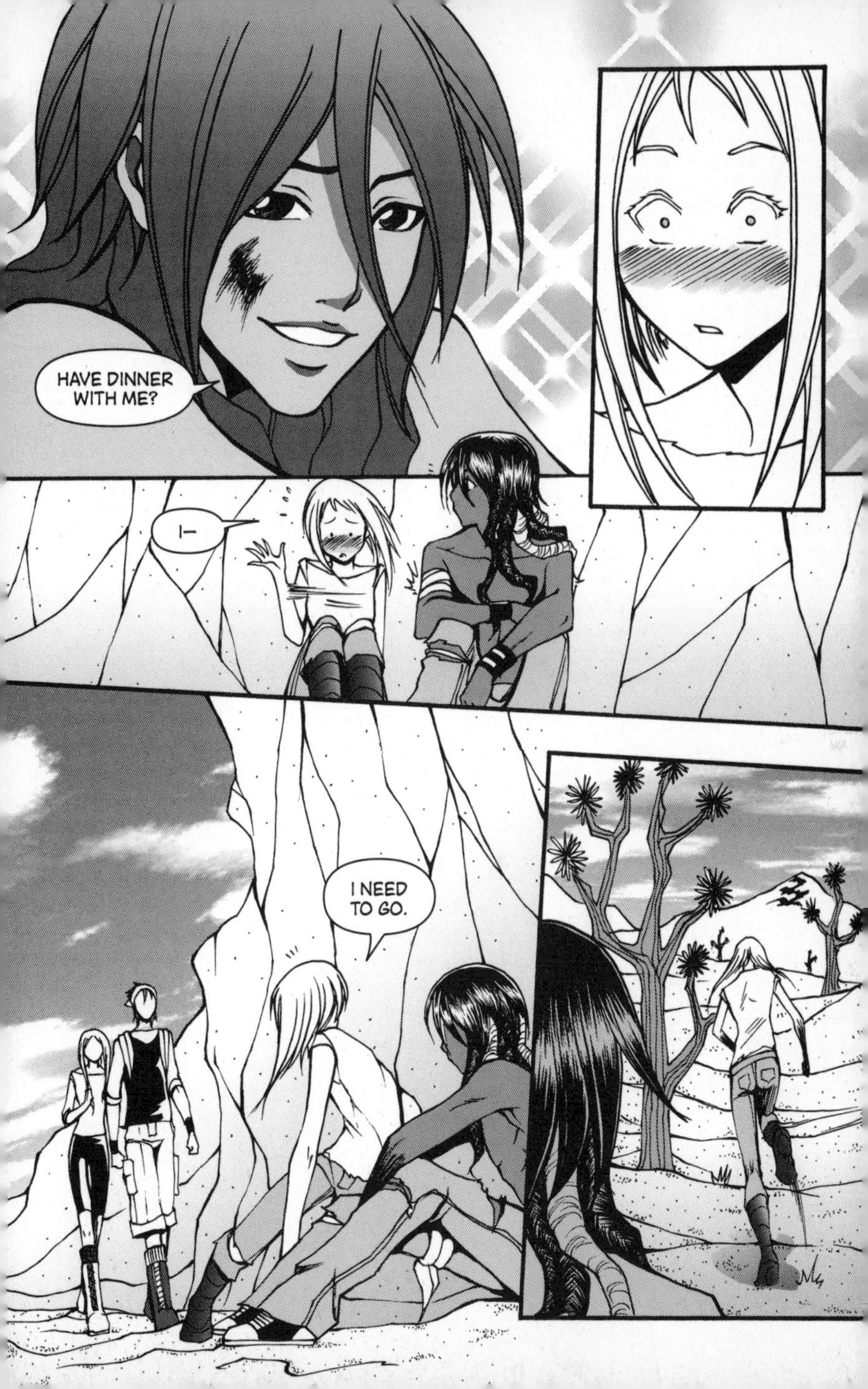
HAVE DINNER WITH ME?
I—
I NEED TO GO.

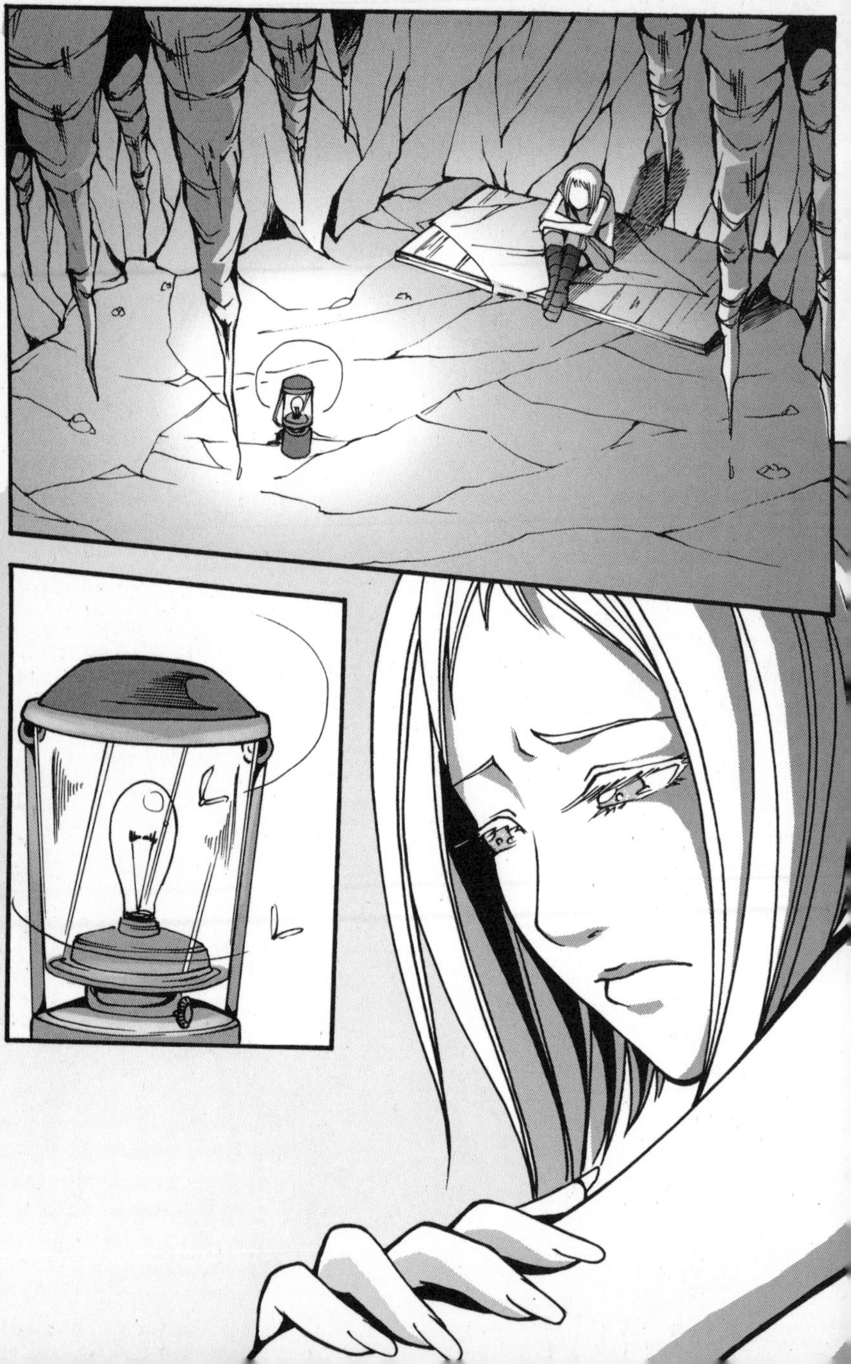

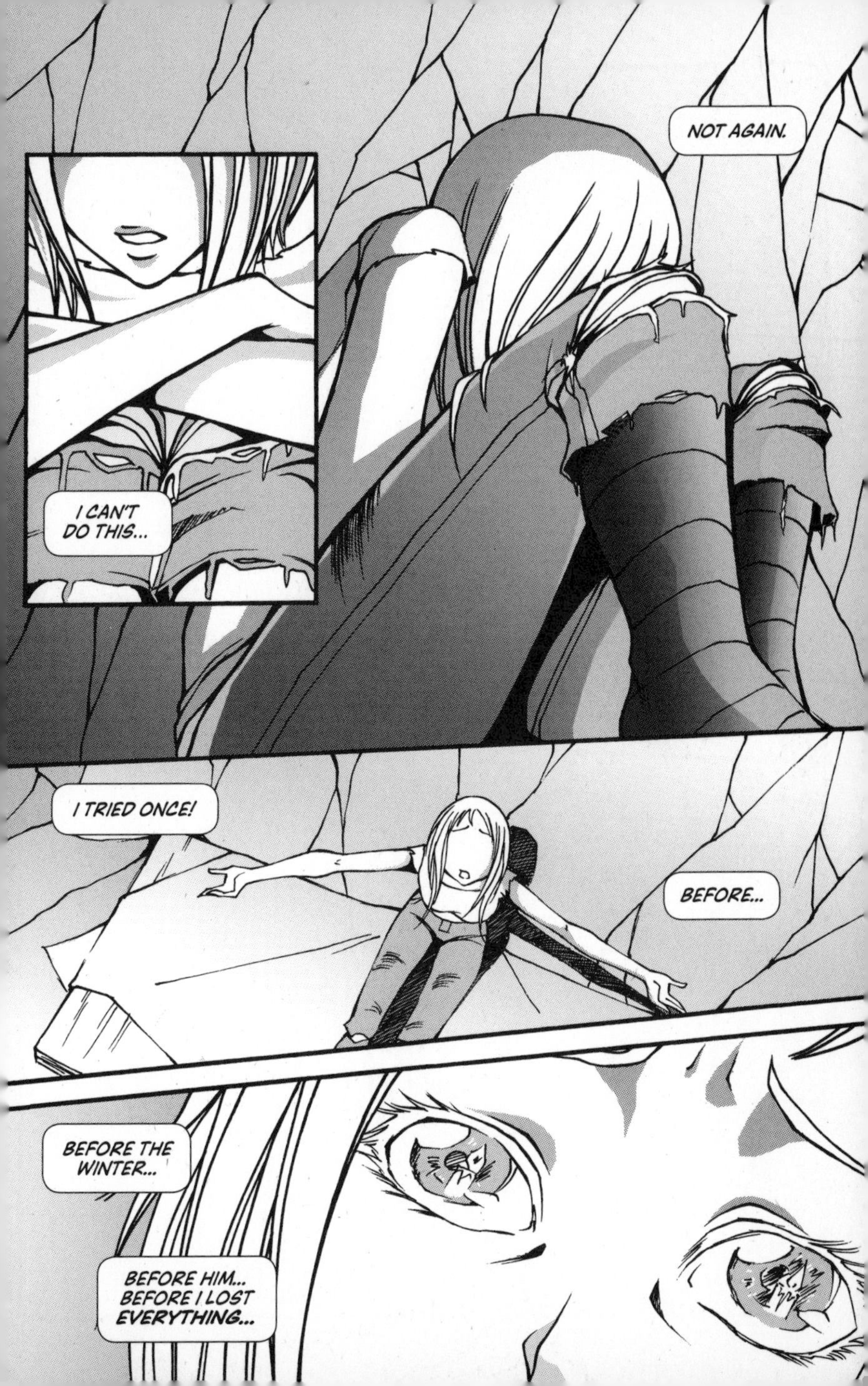
I CAN'T DO THIS...
NOT AGAIN.
I TRIED ONCE!
BEFORE...
BEFORE THE WINTER...
BEFORE HIM... BEFORE I LOST EVERYTHING...

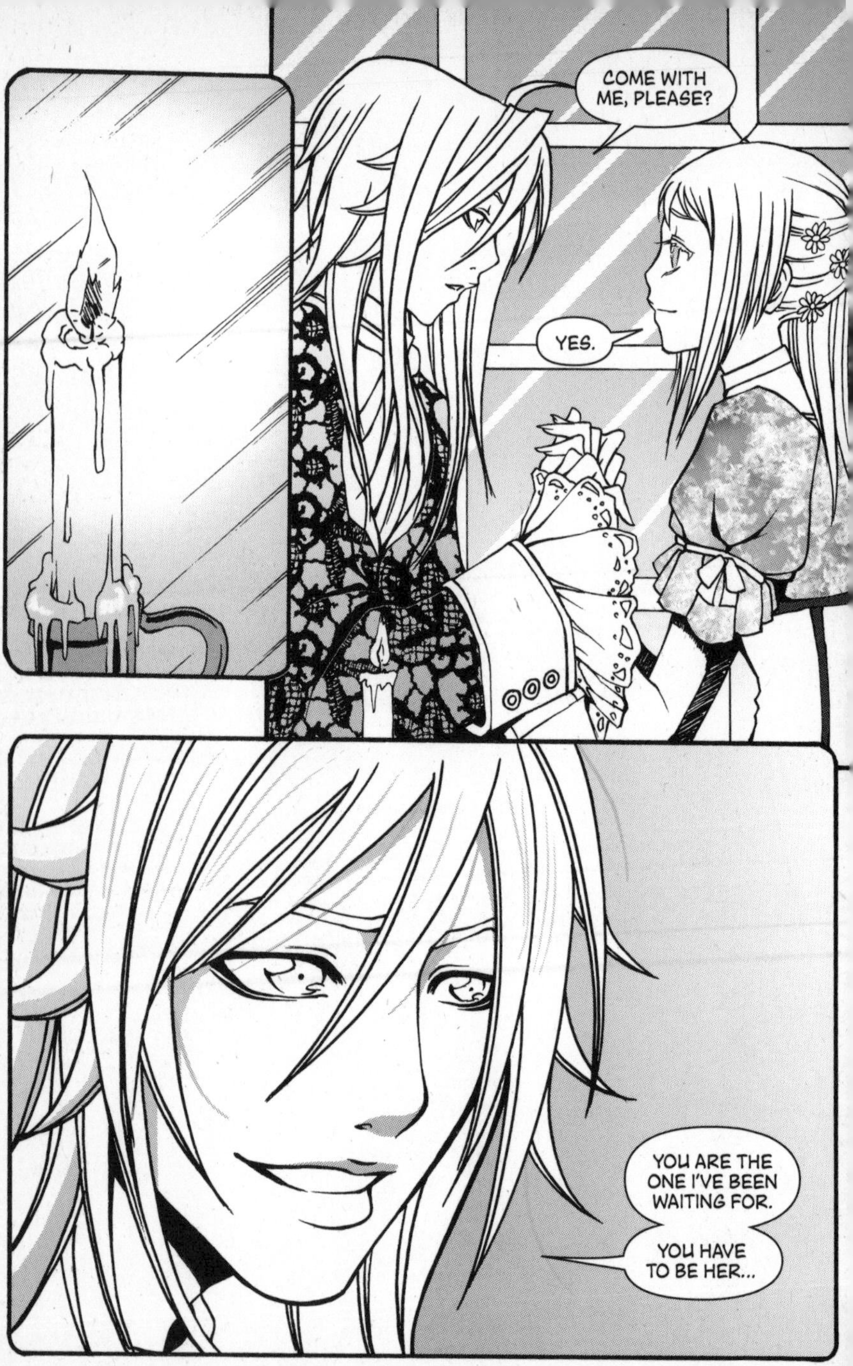
COME WITH ME, PLEASE?
YES.
YOU ARE THE ONE I'VE BEEN WAITING FOR.
YOU HAVE TO BE HER...

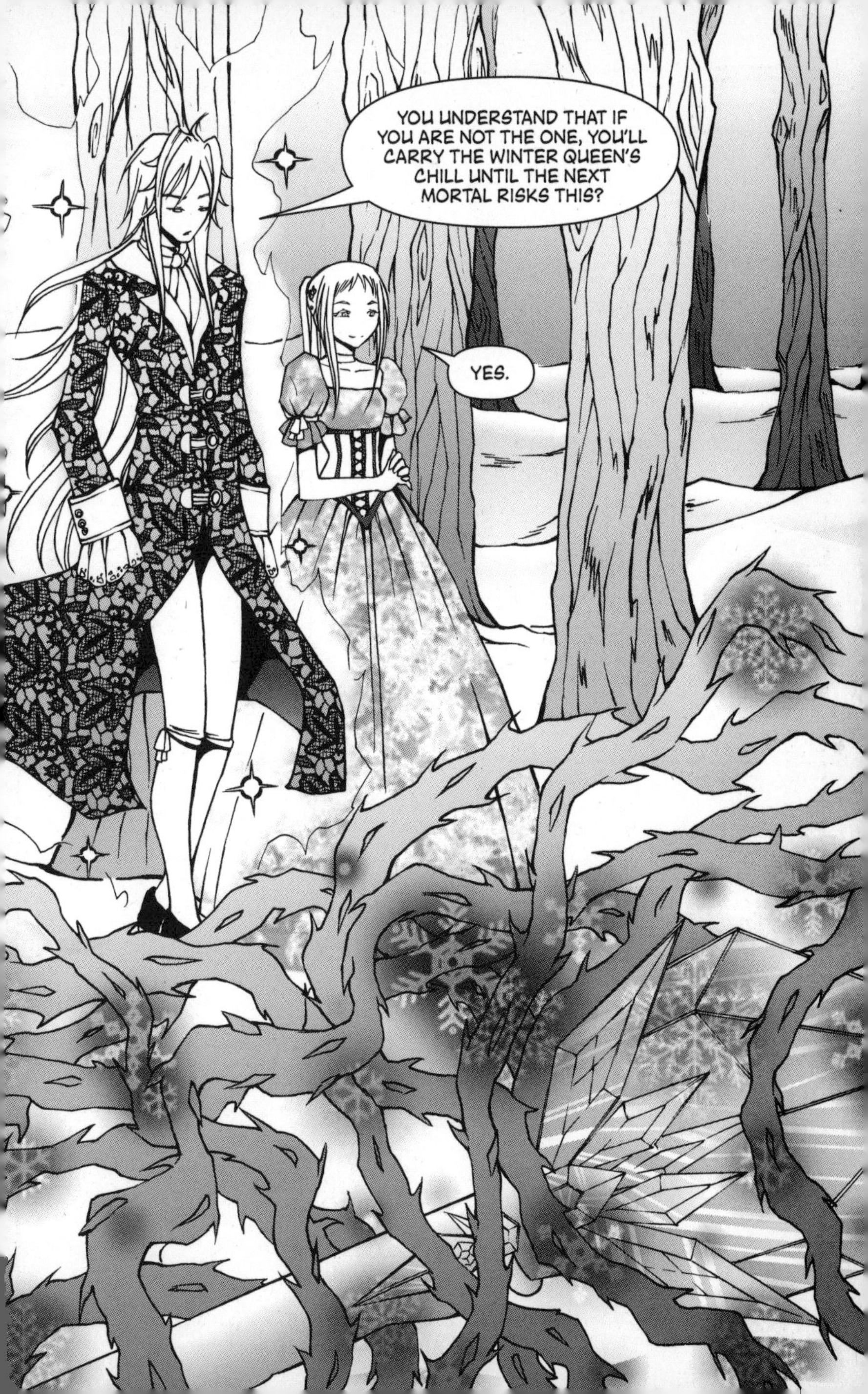
YOU UNDERSTAND THAT IF YOU ARE NOT THE ONE, YOU'LL CARRY THE WINTER QUEEN'S CHILL UNTIL THE NEXT MORTAL RISKS THIS?
YES.

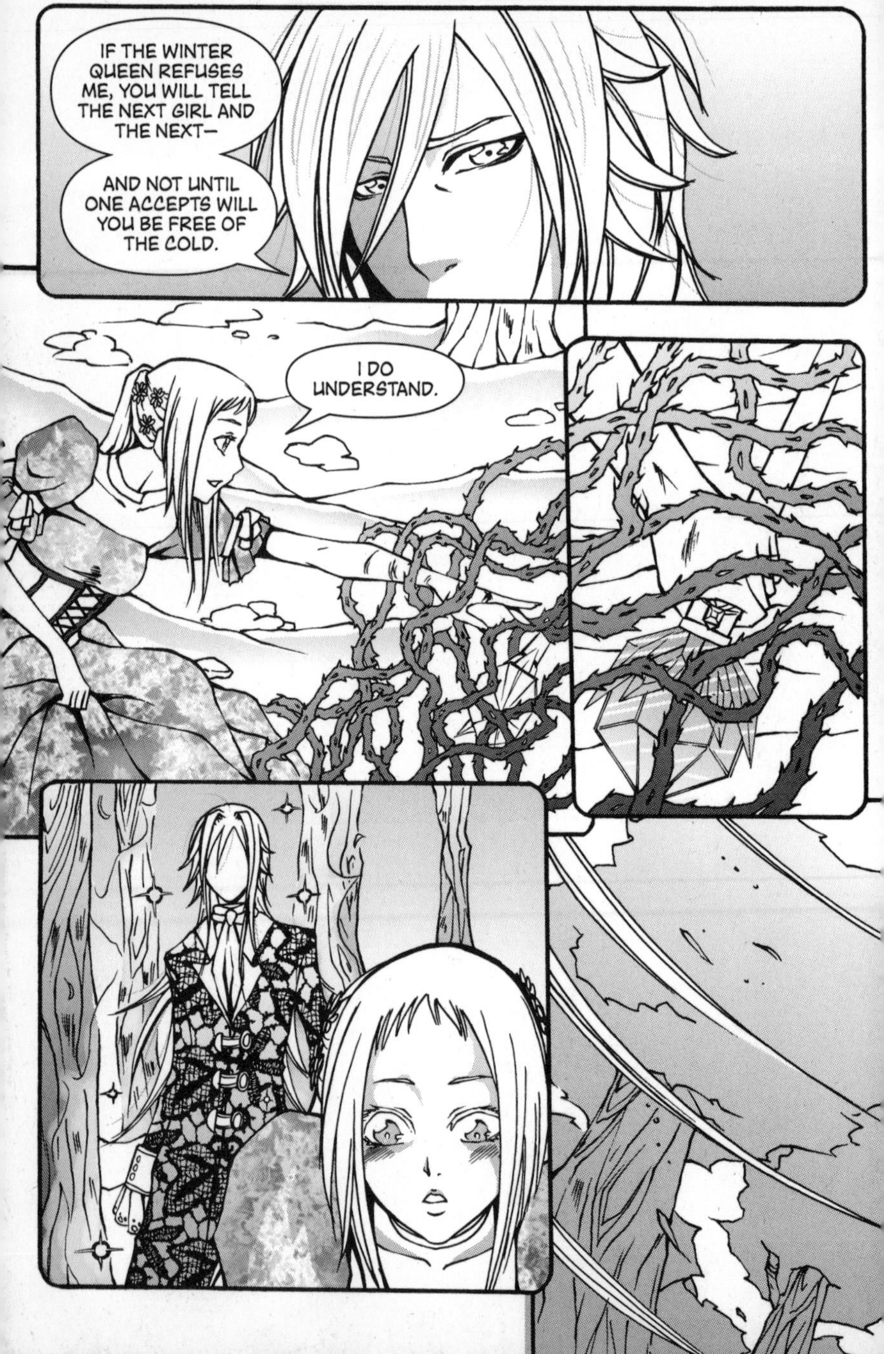
IF THE WINTER QUEEN REFUSES ME, YOU WILL TELL THE NEXT GIRL AND THE NEXT—
AND NOT UNTIL ONE ACCEPTS WILL YOU BE FREE OF THE COLD.
I DO UNDERSTAND.

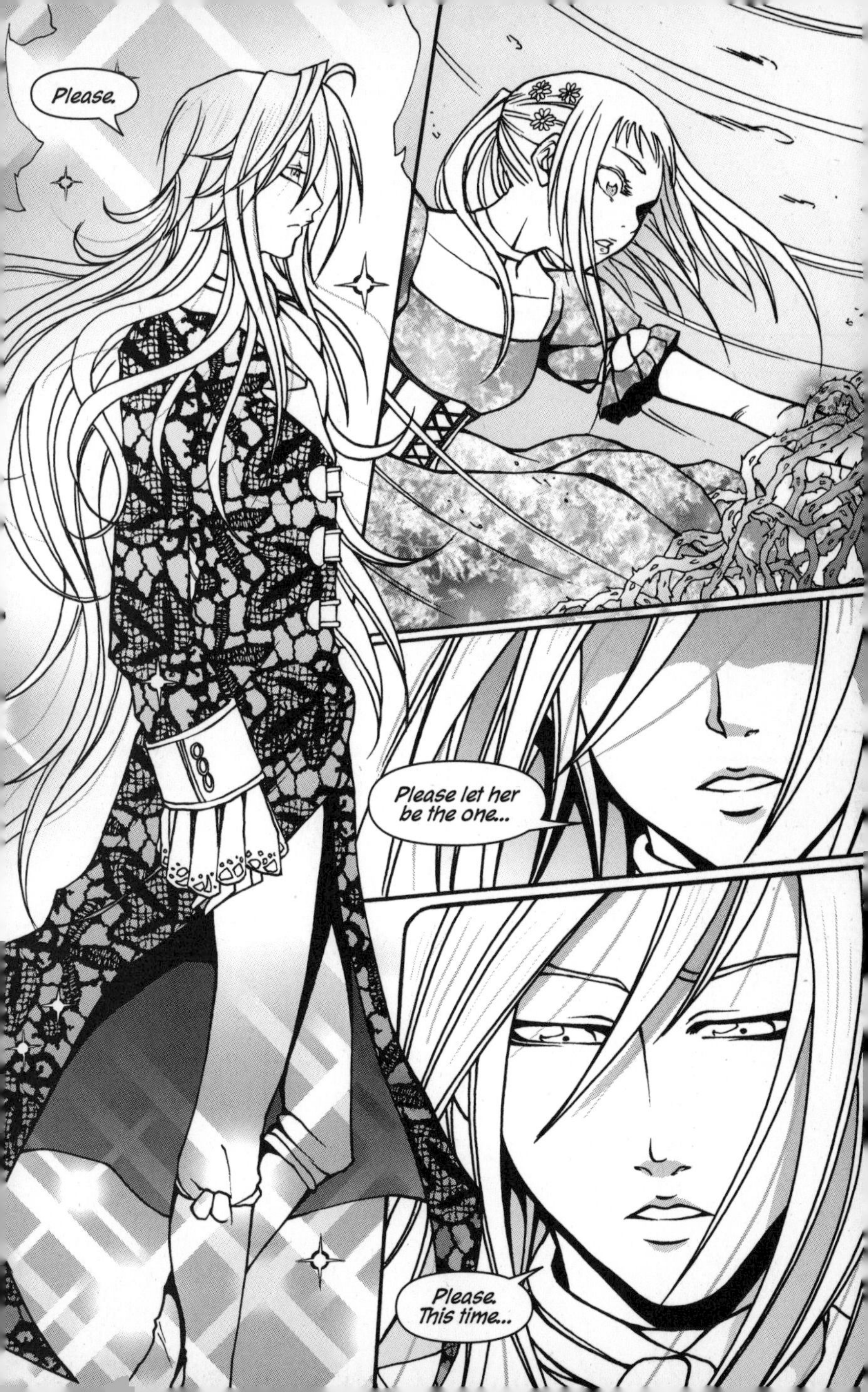
Please.
Please let her be the one...
Please. This time...

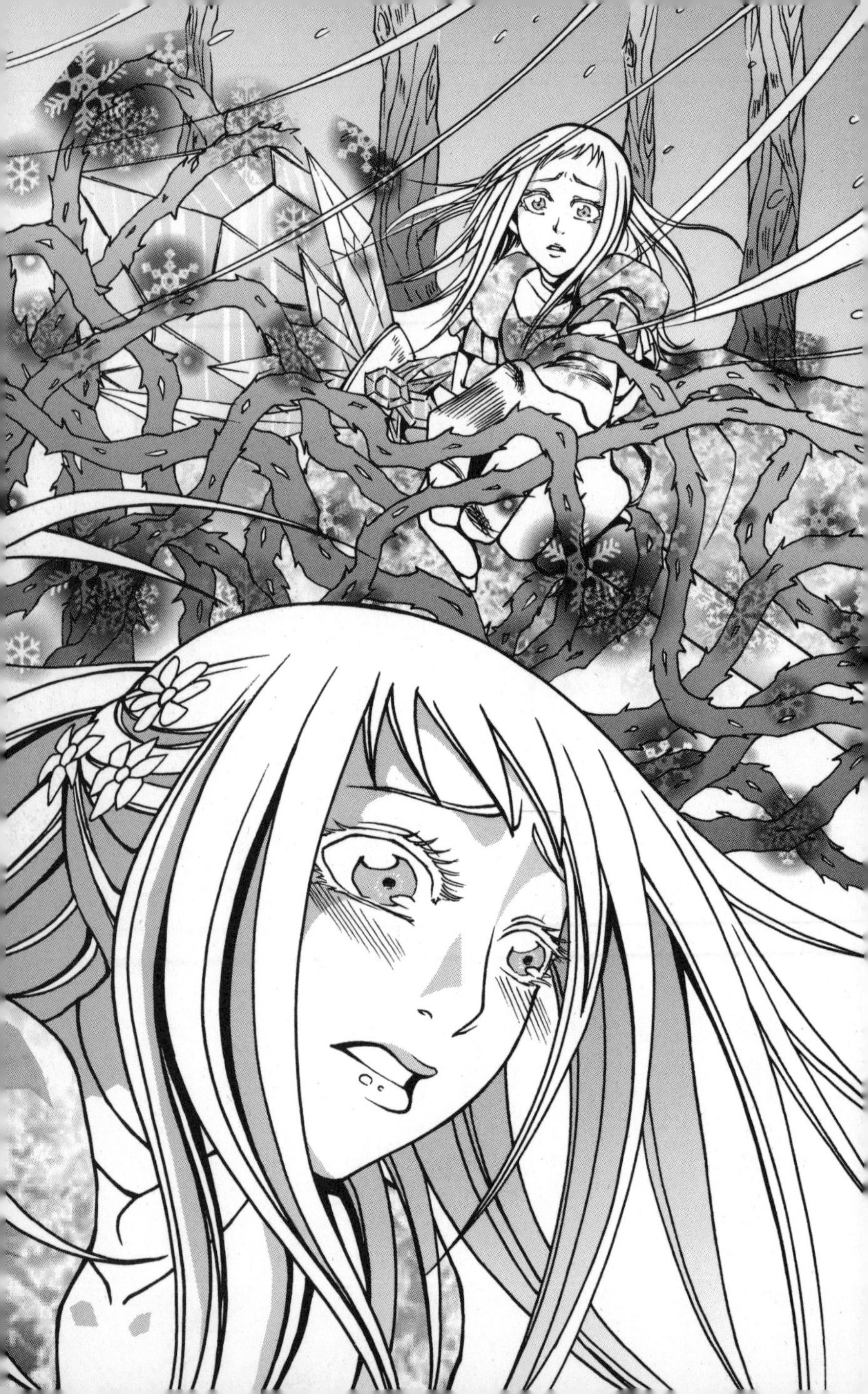

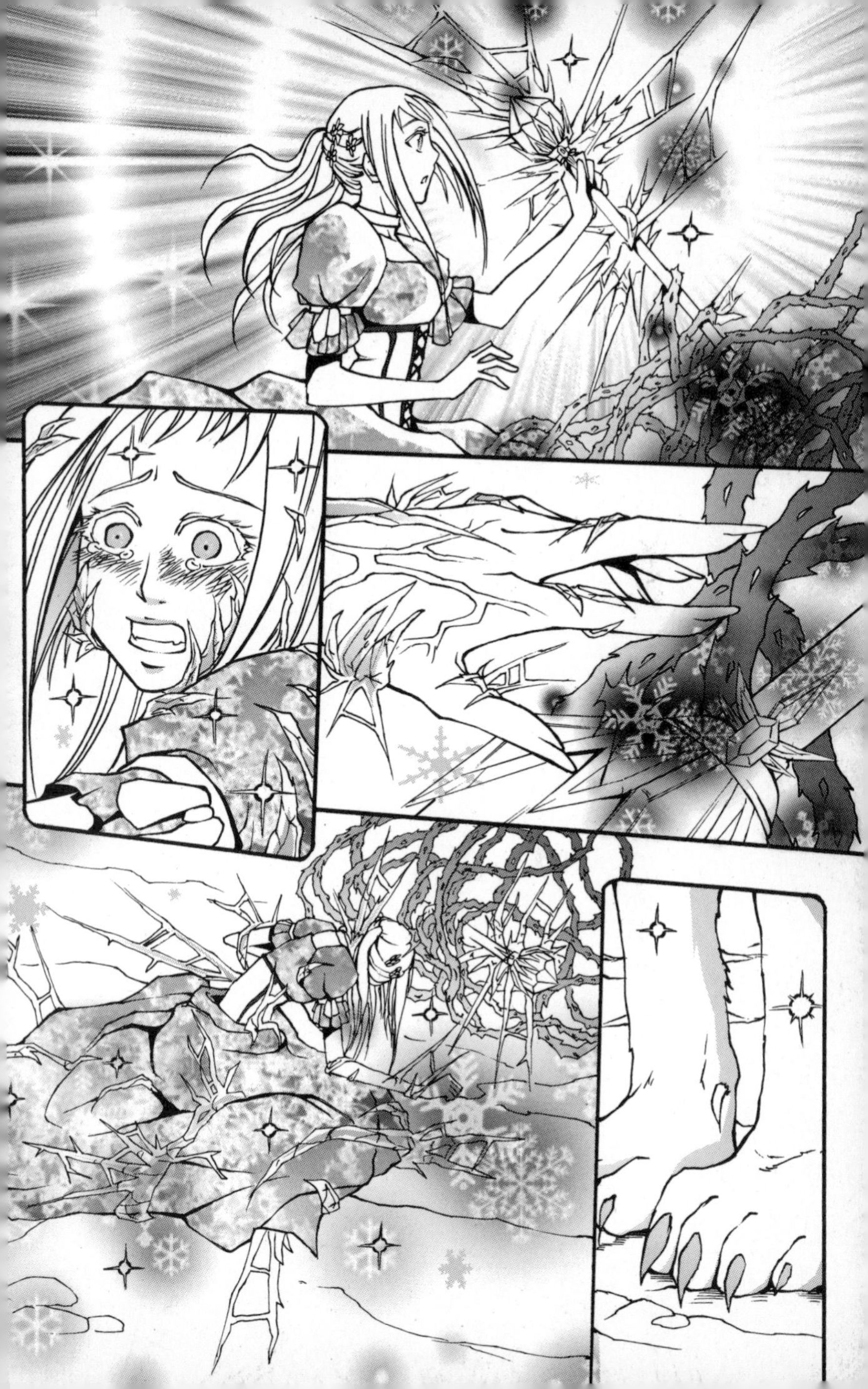

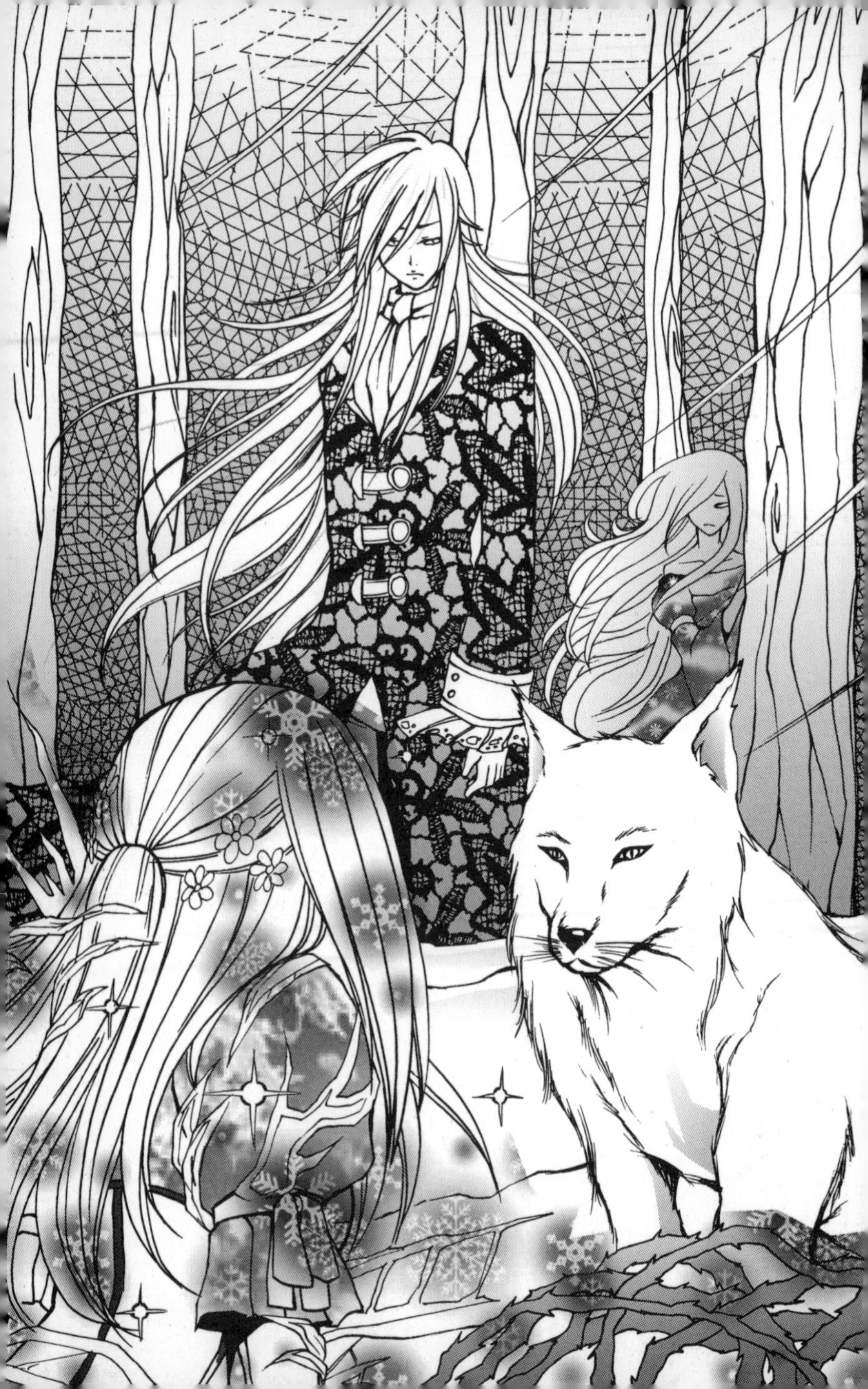

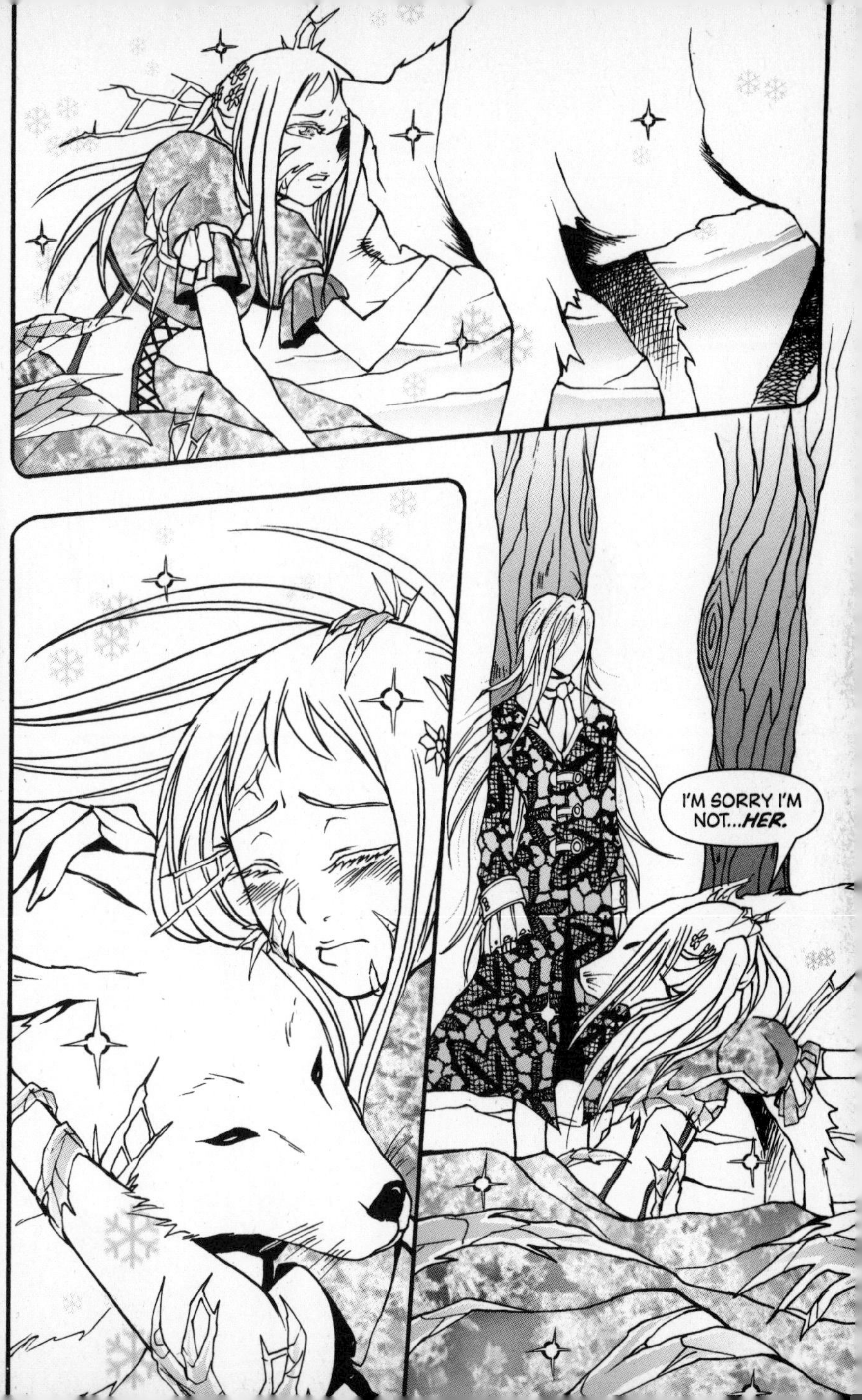
I'M SORRY I'M NOT...*HER.*

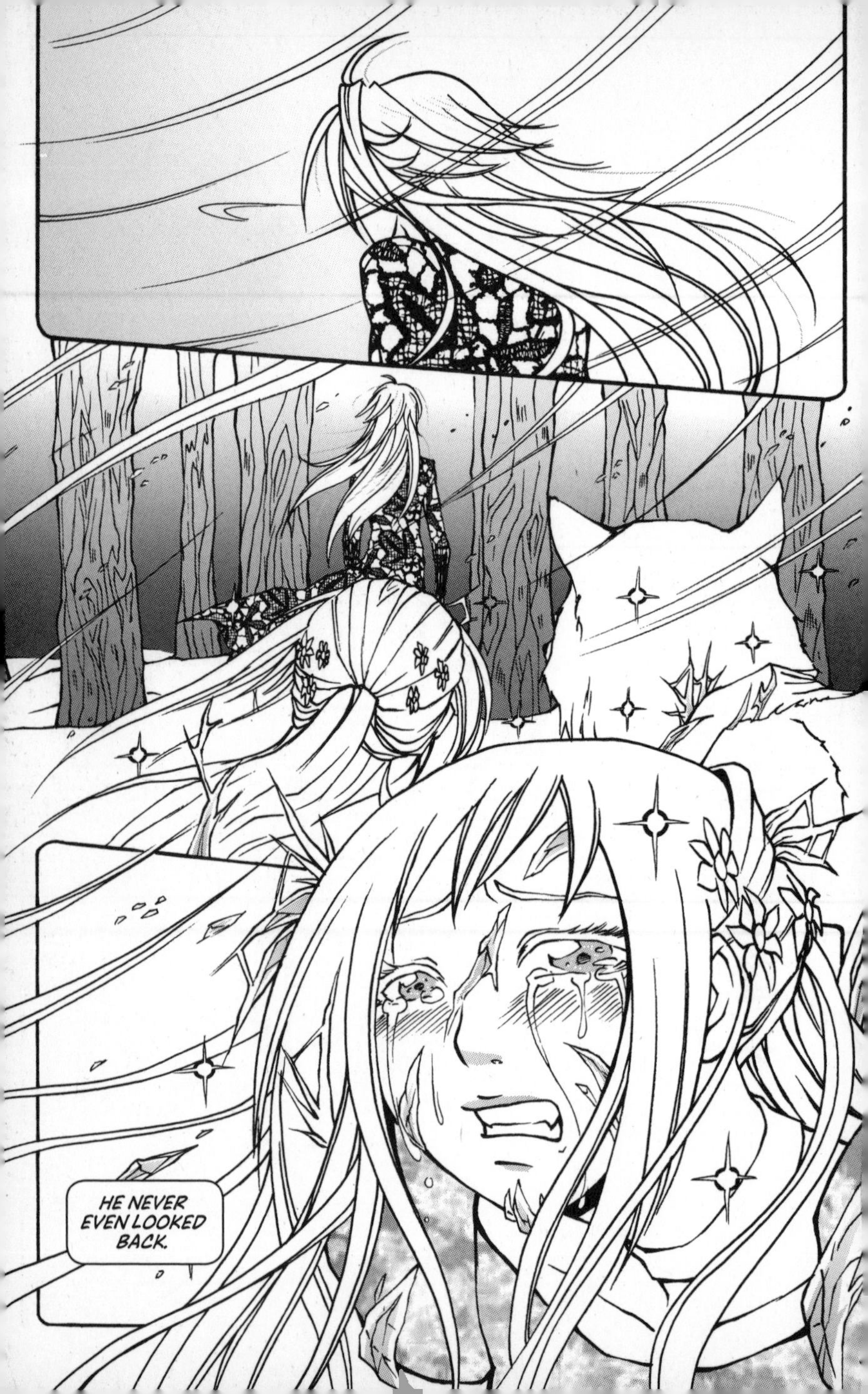
HE NEVER EVEN LOOKED BACK.

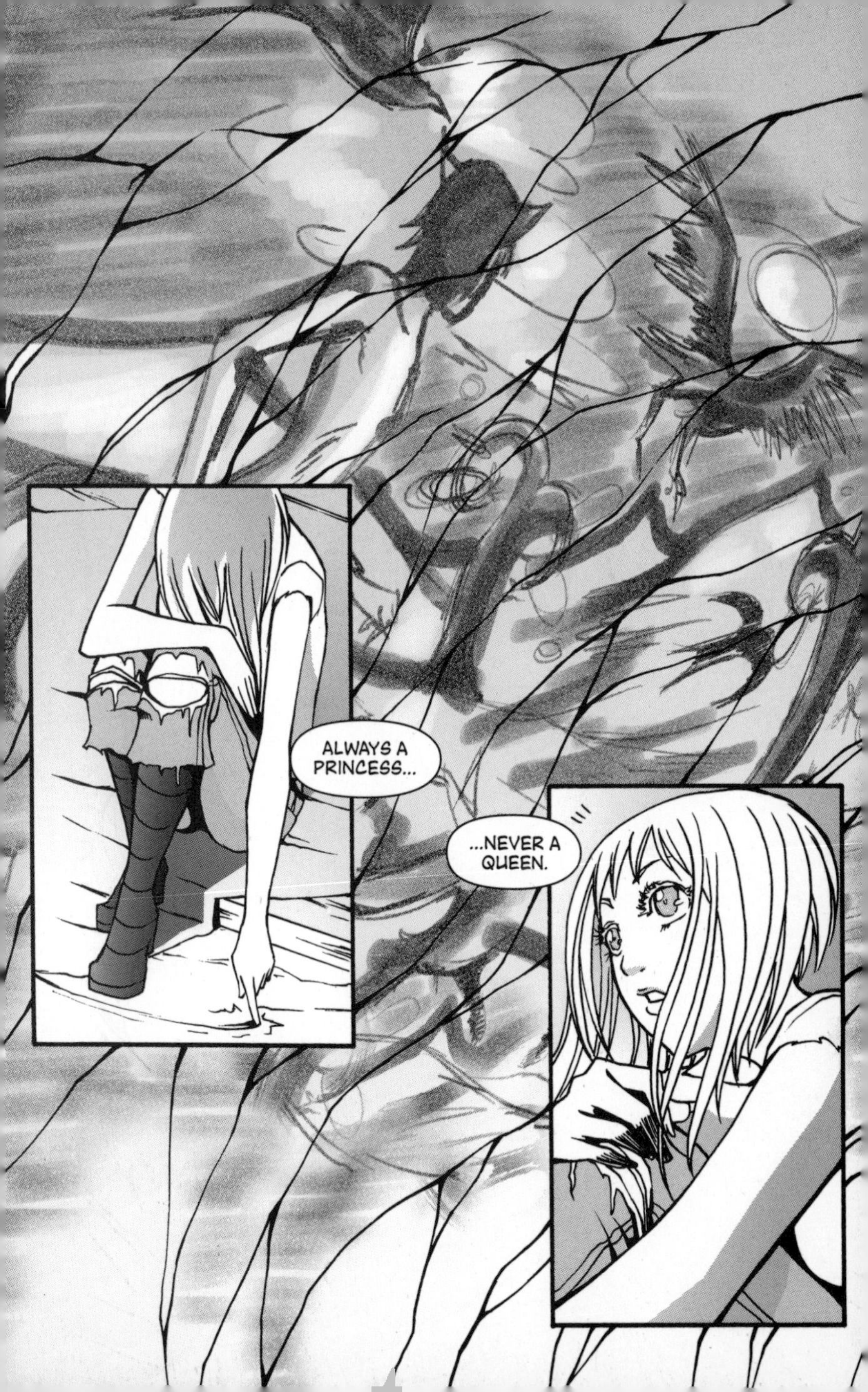
ALWAYS A PRINCESS...
...NEVER A QUEEN.

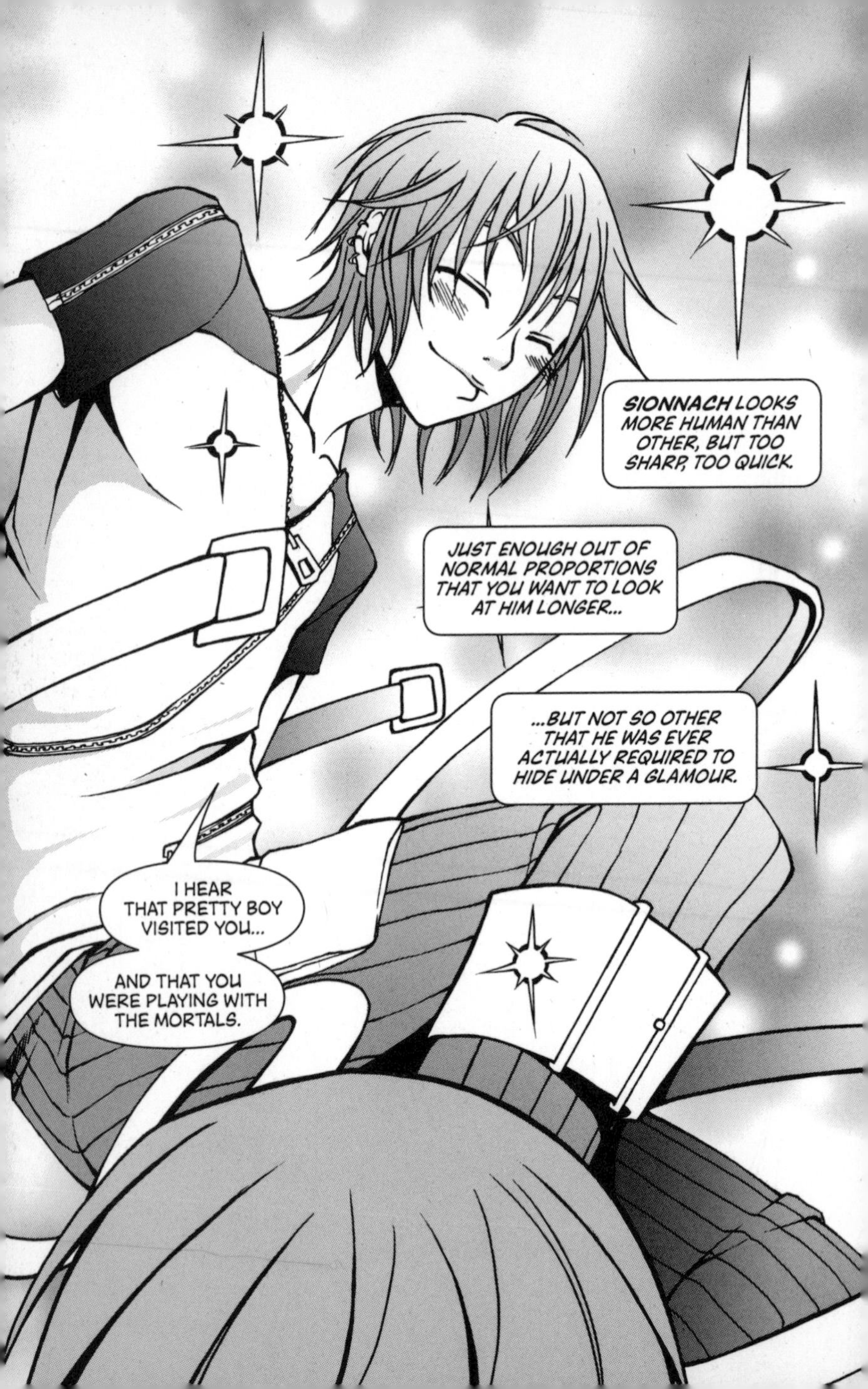
SIONNACH LOOKS MORE HUMAN THAN OTHER, BUT TOO SHARP, TOO QUICK.
JUST ENOUGH OUT OF NORMAL PROPORTIONS THAT YOU WANT TO LOOK AT HIM LONGER...
...BUT NOT SO OTHER THAT HE WAS EVER ACTUALLY REQUIRED TO HIDE UNDER A GLAMOUR.
I HEAR THAT PRETTY BOY VISITED YOU...
AND THAT YOU WERE PLAYING WITH THE MORTALS.

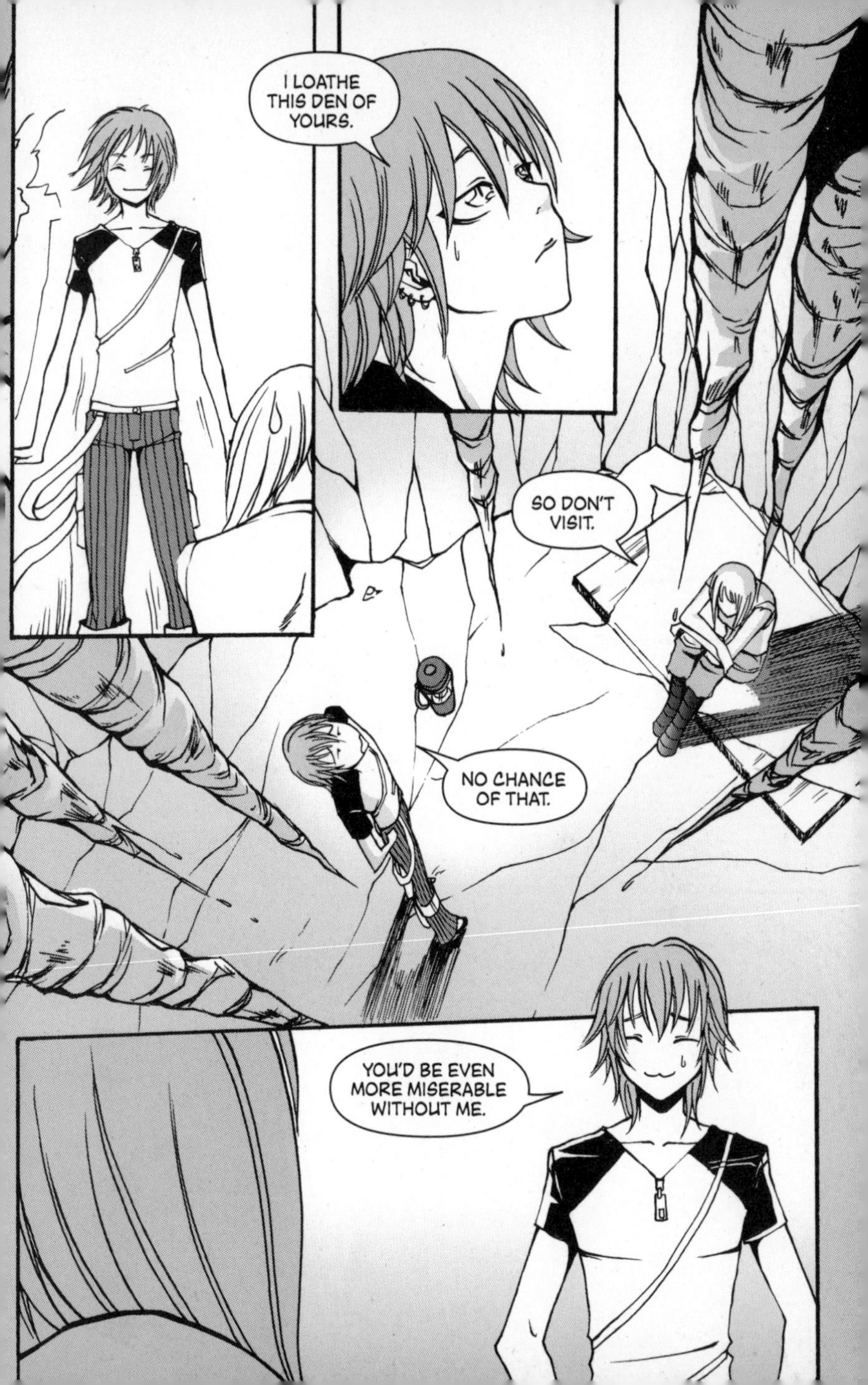
I LOATHE THIS DEN OF YOURS.
SO DON'T VISIT.
NO CHANCE OF THAT.
YOU'D BE EVEN MORE MISERABLE WITHOUT ME.

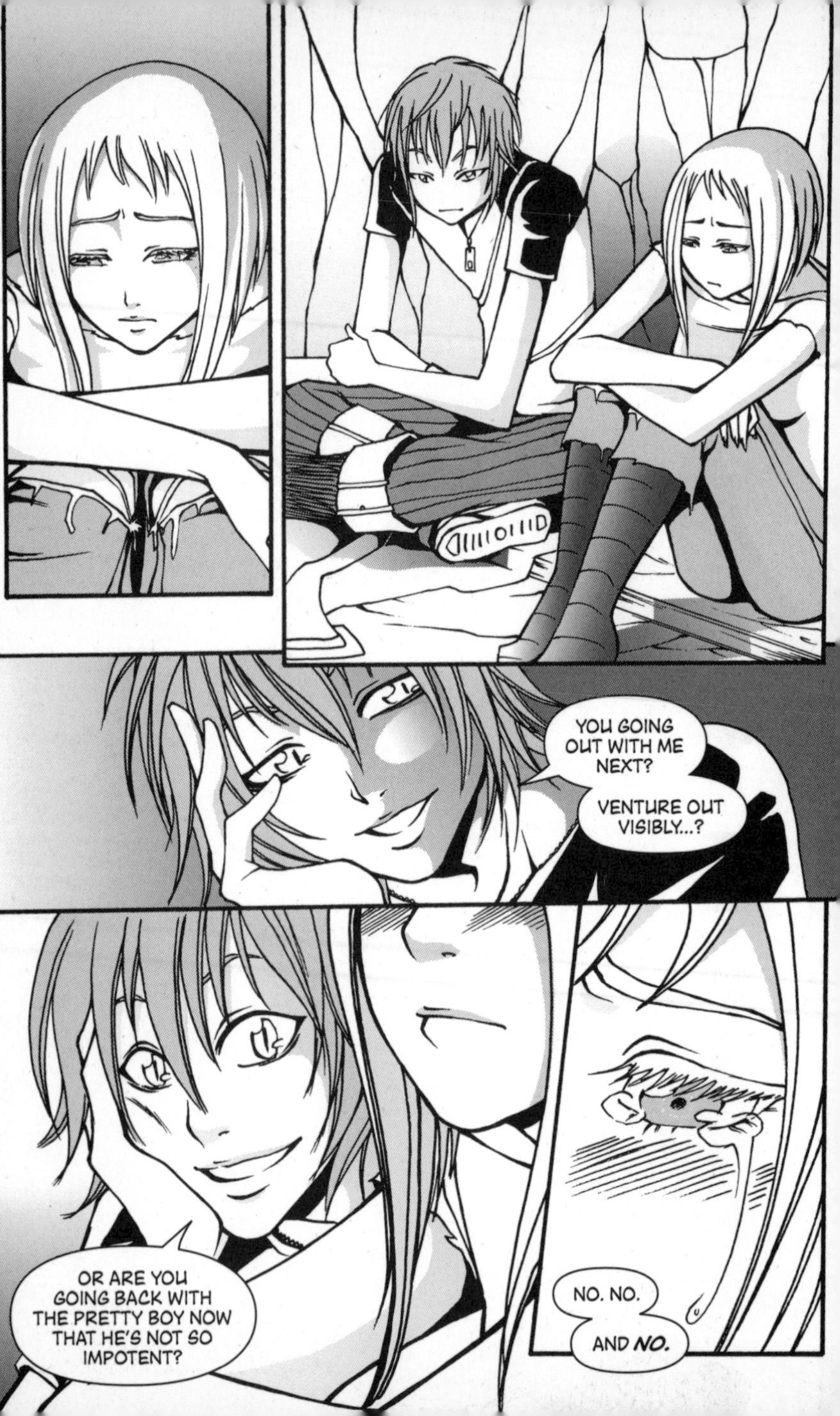
YOU GOING OUT WITH ME NEXT?
VENTURE OUT VISIBLY...?
OR ARE YOU GOING BACK WITH THE PRETTY BOY NOW THAT HE'S NOT SO IMPOTENT?
NO. NO.
AND *NO.*

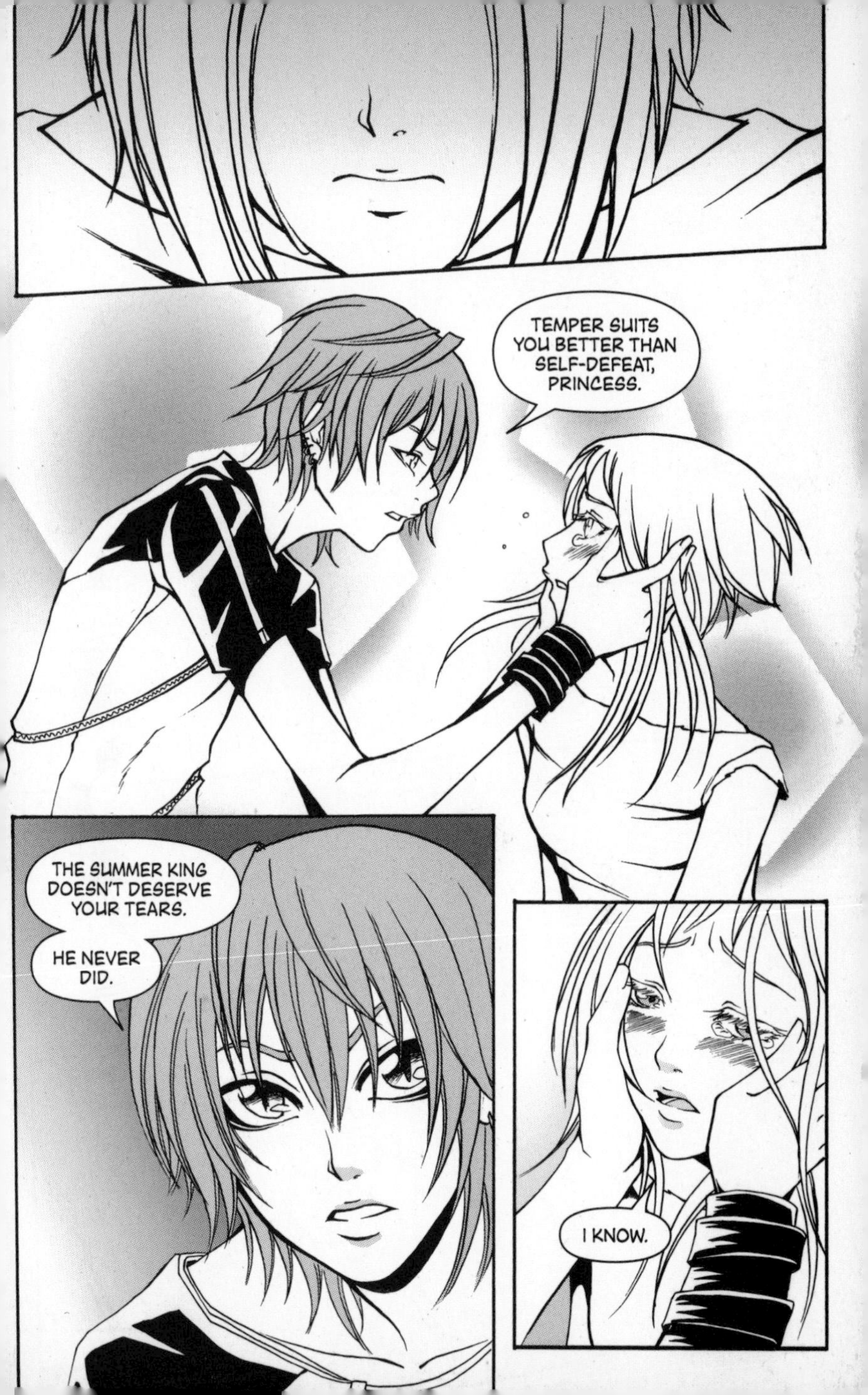
TEMPER SUITS YOU BETTER THAN SELF-DEFEAT, PRINCESS.
THE SUMMER KING DOESN'T DESERVE YOUR TEARS.
HE NEVER DID.
I KNOW.

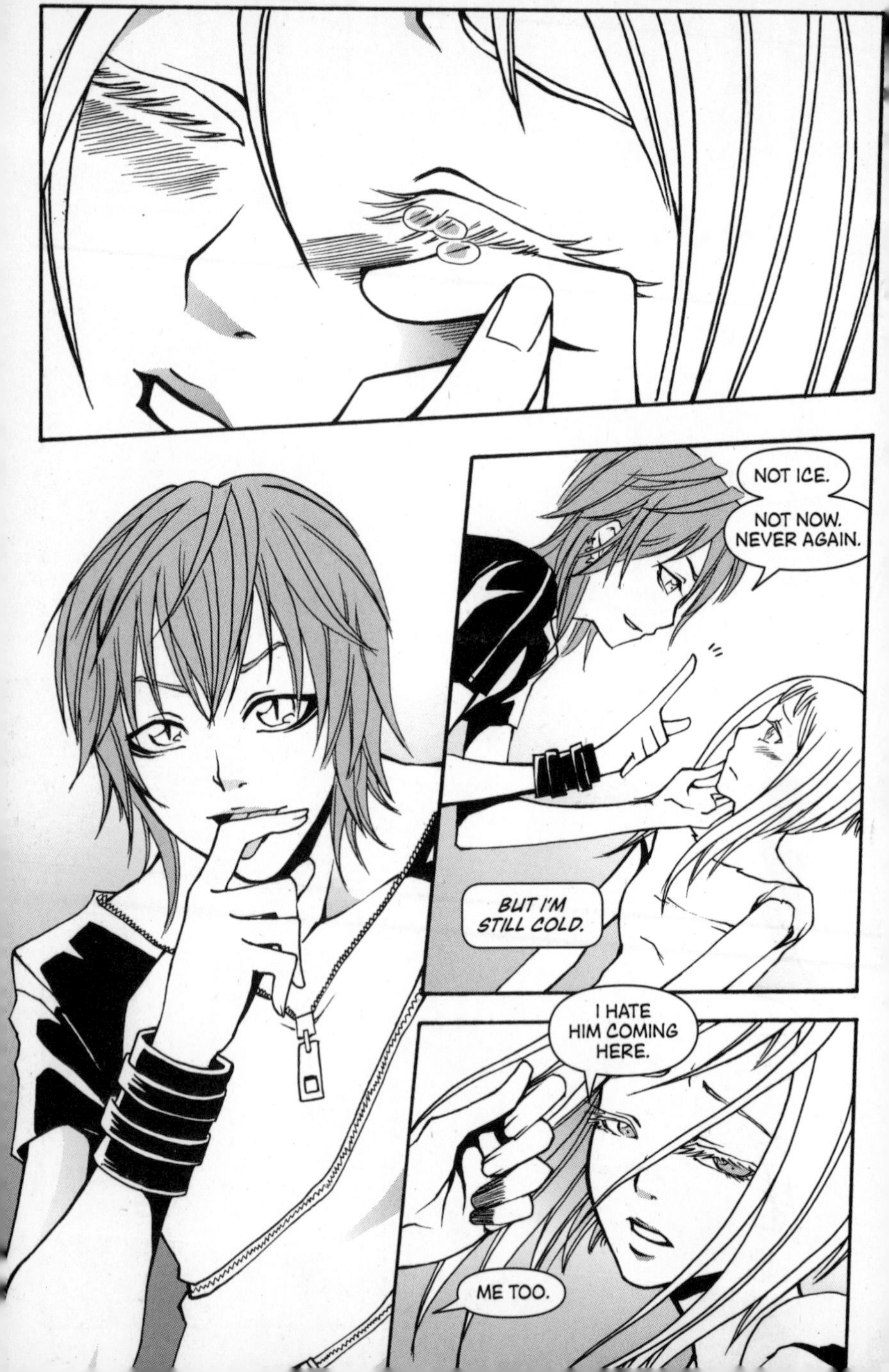
NOT ICE.
NOT NOW. NEVER AGAIN.
BUT I'M STILL COLD.
I HATE HIM COMING HERE.
ME TOO.

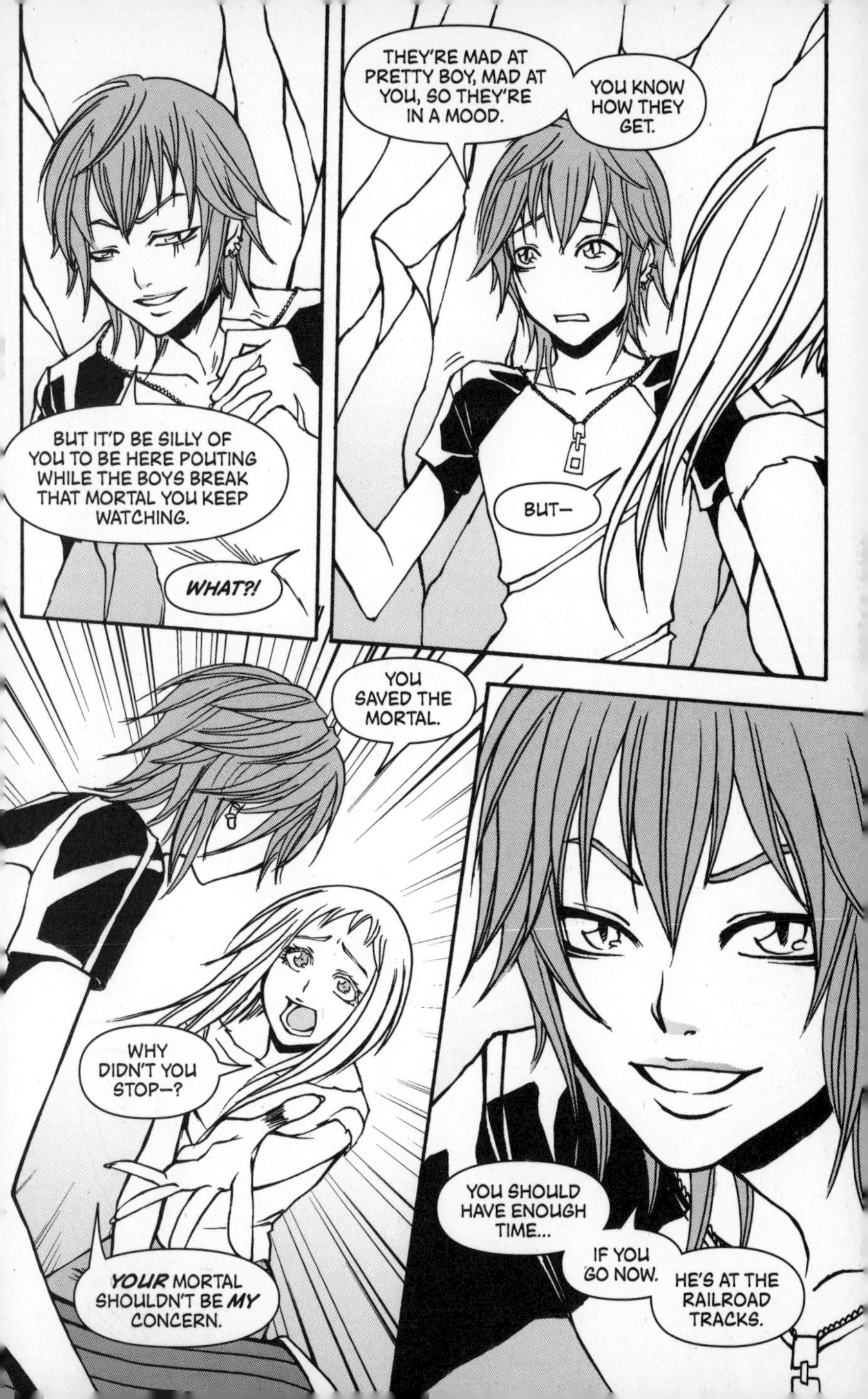
BUT IT'D BE SILLY OF YOU TO BE HERE POUTING WHILE THE BOYS BREAK THAT MORTAL YOU KEEP WATCHING.
WHAT?!
THEY'RE MAD AT PRETTY BOY, MAD AT YOU, SO THEY'RE IN A MOOD.
YOU KNOW HOW THEY GET.
BUT–
YOU SAVED THE MORTAL.
WHY DIDN'T YOU STOP–?
YOUR MORTAL SHOULDN'T BE ***MY*** CONCERN.
YOU SHOULD HAVE ENOUGH TIME...
IF YOU GO NOW.
HE'S AT THE RAILROAD TRACKS.

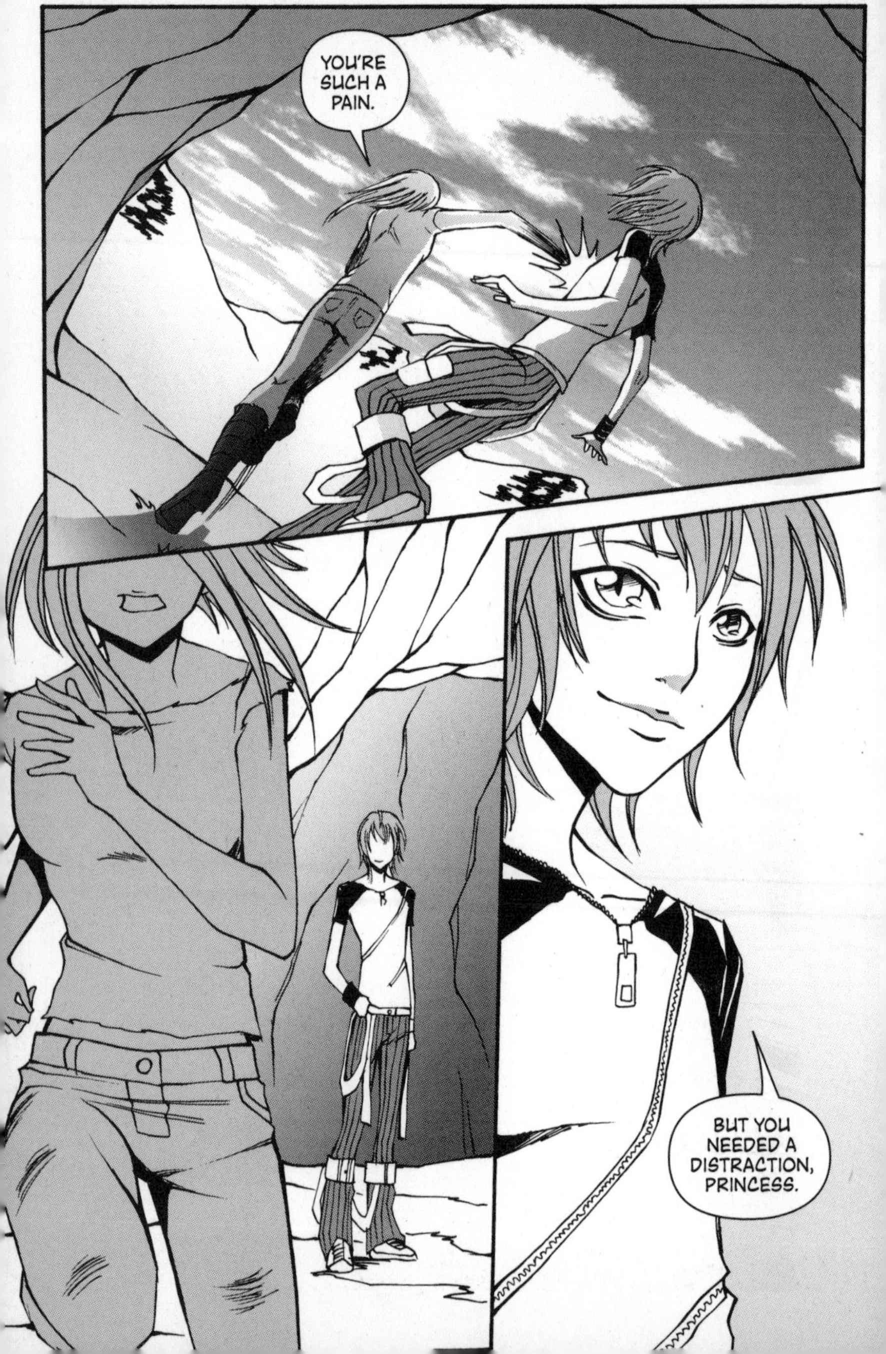
YOU'RE SUCH A PAIN.
BUT YOU NEEDED A DISTRACTION, PRINCESS.

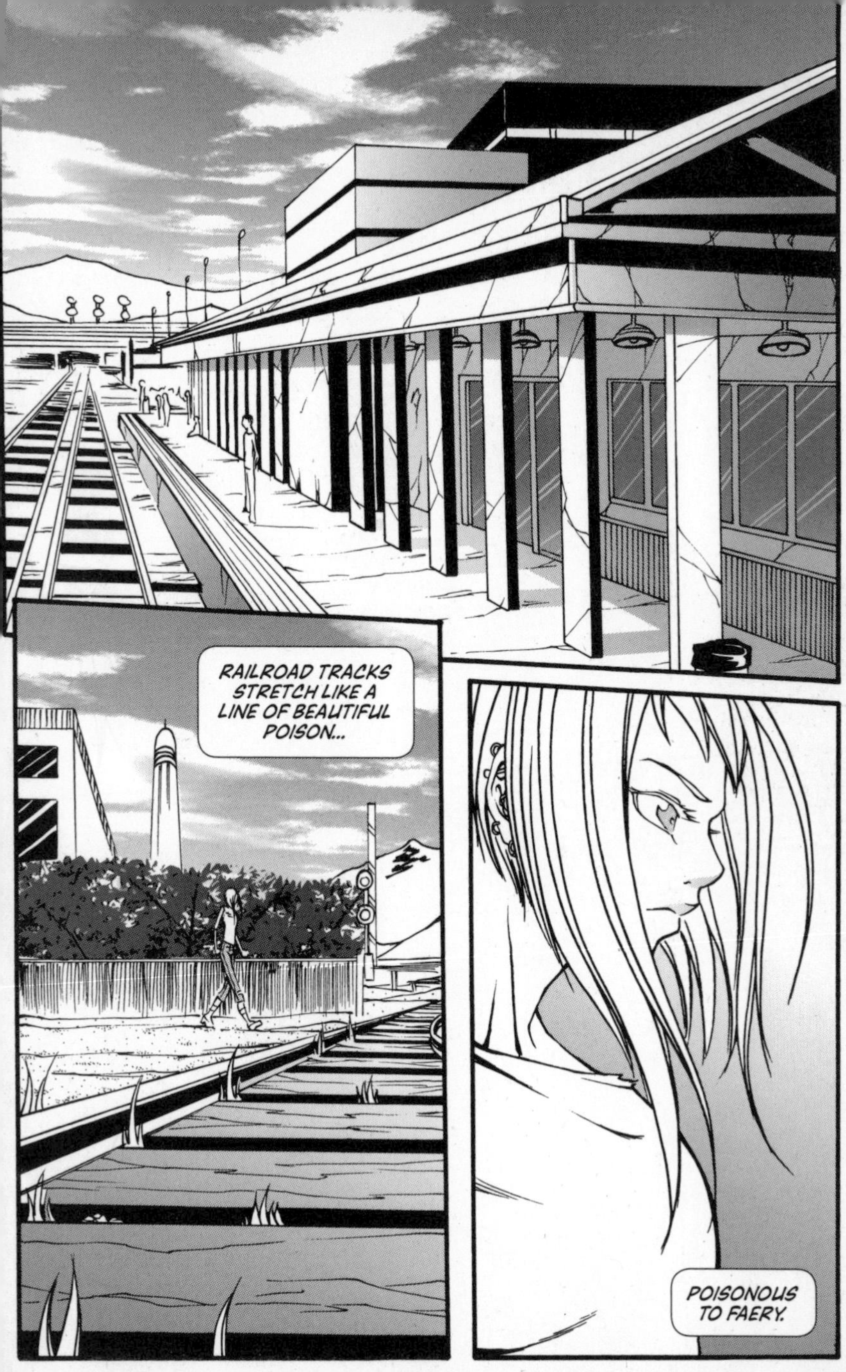
RAILROAD TRACKS STRETCH LIKE A LINE OF BEAUTIFUL POISON...
POISONOUS TO FAERY.

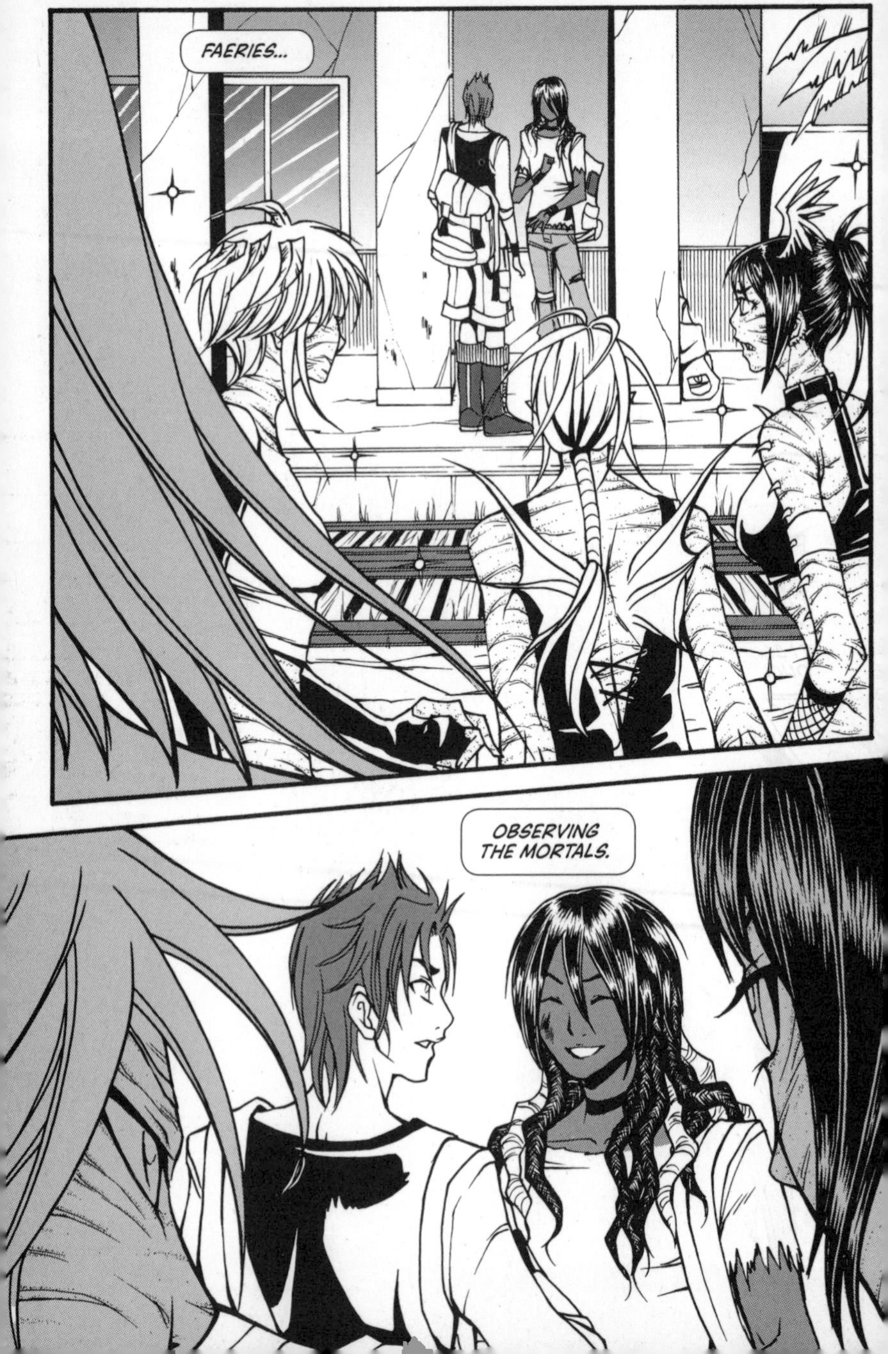
FAERIES...
OBSERVING THE MORTALS.

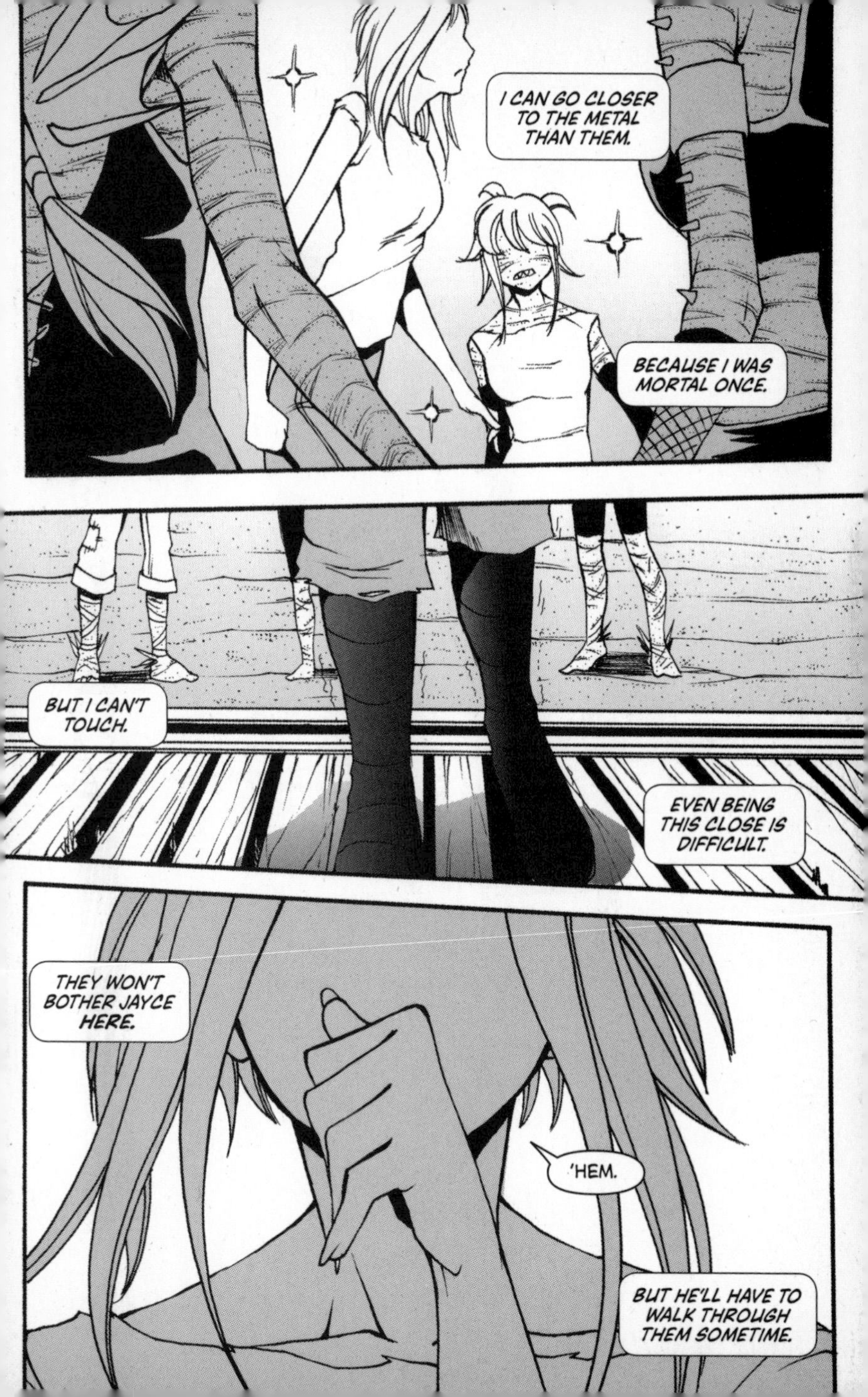
I CAN GO CLOSER TO THE METAL THAN THEM.
BECAUSE I WAS MORTAL ONCE.
BUT I CAN'T TOUCH.
EVEN BEING THIS CLOSE IS DIFFICULT.
THEY WON'T BOTHER JAYCE HERE.
'HEM.
BUT HE'LL HAVE TO WALK THROUGH THEM SOMETIME.

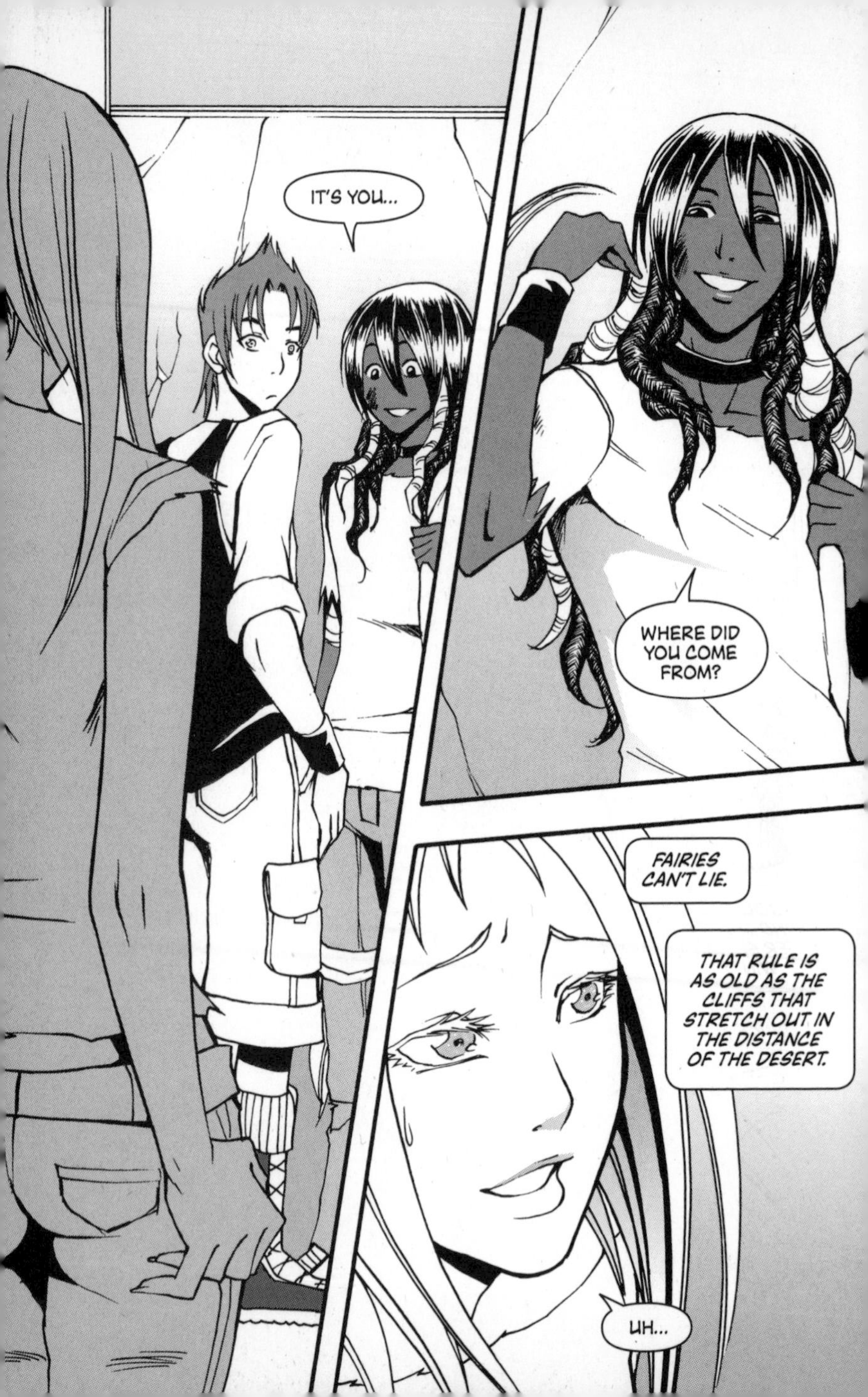
IT'S YOU...
WHERE DID YOU COME FROM?
FAIRIES CAN'T LIE.
THAT RULE IS AS OLD AS THE CLIFFS THAT STRETCH OUT IN THE DISTANCE OF THE DESERT.
UH...

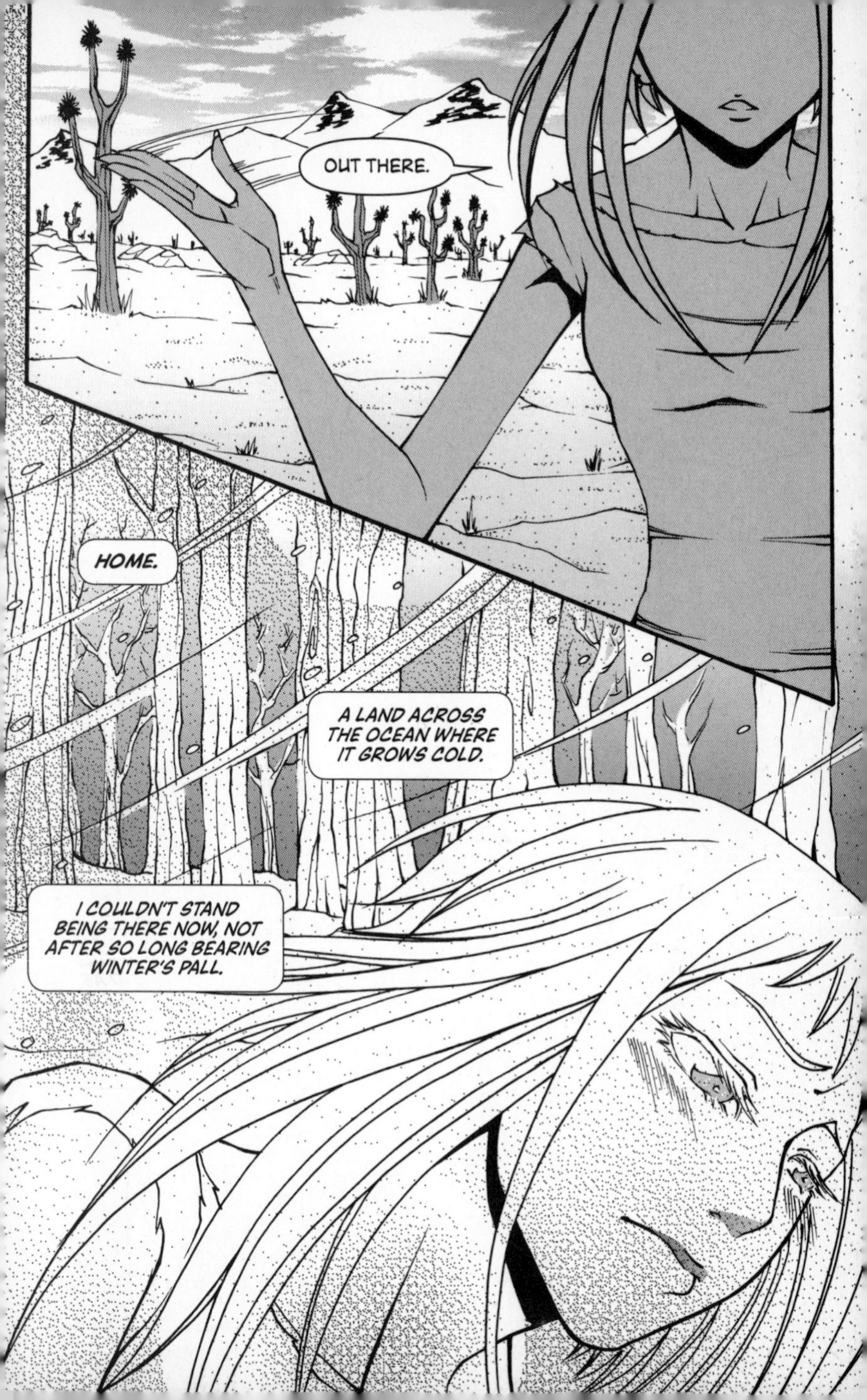
OUT THERE.
HOME.
A LAND ACROSS THE OCEAN WHERE IT GROWS COLD.
I COULDN'T STAND BEING THERE NOW, NOT AFTER SO LONG BEARING WINTER'S PALL.

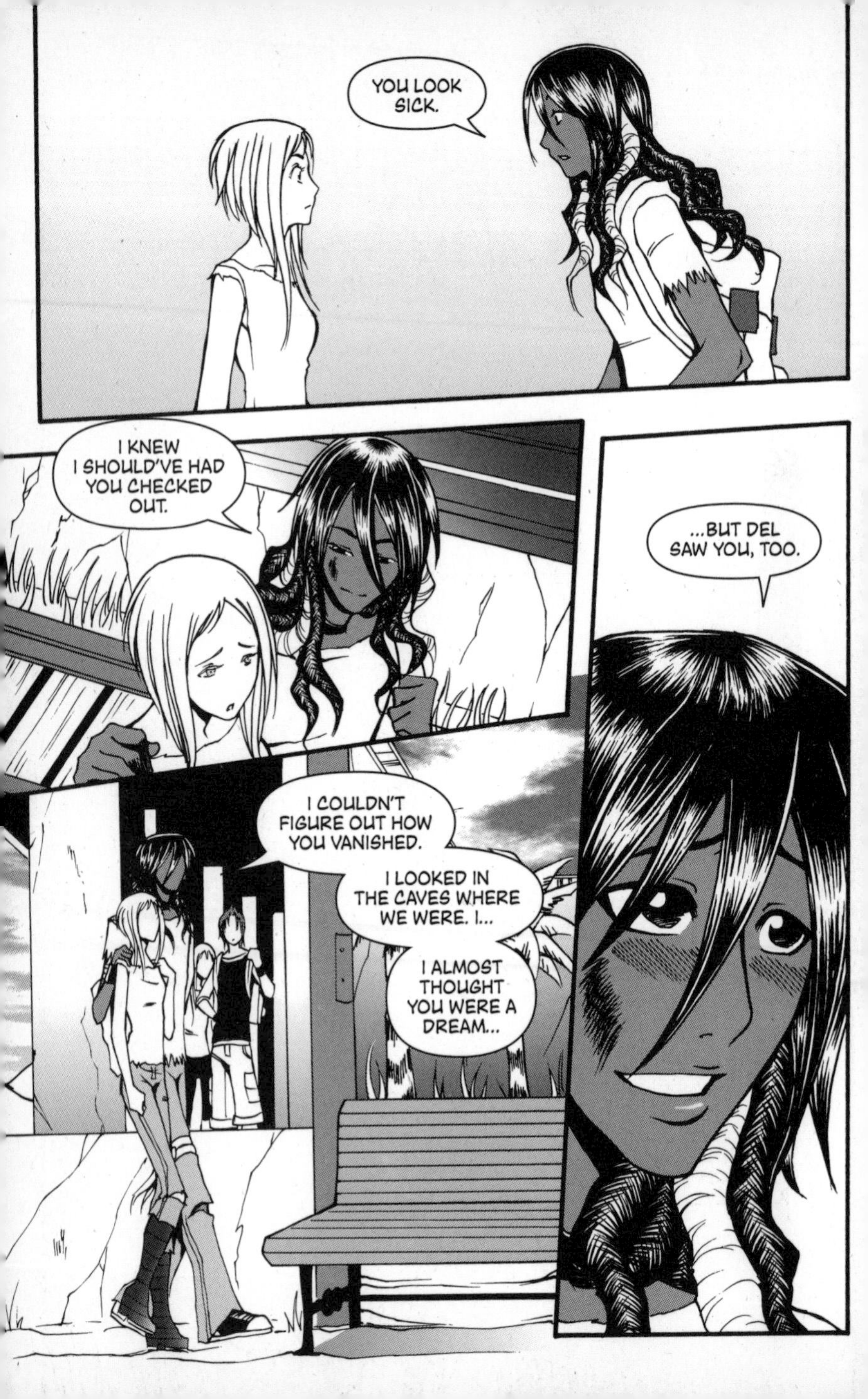
YOU LOOK SICK.
I KNEW I SHOULD'VE HAD YOU CHECKED OUT.
...BUT DEL SAW YOU, TOO.
I COULDN'T FIGURE OUT HOW YOU VANISHED.
I LOOKED IN THE CAVES WHERE WE WERE. I...
I ALMOST THOUGHT YOU WERE A DREAM...

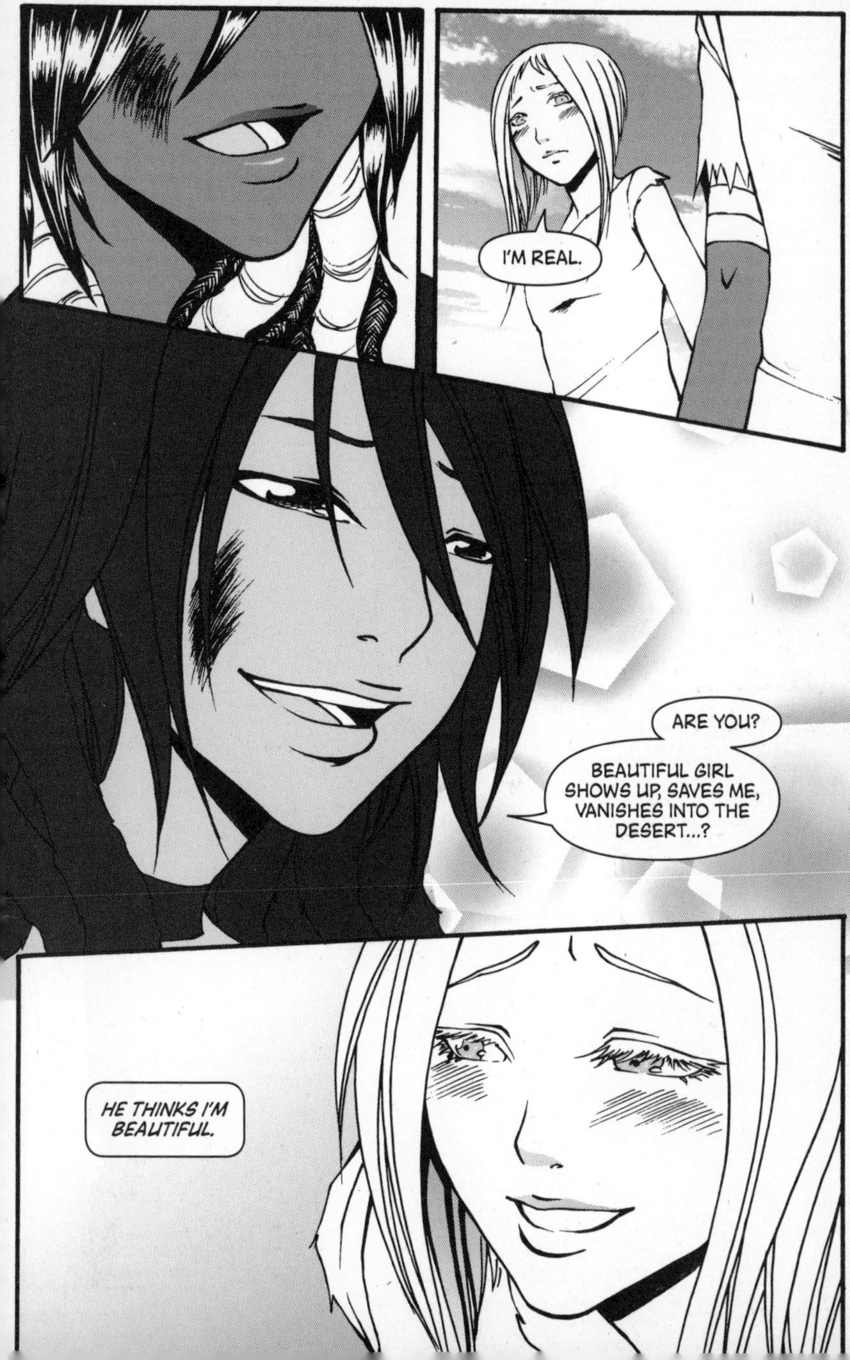
I'M REAL.
ARE YOU?
BEAUTIFUL GIRL SHOWS UP, SAVES ME, VANISHES INTO THE DESERT...?
HE THINKS I'M BEAUTIFUL.

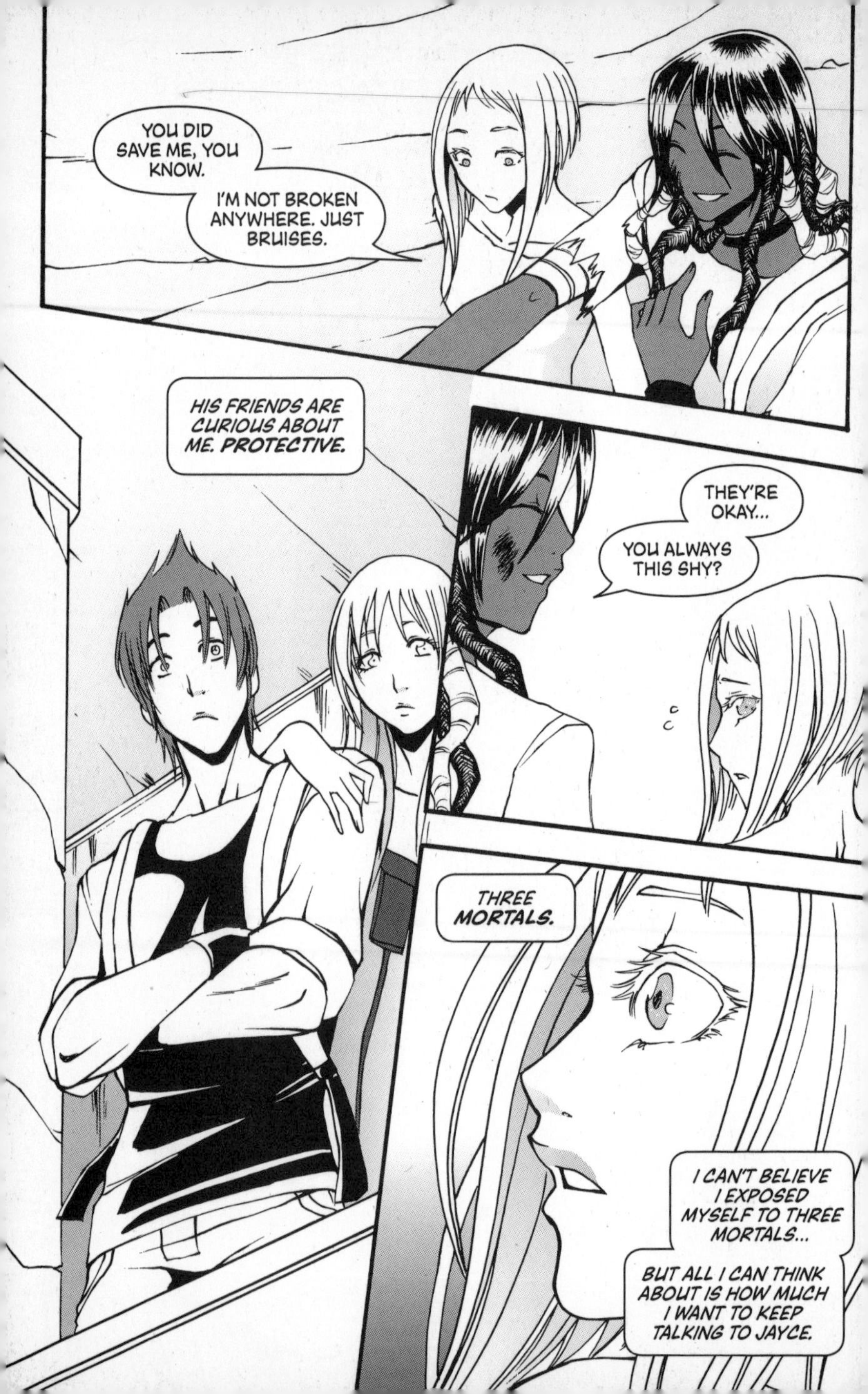
YOU DID SAVE ME, YOU KNOW.
I'M NOT BROKEN ANYWHERE. JUST BRUISES.
HIS FRIENDS ARE CURIOUS ABOUT ME. PROTECTIVE.
THEY'RE OKAY...
YOU ALWAYS THIS SHY?
THREE MORTALS.
I CAN'T BELIEVE I EXPOSED MYSELF TO THREE MORTALS...
BUT ALL I CAN THINK ABOUT IS HOW MUCH I WANT TO KEEP TALKING TO JAYCE.

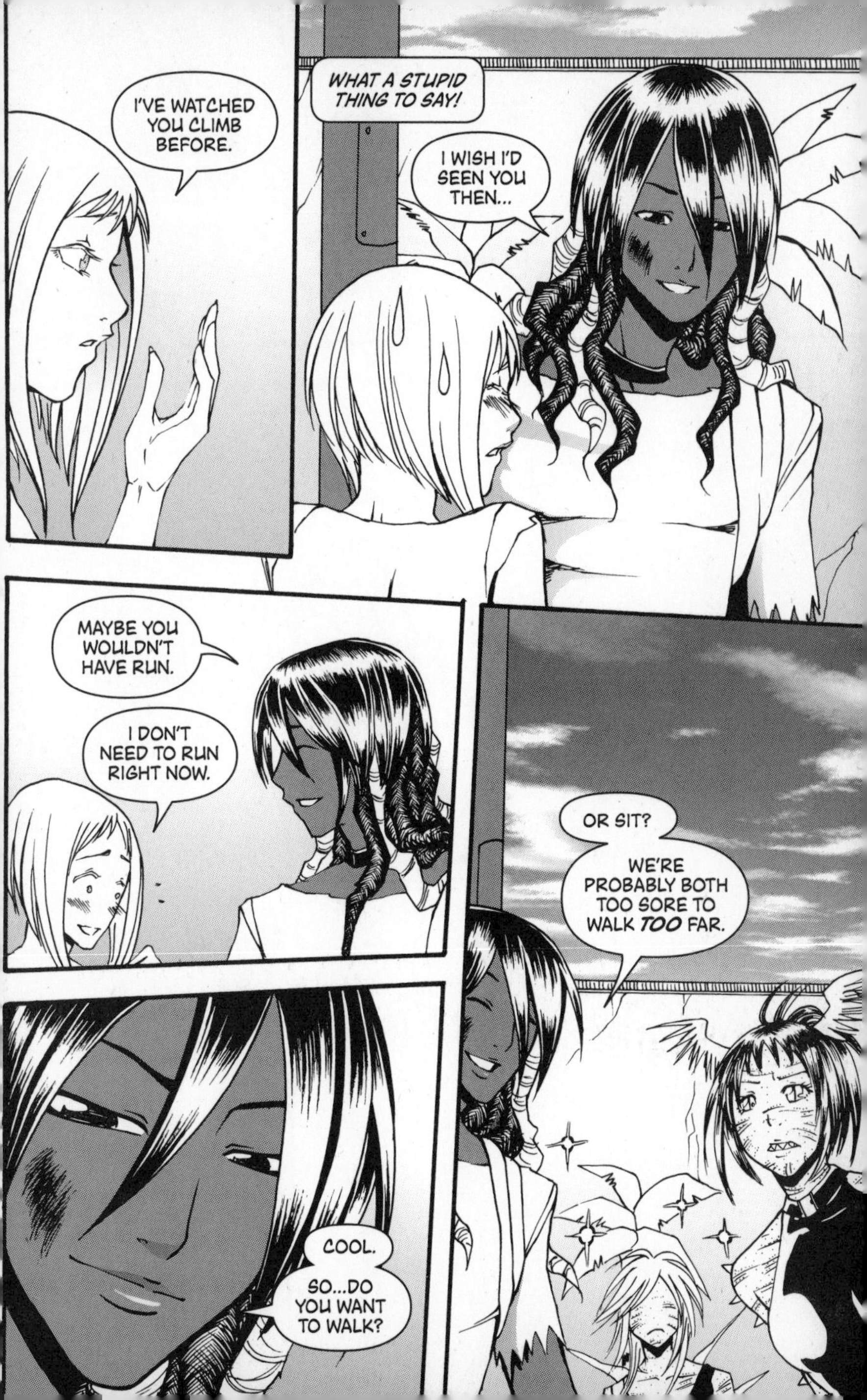
I'VE WATCHED YOU CLIMB BEFORE.
WHAT A STUPID THING TO SAY!
I WISH I'D SEEN YOU THEN...
MAYBE YOU WOULDN'T HAVE RUN.
I DON'T NEED TO RUN RIGHT NOW.
COOL.
SO...DO YOU WANT TO WALK?
OR SIT?
WE'RE PROBABLY BOTH TOO SORE TO WALK TOO FAR.

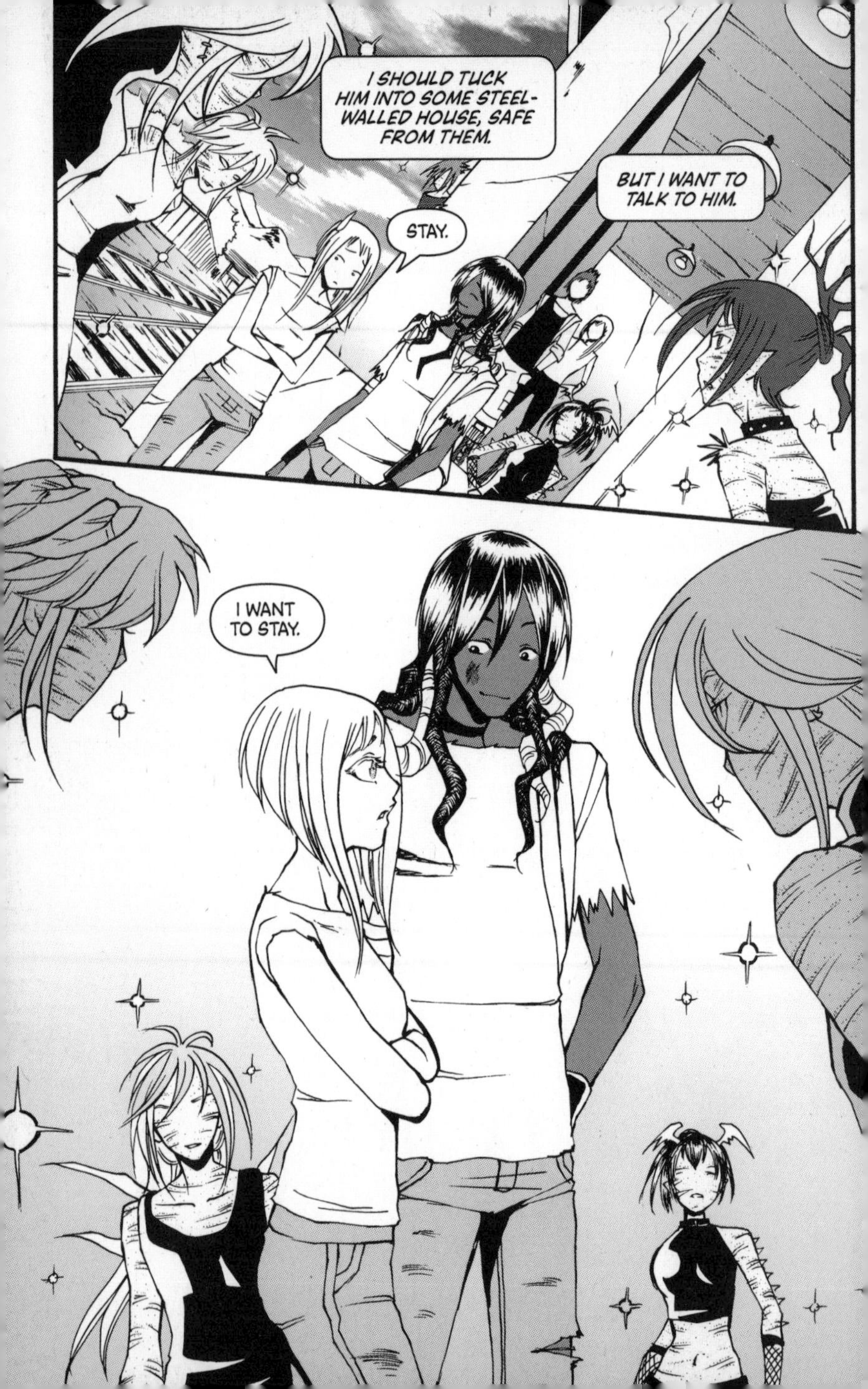
I SHOULD TUCK HIM INTO SOME STEEL-WALLED HOUSE, SAFE FROM THEM.
STAY.
BUT I WANT TO TALK TO HIM.
I WANT TO STAY.

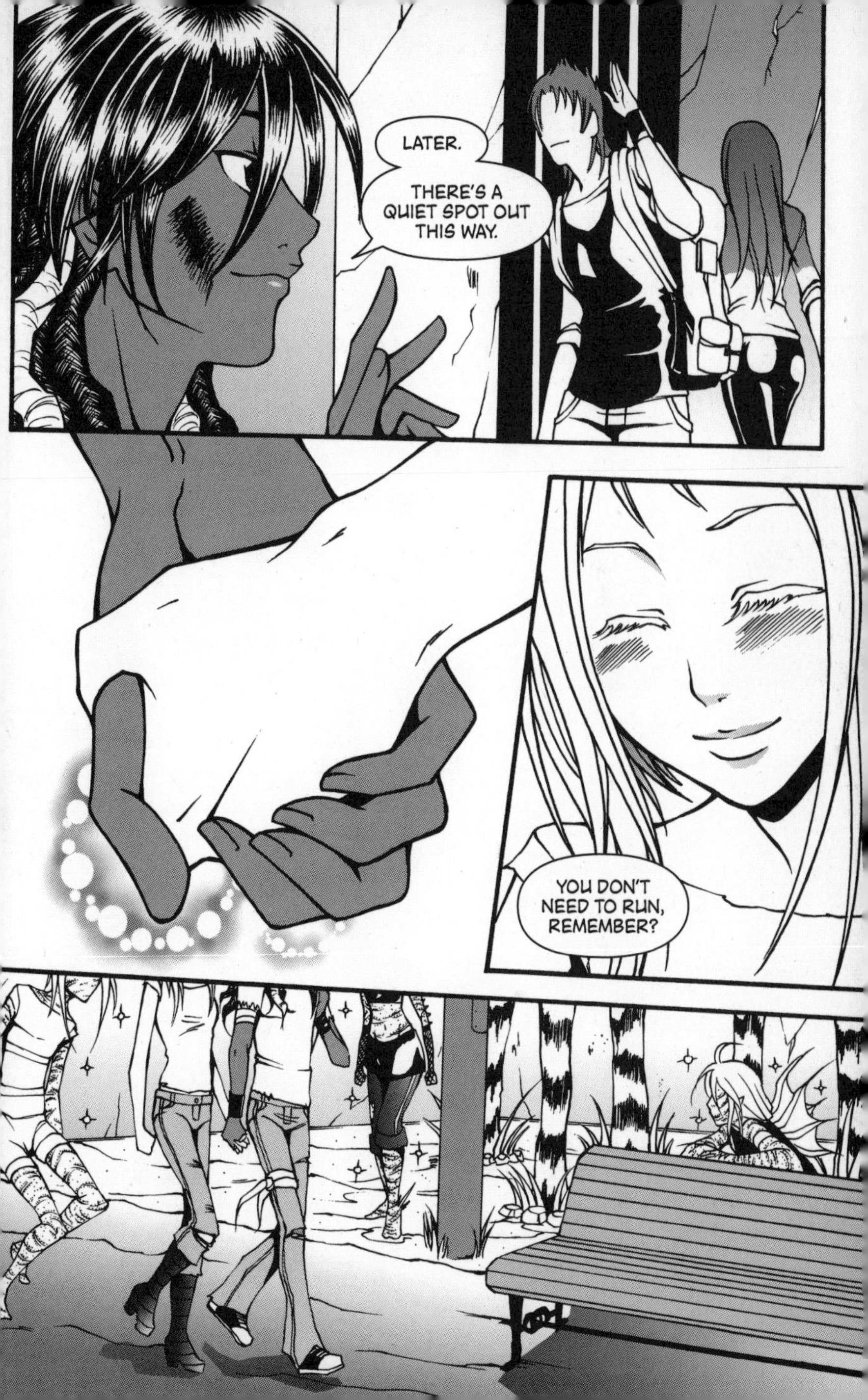
LATER.
THERE'S A QUIET SPOT OUT THIS WAY.
YOU DON'T NEED TO RUN, REMEMBER?

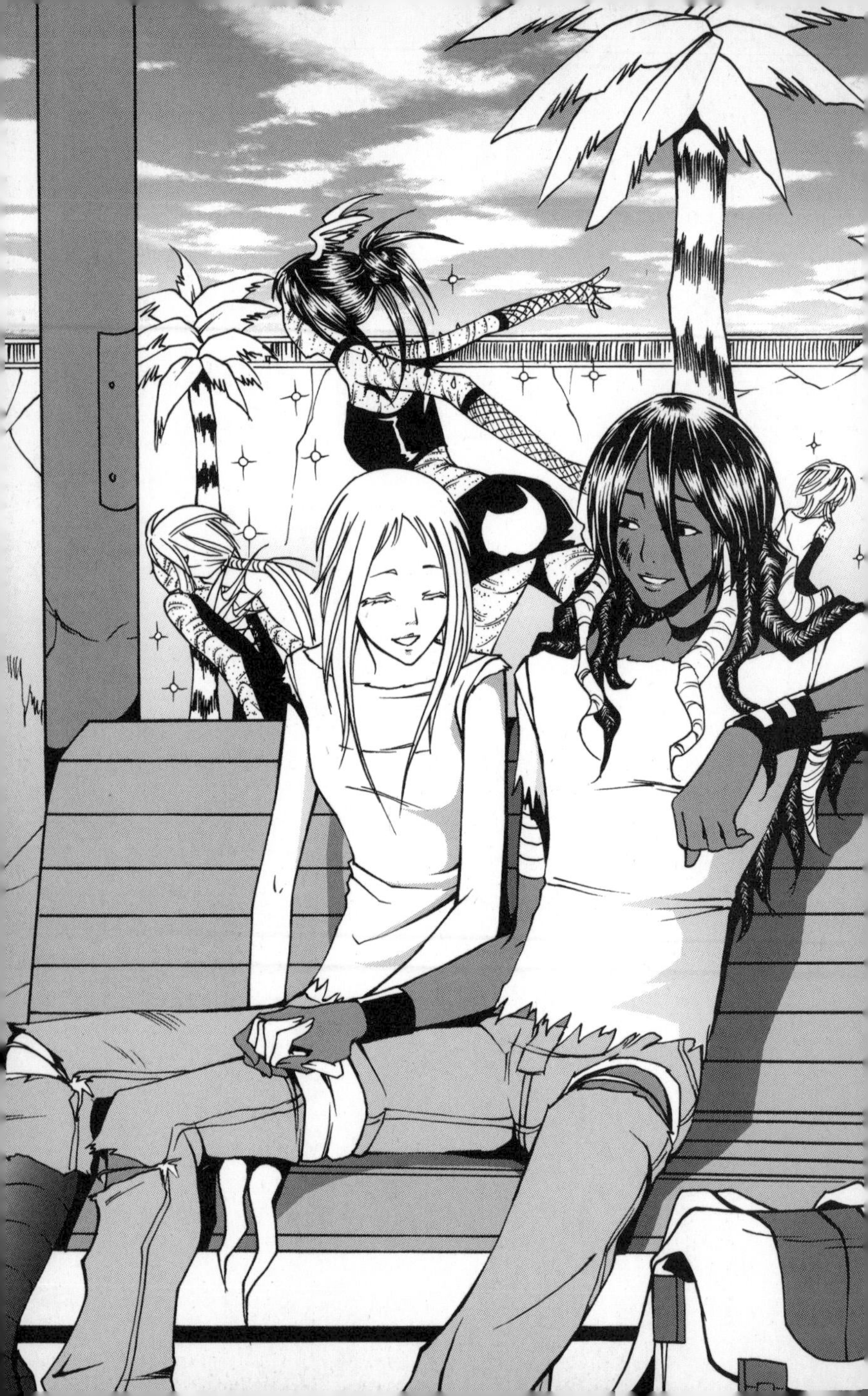

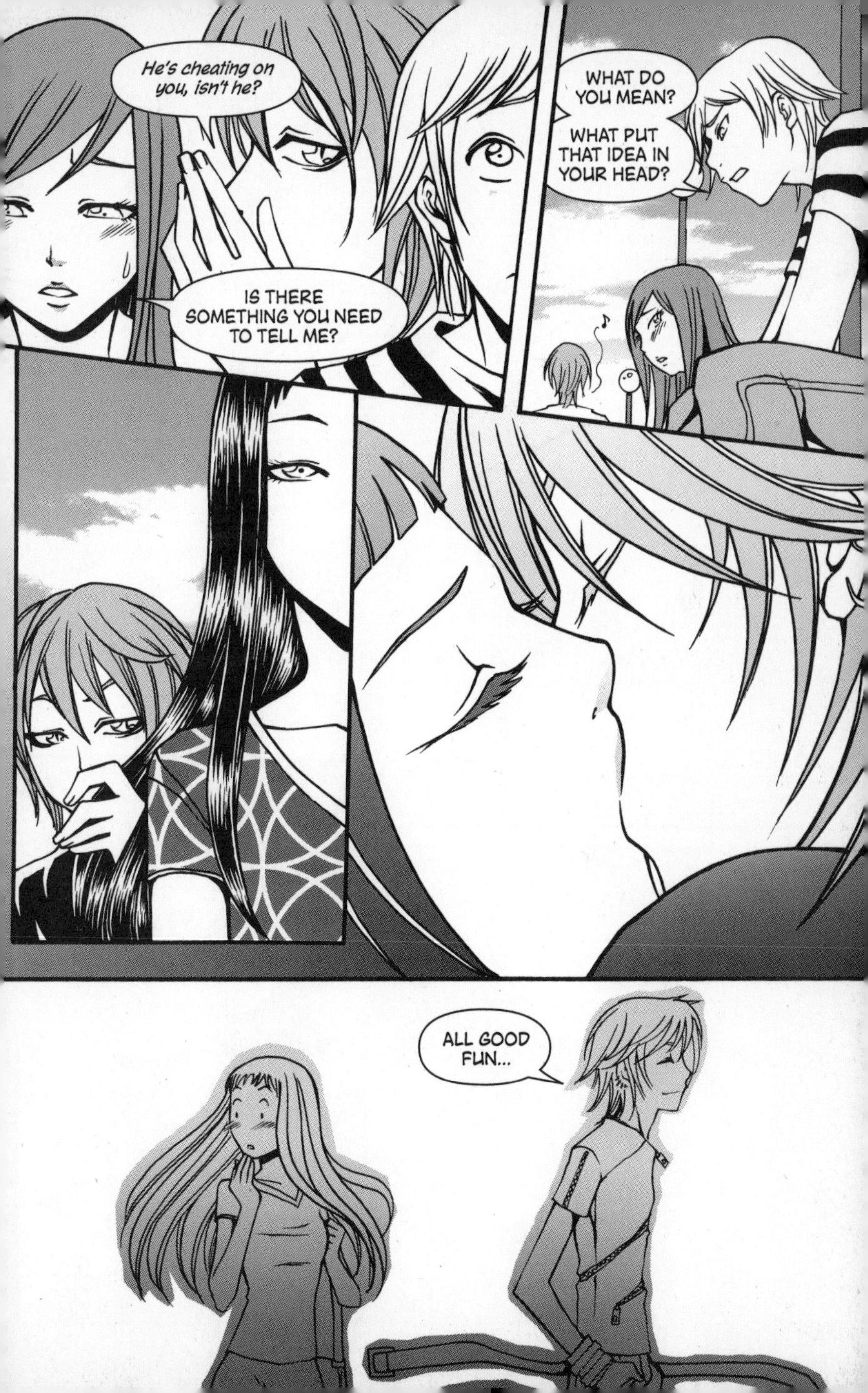
He's cheating on you, isn't he?
IS THERE SOMETHING YOU NEED TO TELL ME?
WHAT DO YOU MEAN?
WHAT PUT THAT IDEA IN YOUR HEAD?
ALL GOOD FUN...

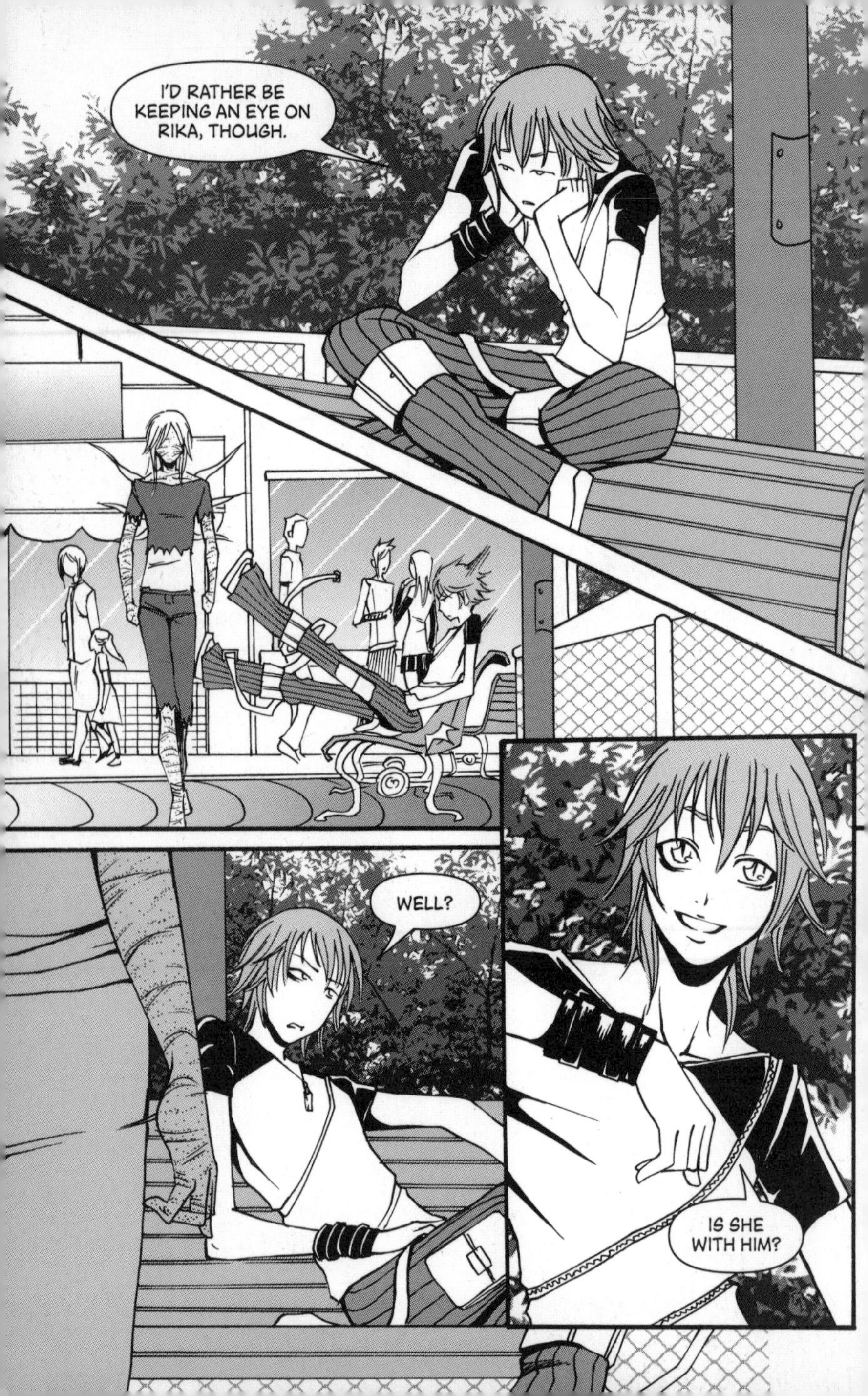
I'D RATHER BE KEEPING AN EYE ON RIKA, THOUGH.
WELL?
IS SHE WITH HIM?

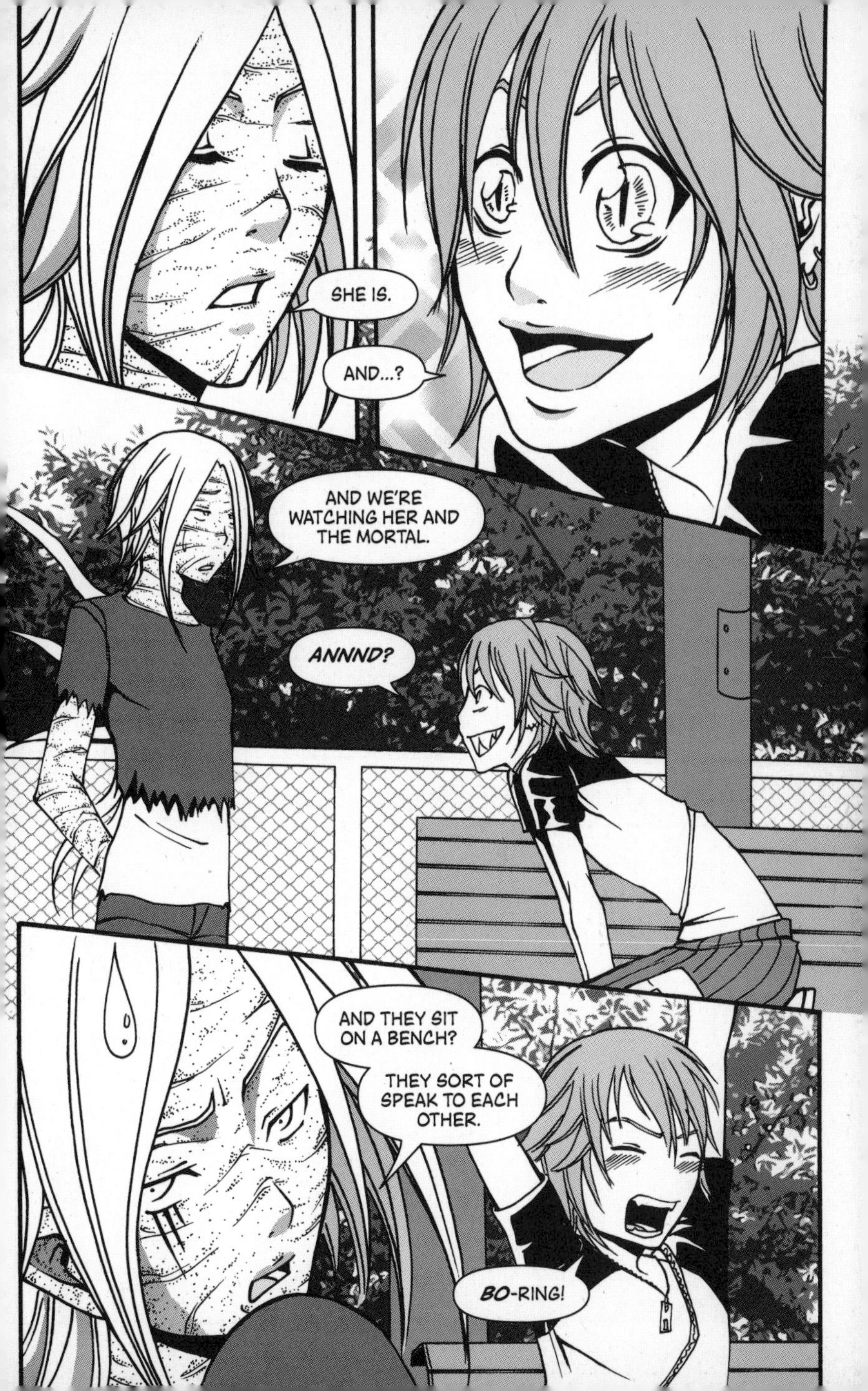
SHE IS.
AND...?
AND WE'RE WATCHING HER AND THE MORTAL.
ANNND?
AND THEY SIT ON A BENCH?
THEY SORT OF SPEAK TO EACH OTHER.
BO-RING!

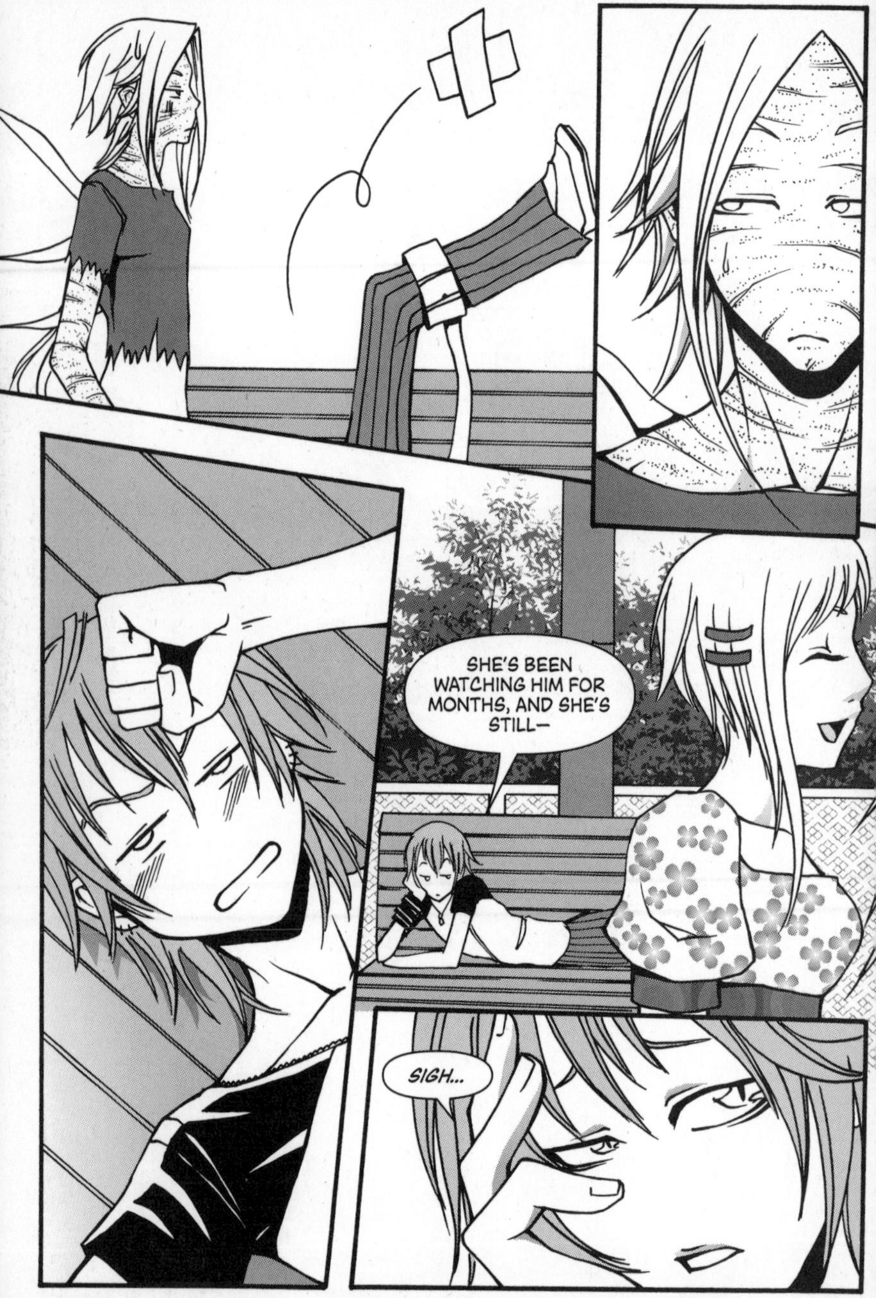
SHE'S BEEN WATCHING HIM FOR MONTHS, AND SHE'S STILL—
SIGH...

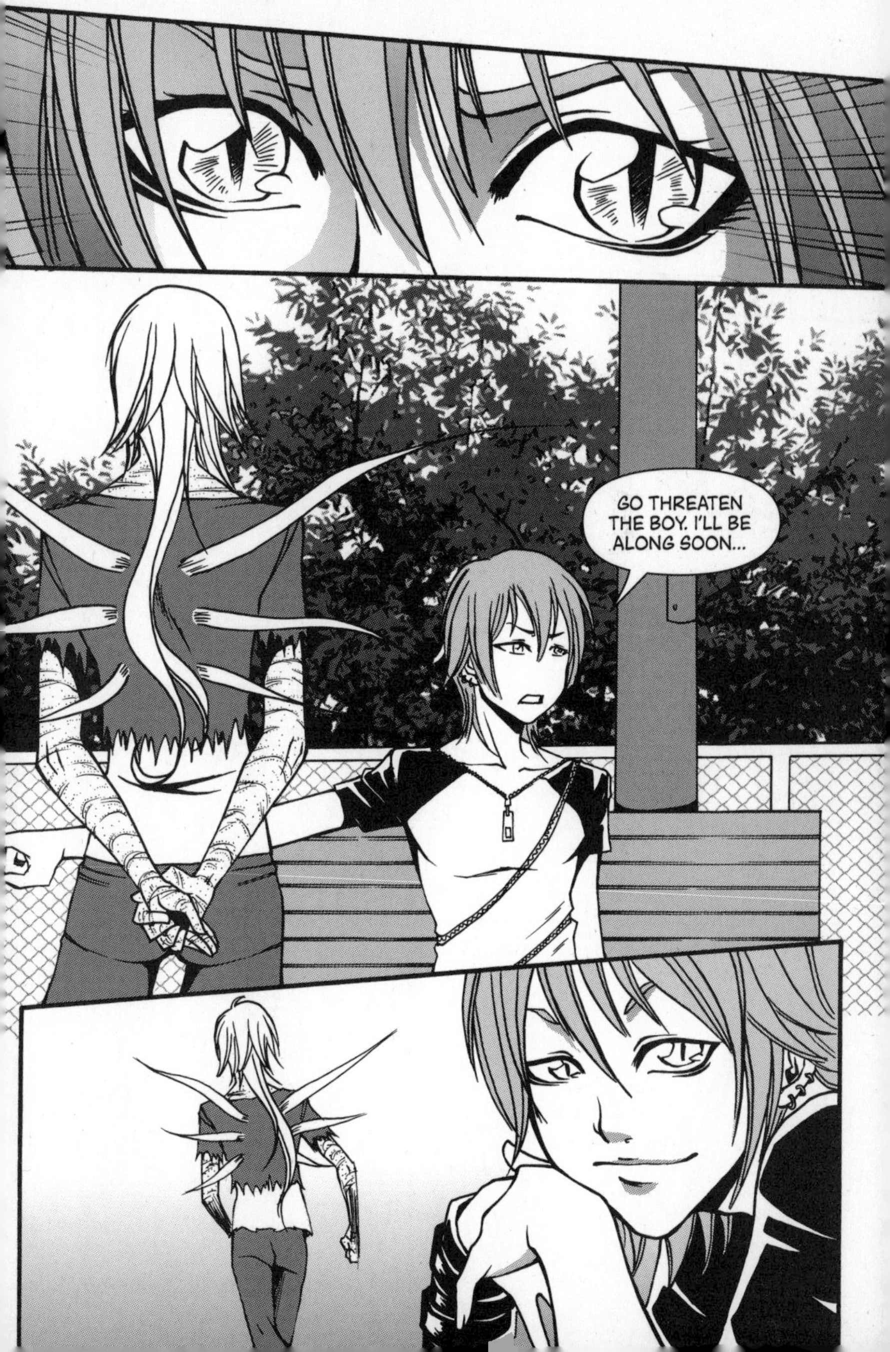
GO THREATEN THE BOY. I'LL BE ALONG SOON...

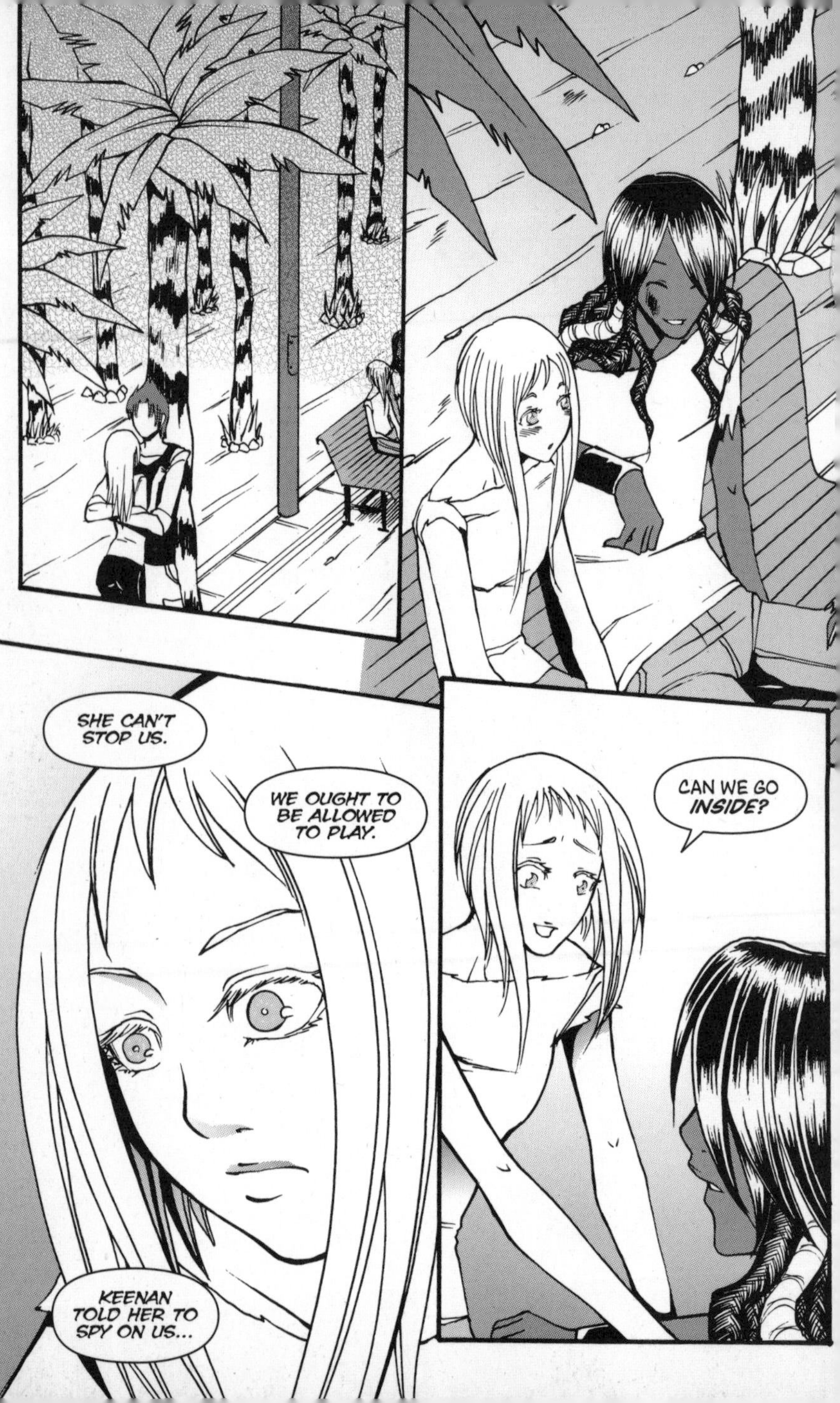
SHE CAN'T STOP US.
WE OUGHT TO BE ALLOWED TO PLAY.
KEENAN TOLD HER TO SPY ON US...
CAN WE GO *INSIDE?*

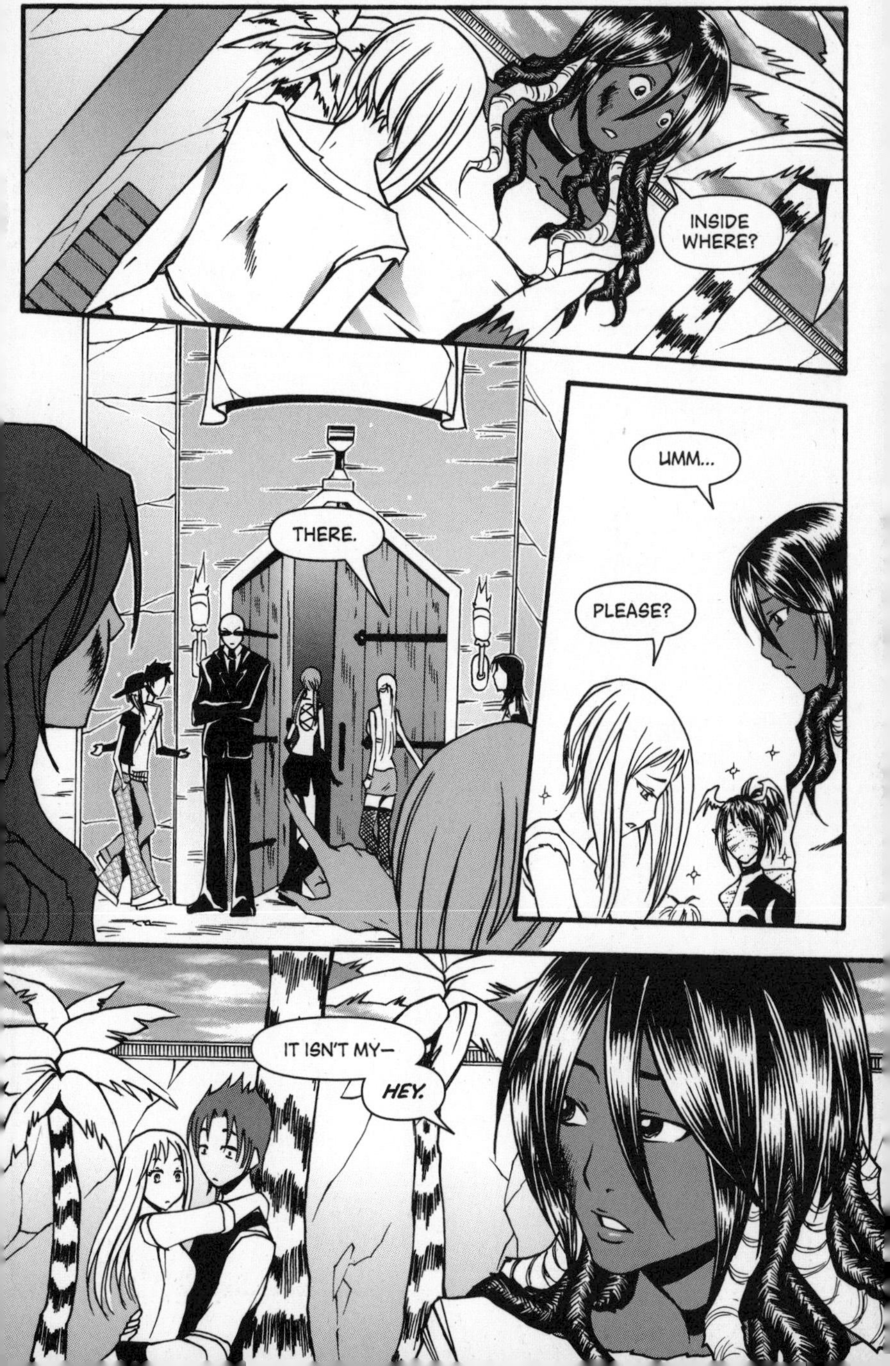
INSIDE WHERE?
THERE.
UMM...
PLEASE?
IT ISN'T MY—
HEY.

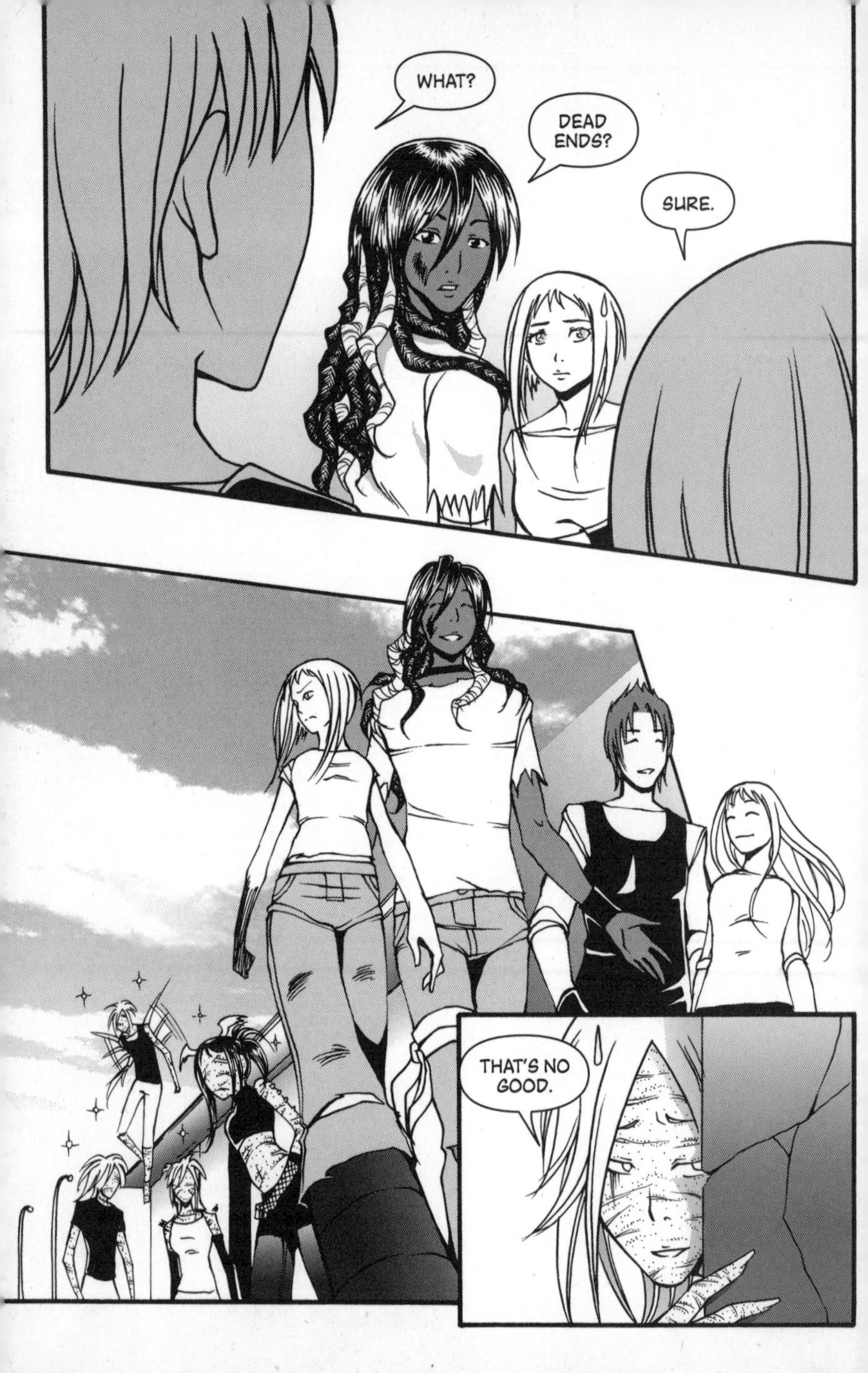
WHAT?
DEAD ENDS?
SURE.
THAT'S NO GOOD.

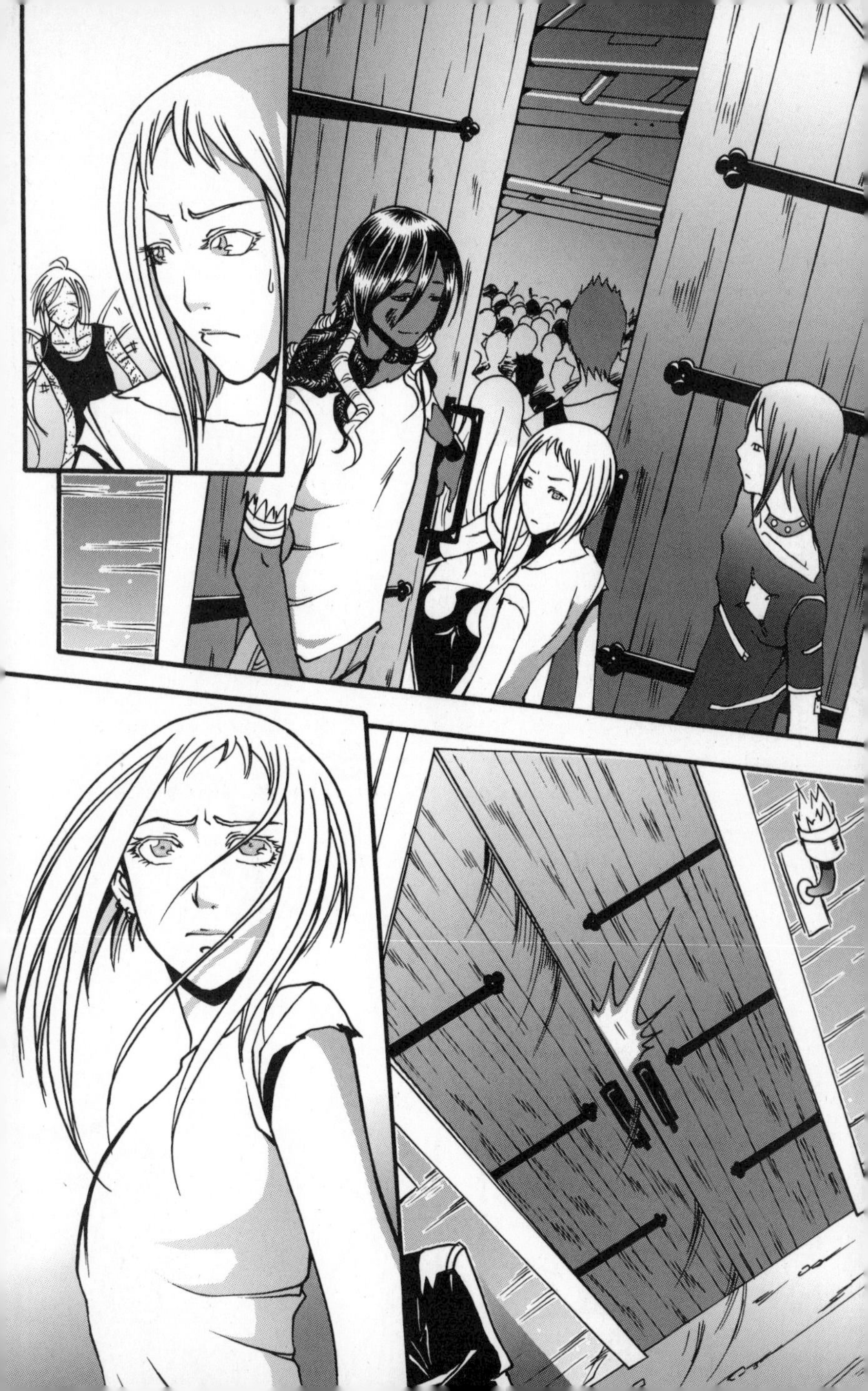

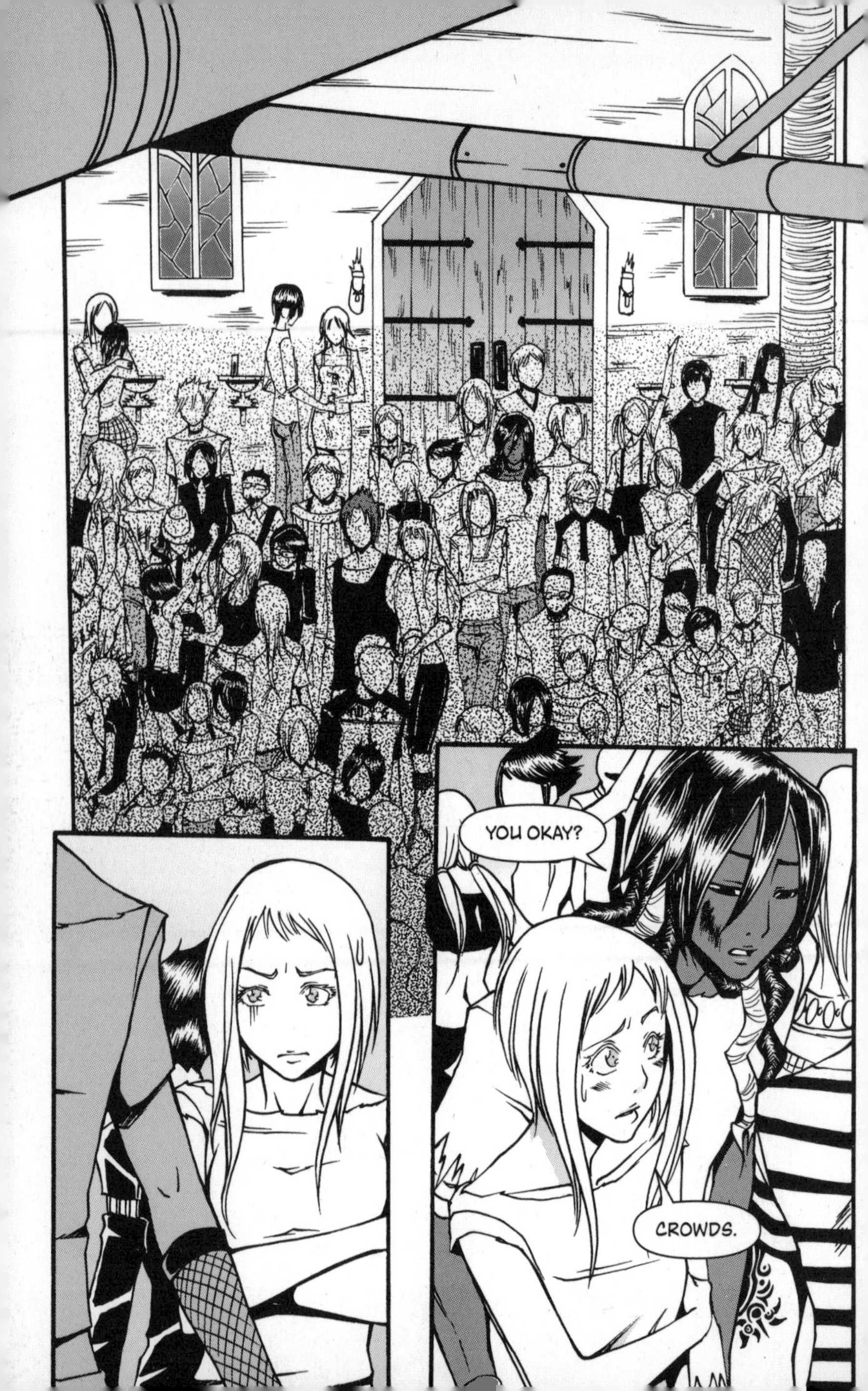
YOU OKAY?
CROWDS.

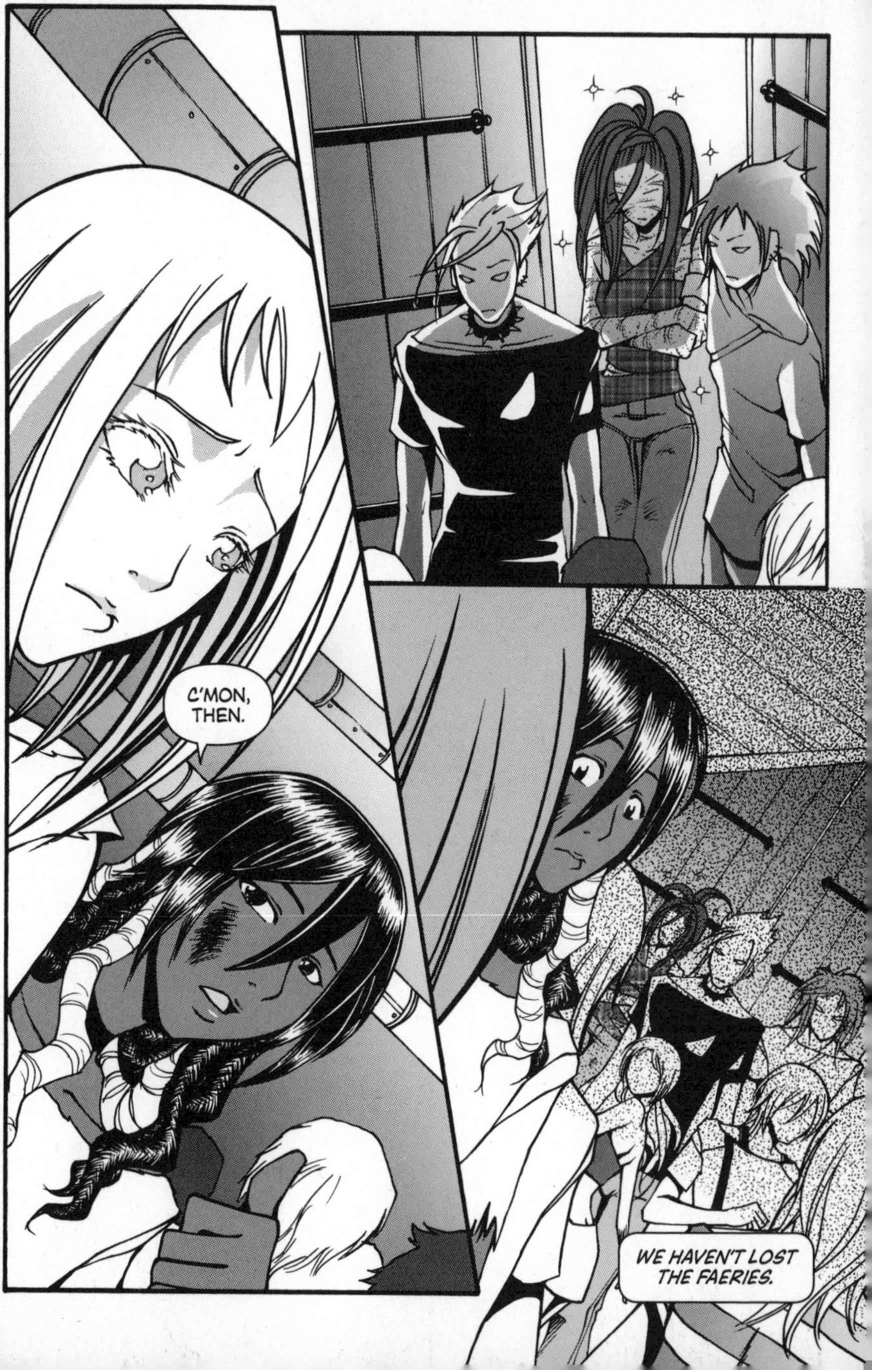
C'MON, THEN.
WE HAVEN'T LOST THE FAERIES.

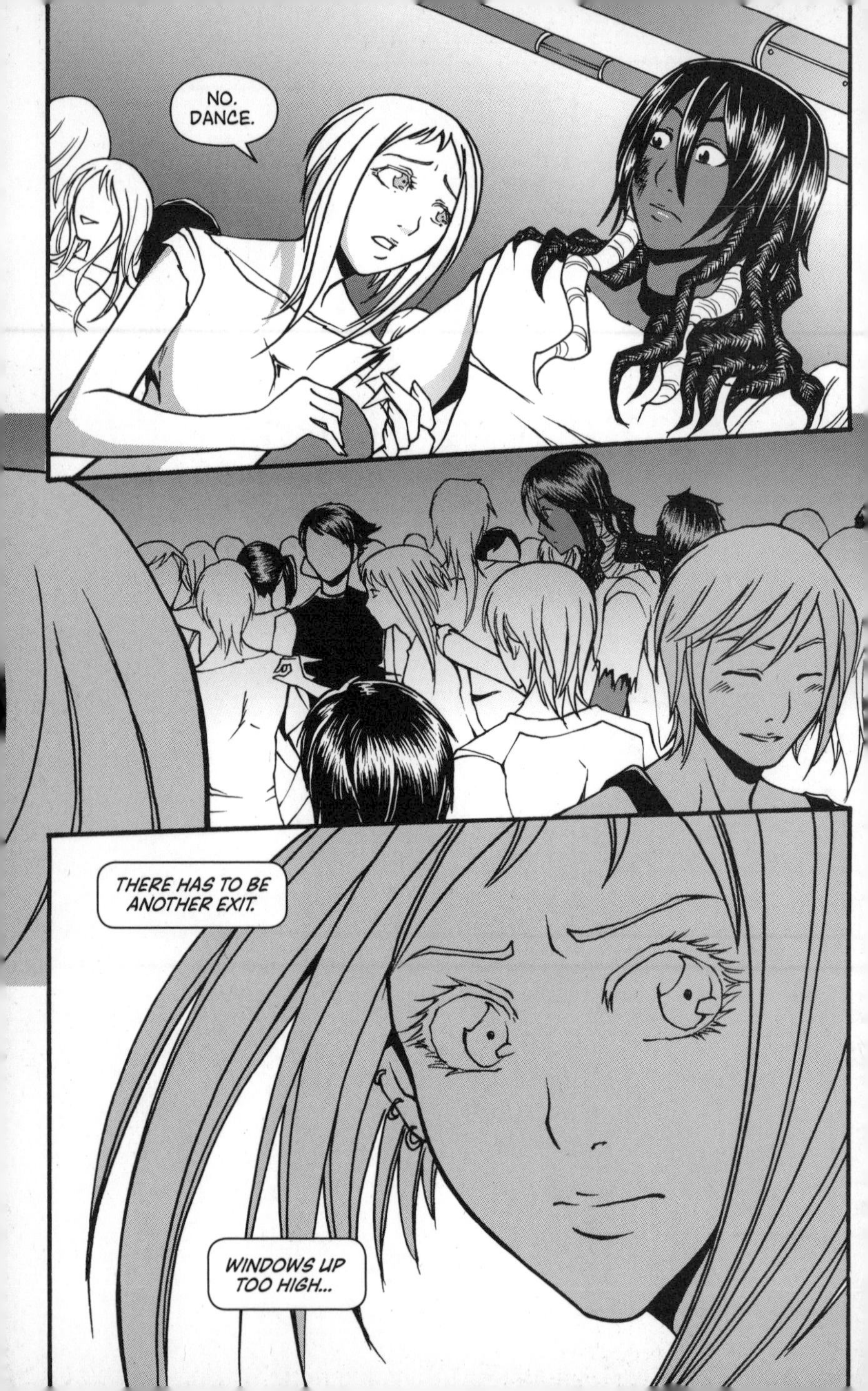
NO. DANCE.
THERE HAS TO BE ANOTHER EXIT.
WINDOWS UP TOO HIGH...

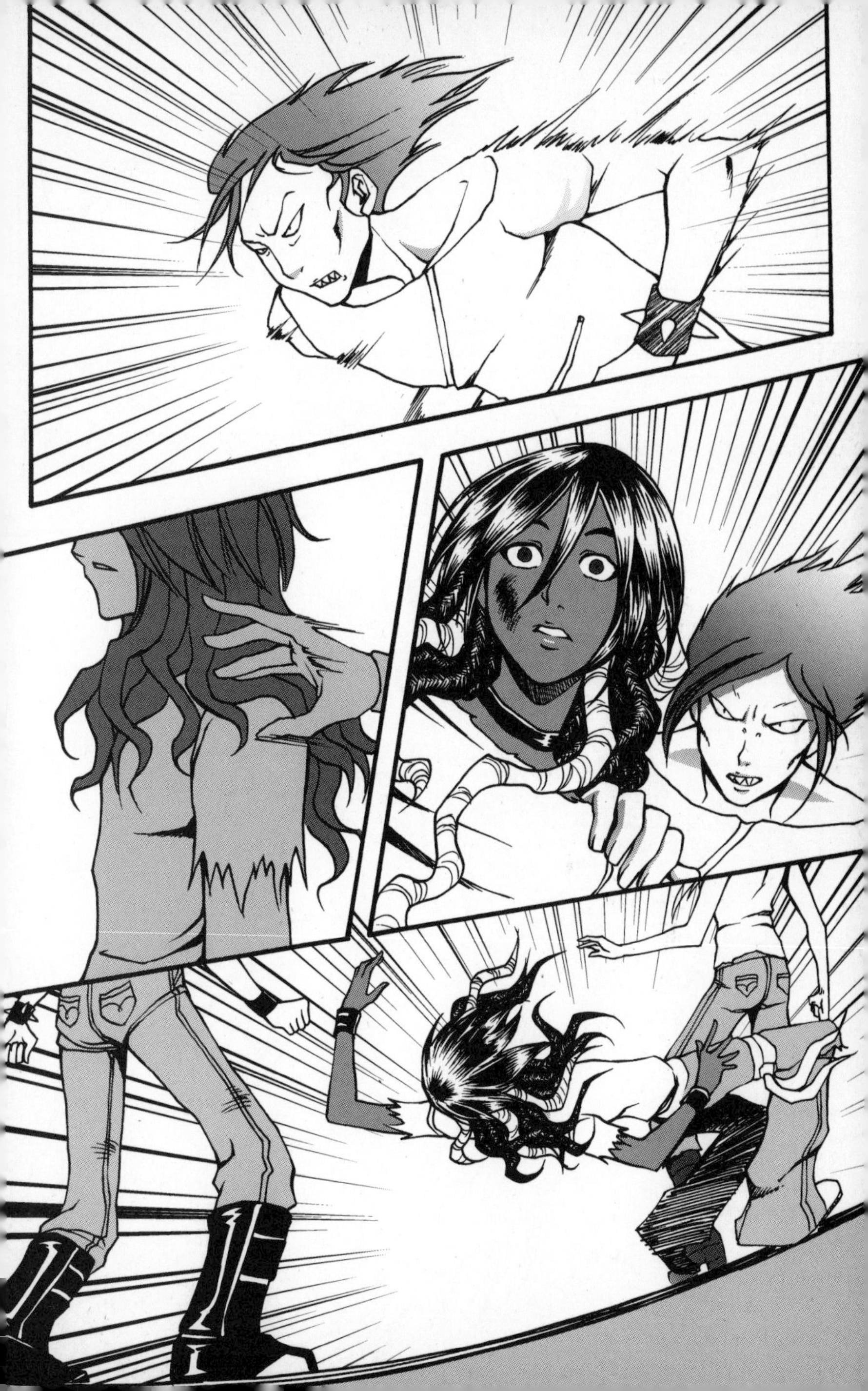

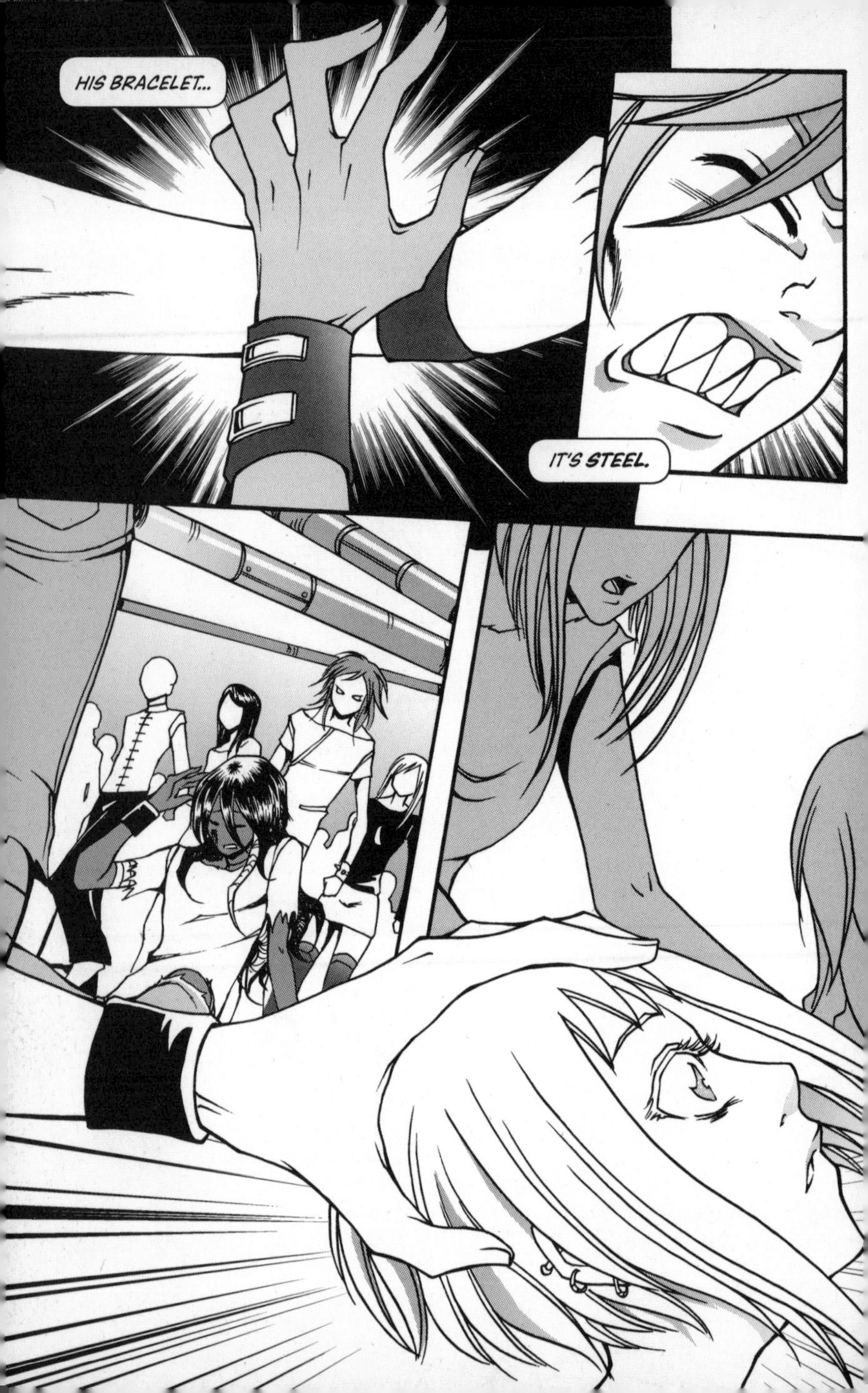
HIS BRACELET...
IT'S STEEL.

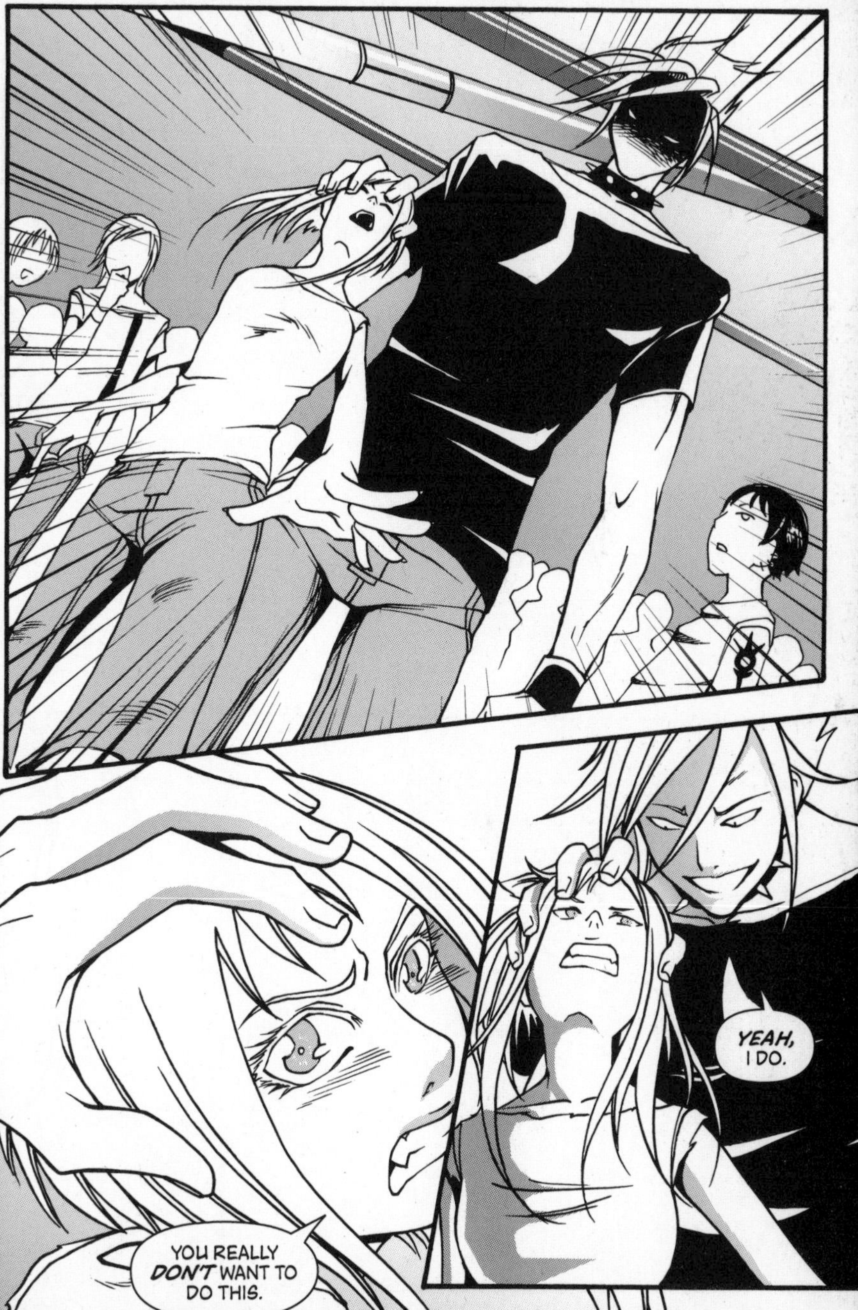
YOU REALLY DON'T WANT TO DO THIS.
YEAH, I DO.

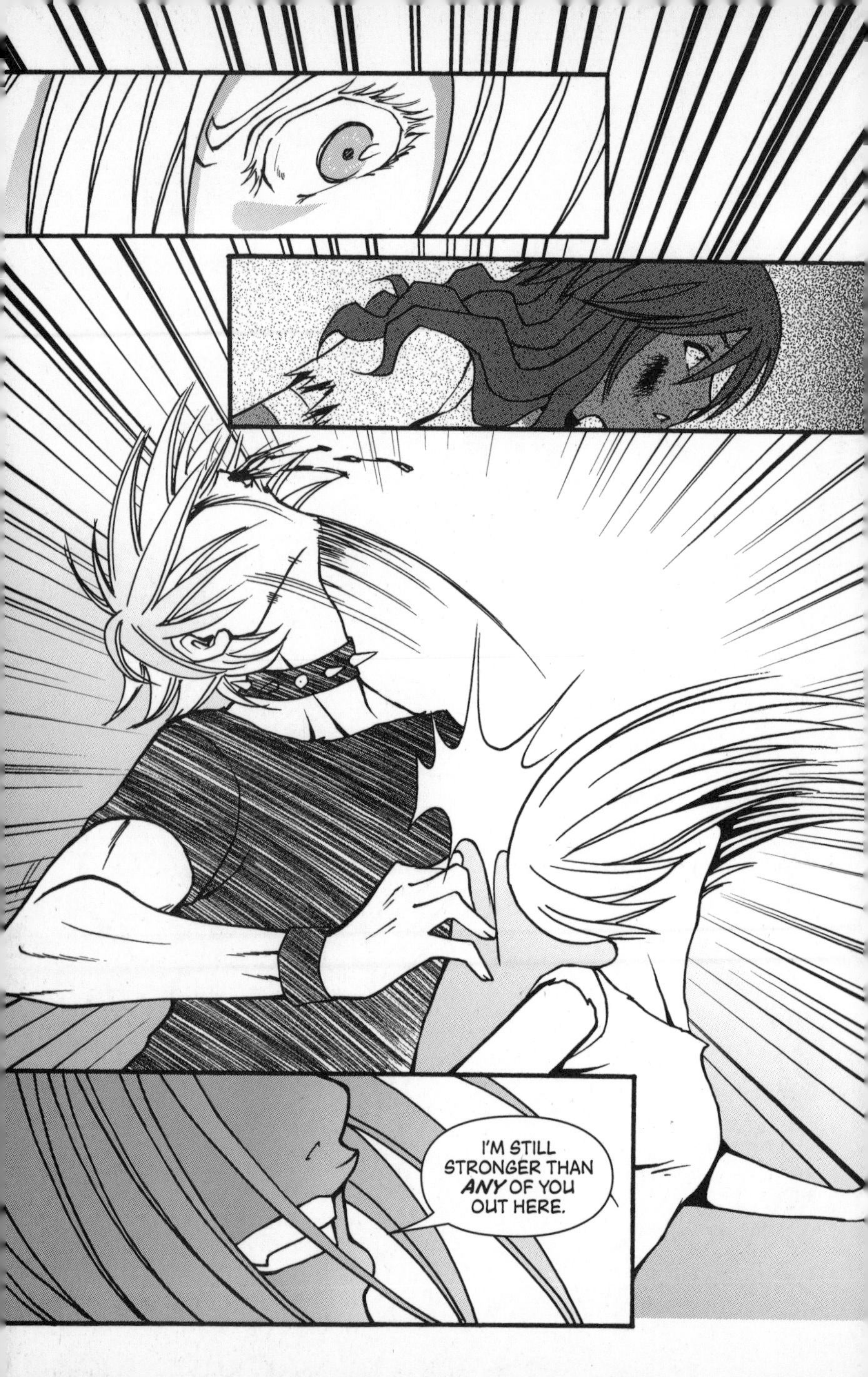
I'M STILL STRONGER THAN *ANY* OF YOU OUT HERE.

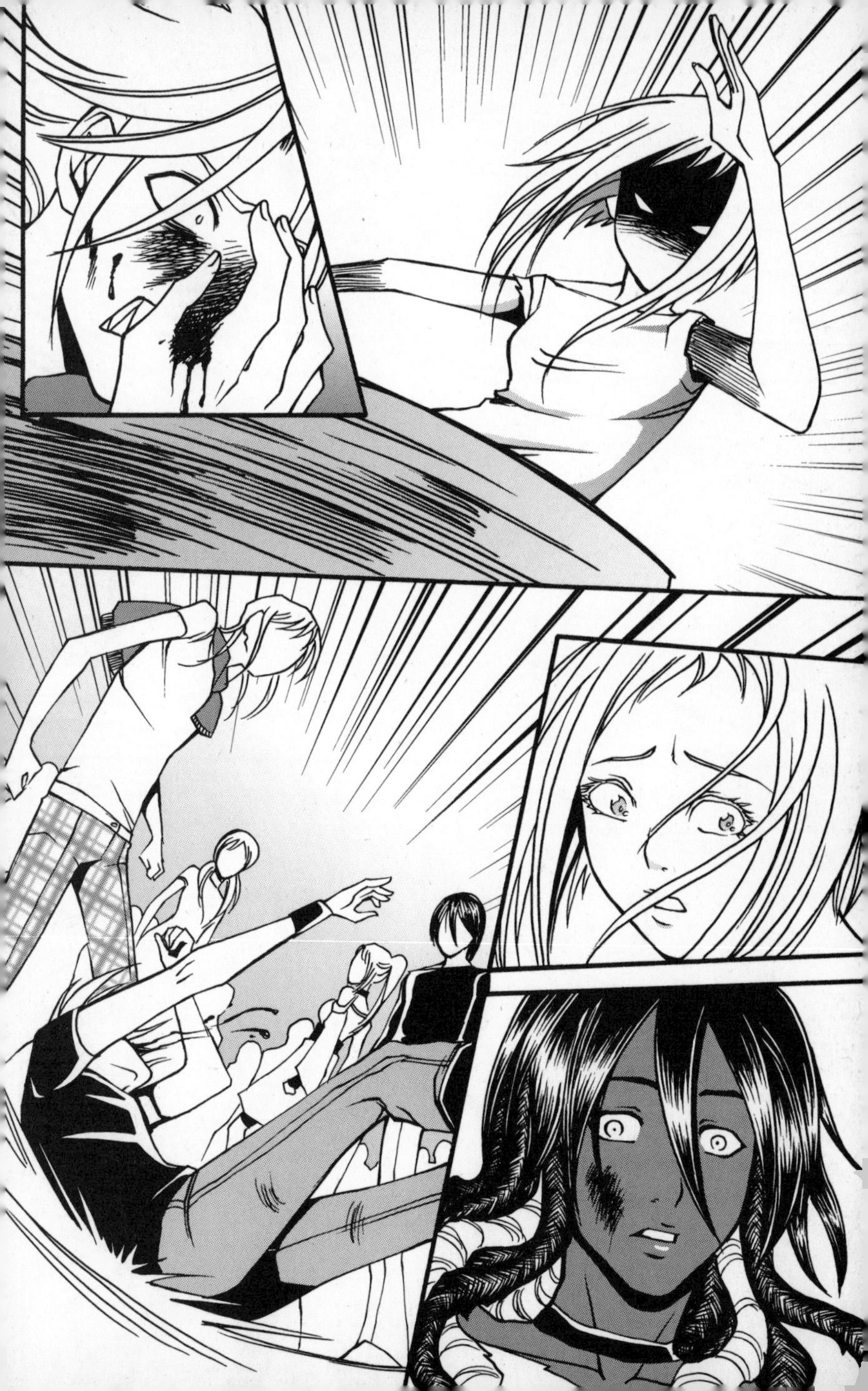

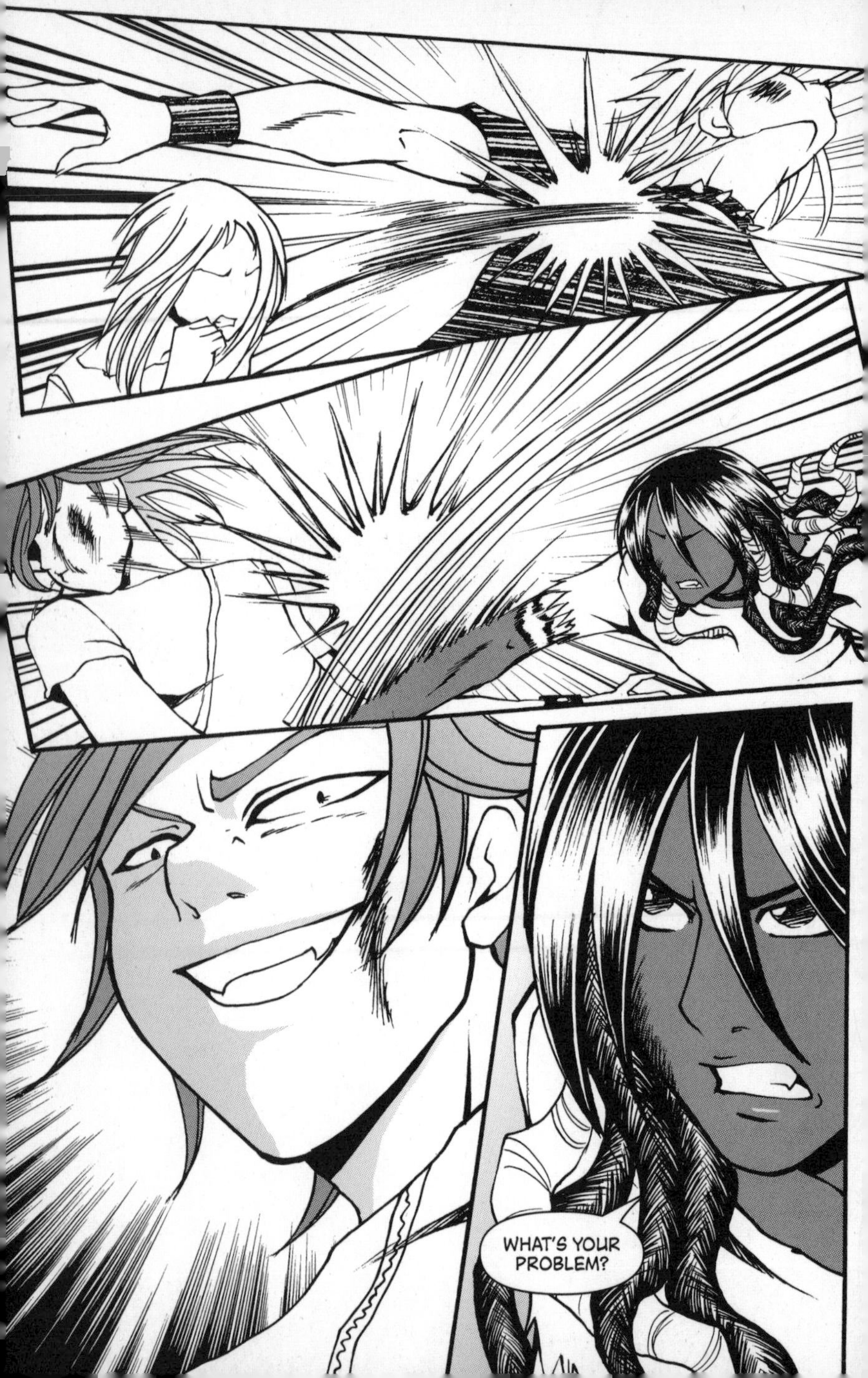
WHAT'S YOUR PROBLEM?

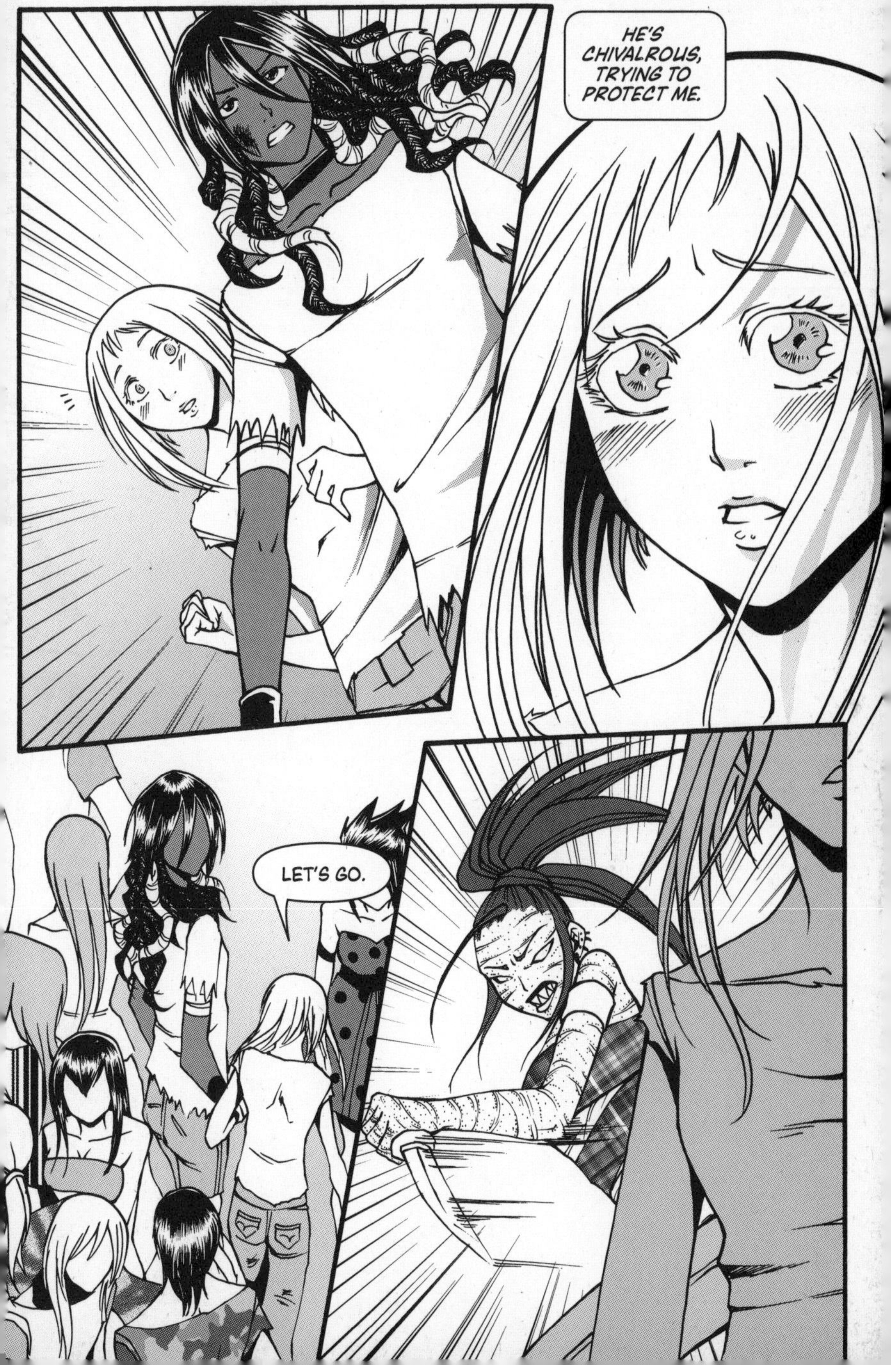
HE'S CHIVALROUS, TRYING TO PROTECT ME.
LET'S GO.

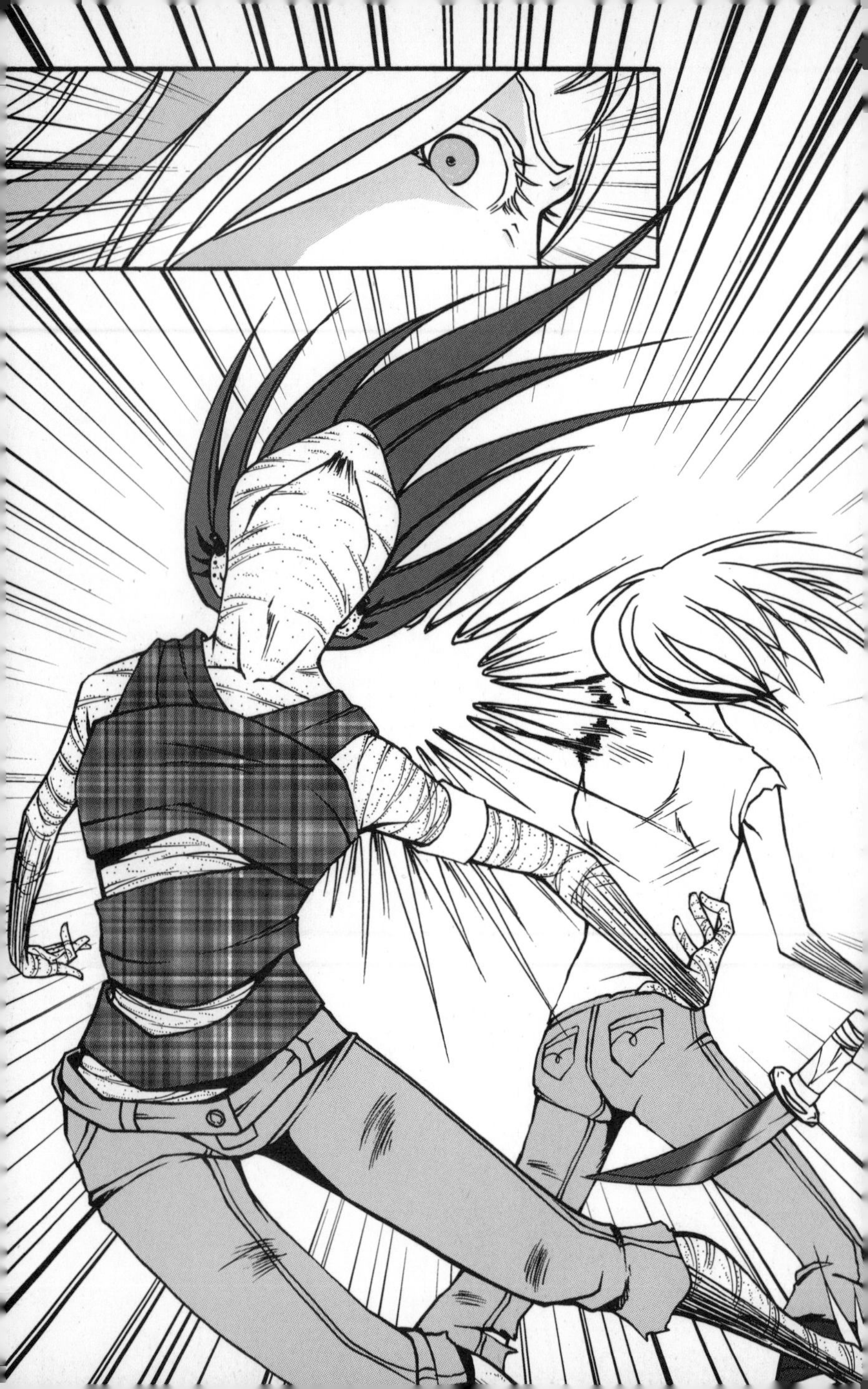

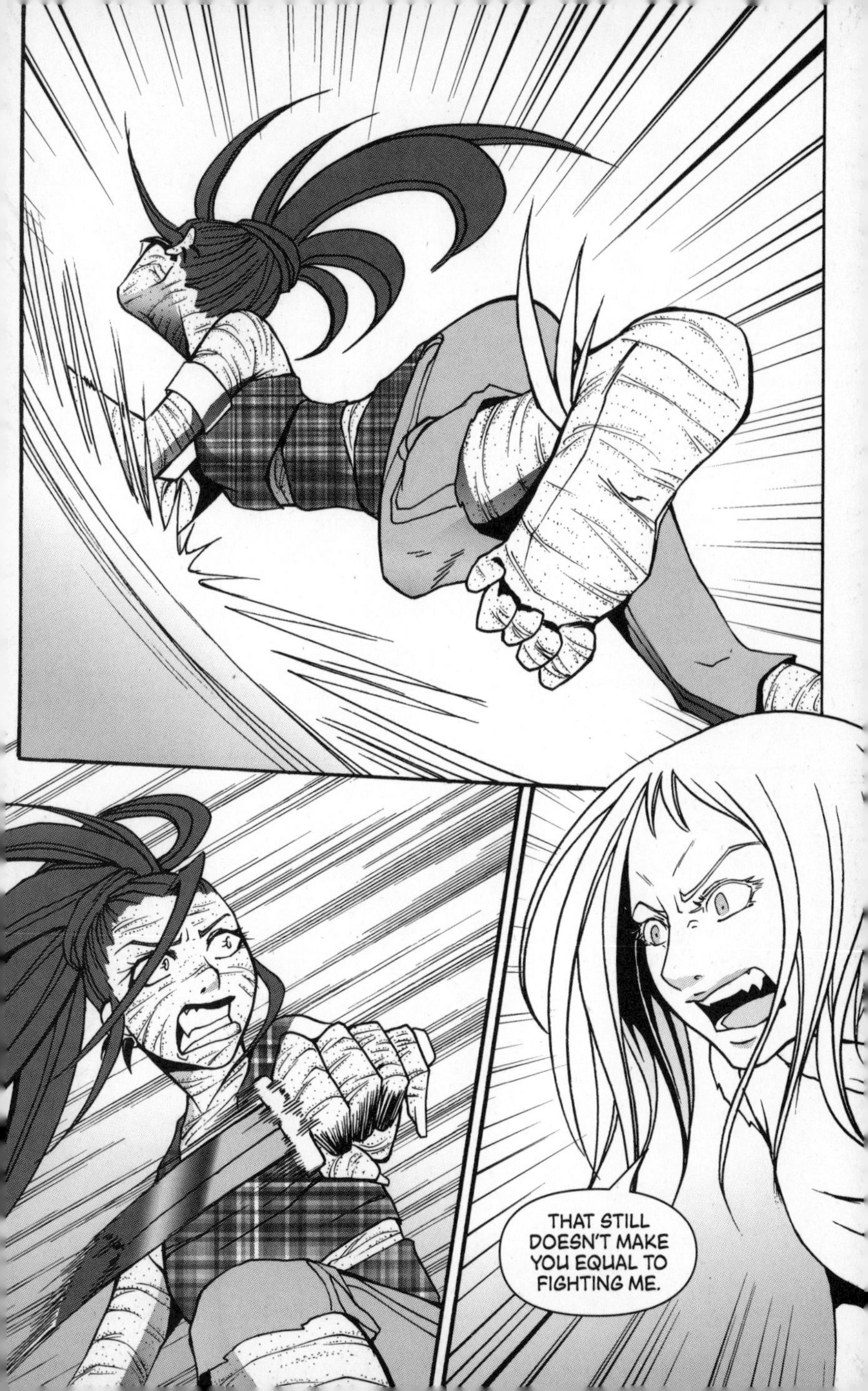
THAT STILL DOESN'T MAKE YOU EQUAL TO FIGHTING ME.

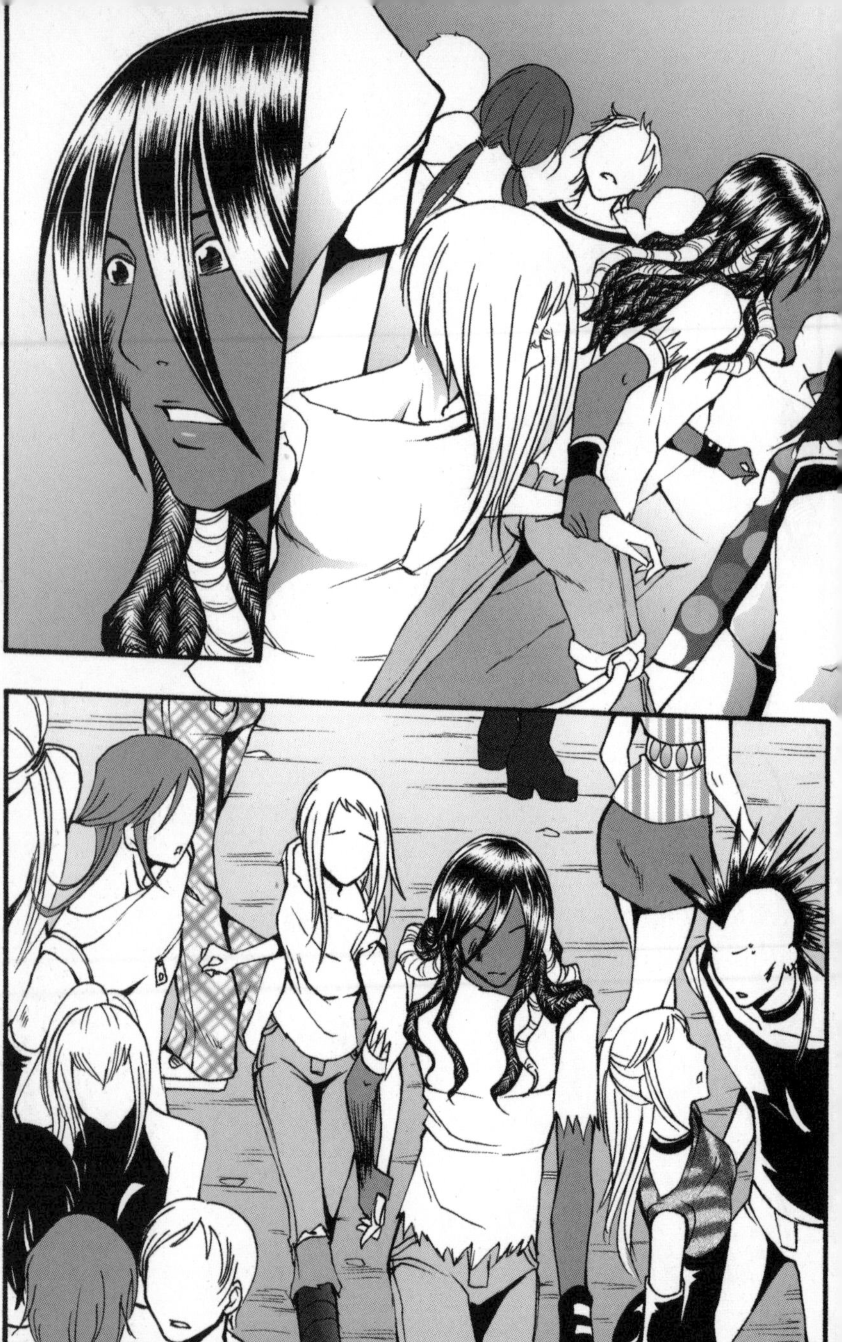

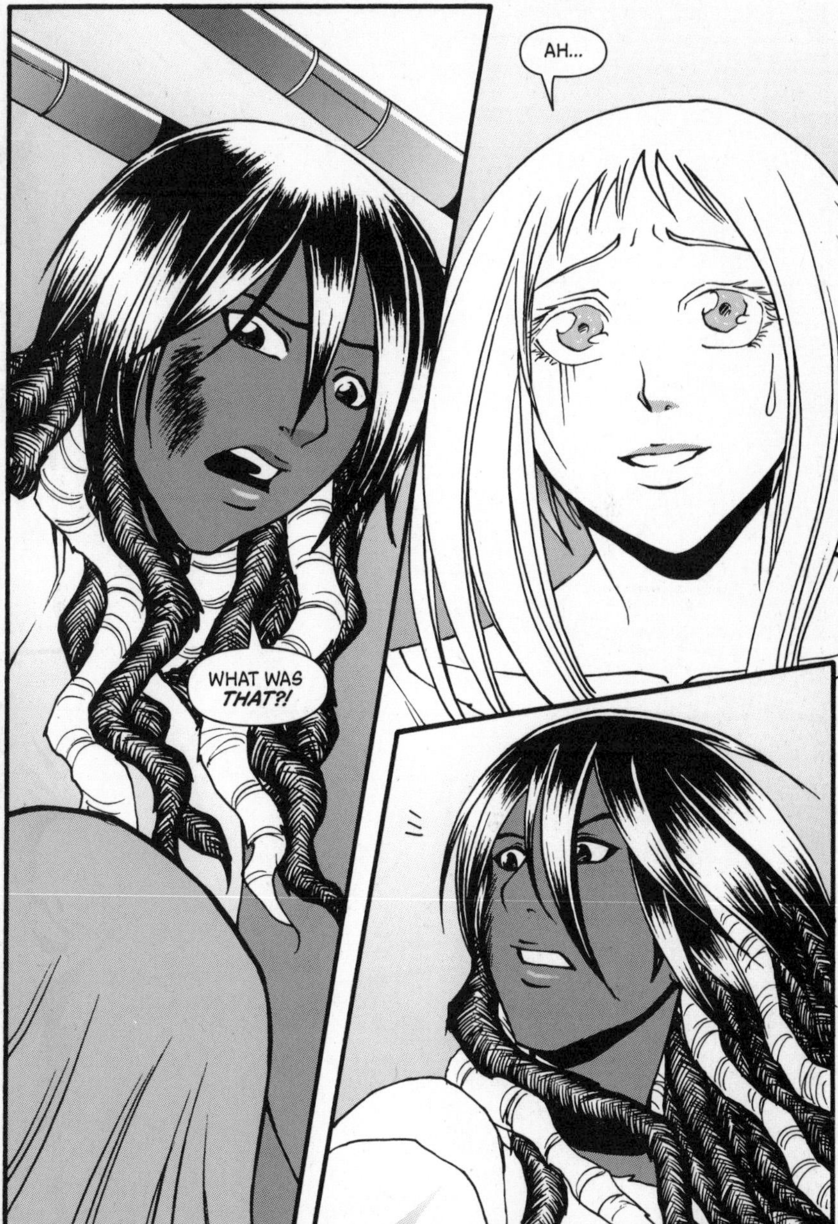
AH...
WHAT WAS THAT?!

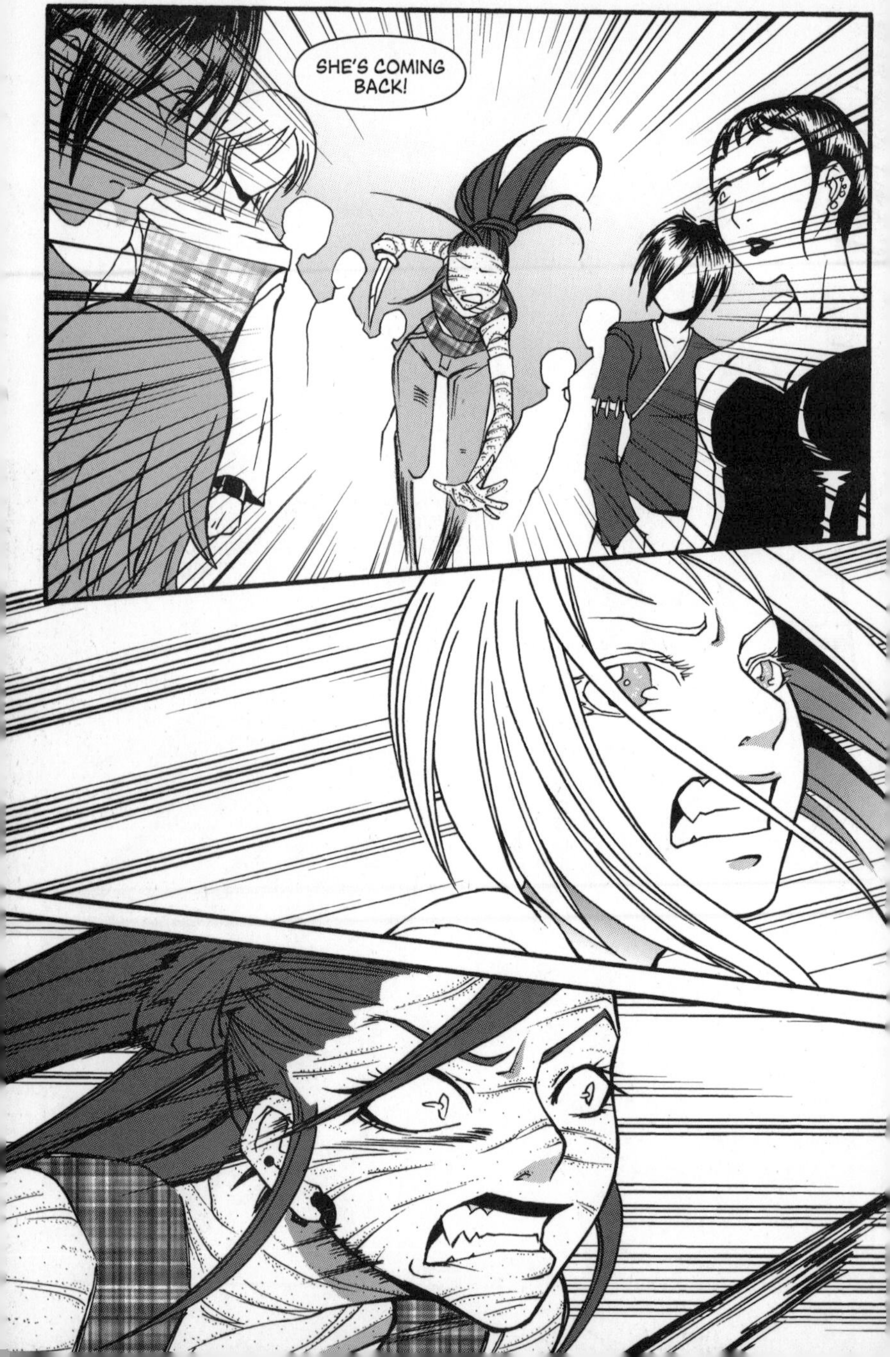

SHE'S COMING BACK!

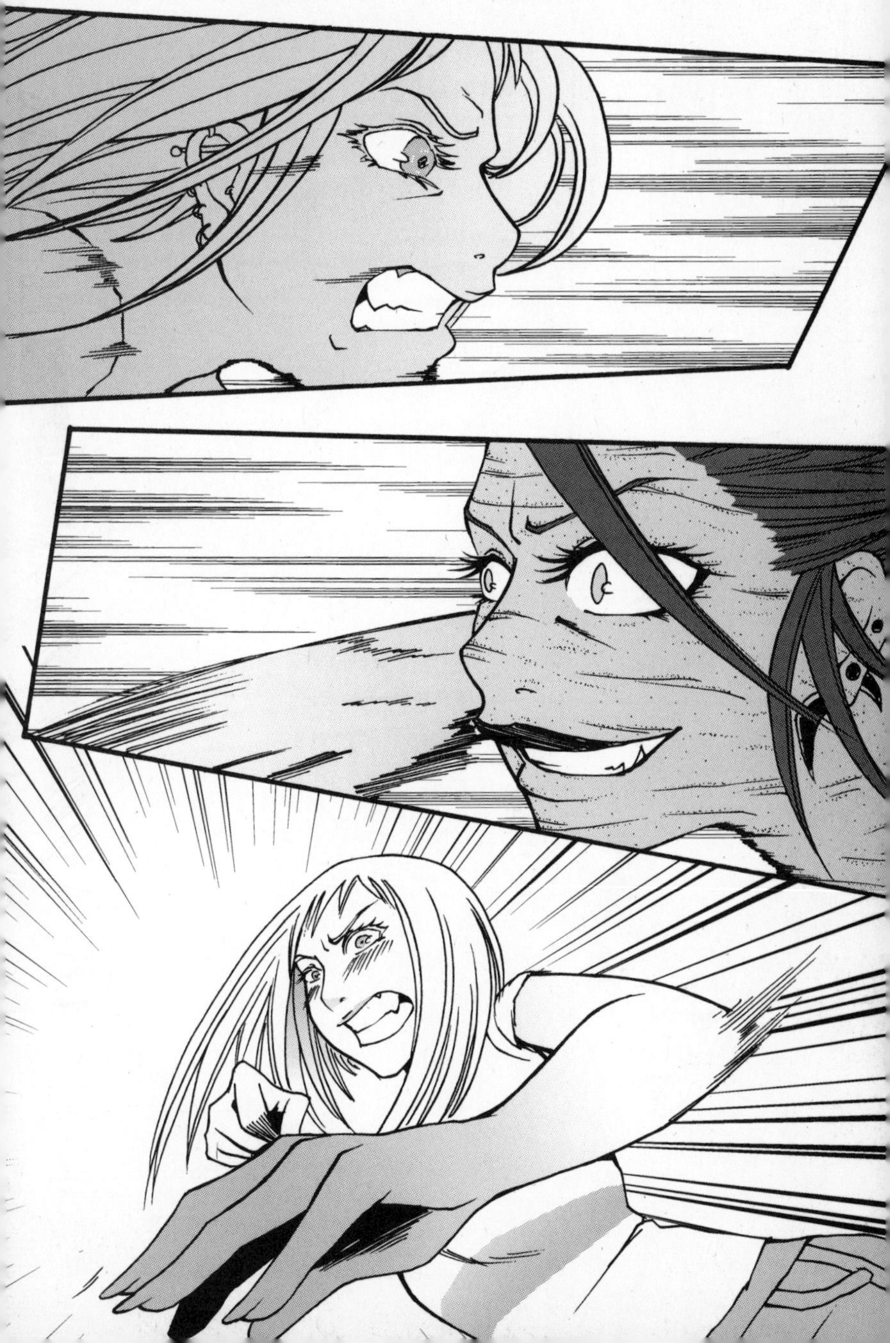

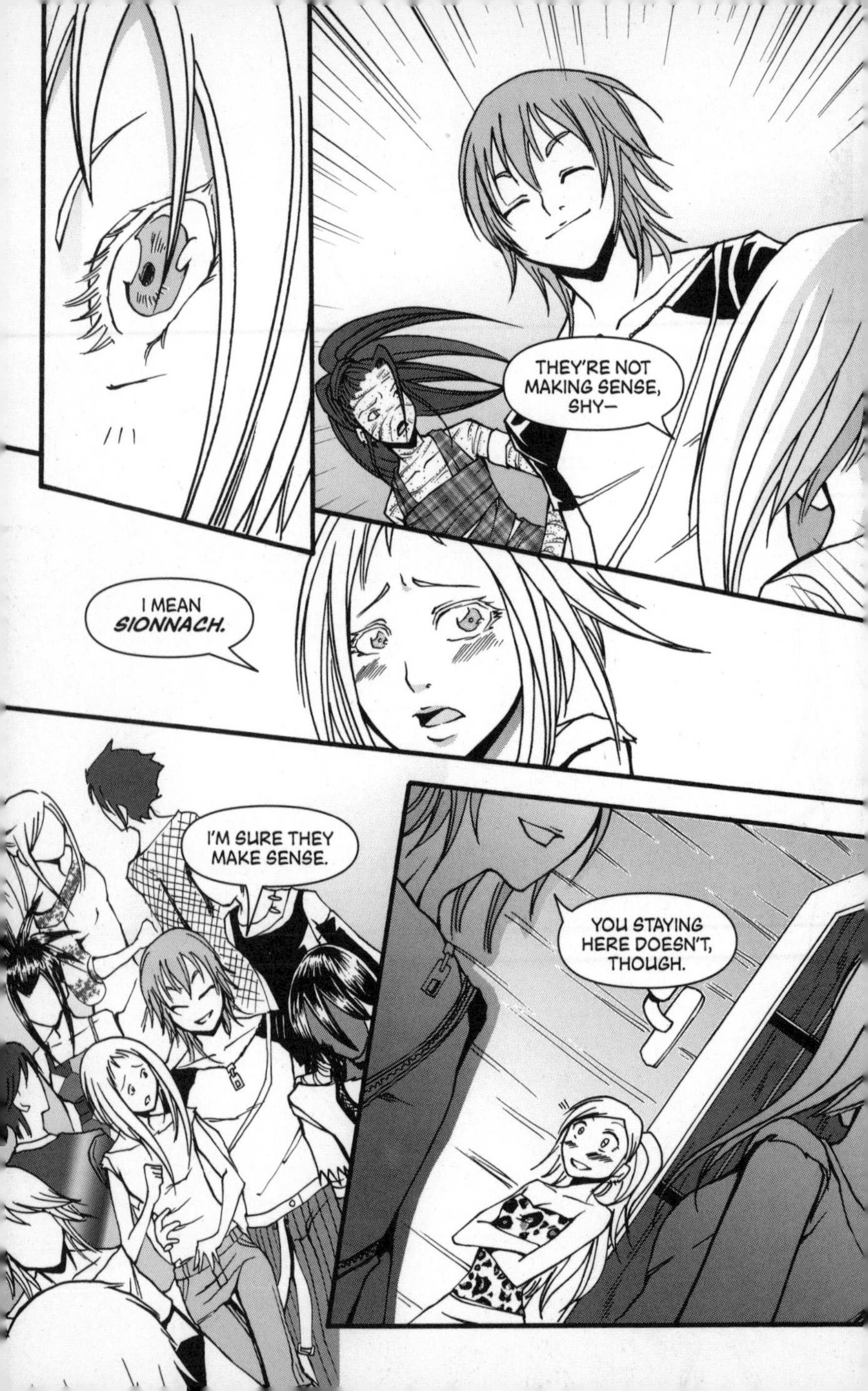
THEY'RE NOT MAKING SENSE, SHY—
I MEAN *SIONNACH.*
I'M SURE THEY MAKE SENSE.
YOU STAYING HERE DOESN'T, THOUGH.

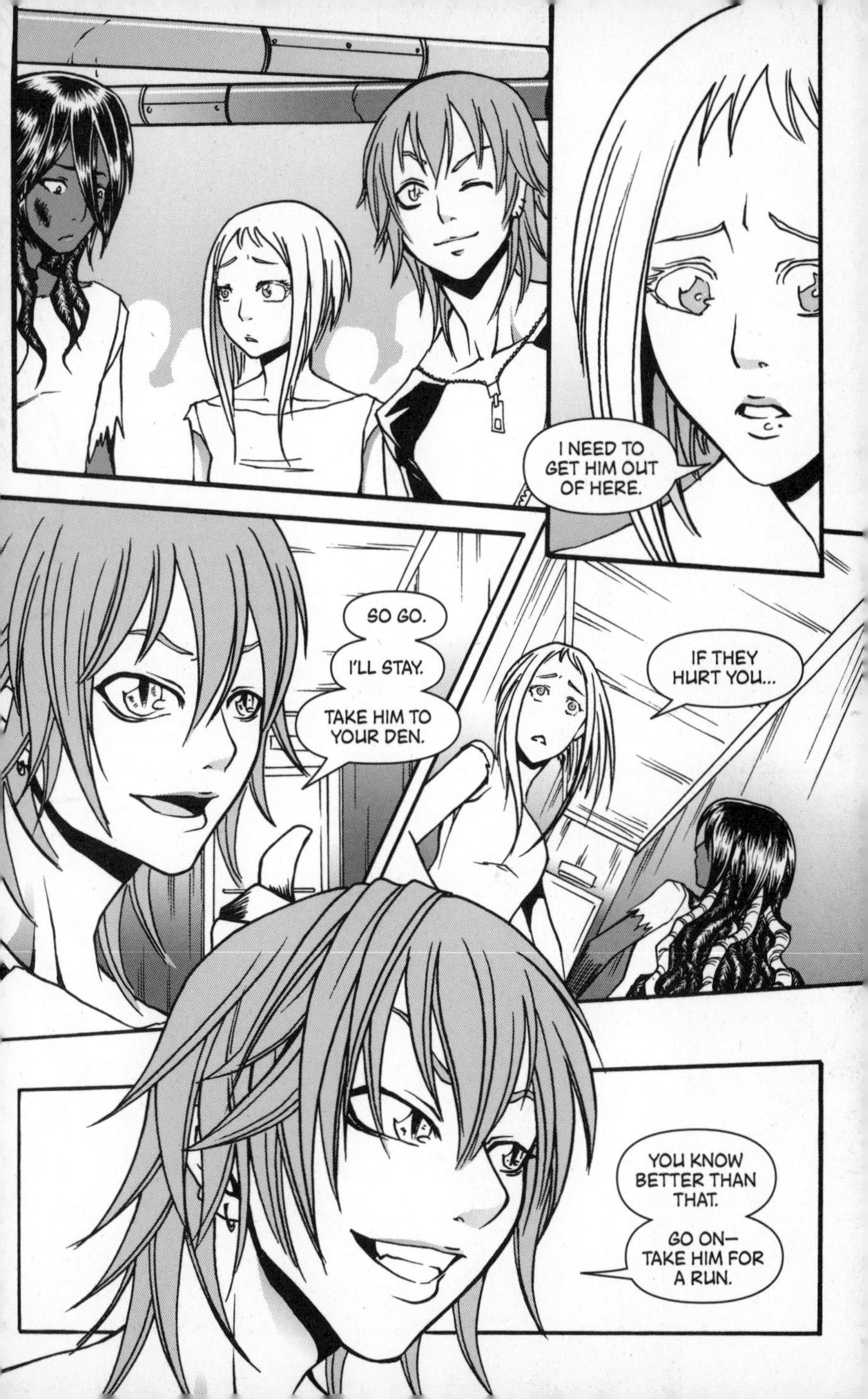
I NEED TO GET HIM OUT OF HERE.
SO GO.
I'LL STAY.
TAKE HIM TO YOUR DEN.
IF THEY HURT YOU...
YOU KNOW BETTER THAN THAT.
GO ON— TAKE HIM FOR A RUN.

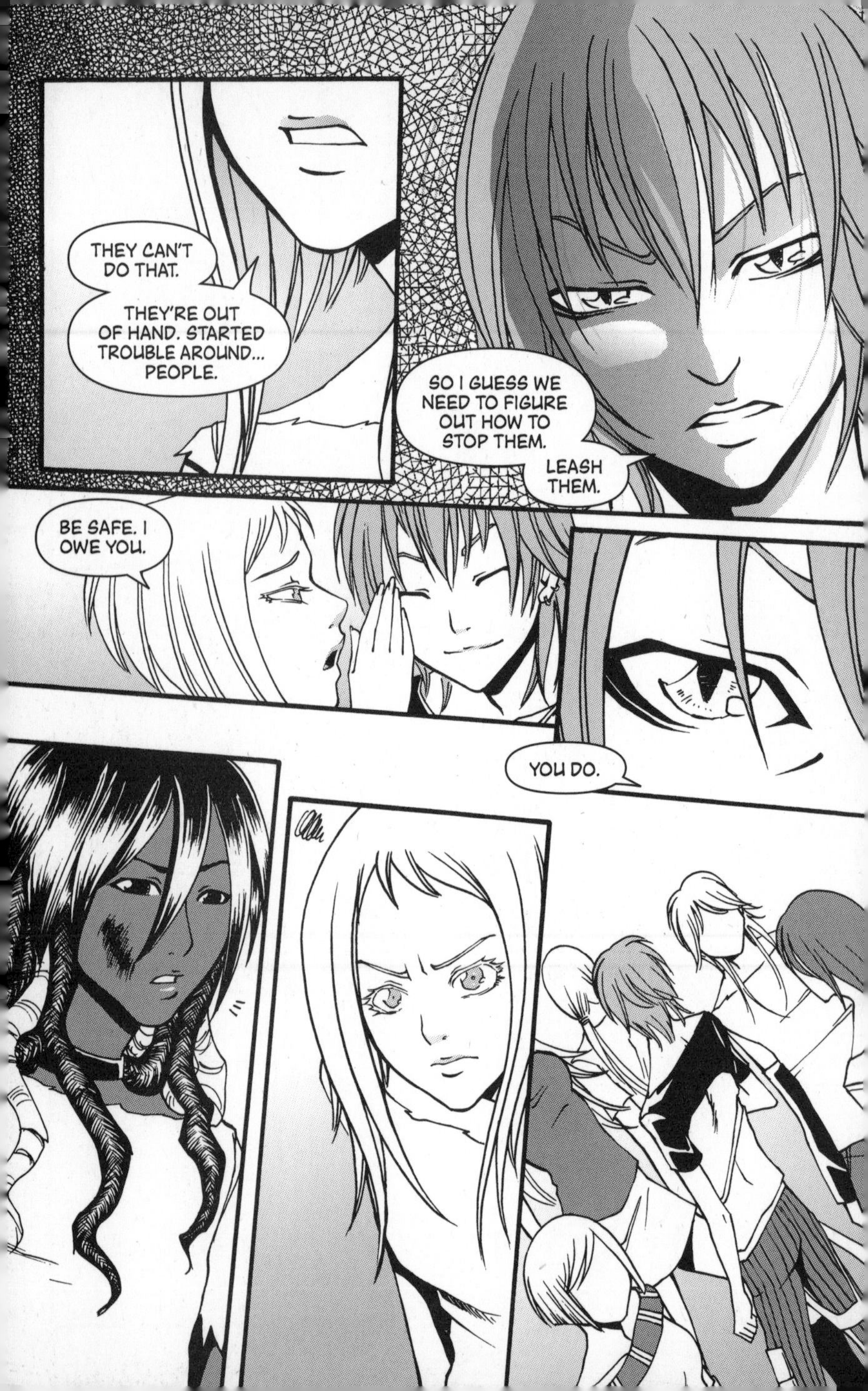

THEY CAN'T DO THAT.
THEY'RE OUT OF HAND. STARTED TROUBLE AROUND... PEOPLE.
SO I GUESS WE NEED TO FIGURE OUT HOW TO STOP THEM.
LEASH THEM.
BE SAFE. I OWE YOU.
YOU DO.

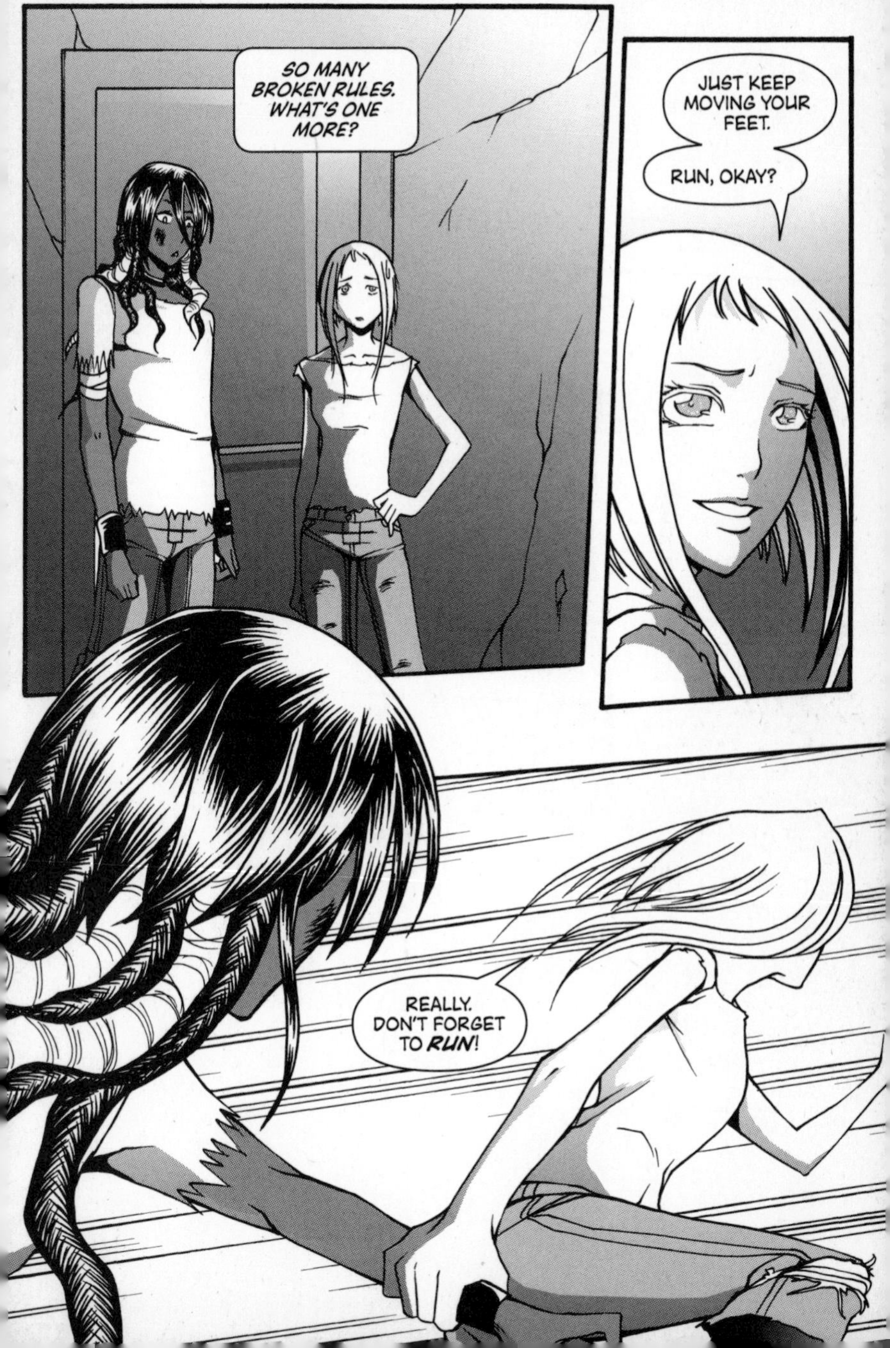
SO MANY BROKEN RULES. WHAT'S ONE MORE?
JUST KEEP MOVING YOUR FEET.
RUN, OKAY?
REALLY. DON'T FORGET TO *RUN*!

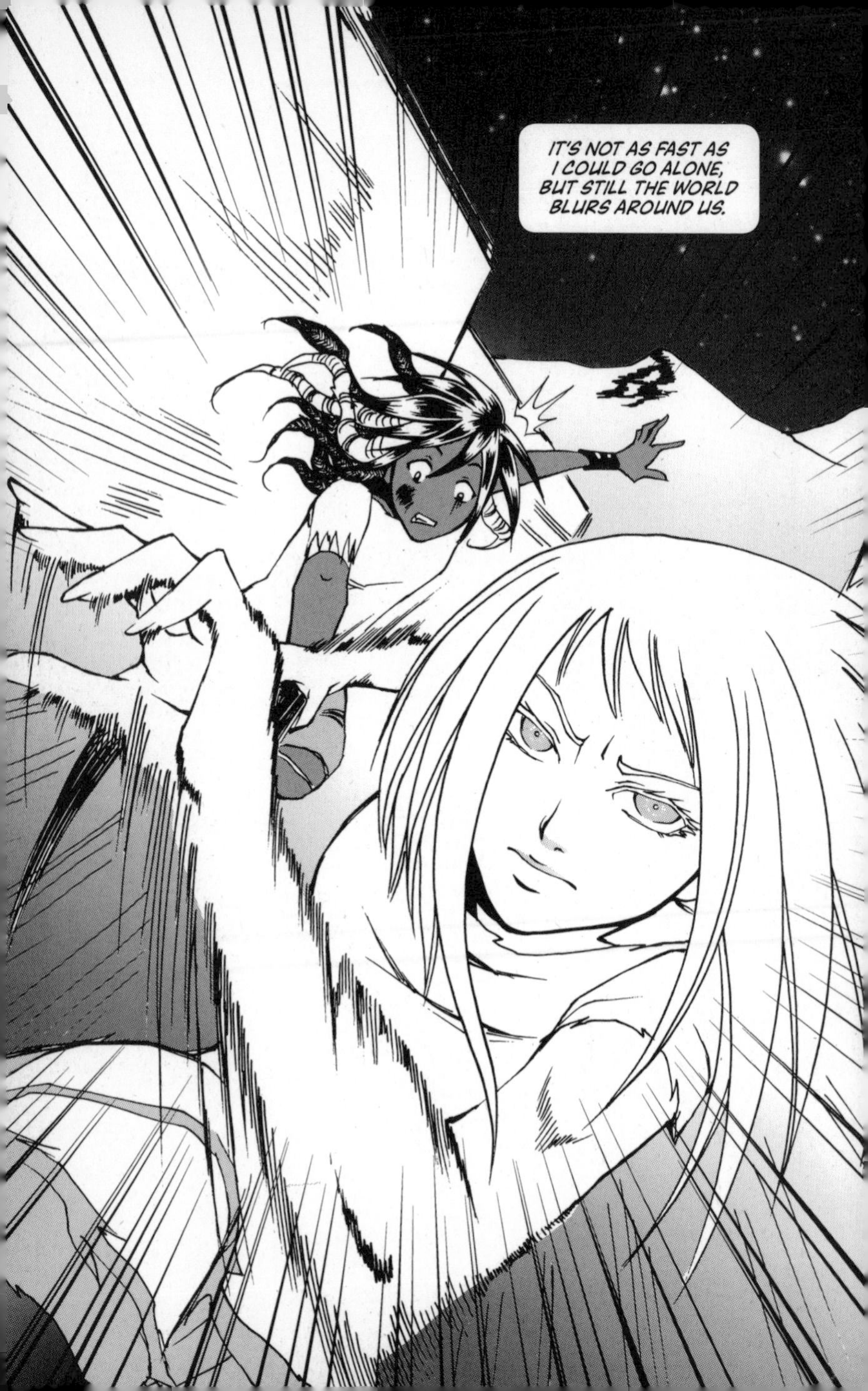
IT'S NOT AS FAST AS I COULD GO ALONE, BUT STILL THE WORLD BLURS AROUND US.

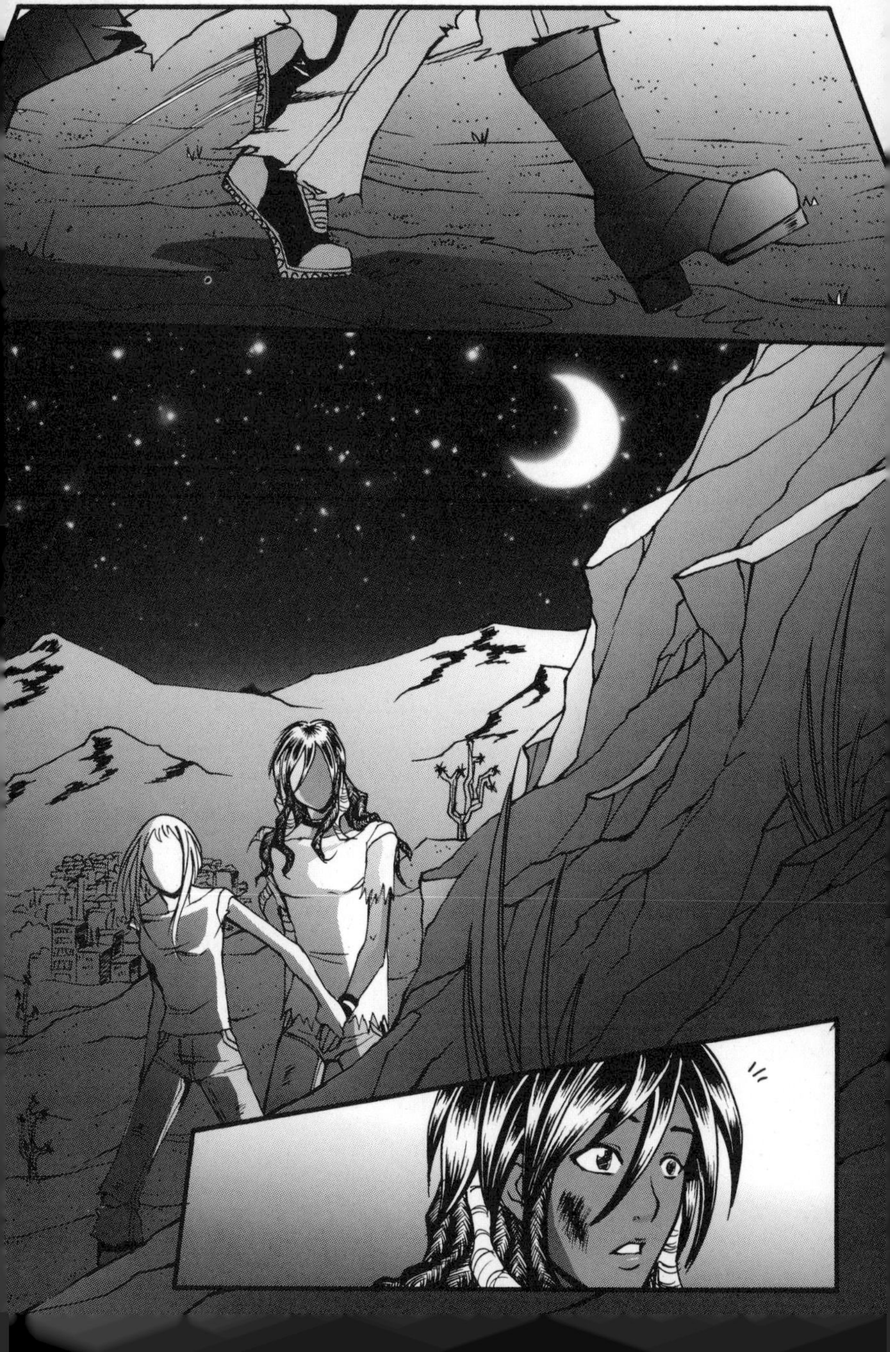

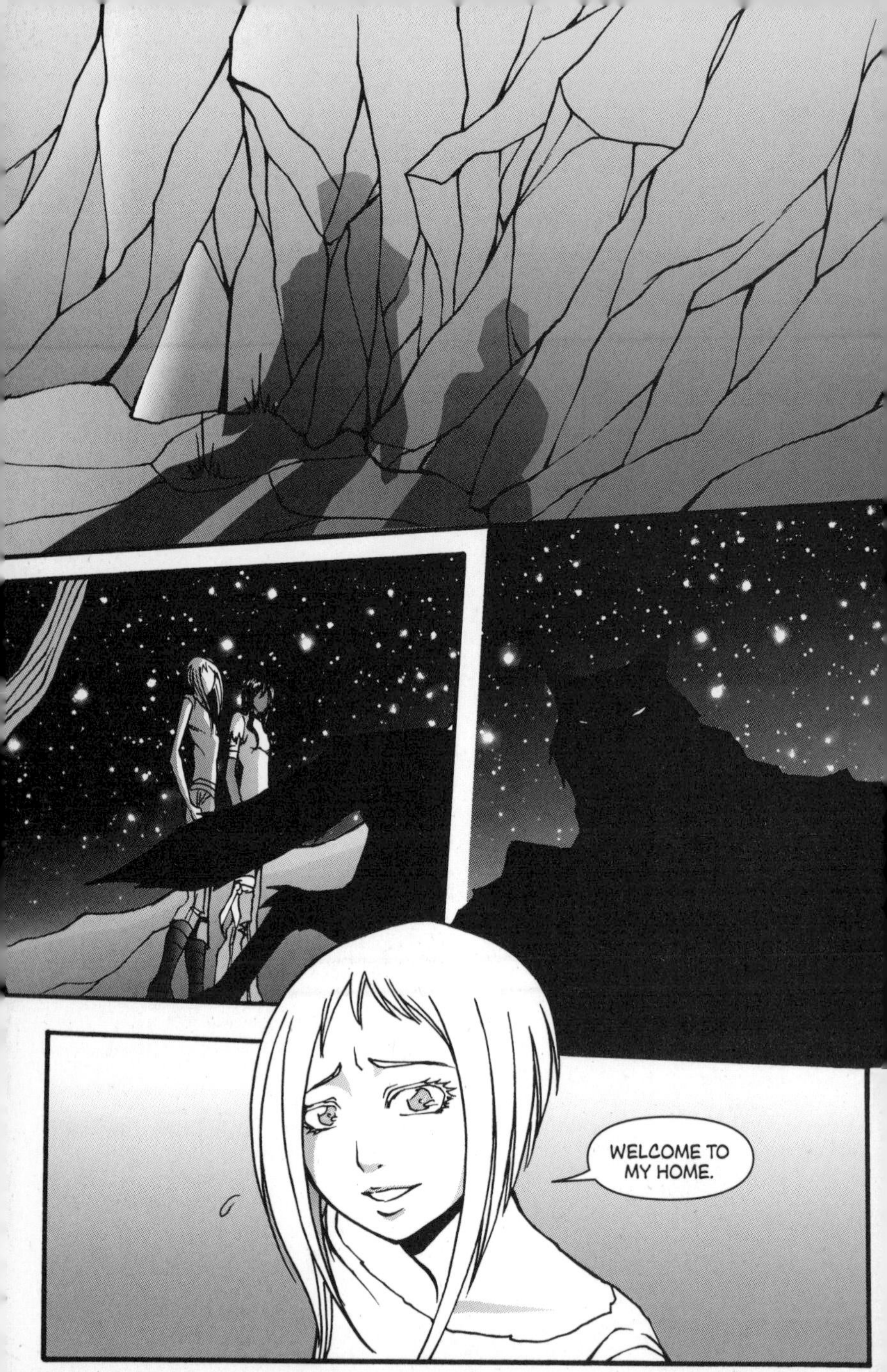
WELCOME TO
MY HOME.

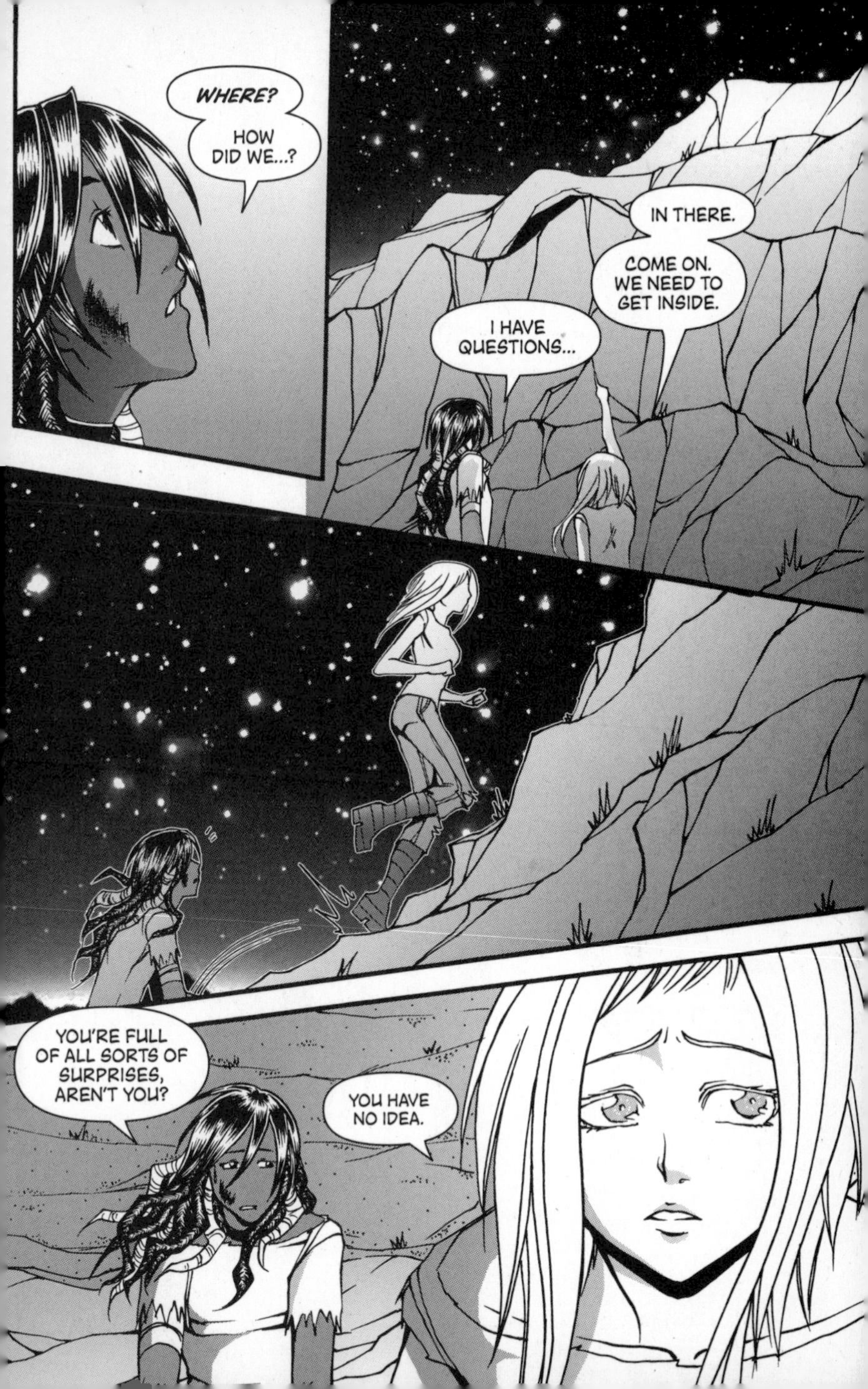
WHERE?
HOW DID WE...?
I HAVE QUESTIONS...
IN THERE.
COME ON. WE NEED TO GET INSIDE.
YOU'RE FULL OF ALL SORTS OF SURPRISES, AREN'T YOU?
YOU HAVE NO IDEA.

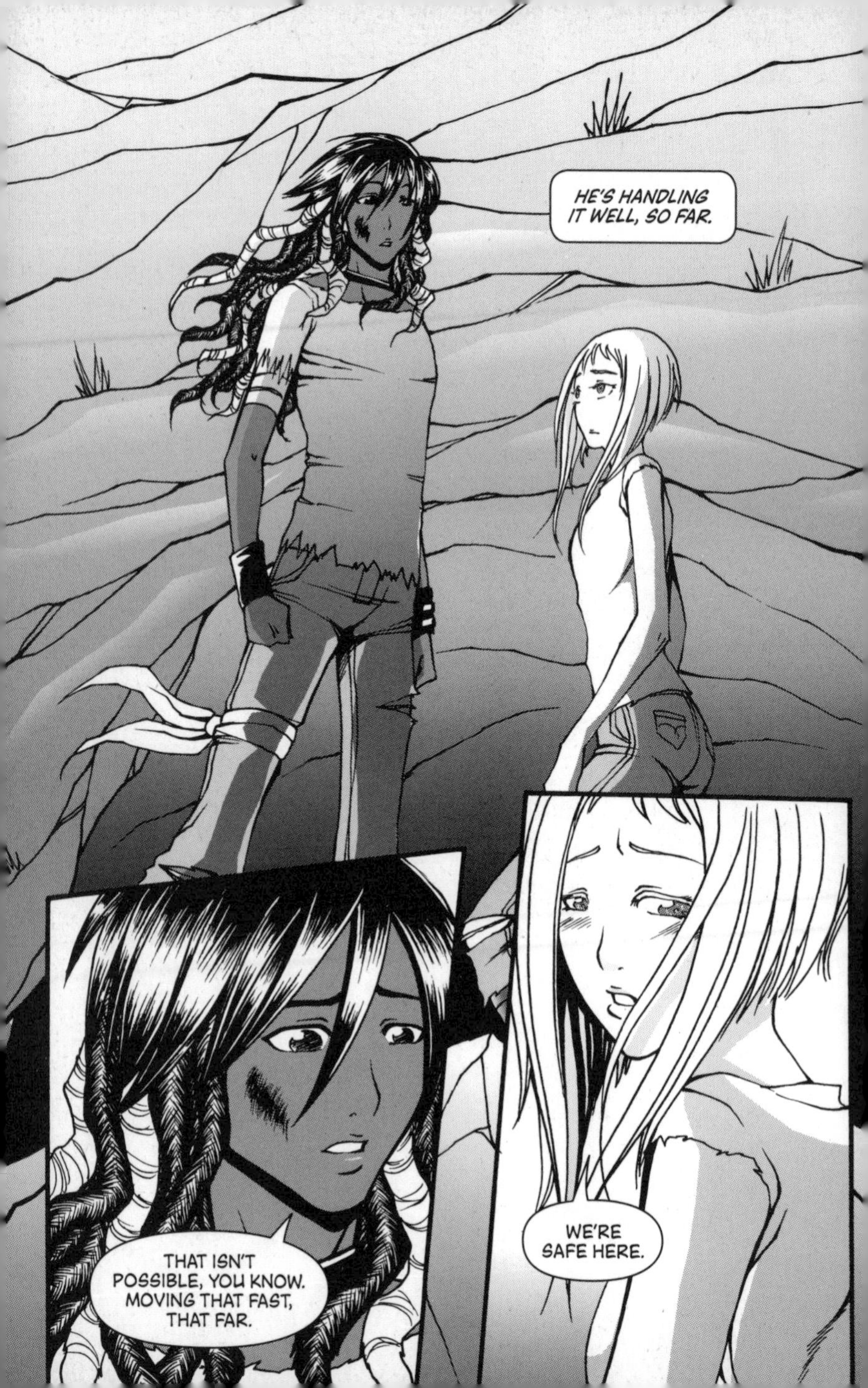
HE'S HANDLING IT WELL, SO FAR.
THAT ISN'T POSSIBLE, YOU KNOW. MOVING THAT FAST, THAT FAR.
WE'RE SAFE HERE.

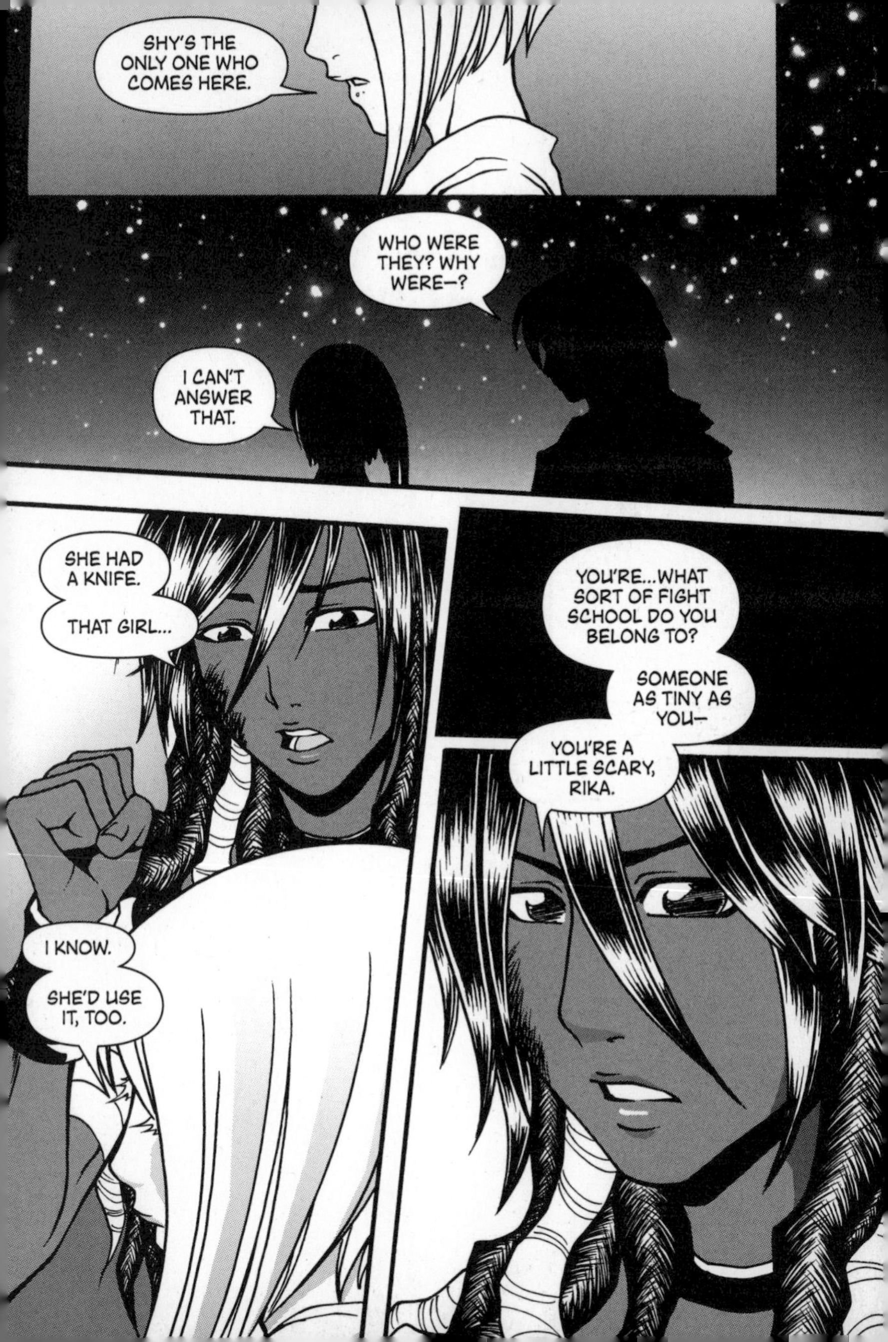

SHY'S THE ONLY ONE WHO COMES HERE.
WHO WERE THEY? WHY WERE—?
I CAN'T ANSWER THAT.
SHE HAD A KNIFE.
THAT GIRL...
I KNOW.
SHE'D USE IT, TOO.
YOU'RE...WHAT SORT OF FIGHT SCHOOL DO YOU BELONG TO?
SOMEONE AS TINY AS YOU—
YOU'RE A LITTLE SCARY, RIKA.

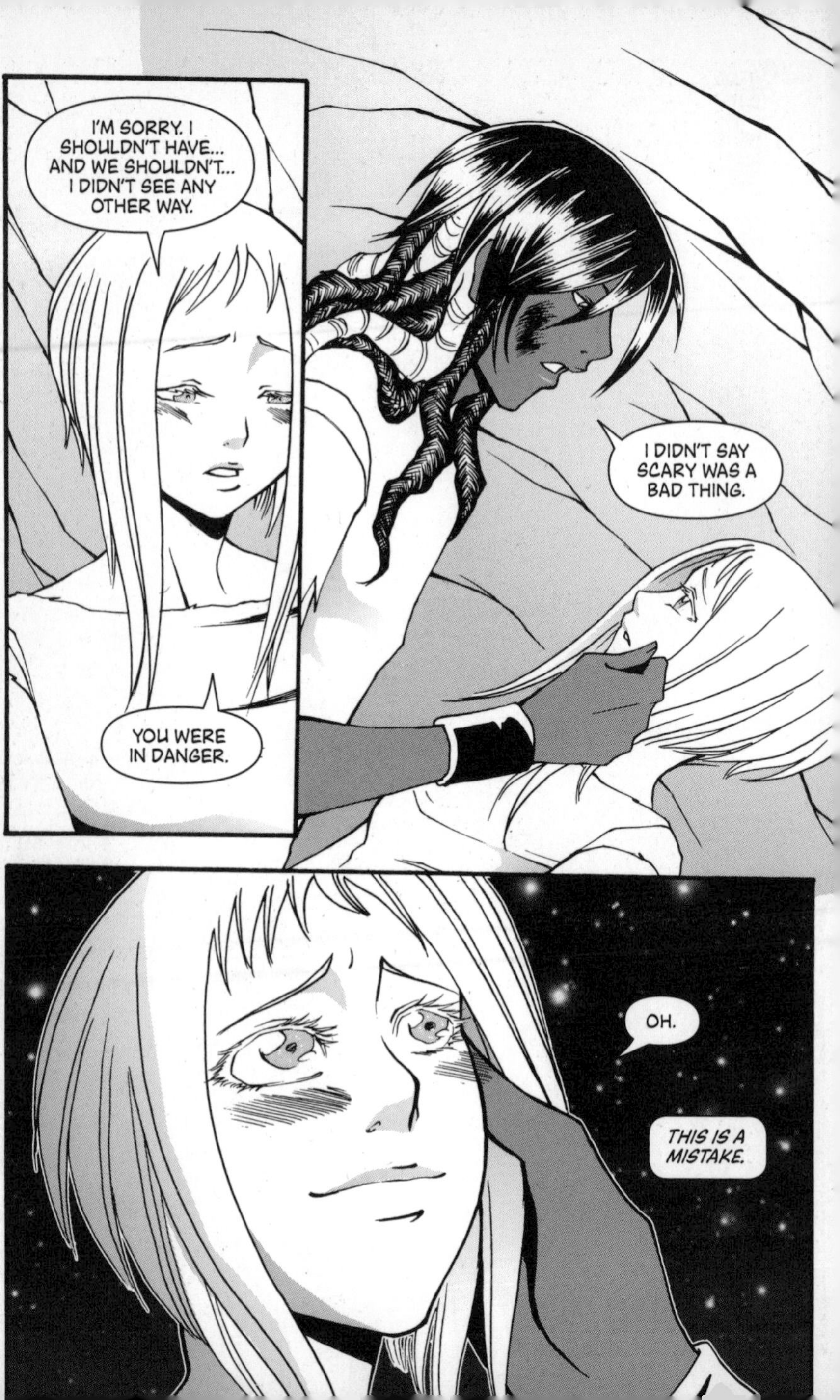
I'M SORRY. I SHOULDN'T HAVE... AND WE SHOULDN'T... I DIDN'T SEE ANY OTHER WAY.
YOU WERE IN DANGER.
I DIDN'T SAY SCARY WAS A BAD THING.
OH.
THIS IS A MISTAKE.

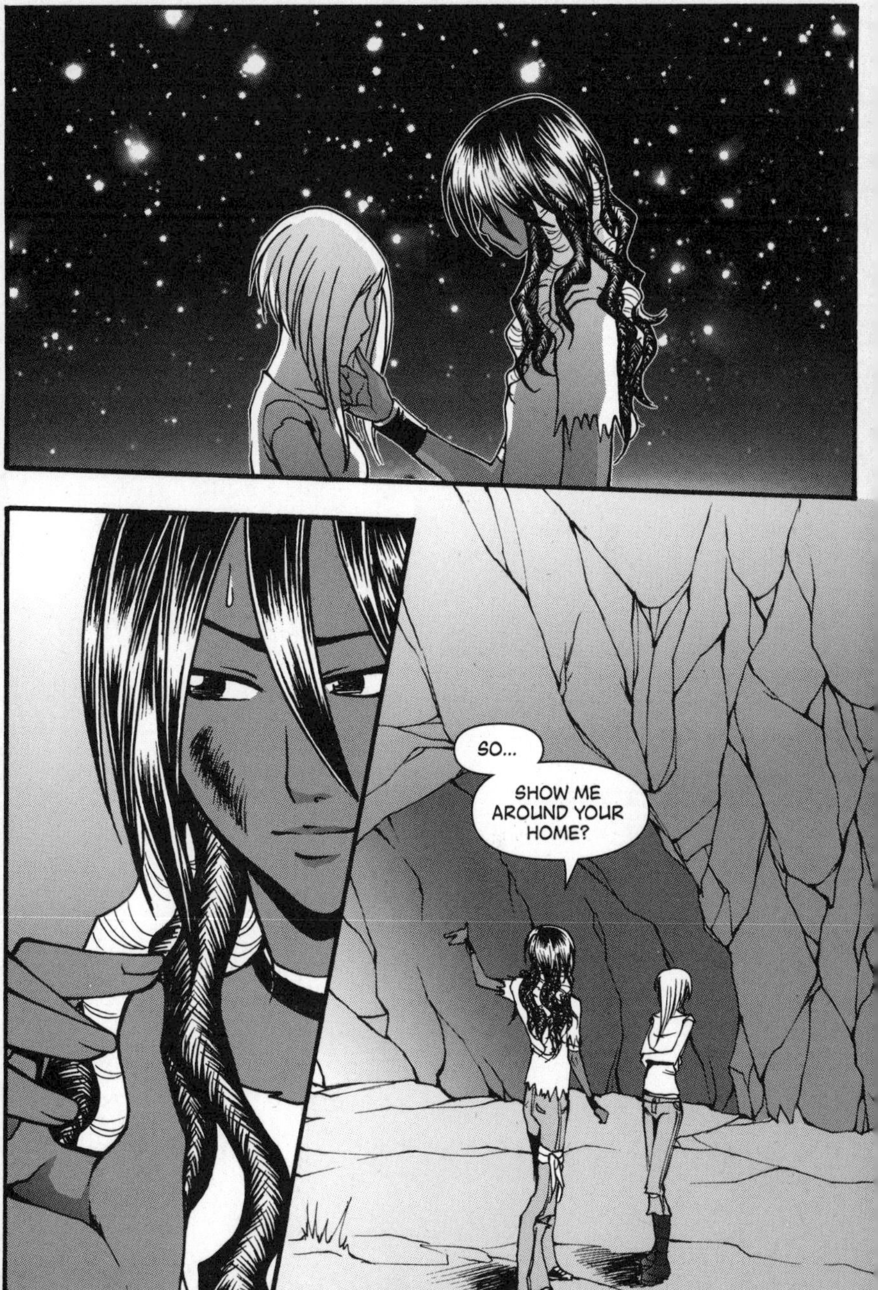
SO...
SHOW ME AROUND YOUR HOME?

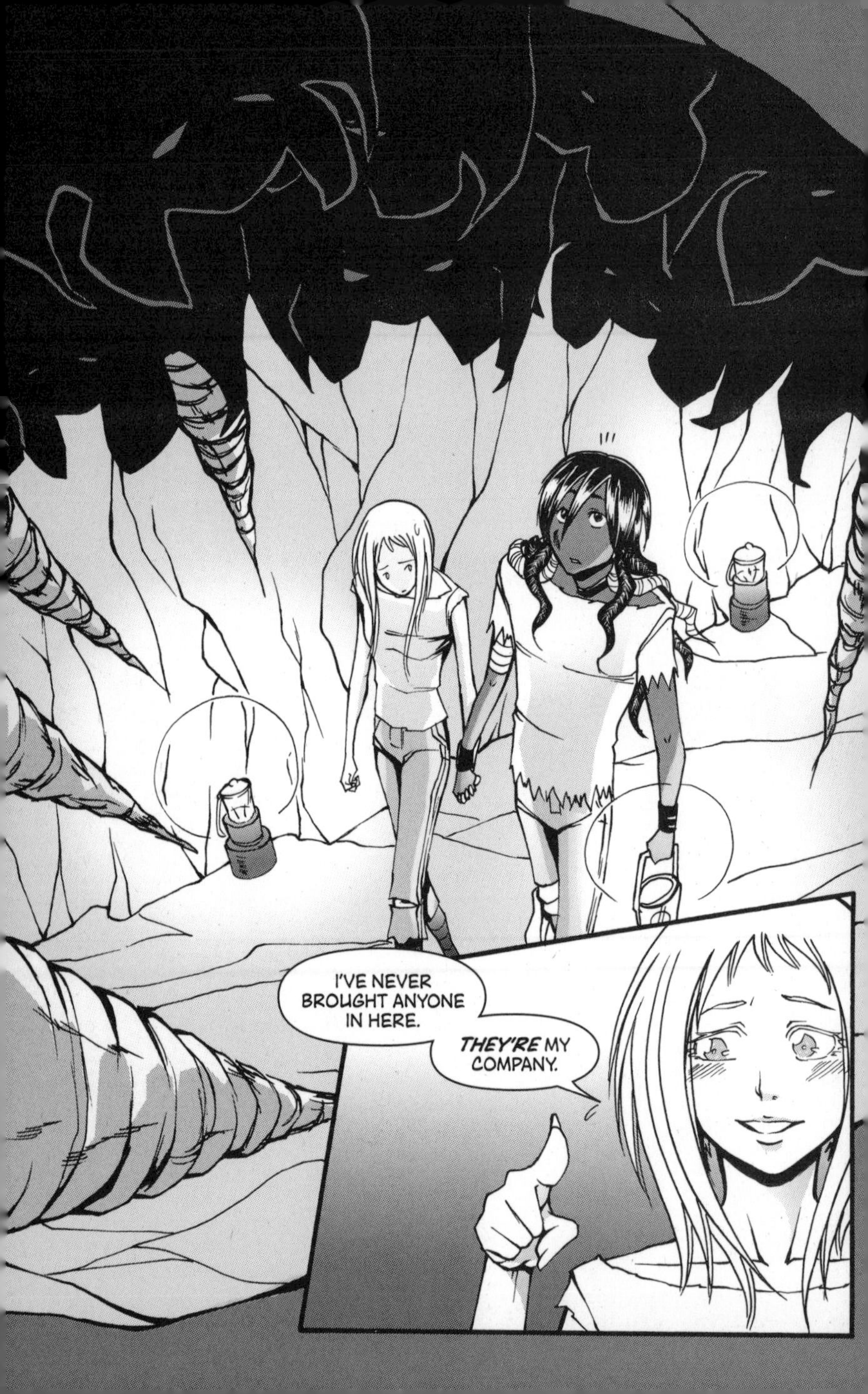
I'VE NEVER BROUGHT ANYONE IN HERE.
THEY'RE MY COMPANY.

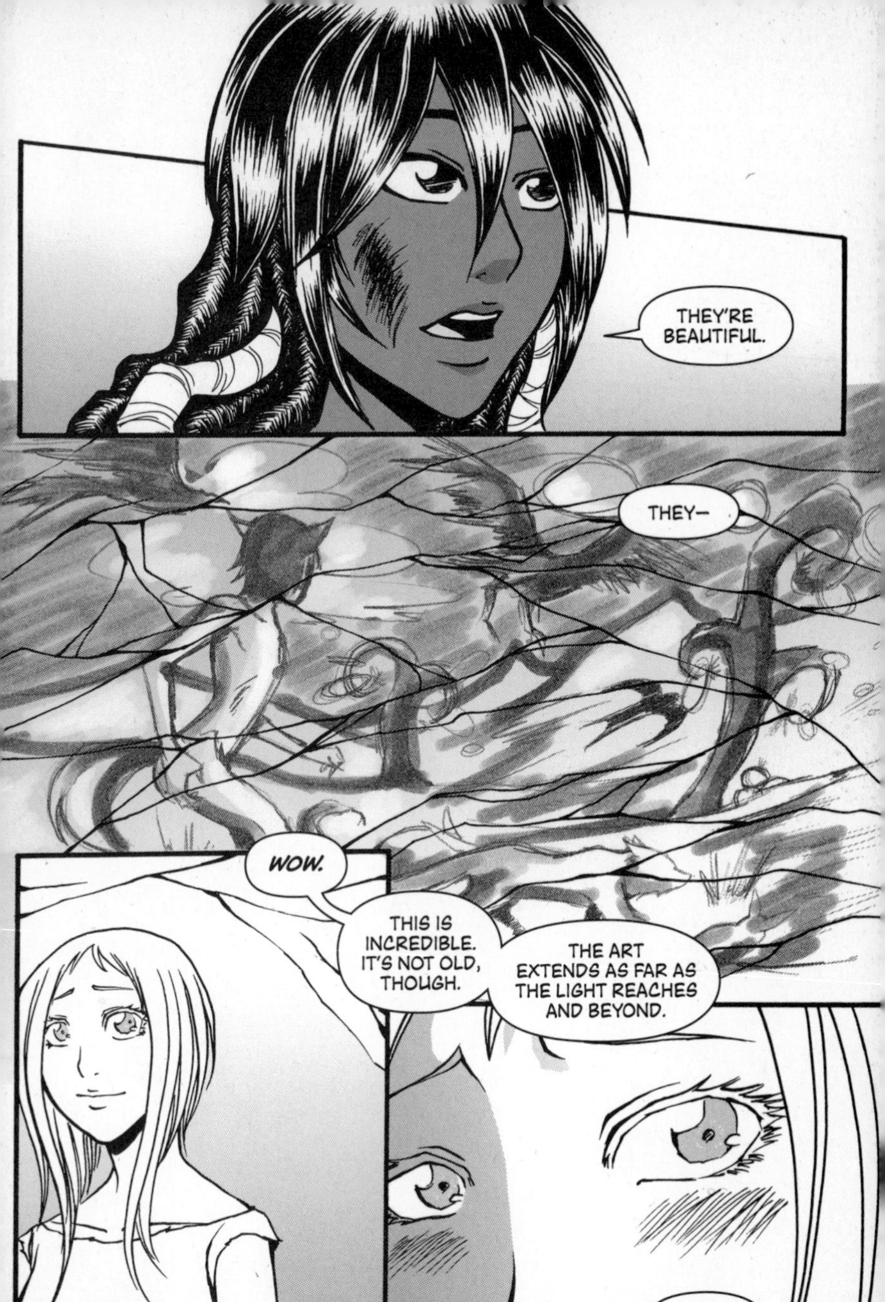
THEY'RE BEAUTIFUL.
THEY—
WOW.
THIS IS INCREDIBLE. IT'S NOT OLD, THOUGH.
THE ART EXTENDS AS FAR AS THE LIGHT REACHES AND BEYOND.
DID *YOU* DO THIS?

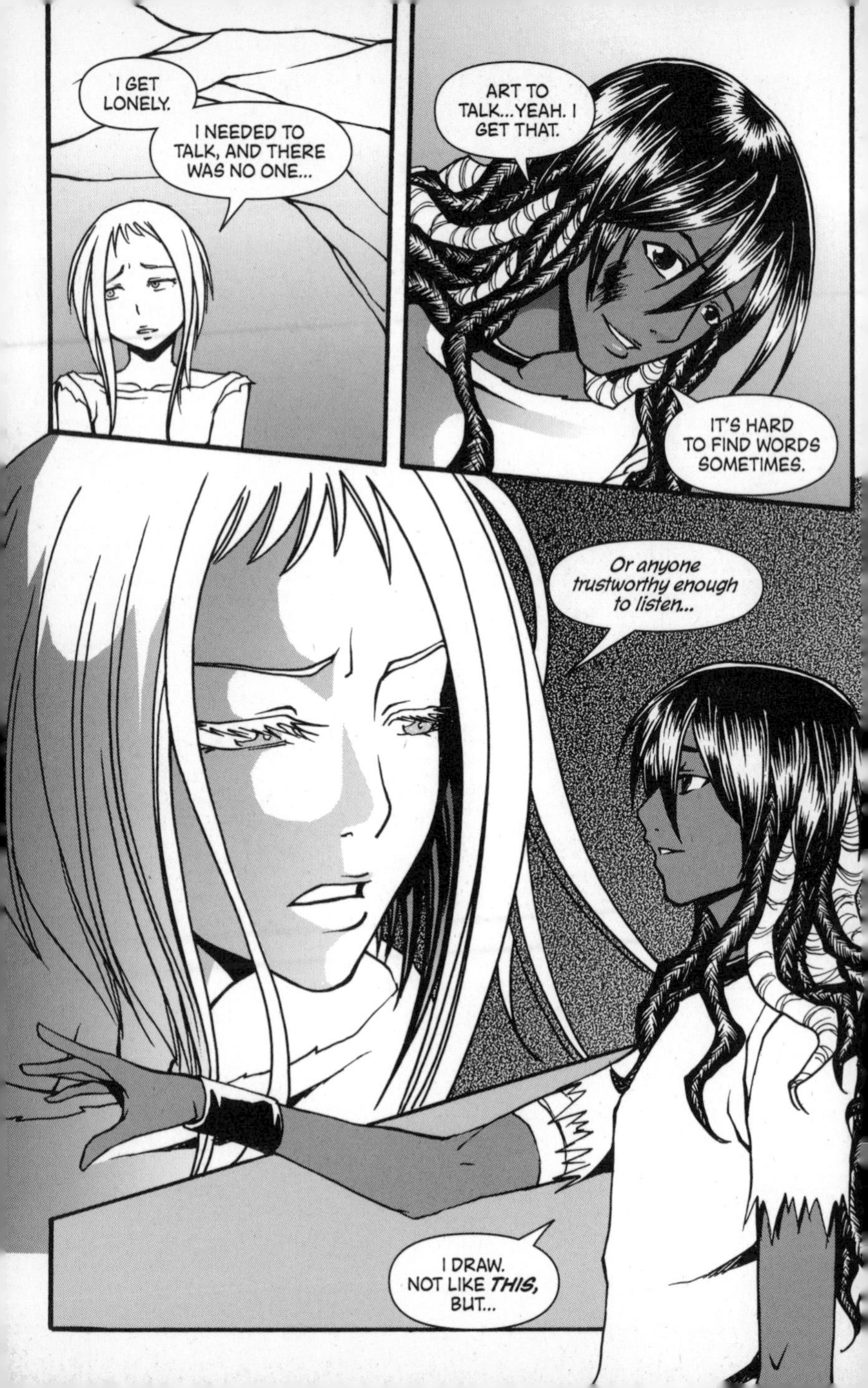
I GET LONELY.
I NEEDED TO TALK, AND THERE WAS NO ONE...
ART TO TALK...YEAH. I GET THAT.
IT'S HARD TO FIND WORDS SOMETIMES.
Or anyone trustworthy enough to listen...
I DRAW. NOT LIKE ***THIS,*** BUT...

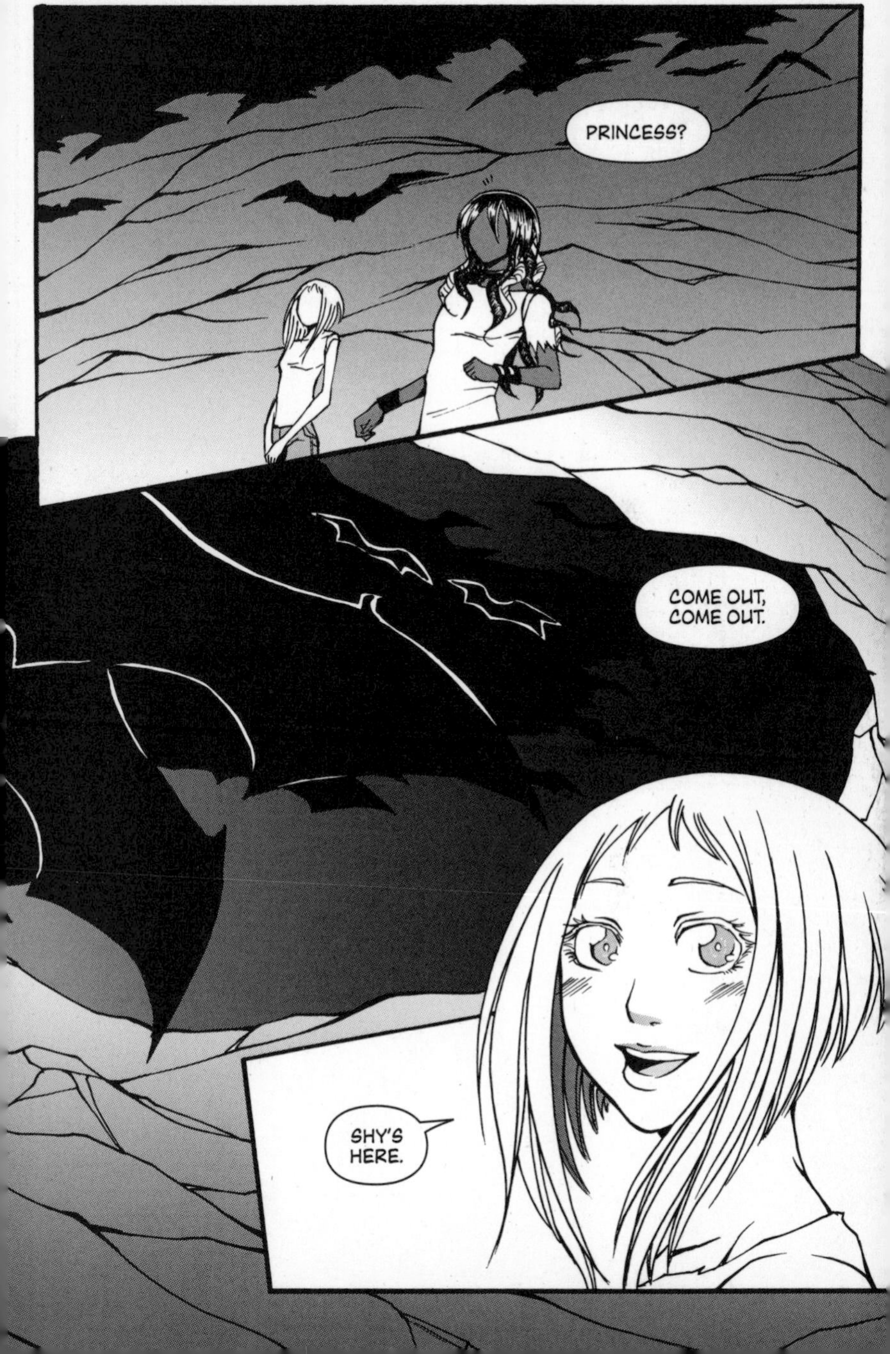
PRINCESS?
COME OUT, COME OUT.
SHY'S HERE.

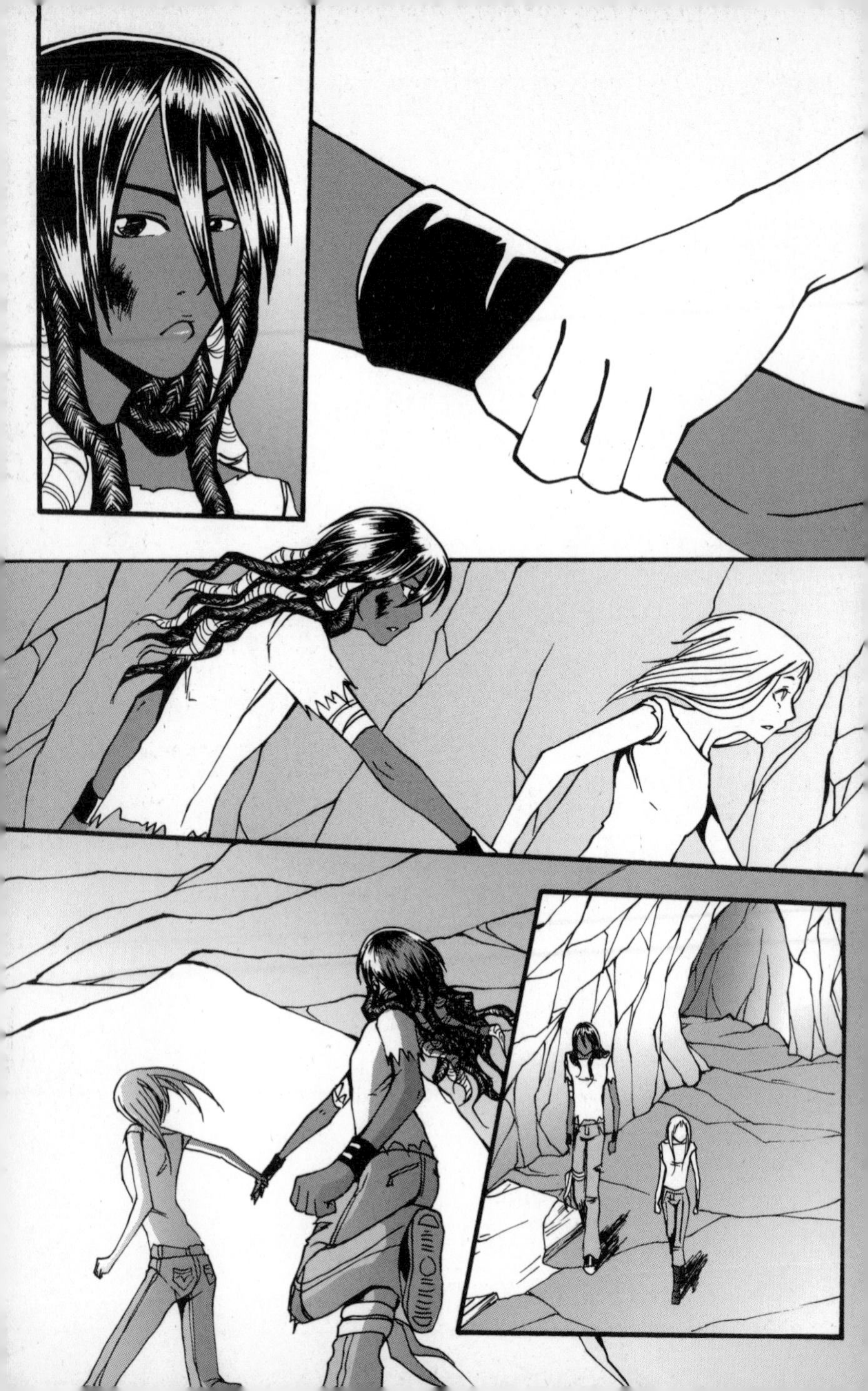

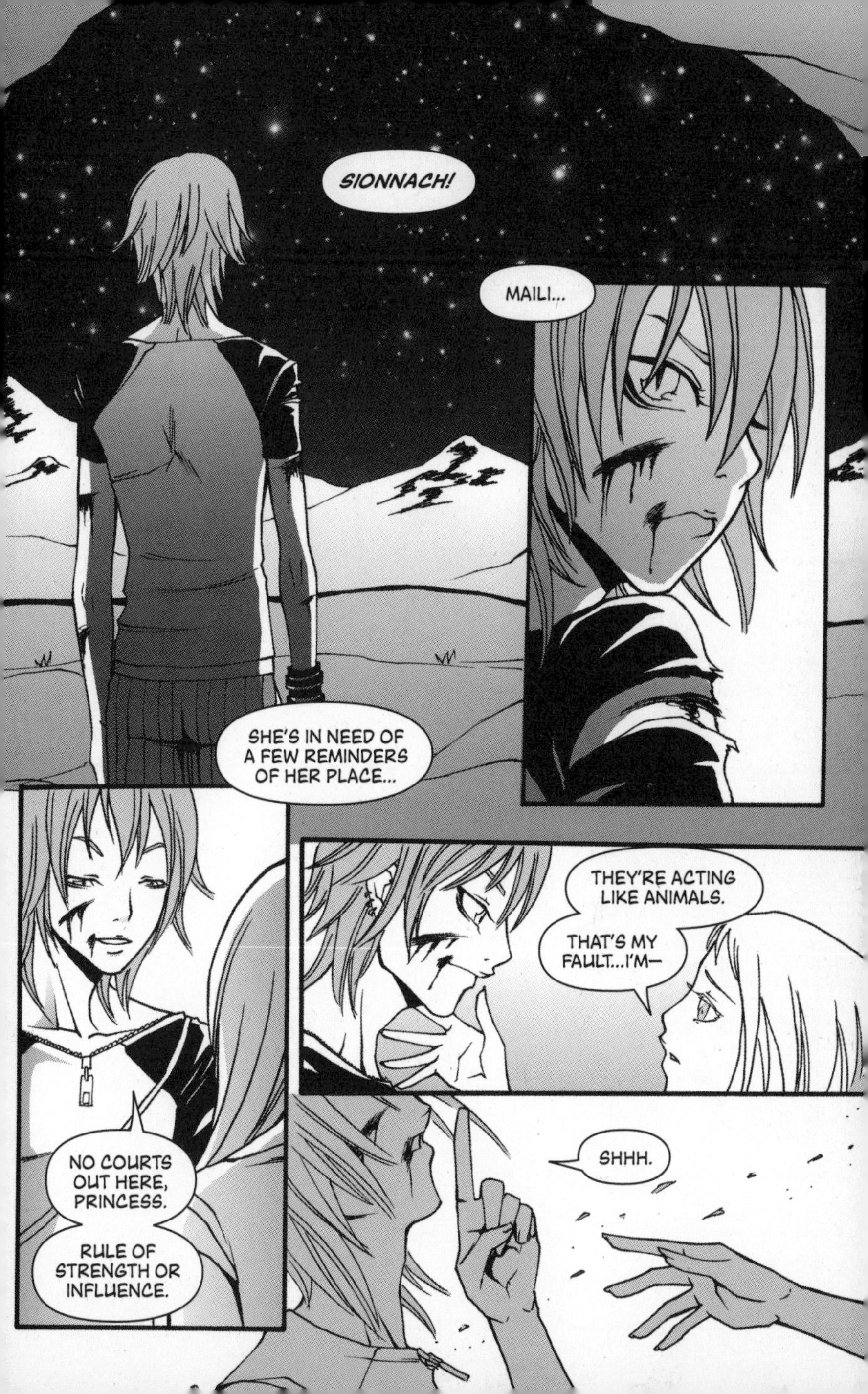
SIONNACH!
MAILI...
SHE'S IN NEED OF A FEW REMINDERS OF HER PLACE...
NO COURTS OUT HERE, PRINCESS.
RULE OF STRENGTH OR INFLUENCE.
THEY'RE ACTING LIKE ANIMALS.
THAT'S MY FAULT...I'M—
SHHH.

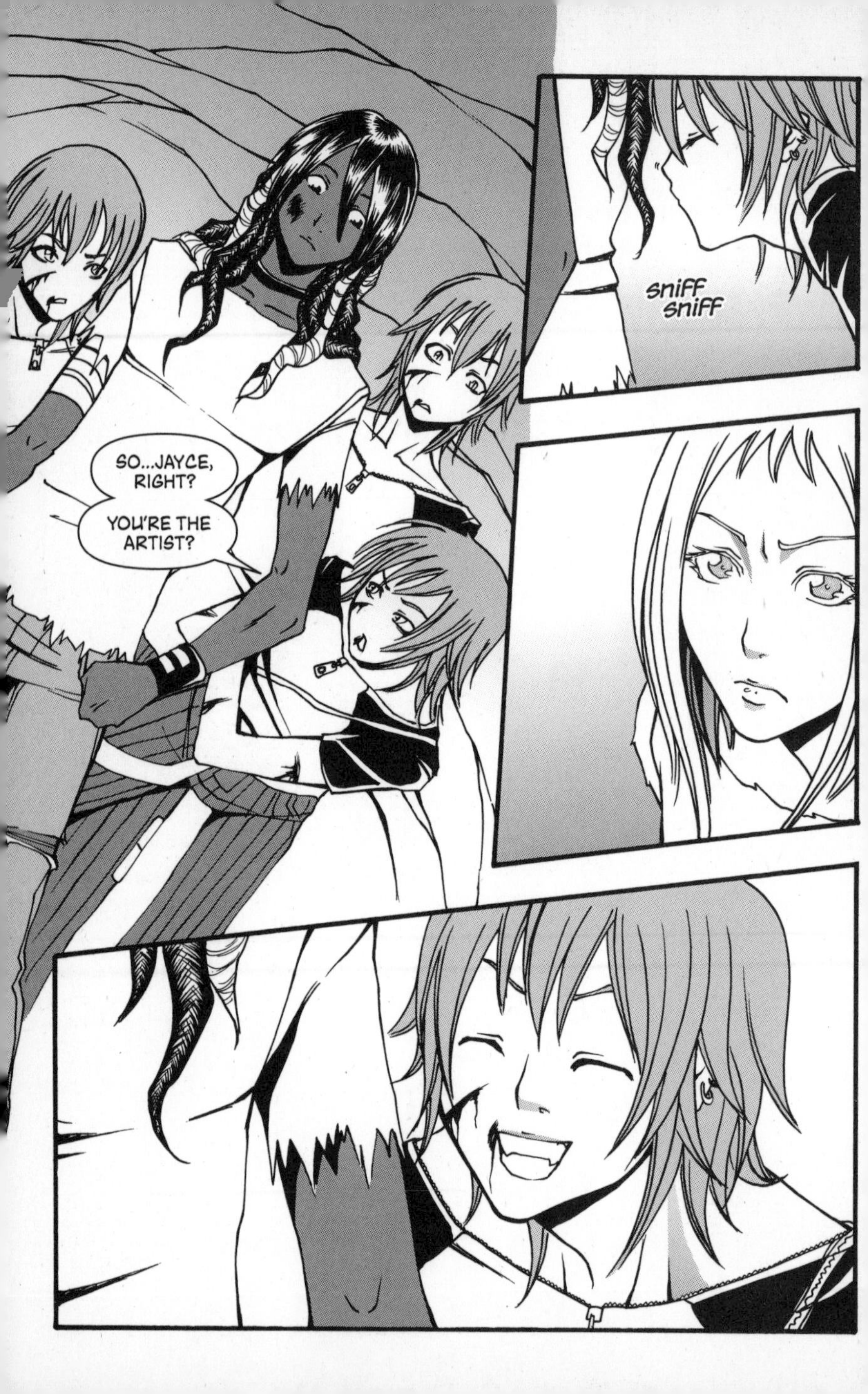
SO...JAYCE, RIGHT?
YOU'RE THE ARTIST?
SNIFF SNIFF

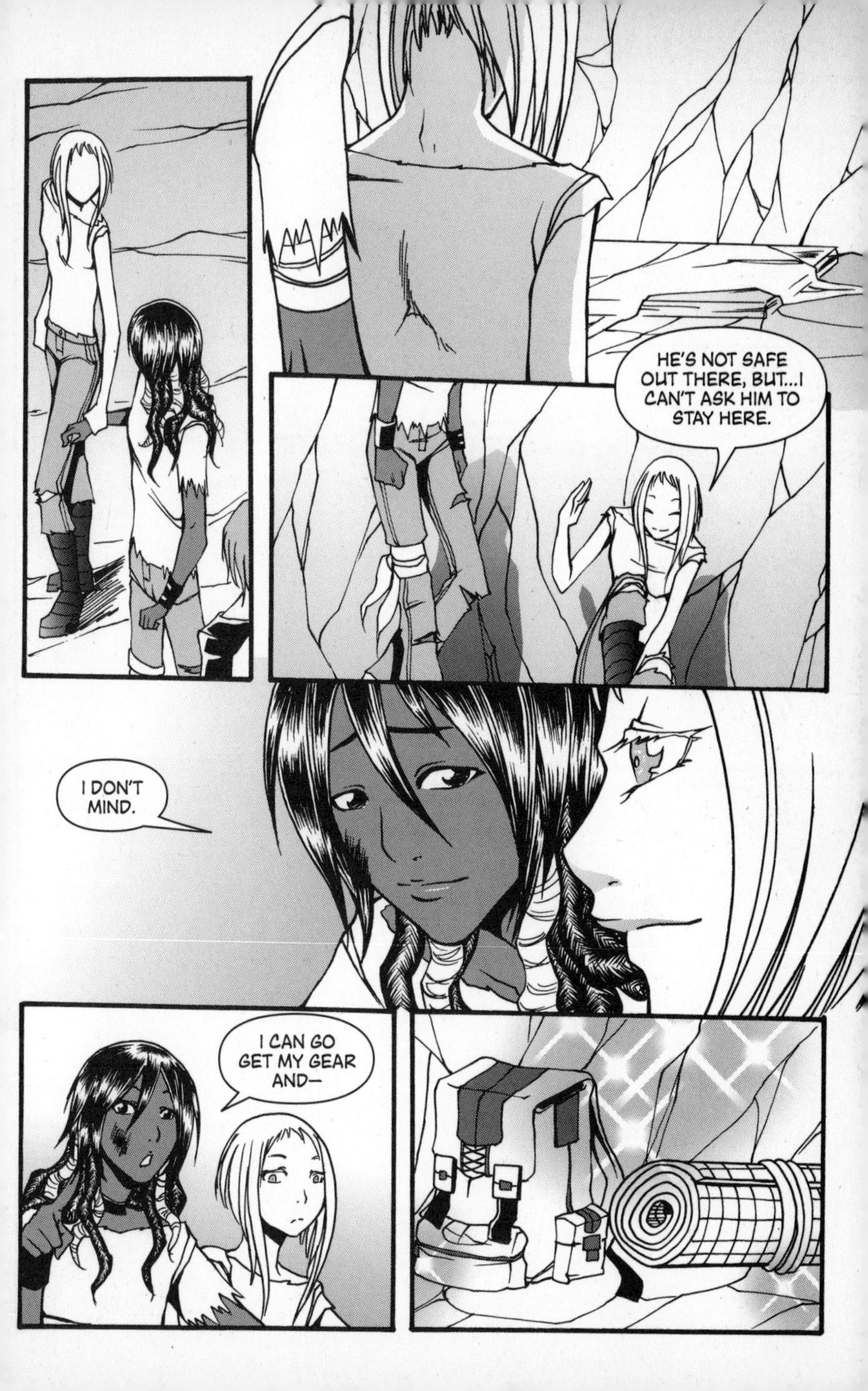
HE'S NOT SAFE OUT THERE, BUT...I CAN'T ASK HIM TO STAY HERE.
I DON'T MIND.
I CAN GO GET MY GEAR AND—

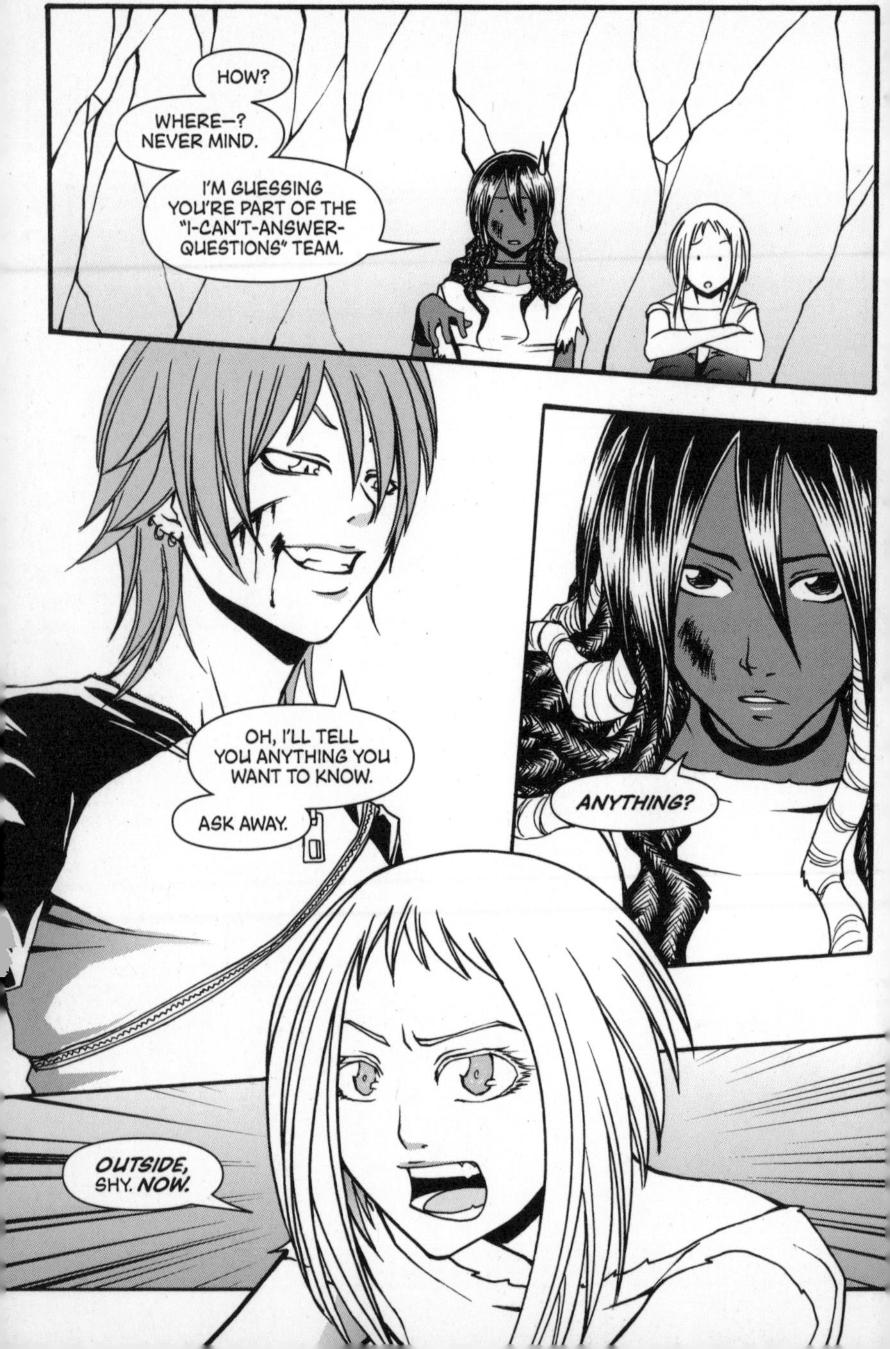
HOW?
WHERE—? NEVER MIND.
I'M GUESSING YOU'RE PART OF THE "I-CAN'T-ANSWER-QUESTIONS" TEAM.
OH, I'LL TELL YOU ANYTHING YOU WANT TO KNOW.
ASK AWAY.
ANYTHING?
OUTSIDE, SHY. ***NOW.***

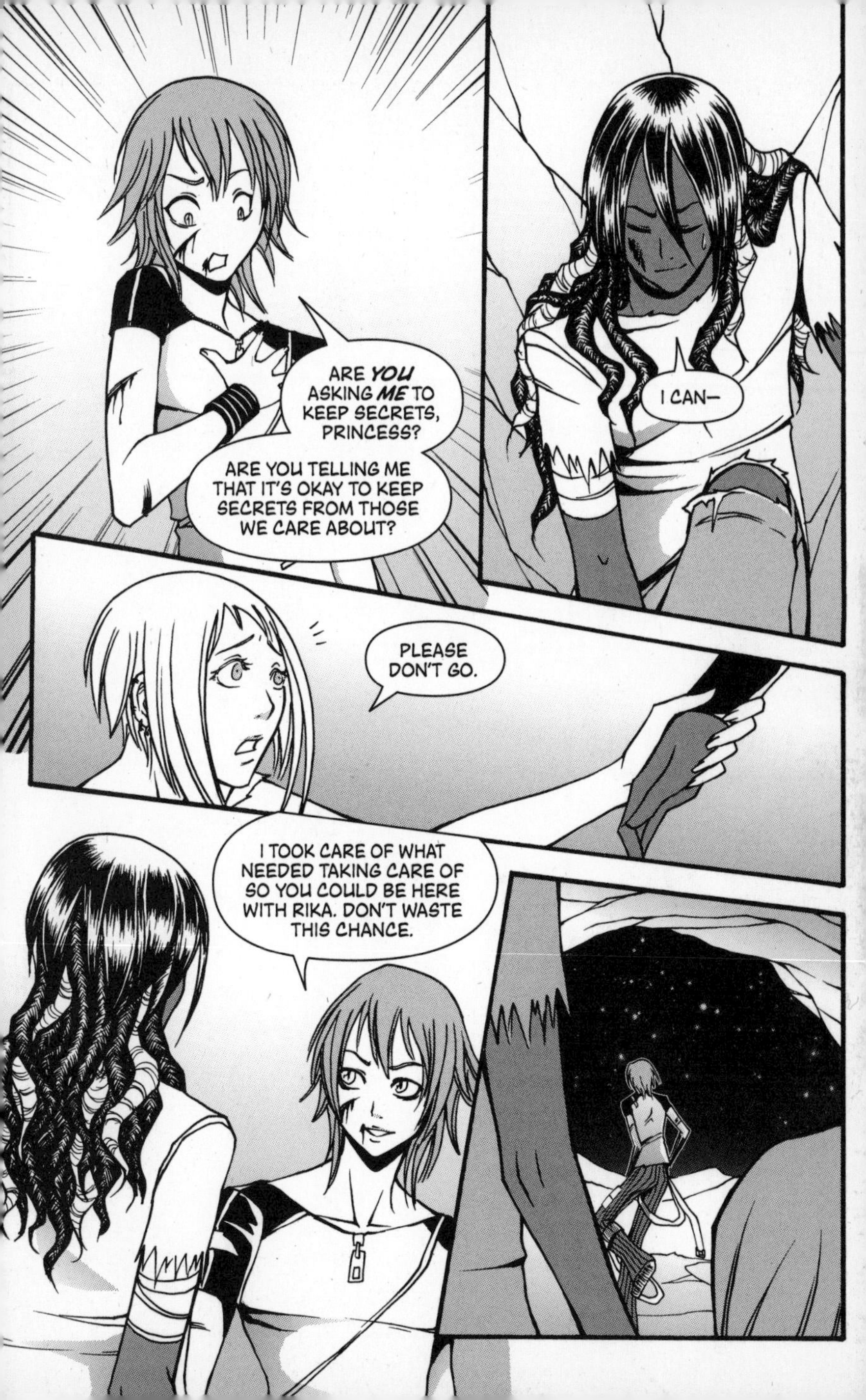
ARE *YOU* ASKING *ME* TO KEEP SECRETS, PRINCESS?
ARE YOU TELLING ME THAT IT'S OKAY TO KEEP SECRETS FROM THOSE WE CARE ABOUT?
I CAN—
PLEASE DON'T GO.
I TOOK CARE OF WHAT NEEDED TAKING CARE OF SO YOU COULD BE HERE WITH RIKA. DON'T WASTE THIS CHANCE.

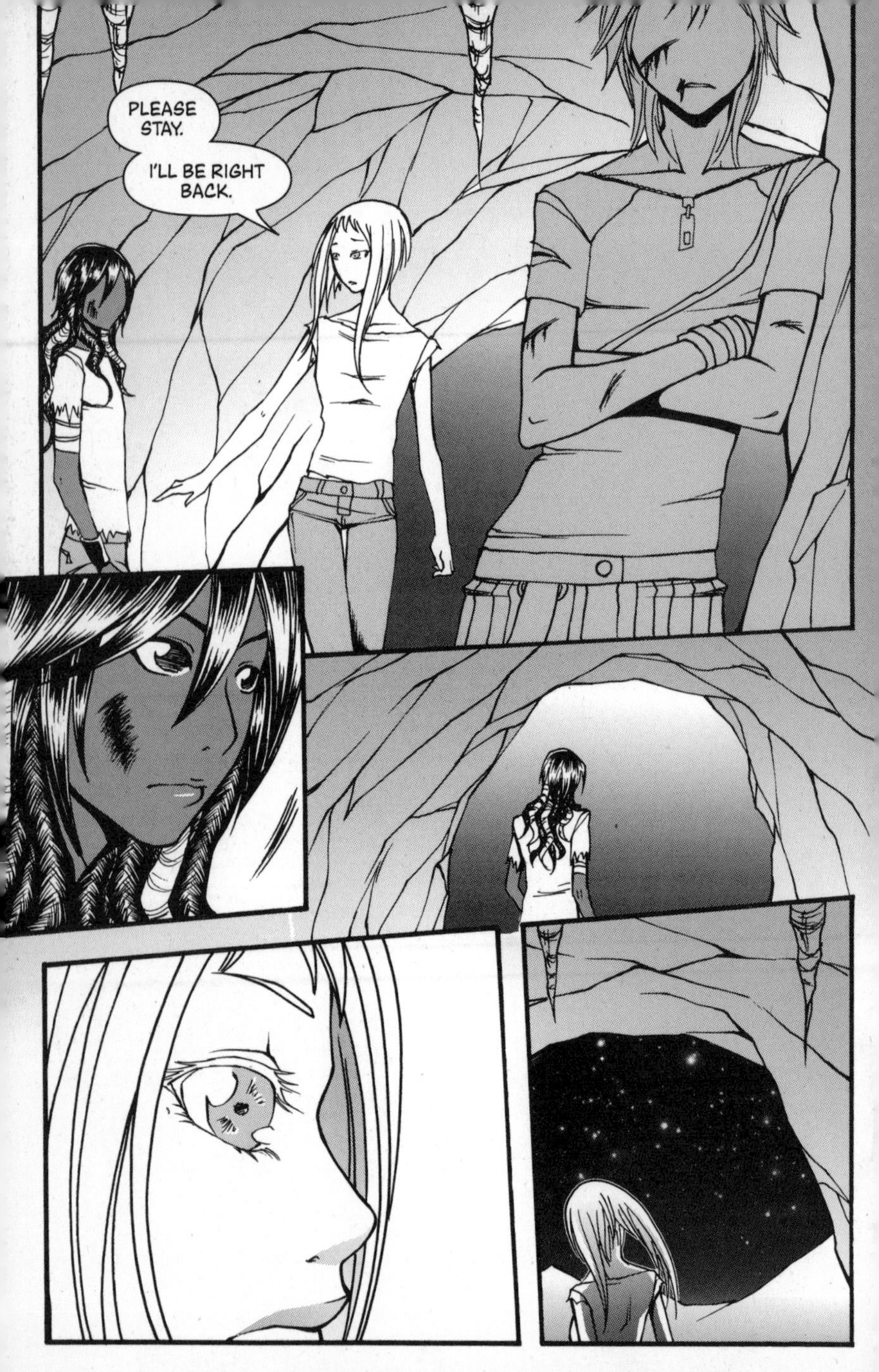
PLEASE STAY.
I'LL BE RIGHT BACK.

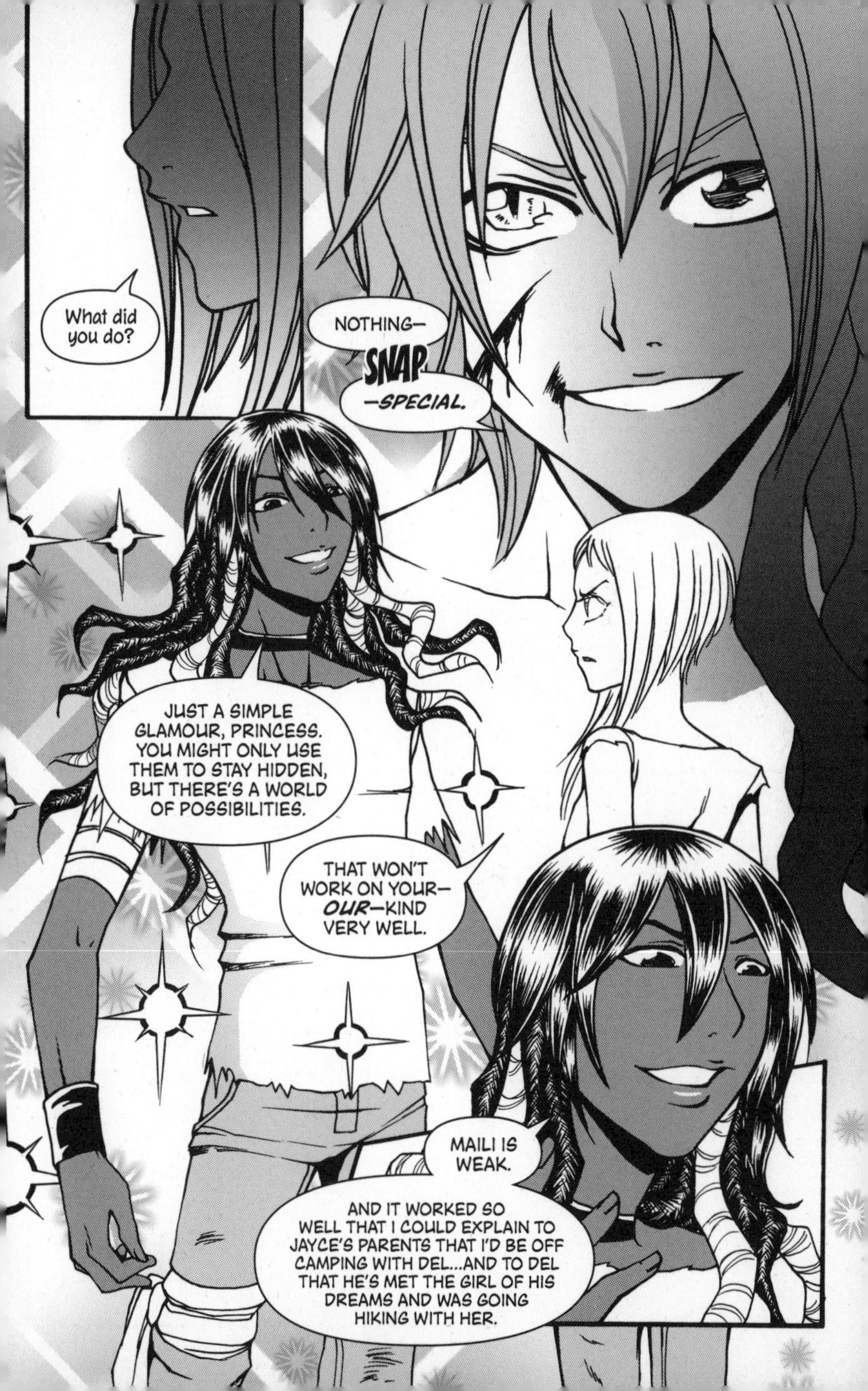
What did you do?
NOTHING—
SNAP
—SPECIAL.
JUST A SIMPLE GLAMOUR, PRINCESS. YOU MIGHT ONLY USE THEM TO STAY HIDDEN, BUT THERE'S A WORLD OF POSSIBILITIES.
THAT WON'T WORK ON YOUR— OUR—KIND VERY WELL.
MAILI IS WEAK.
AND IT WORKED SO WELL THAT I COULD EXPLAIN TO JAYCE'S PARENTS THAT I'D BE OFF CAMPING WITH DEL...AND TO DEL THAT HE'S MET THE GIRL OF HIS DREAMS AND WAS GOING HIKING WITH HER.

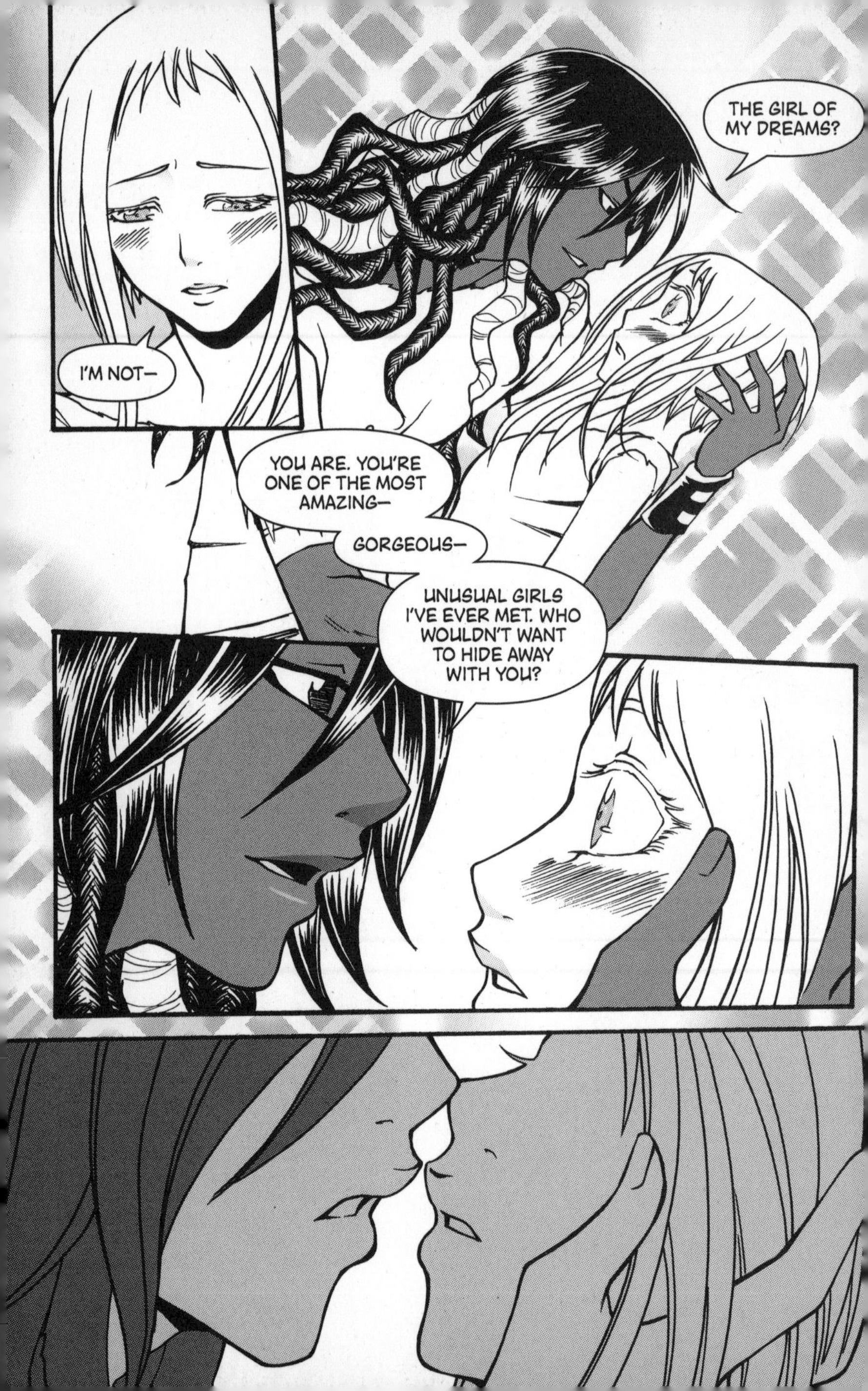
I'M NOT—
THE GIRL OF MY DREAMS?
YOU ARE. YOU'RE ONE OF THE MOST AMAZING—
GORGEOUS—
UNUSUAL GIRLS I'VE EVER MET. WHO WOULDN'T WANT TO HIDE AWAY WITH YOU?

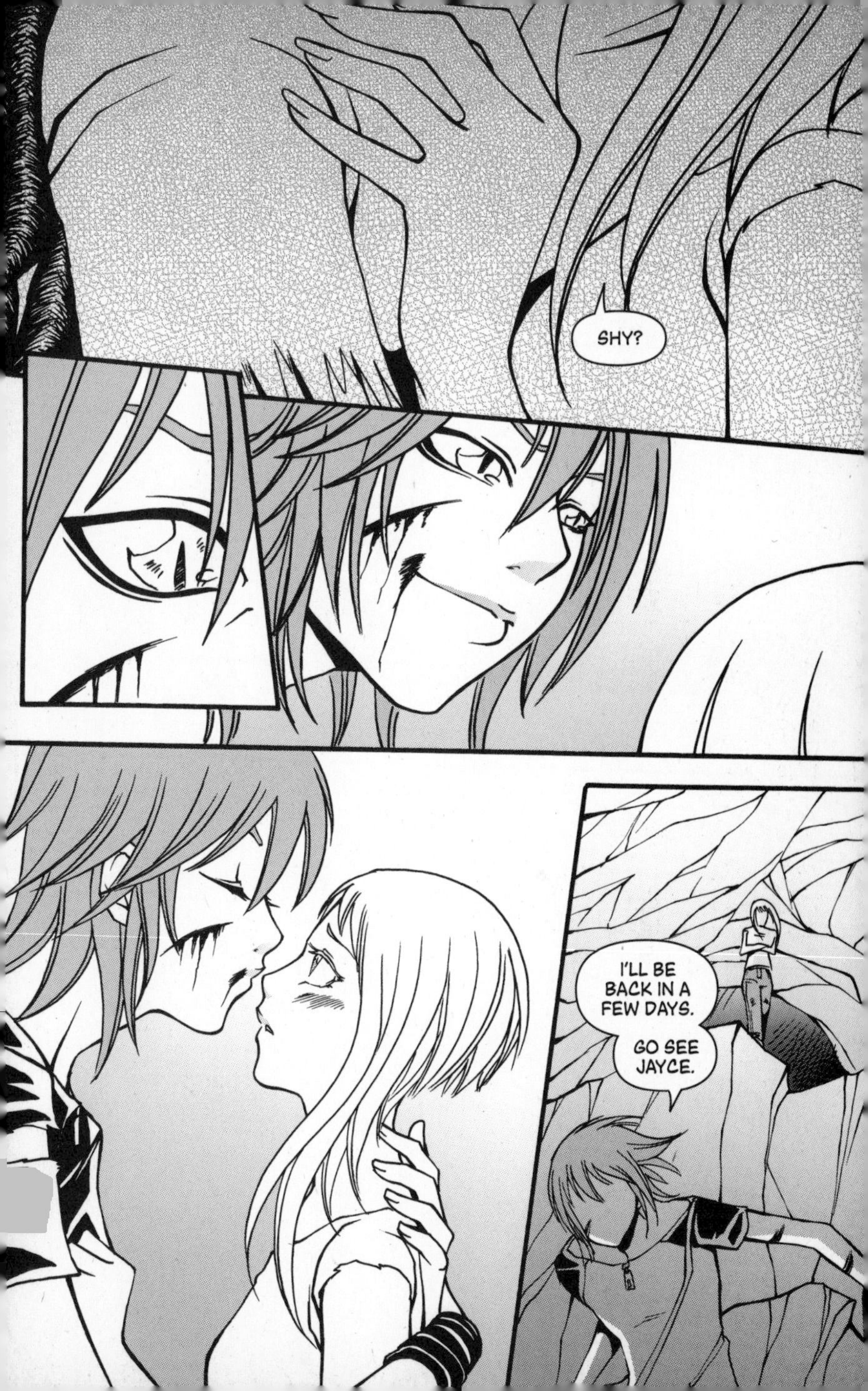
SHY?
I'LL BE BACK IN A FEW DAYS.
GO SEE JAYCE.

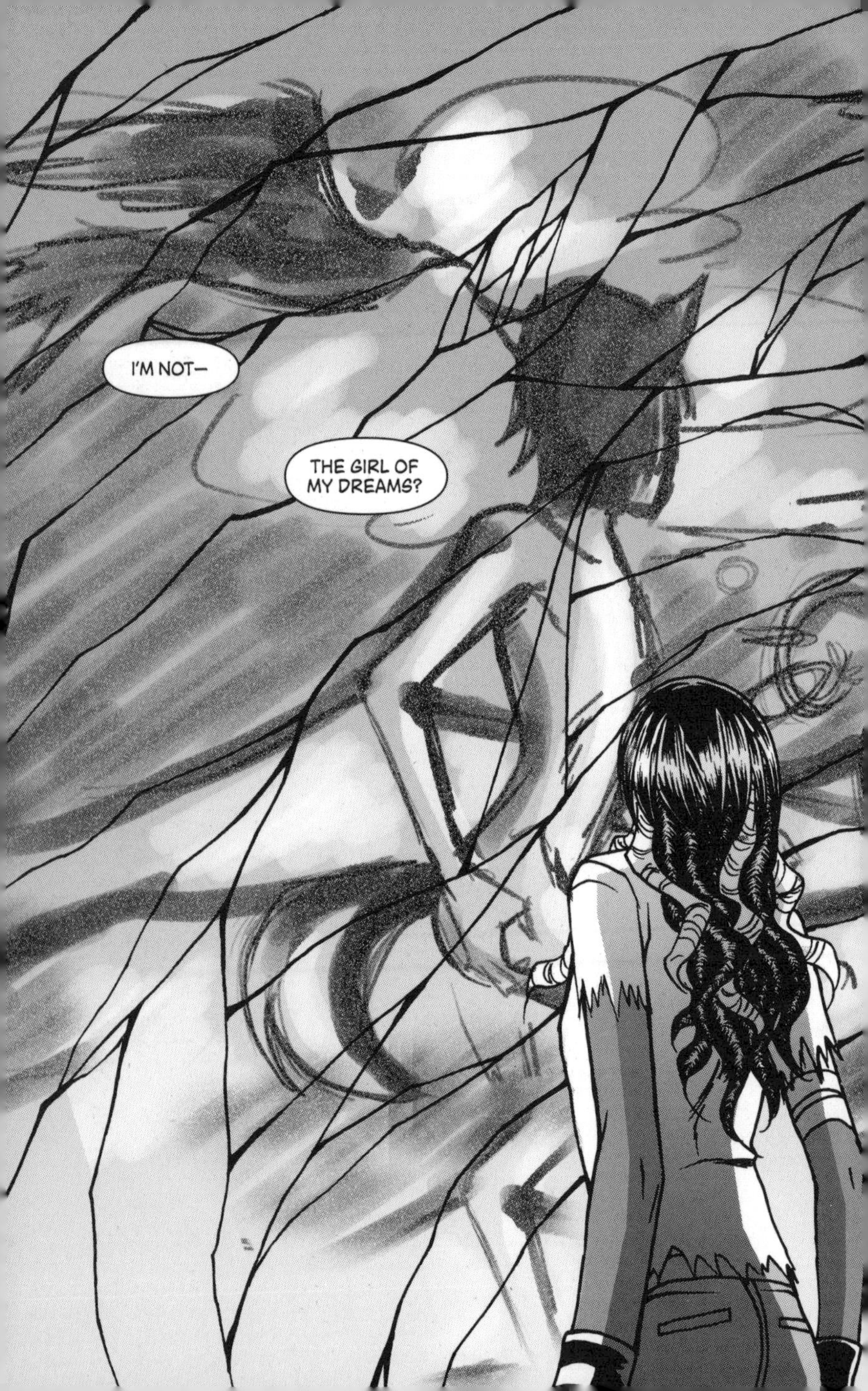
I'M NOT—
THE GIRL OF MY DREAMS?

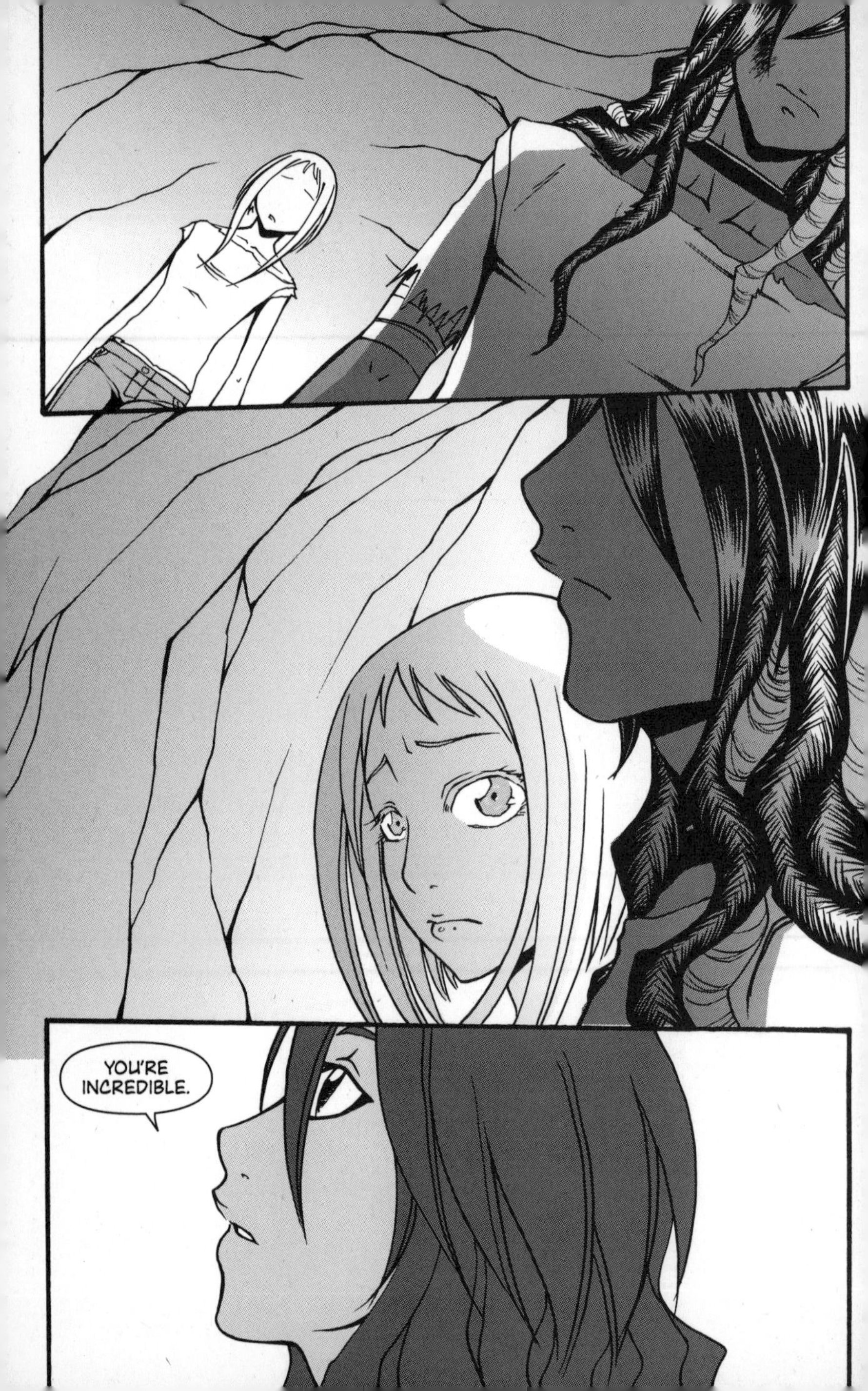
YOU'RE INCREDIBLE.

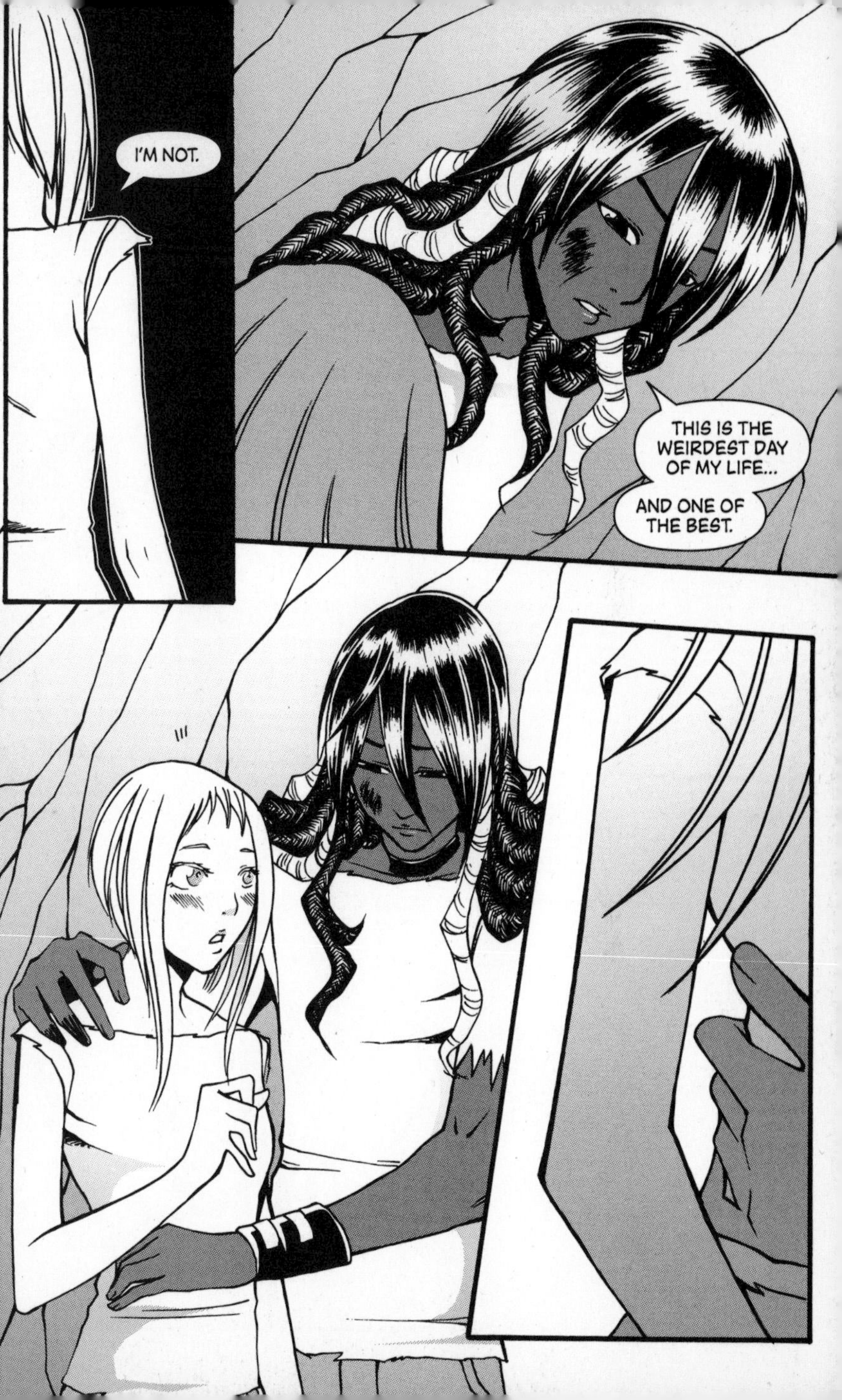
I'M NOT.
THIS IS THE WEIRDEST DAY OF MY LIFE...
AND ONE OF THE BEST.

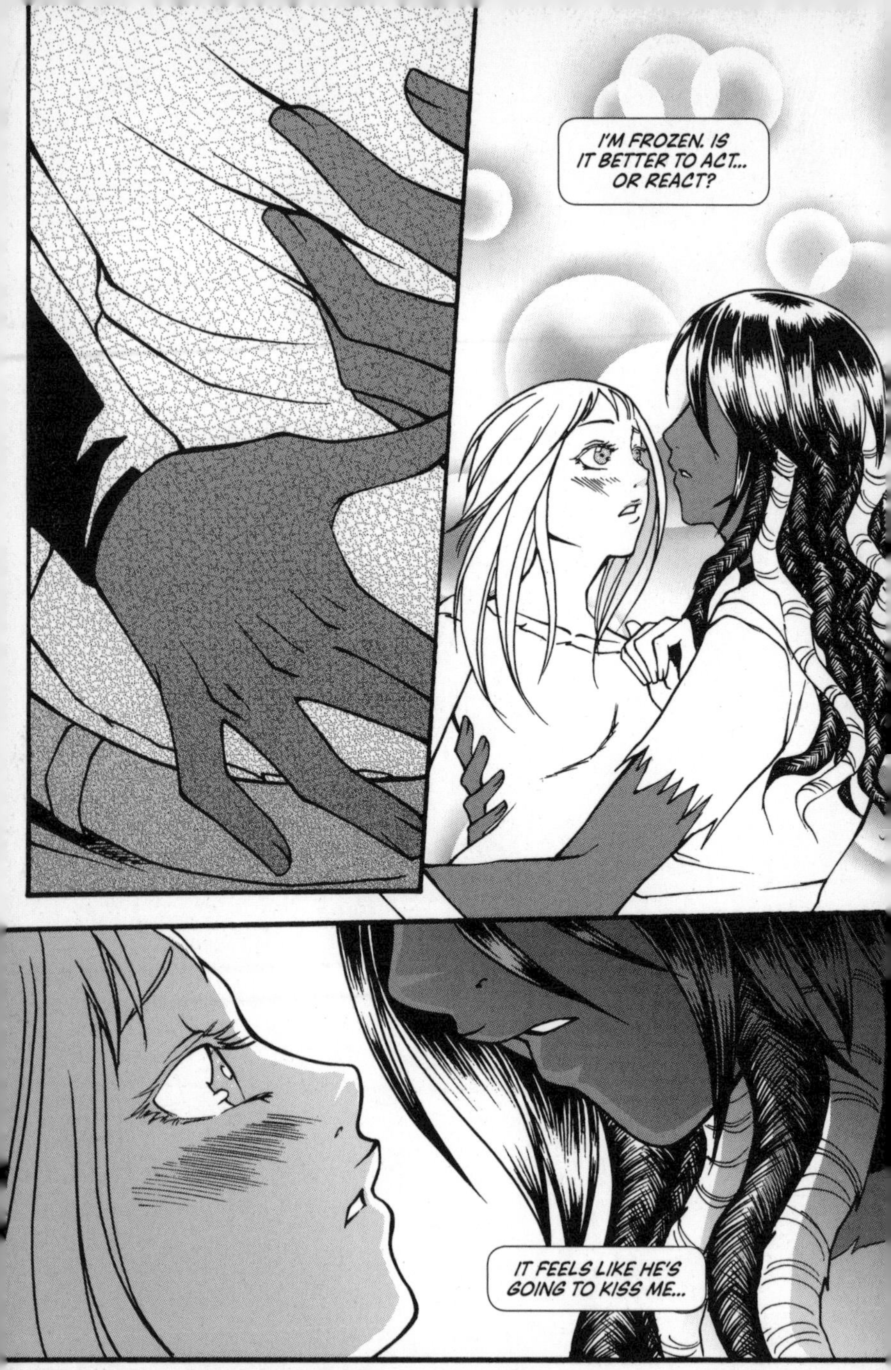
I'M FROZEN. IS IT BETTER TO ACT... OR REACT?
IT FEELS LIKE HE'S GOING TO KISS ME...

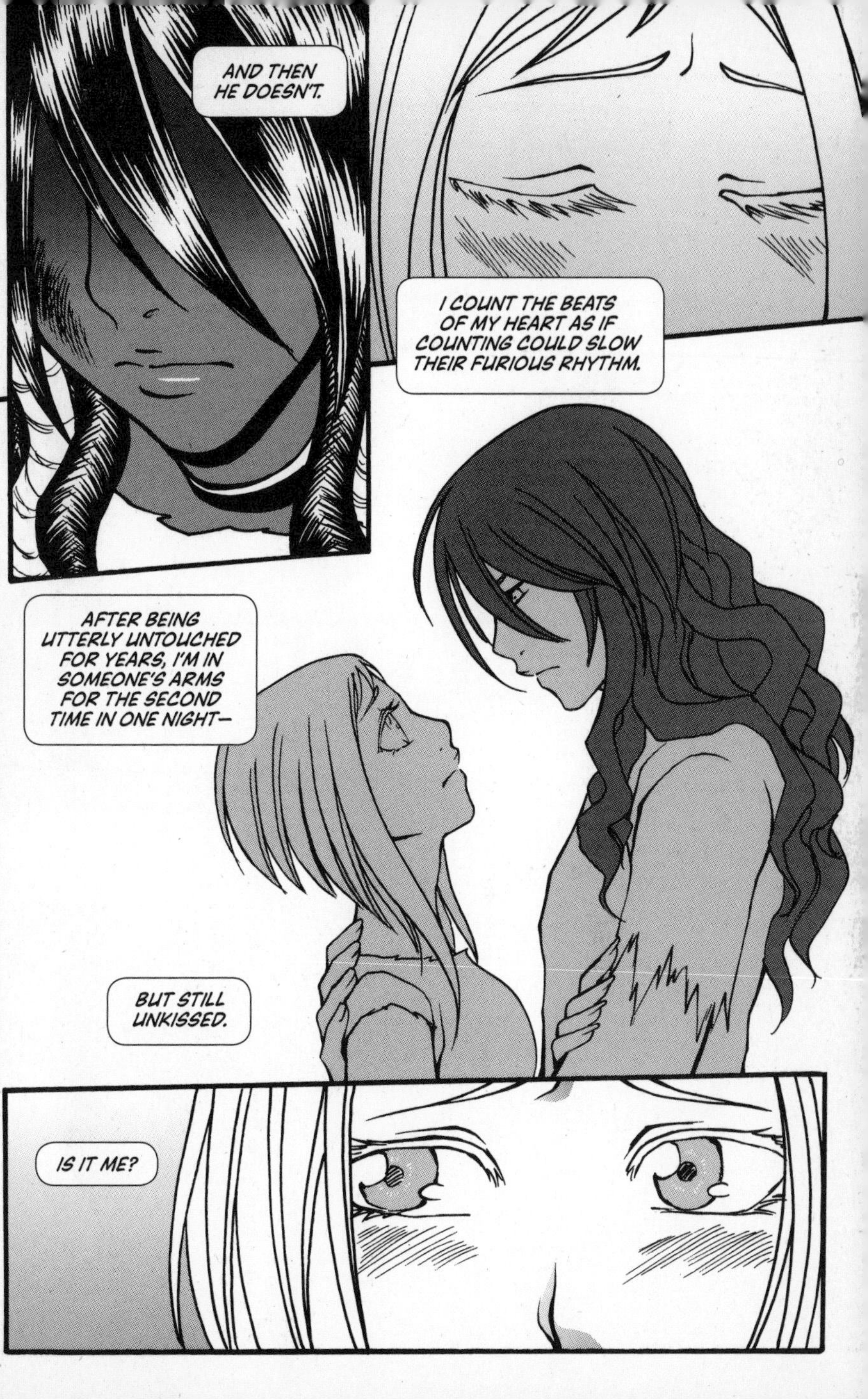
AND THEN HE DOESN'T.
I COUNT THE BEATS OF MY HEART AS IF COUNTING COULD SLOW THEIR FURIOUS RHYTHM.
AFTER BEING UTTERLY UNTOUCHED FOR YEARS, I'M IN SOMEONE'S ARMS FOR THE SECOND TIME IN ONE NIGHT—
BUT STILL UNKISSED.
IS IT ME?

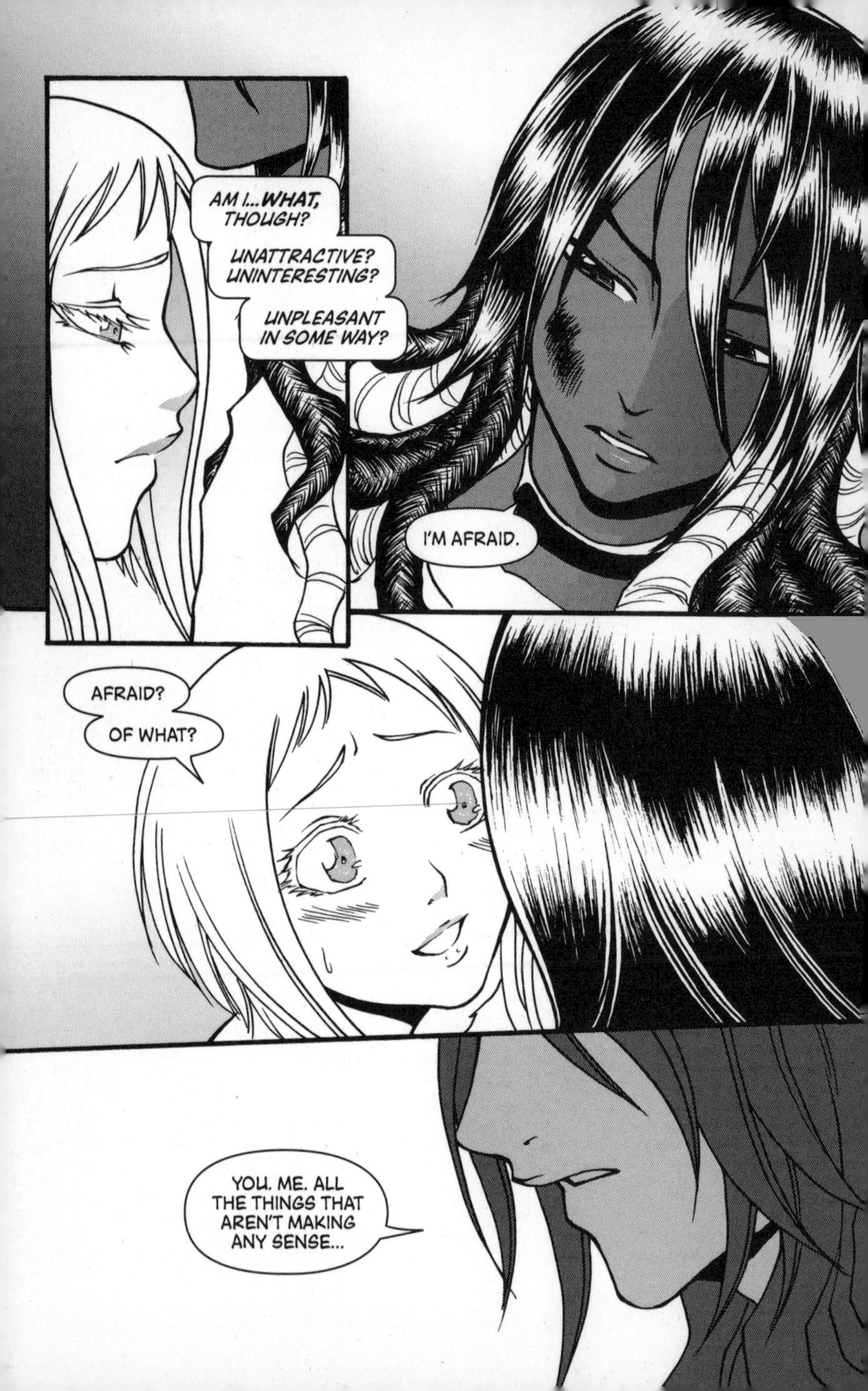
AM I...WHAT, THOUGH?
UNATTRACTIVE? UNINTERESTING?
UNPLEASANT IN SOME WAY?
I'M AFRAID.
AFRAID?
OF WHAT?
YOU. ME. ALL THE THINGS THAT AREN'T MAKING ANY SENSE...

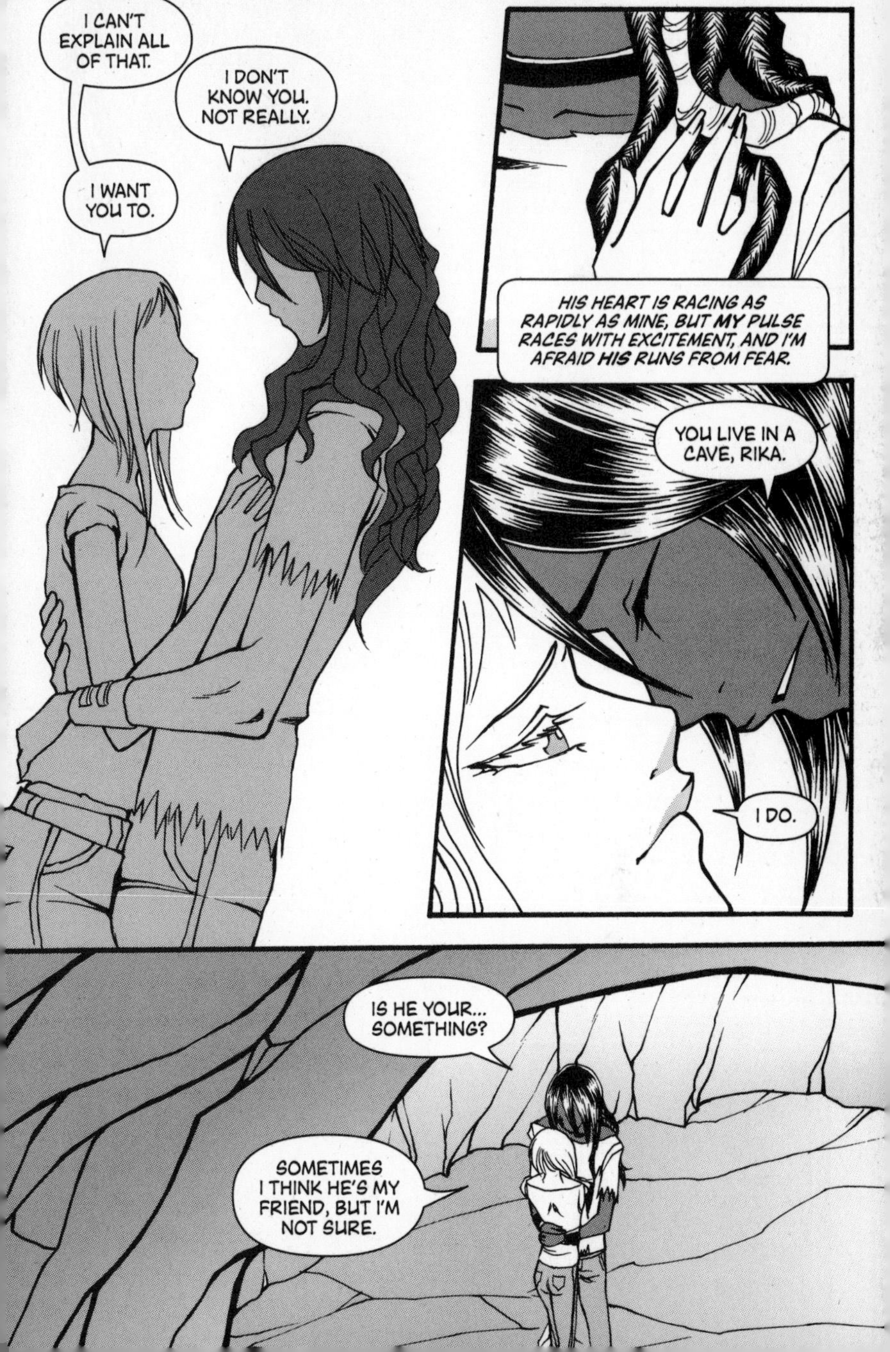
I CAN'T EXPLAIN ALL OF THAT.
I DON'T KNOW YOU. NOT REALLY.
I WANT YOU TO.
HIS HEART IS RACING AS RAPIDLY AS MINE, BUT MY PULSE RACES WITH EXCITEMENT, AND I'M AFRAID HIS RUNS FROM FEAR.
YOU LIVE IN A CAVE, RIKA.
I DO.
IS HE YOUR... SOMETHING?
SOMETIMES I THINK HE'S MY FRIEND, BUT I'M NOT SURE.

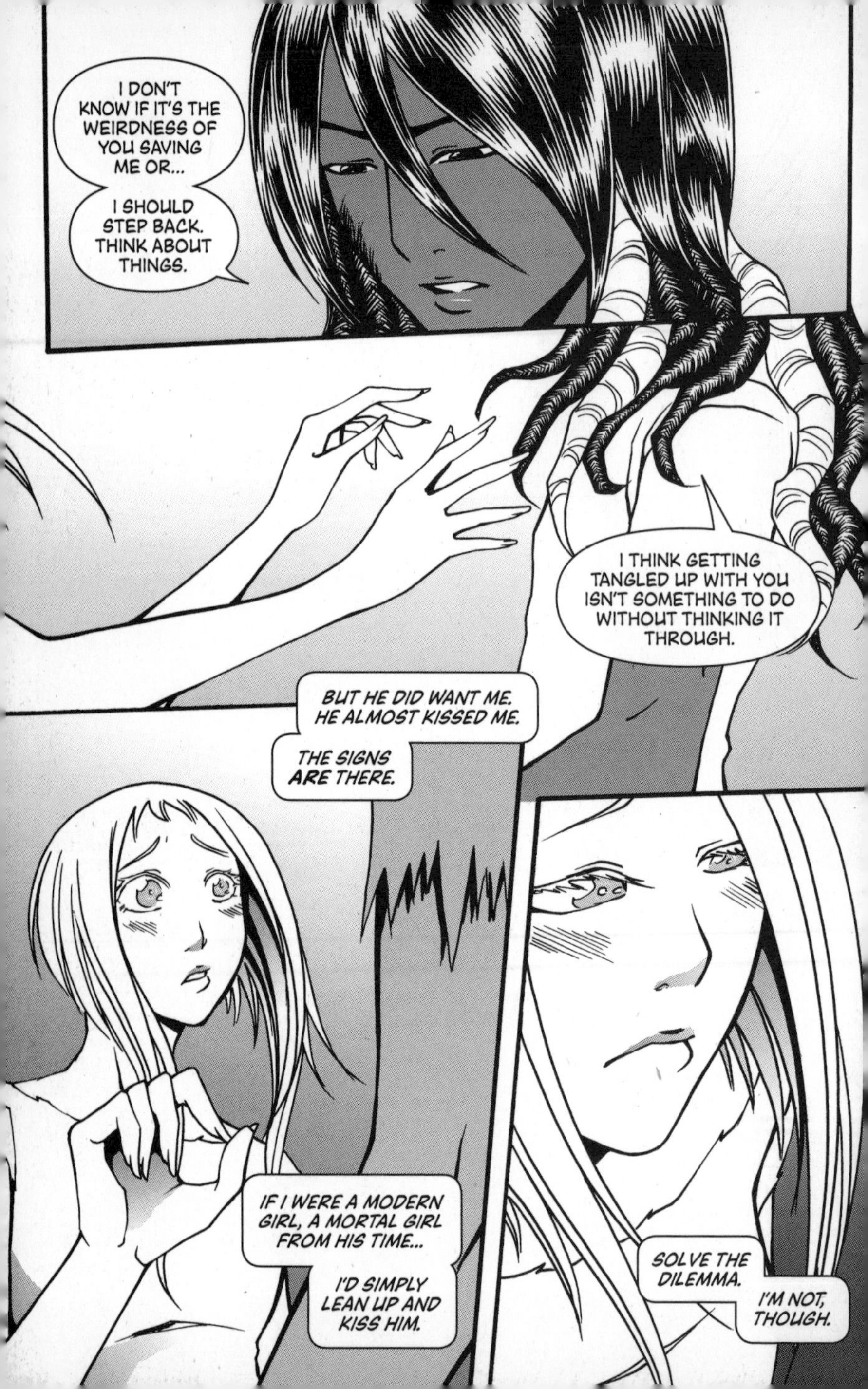
I DON'T KNOW IF IT'S THE WEIRDNESS OF YOU SAVING ME OR...
I SHOULD STEP BACK. THINK ABOUT THINGS.
I THINK GETTING TANGLED UP WITH YOU ISN'T SOMETHING TO DO WITHOUT THINKING IT THROUGH.
BUT HE DID WANT ME. HE ALMOST KISSED ME.
THE SIGNS ARE THERE.
IF I WERE A MODERN GIRL, A MORTAL GIRL FROM HIS TIME...
I'D SIMPLY LEAN UP AND KISS HIM.
SOLVE THE DILEMMA.
I'M NOT, THOUGH.

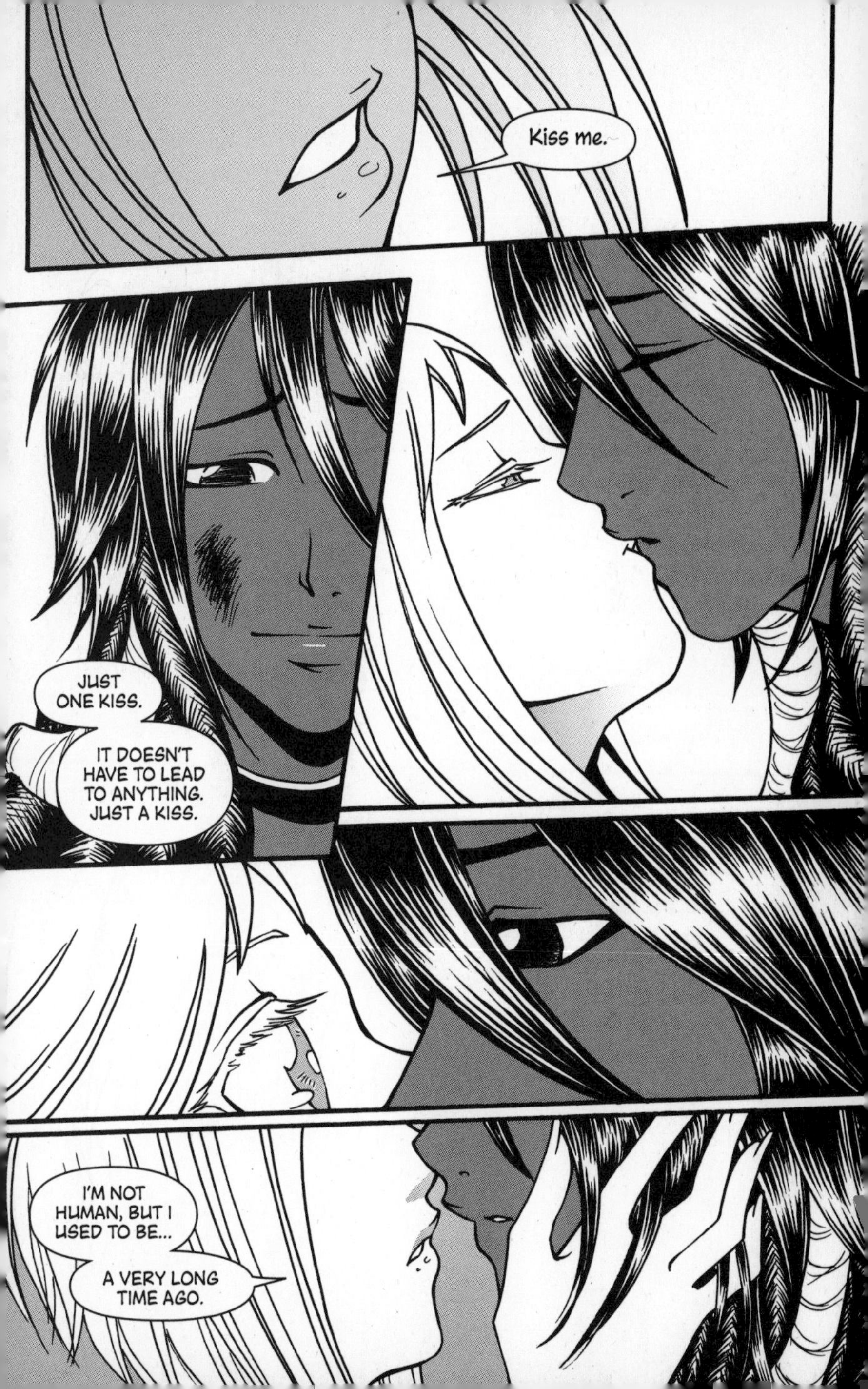
Kiss me.
JUST ONE KISS.
IT DOESN'T HAVE TO LEAD TO ANYTHING. JUST A KISS.
I'M NOT HUMAN, BUT I USED TO BE...
A VERY LONG TIME AGO.

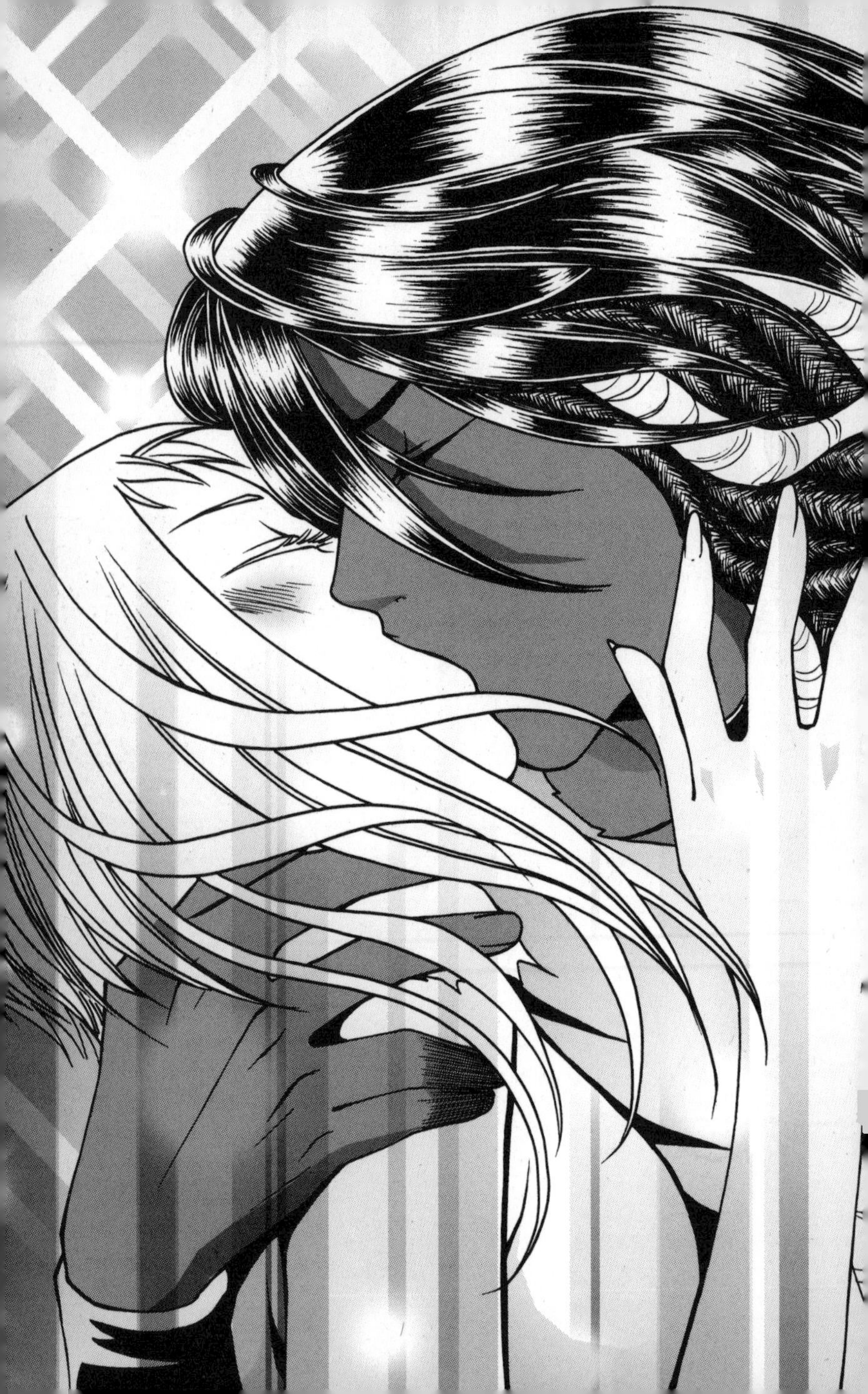

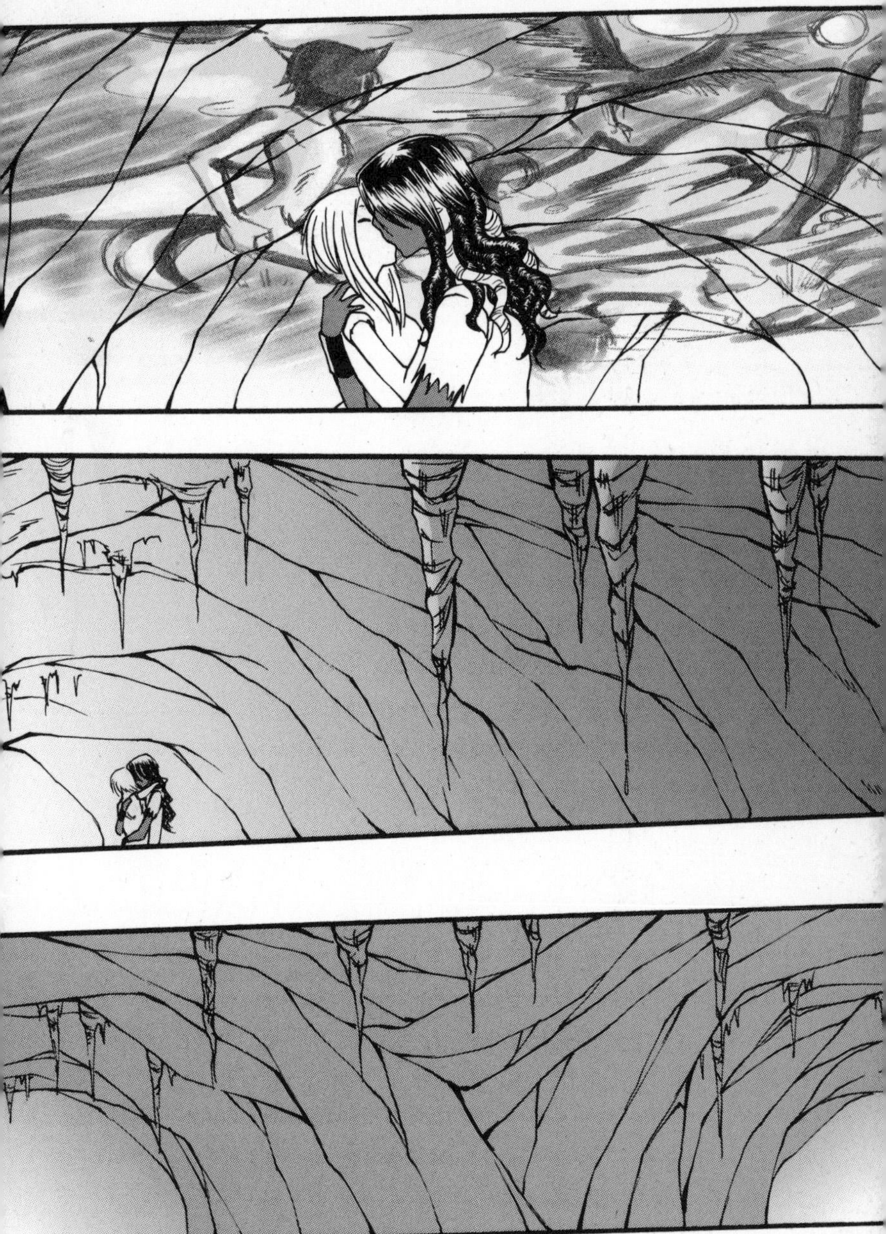

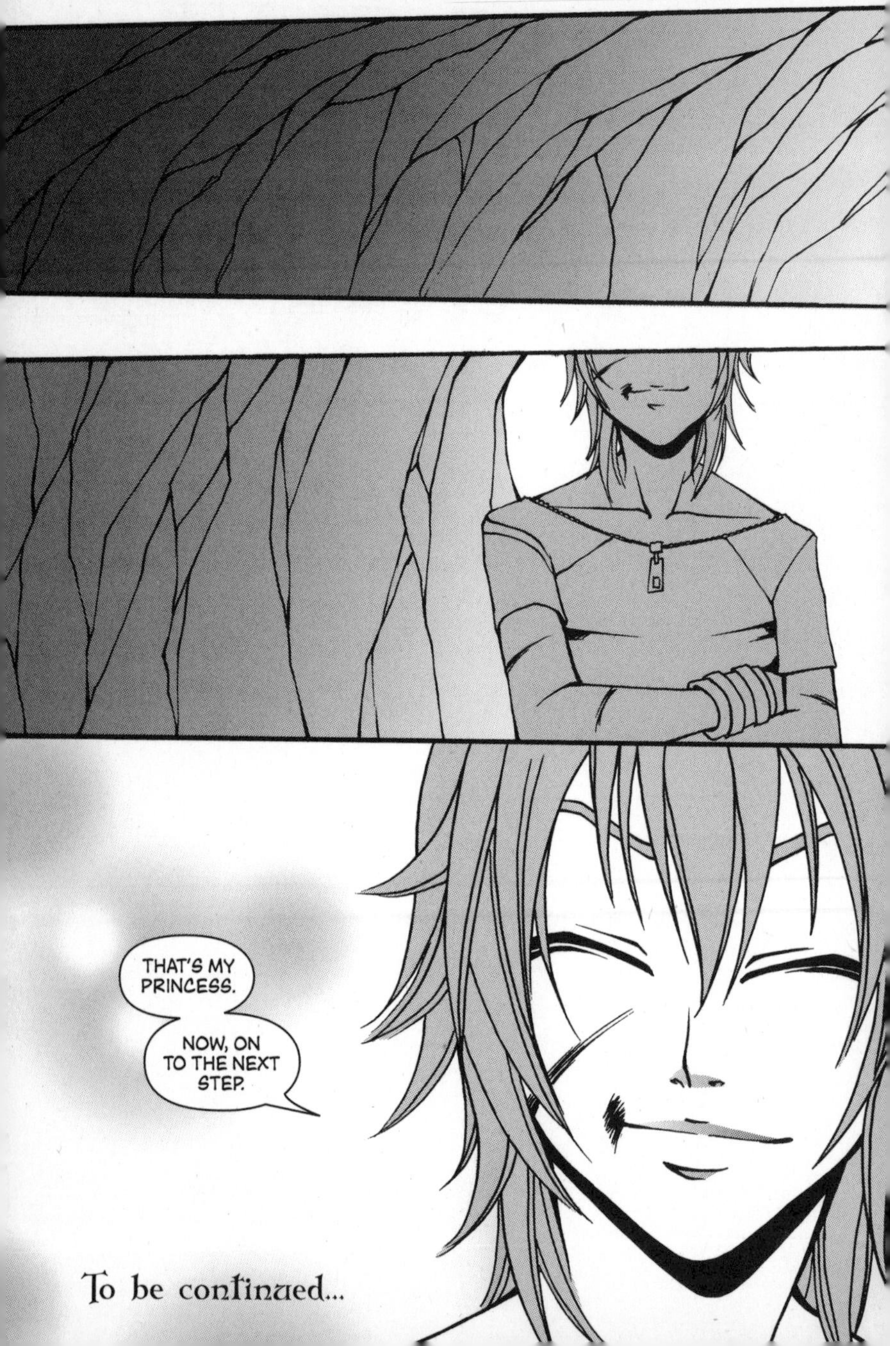
THAT'S MY PRINCESS.
NOW, ON TO THE NEXT STEP.
To be continued...

Read on for a taste of
Melissa Marr's newest tale of Faerie,

FRAGILE ETERNITY

Seth knew the moment Aislinn slipped into the house; the slight rise in temperature would've told him even if he hadn't seen the glimmer of sunlight in the middle of the night. *Better than a lantern.* He smiled at the thought of his girlfriend's likely reaction to being called a lantern, but his smile fled a heartbeat later when she came into his doorway.

Her shoes were already gone. Her hair was loosened from whatever arrangement it had been forced into for the Summer revels she'd been at earlier that night. *With Keenan.* The thought of her in Keenan's arms made Seth tense. She had these all-night dances with the Summer King every month, and try as he might, Seth was still jealous.

But she's not with him now. She's here.

She unfastened the bodice of an old-fashioned dress as she stared at him. "Hey."

He might've spoken; he wasn't really sure. It didn't matter. Not much did in these moments, just her, just them, just what they meant to each other.

The rest of the dress fell away, and she was in his arms.

He knew he didn't speak then, not with sunlight like warm honey against his skin. The Summer Court revel had ended, and she was here.

Not with him. *With me.*

The monthly revels weren't mortal-friendly. Afterward, she came to him, though, too filled with sunlight and celebration to simply sleep, too afraid of herself to stay with the rest of the Summer Court all night. So she came to his arms, sun-drunk and forgetting to be as careful with him as she was on other nights.

She kissed him, and he tried to ignore the tropical heat. Orchids, a small ylang-ylang tree, and golden goddess branches clustered in the room. The perfumed scents were heavy in the humid air, but it was better than the waterfall a few months ago.

When she was here, in his arms, the consequences didn't matter. All that mattered was them.

Mortals weren't made to love faeries; he knew it each month when she forgot just how breakable he was. If he could be strong enough, he'd be at the revels. Instead, he admitted that mortals weren't safe in throngs of unrestrained faeries. Instead, he hoped that after the revels she wouldn't injure him too badly. Instead, he waited in the dark, hoping that this month wasn't the month that she stayed with Keenan.

∞⟨×⟩∞

Later, when speech returned, he plucked orchid petals from her hair. "Love you."

"You too." She blushed and ducked her head. "Are you okay?"

"When you're here, I am." He dropped the flower petals to the floor. "If I had my way, you'd be here every night."

"I'd like that." She snuggled in and closed her eyes. There was no light in her skin now—not when she was calm and relaxed—and Seth was grateful for it. In a couple hours day would break; she would see the burns on his sides and back where her hands had touched him too much and she'd forgotten herself. Then, she'd look away. She'd suggest things he hated to hear.

The Winter Queen, Donia, had given him a recipe for a salve that healed sunlight burns. It didn't work as well on mortals as it did on faeries, but if he put it on soon enough, it would heal the burns within the day. He glanced at the clock. "Almost breakfast time."

"No," Aislinn murmured, "'s time to sleep."

"Okay." He kissed her and held her as long as he safely could. He watched the clock, listened to her even breaths as she fell deeper into sleep. Then, when he could wait no longer, he started to slide out of the bed.

She opened her eyes. "Stay."

"Bathroom. Be right back." He gave her a sheepish grin in hopes that she wouldn't ask any questions. Since she couldn't lie, he did his best to avoid lying to her in return, but they'd been down this road a few times.

She started to look at his arms, and he knew neither of them wanted to have the conversation that would follow—the one where she told him she shouldn't come when she was like this and he panicked at the thought of her being at the loft with the Summer King instead.

She winced. "I'm sorry I thought you meant you weren't hurt—"

He could argue, or he could distract her.

It wasn't a difficult choice to make.

When Aislinn woke, she propped herself up on one arm and watched Seth sleep. She wasn't sure what she'd do if she ever lost him. Sometimes she felt like he was all that held her together; he was her version of the vine that wrapped around the Summer Girls—the thread that kept her from unraveling.

And I hurt him. Again.

She could see the shadowed bruises and bright burns on his skin from her hands. He'd never complain about it, but she worried. He was so breakable in comparison to even the weakest faeries. She traced her fingertips over his shoulder, and he moved closer. In all the weirdness of the past few months since she'd become Summer Queen, he'd been there. He didn't ask her to be all mortal or all faery; instead, he let her be herself. It was a gift she couldn't ever repay him for. *He* was a gift. He'd been essential to her when she was a mortal, and he had only grown more important as she'd tried to keep steady in her new life as a faery queen.

He opened his eyes to stare up at her. "You look like you're far away."

"Just thinking."

"About?" He quirked his pierced brow.

And her heart fluttered exactly as it had when she'd tried to be just friends with him. "The usual . . ."

"Everything will be fine." He rolled her under him. "We'll figure it out."

She wrapped her arms around him so she could tangle her fingers in his hair. She told herself to be careful, to moderate her strength, to not remind him that she was so much stronger than a mortal. *That I'm not what he is.*

"I *want* it to be fine," she whispered, trying to force away thoughts of his mortality, of his transience now that she was eternal, of how very finite he was—and she wasn't. "Tell me again?"

He lowered his lips to hers and told her things that didn't require words. When he pulled back, he whispered, "Something this good can last forever."

She ran her hand down his spine, wondering if he'd think she was weird for wanting to let sunlight into her fingertips as she did so, wondering if it would only remind him of how not-mortal she was now. "I wish it could always be like this. Just us."

There was something she couldn't read in his expression, but then he pulled her to him and she let go of thoughts and words.

———◆———

Seth watched Aislinn argue with the court's advisors, far more vocal with the fey than she ever was with humans. On the table in front of them, Aislinn had the pages of her new plan, complete with charts, spread out.

When she sat in Keenan's loft, with the tall plants and crowds of faeries overfilling the place, it was easy to forget that she hadn't always been one of them. The plants leaned toward her, blooming in her presence. The birds that roosted in the columns greeted her when she walked into a room. Faeries vied for her attention, seeking a few moments in her presence. After centuries without strength, the Summer Court was beginning to thrive—because of Aislinn. At first, she had seemed uncomfortable with being in the center of it, but she'd grown so at ease with her position that Seth wondered how long it'd be until she abandoned the mortal world, including him.

"If we assign different regions like this—" She pointed to her diagram again, but Quinn excused himself, leaving

Tavish to explain once more why he thought her plan was unnecessary.

Quinn, the advisor who'd replaced Niall recently, plopped down on the sofa next to Seth. He was as unlike Niall in appearance as he was in temperament. Where Niall had highlighted his almost common features, Quinn seemed to strive for some degree of polish and posturing. He kept his hair sun-streaked, his skin tanned, his clothes hinting at wealth. More important, though, where Niall had been a voice that could pull Keenan from his melancholia or dissipate the Summer King's temper, Quinn seemed to fuel Keenan's mood of the moment. *That* made Seth leery of the new guard.

Quinn scowled. "She's being unreasonable. The king can't expect us to—"

Seth simply looked at him.

"What?"

"You think Keenan's going to tell her *no*? To anything?" Seth almost laughed aloud at the idea.

Quinn looked affronted. "Of course."

"Wrong." Seth watched his girlfriend, the queen of the Summer Court, glow like small suns were trapped inside her skin. "You have a lot to learn. Unless Ash changes her mind, Keenan will give her plan a try."

"But the court has always been run like this," Tavish, the court's oldest advisor, was repeating yet again.

"The court has also always been ruled by a monarch, hasn't it? It still is. You don't *need* to agree, but I'm asking for your support." Aislinn flicked her hair over her shoulder. It was still as black as Seth's, just as it had been when she was a human, but now that she'd become one of them, her hair had golden streaks in it.

Tavish raised his voice, a habit he'd apparently not been prone to before Aislinn joined the court. "My Queen, surely—"

"Don't 'my Queen' me, Tavish." She poked him in the shoulder. Tiny sparks flickered from her skin.

"I don't mean to offend you, but the idea of local rulers seems foolish." Tavish smiled placatingly.

Aislinn's temper sent rainbows flashing across the room. "Foolish? Structuring our court so our faeries are safe and have access to help when they need us is foolish? We have a responsibility to take care of our court. How are we to do that if we don't have contact with them?"

But Tavish didn't back down. "Such a major change . . ."

Seth tuned them out. He'd hear Aislinn recount it all later when she tried to make sense of it. *No need to hear it twice.* He picked up a remote and flicked through the music. Someone had added the Living Zombies song he'd mentioned the other week. He selected it and turned the volume up.

Tavish had a please-help-me look on his face. Seth

ignored it, but Quinn didn't. Grumbling, but eager to prove his worth, the new advisor went back over to the table.

Then Keenan walked in the door with several of the Summer Girls beside him. They looked more beautiful by the day. As summer approached—and as Aislinn and Keenan grew stronger—their faeries seemed to blossom.

Tavish immediately began, "Keenan, my King, perhaps you could explain to her grace that . . ." But his words died after a glimpse at the expression of ire the Summer King wore.

In response to his volatile mood, Aislinn's already-glowing skin radiated enough light that it hurt Seth to look at her. Without even realizing she was doing it, she'd extended sunbeams like insubstantial hands reaching toward Keenan. Over the past few months, she'd developed an increasingly strong connection with the Summer King.

Which sucks.

All Keenan had to do was look her way and she was at his side, papers forgotten, argument forgotten, everything but Keenan forgotten. She went to him, and the rest of the world went on pause at Keenan's look of upset.

It's her job. Court things have to come first.